PAIR BONDING

Casey Bourne

It is said that long ago in Ancient Greece, humans were so complete, so perfect, and so utterly content, that even the gods envied them.

The story goes that Zeus, the Almighty father of god and men, had created humans whole; with four hands, four legs, and two faces on opposite sides of the head. But over time, Zeus' envy grew until he began to fear these creatures that were once his most proud creation. No creature ought to be more powerful than the gods.

Zeus asked Hermes to summon the gods from all over the land and sky to meet on Mount Olympus and find a way to restore the natural balance. It is said that the gods debated for five days and nights as they tried to find a way to foil the humans. Finally, Zeus stood before his fellow gods and declared, "I have an answer. I will split each human into two separate beings. Without half of their body and soul, they will be cursed to spend their lives searching for their other half, and become too weak to challenge us."

The gods cheered for this seemed like a fair and wise solution.

And so Zeus asked Apollo to make this divide and heal the humans' wounds, thus creating the beings that we are today. The separation was unbearable but the gods were still not pleased for as long as the two separate beings remained close – remained touching – then they were still content and powerful in their wholeness.

Desperately, Zeus tried to cast the two halves to opposite sides of the globe, only to watch them perish from separation, too anxious to even eat alone having once been whole. Then, he tried to erase the memory of their Pair, only to make the connection in their minds even stronger. The Bond between them was not so easily abated it seemed.

Zeus was wandering the lands contemplating defeat when he found the goddess of beauty, Aphrodite – not with her husband, but with a new lover – and it was then that Zeus became enlightened as to the solution.

The gods were called once more to Mount Olympus and Zeus stood before them and said, "I have an answer; a way to make the humans weak, pitiful, and wholly inferior to their creators. I will give them… love."

And the gods rejoiced because nothing made more chaos than love.

And so Aphrodite cursed the humans to fall in love and lust with each other, so that they might never find their other half, and would never again find the true happiness that the gods feared. It was a success. To this day, the gods watch from afar at the chaos that Aphrodite inflicts; the power that humans once possessed almost forgotten.

But sometimes, it is said, that Zeus takes pity on his creations; that he leads two worthy beings to their Pair, who Bond upon their touch, fusing their souls together for eternity, so that all can witness the almighty power of the gods.

Rebecca

"The weight of the world is love. Under the burden of solitude, under the burden of dissatisfaction / the weight, the weight we carry is love."

— Allen Ginsberg

On a warm pleasant day in 1992, Rebecca Brighton comes home to find her husband dead in the bathtub. He is floating in his own blood; naked, except for the thick black bracelet around his wrist.

Her first thought, strangely, is for the people in the flat below them. She imagines the retired couple sitting in front of their small television; Mrs Meyer viciously knitting a jumper and Mr Meyer languidly reading Dickens, unaware of the morbid scene above them until a drop of blood obscures a word on page seventy-two.

The bath tap is still gushing water between Matthew's feet. It makes his corpse bob up and down like one of Lizzie's plastic bath toys. Rebecca wonders if his gaunt body will become so light that it will slip over the edge of the bathtub and swim towards her shoes like a wave on the shoreline. The kitchen knife he used floats halfway between them on the blood-soaked tiles.

Rebecca drops in front of the toilet and heaves. The iron tang of his blood assaults her nostrils but when her eyes open once more, there is only vomit in the toilet bowl.

She stands and sees a stranger in the mirror before her; a ghostly white woman with her husband's blood on her cotton trousers; an eerie sight in a familiar place. This is where her family used to navigate around each other in years of shared morning routines. Now she stands ankle-deep in a red ocean.

It's mid-afternoon now. She still has to pick up Lizzie from nursery. If Rebecca hadn't finished her shift early, Matthew would have spent the entire day floating here. Would the bathwater be clear again in an hour's time? Two? The body only has a limited amount of blood after all.

Rebecca turns off the tap.

She looks down at the plughole, visible between his bobbing legs. She cannot bear to look at the wound in his chest; a wound cut with such depth and precision. No hesitation. She has been a nurse for ten years and knows a determined suicide when she sees one.

The telephone is ringing down the hall.

Rebecca steps away from the bathtub, closing the door behind her. A wave of red pulses out into the corridor. She walks down the hall in her wet trousers and picks up the phone.

"Hello," she says. Her voice is lifeless, like it too is floating in water.

"Hi, Mrs Brighton? It's Rob here, Matt's boss. We were at a meeting this morning and we haven't seen him since. We thought he just might be off celebrating but –"

"Celebrating?"

"Oh yes! Excellent news. Ought to be in the papers tomorrow, but one of our own found their soulmate this afternoon. Shook hands with a client and Bonded right in front of us –"

"Bonded?" Rebecca feels the word tear at her insides. "Did... Did Matthew Witness it?" she whispers even though she already knows the answer.

"I reckon so. We were out at lunch and –"

"Rob – Mr Henry, Sir – Matthew has Severe Dissonance. He shouldn't have been exposed. He shouldn't have..." She pushes her fist against her mouth, trying to block the outpour that threatens to escape.

"Well," Rob says jovially, "we try our hardest but it's not like we can tell when someone's about to Bond now, is it? Or stop it even." He chuckles.

"Of course," Rebecca replies. Numb. She feels numb.

"I realise he was an Outlier but he should be over the shock of it by now surely? We need him back at work pronto."

Rebecca closes her eyes and takes her fist far enough away from her mouth to speak clearly. There are teeth marks on her knuckles. "Mr Henry, sir, Matthew won't be returning to work. Ever. I'm so very sorry."

She hangs up the phone before he can answer, and looks back down the corridor to see more blood seeping under the door.

Somehow she manages to call an ambulance and waits for them to take away the body. She calls the Meyers and asks them to collect Lizzie and take care of her. Later, Rebecca can hear her daughter's screams in the flat below as she scrubs the blood from the bathtub. She's going to have to explain this to her. How do you tell a three-year-old that they no longer have a father? She scrubs the bathtub but no matter how much she bleaches it, she still sees red.

Suddenly, a gentle hand brushes against hers. Rebecca jars and drops the sponge in the bath. It felt like a touch for Recognition. How could anyone think she would want to find her soulmate at a time like this? But it's not the first and middle fingers raised in the standard gesture she realises, but a tentative brush of fingers in comfort. It's Jane, one of the paramedics. She must have stayed because now she is hovering over Rebecca with a frown on her face.

"You're in shock," she says, and Rebecca doesn't doubt it.

Rebecca is given a sedative and falls into a fitful sleep that night. But dreams don't come, only memories.

*

It was the late summer of 1982 and Rebecca was working as a young nurse in a large London hospital.

Rebecca had lived in the capital her whole life but her family had fractured and she doubted any of her colleagues would know her name if not for her badge. She didn't realise how much the loneliness had gotten to her until there was a poster in the staffroom calling for volunteers to attend an Outlie and she had scribbled her name down before she'd even read the conditions.

Like most people, Rebecca had been raised to believe that Outlie communities were backward, simple, and inhumane. In truth, Outlies were small farming communities that raised their villagers without the knowledge of soulmates; an idealistic attempt to reclaim the olden days without something they called 'the burden of knowledge.' There was something about these dark whispers of forbidden places that instilled a deep sense of curiosity within her but there was also part of Rebecca that just wanted to escape the city for a while. She wanted to breathe in the countryside; hear a river without traffic, smell the scent of muddy forests without cigarette smoke, and actually look out of a window and see something other than concrete.

She was among the seven nurses from the hospital chosen to attend the Outlie to help with a suspected flu epidemic. The day before they were due to leave, they were called into a meeting to sign an agreement prohibiting discussion of 'Mainstream' society with the villagers there.

"This is a serious oath concerning the wellbeing of the Outliers," the administrator said. "If you don't think you can keep your trap shut," she added, with a pointed look at Nate, a young ginger-haired male nurse with a reputation for talking his way into trouble, "then don't go."

Nate huffed. "C'mon, that's kronos! What's the worst that could happen?"

Apparently Nate had forgotten his training from medical school but Rebecca remembered it all too well. History had proven that people did not react well to discovering that they had been living a lie. Outliers' curiosity about Mainstream could lead to Dissonance; a dangerous kind of depression brought on by the psychological jarring that the truth caused. The 'worse that could happen,' as Nate put it, was if an Outlier Witnessed two people Bonding. There was a case Rebecca studied in medical school about a group of Lifetimers that Witnessed during the 1950s breaks. There was a black and white picture of their bodies piled in front of a tree with one gun shared between them. No one knew why the Witnesses did it – they were always dead by the time people found them – but the theory was that the Bond was such a momentous sight to behold that it broke something in their minds; that the weight of how much they had been denied was pulled, just like a trigger: sudden and inescapable.

The administrator told Nate as much, but he just huffed again. "Poor buggers. Gotta be seriously messed up that offing yaself seems like the best option."

The administrator clenched her teeth. "Yes, well, I think we can all agree it's best to avoid revealing anything about Mainstream. Perhaps," she said with emphasis, "some ought to avoid talking at all."

The nurses were ferried onto a minibus at the crack of dawn the next morning. Out of the seven of them attending, Rebecca only knew Nate by name; the others were a tight knit group of middle-aged women that gave her no more than a passing glance. They were introduced to their guide, a man from the Outlie Affairs department of the government's Pair Bond Service, named Chris Thompson. Chris drove the minibus and chattered constantly in a manner that Rebecca thought was far too enthusiastic for 6am. Two hours later, the bus was bumbling down a one-track country lane somewhere in the Home Counties when Chris pulled over and turned off the engine.

The whispers of the other nurses travelled back to Rebecca asking much the same questions as she was thinking: *Why have we stopped? Where are we? Is this it?*

"Alright chaps!" Chris shouted back, all too cheerily. "This is as far as this old thing goes. We got a mile or two to walk so grab your bags and let's get moving!"

While the others muddled about, still muttering and complaining, Rebecca grabbed her backpack from beside her and pushed past until she was outside.

A deep forest lay before her, greener and livelier than anything in the city, and it greeted her with birdsong and the rustle of leaves in the breeze. She opened her arms to the countryside, tilted her head towards the sun, and breathed in her first breath of forest air.

She immediately choked on acrid dark fumes.

"Holy Zeus," she wheezed.

"Nuh-uh," Chris tutted, "none of that."

Rebecca cupped her hand over her mouth. She hadn't even realised she'd sworn using a Hellenic god. This was going to be hard. "What's with the –?" she asked and gestured to the smoke coming out of the engine that had caused her to choke.

"Oh that," Chris said, peering round the back of the minibus with disinterest. "It does that."

"Reassuring," Nate grunted in Rebecca's ear as he pushed past.

They loaded up their bags and followed Chris through a trail of snapped twigs that someone might optimistically call a footpath. It felt surreal, like she was in an action movie on the way to infiltrate a secret base. They had been told precautions would have to be made before they set off but it was all things she wouldn't have thought of, such as wearing simple woven clothing and leather boots so that questions weren't raised about manufacturers, and the fact that all their medical supplies were repackaged into cloth pouches and wooden boxes. Rebecca had read that some Outlies moved with the times but clearly not this one if they had to take so many precautions.

After ten minutes of walking, Chris approached a dilapidated brick wall covered in ivy that stretched as far as the eye could see through the forest.

Nate exchanged a sceptical look with Rebecca as Chris confidently walked up to the wall and pressed firmly against it.

Rebecca was about to raise her concerns when a vertical strip of light appeared in the wall and widened before her eyes. It was a door. They'd hidden a door in the wall.

Nate gasped beside her. "How frickin' rad is that?"

He ran past her and through the door before the guide had even fully opened it. Rebecca watched in amusement as he darted in and around it, presumably trying to find signs of the join.

"How d'ya know where to push?" Nate asked Chris.

Chris wiggled his fingers with a manic grin. "Magic."

Rebecca rolled her eyes and pointed to the carving in the door, a simple cross that obviously marked the spot. "Like that?"

"Oh," Nate said, sounding disappointed. "Well… still, a secret door. *Kinda* rad."

She couldn't find it in herself to disagree.

They kept walking until eventually the trees cleared and Rebecca was afforded her first view of Petersville. Hundreds of clay houses spiralled up the large central hill like a helter-skelter culminating in a large building at the top adorned with spires. The entire village was encased by a defensive wooden wall, tall enough that as they approached, it hid the hill behind it completely. The man on the gates nodded when Chris handed over the paperwork and then they were introduced to the Outlie's figurehead, a man called Master Peter.

Rebecca had to fight to keep her hands to herself. It had been ingrained in her since childhood to touch for Recognition with every stranger but it was a tradition based on soulmate recognition and they couldn't do that here. They had been warned repeatedly that touch was to be kept to a minimum.

Master Peter was a tall, gaunt, white man dressed in cloth robes, with short greying hair and a chin covered in week-length stubble. Apparently the name 'Peter' was passed down between the leaders of the village but looking at him she could think of no better name for the man. He reminded her of a school teacher; straight-backed and straight-talking. There was a tiredness to his eyes though, something behind the steel resolve that looked broken. The flu epidemic must be causing him great stress, she thought. His eyes roamed over them, taking time to examine each nurse before him. She bowed her head when he got to her. There was something about his manner that made her feel ashamed for even being there.

"I am Master Peter, elected leader of this village. We appreciate you coming here at such short notice to treat our community," he said, although his monotone did not reflect any gratitude at all. "My people have been told that you are from a nearby village named Easton. I trust you all to follow the instructions you have been given. I am the only one here who is burdened with the knowledge of your world and I cannot stress to you the importance that this remain true." He paused, presumably to glare at them again, but she wouldn't know; her eyes still fixed on the dusty ground. "I will give you a brief tour of the village and then you shall get to work."

Master Peter turned on his heel and strode through the open gates. Rebecca exchanged a wary glance with Nate, who had miraculously been stunned into silence by the intimidating leader. Then, Nate shrugged his shoulders and followed Master Peter, the others following shortly after. Rebecca turned around, looked at the berth of forest and blue sky that she had been craving, and with one last look at the still overly-enthusiastic Chris waving them goodbye, stepped through to the other side.

Silence followed them up the spiral hill.

The Outliers stopped what they were doing; all staring at the newcomers as they passed. The nurses were equally as stilted, wary of the Outliers' innocence and what medical disaster awaited them. Rebecca clenched her hands behind her back, suppressing the instinct to reach out for them in Recognition.

She couldn't help but notice how homogenous the population was: barring a couple of faces, they were all white men and women, probably stemming from only a few families. There was something similar in the Outliers' behaviour too, though she couldn't put her finger on exactly what it was: a guardedness, perhaps. They all wore similar cloth robes that reminded her of the Hellenic Priests in Mainstream, but theirs were the simplest of cuts and with plain material; not the bright silk colours that the Priests favoured. The villagers thinned as they moved away from the market and public house and up the hill through the settlements.

Upon closer inspection, Rebecca could see that most of the houses were small and made out of clay but sometimes thatch and wood were used as well. About halfway up the hill, they came across a notable exception. It was a large wooden cabin with a golden sun painted over the doorway. Master Peter called it the 'Prayer House' but it was unlike any of the grandiose Hellenic stone Temples that peppered Mainstream.

"Many people here subscribe to Biblia, an Abrahamic religion," Master Peter continued. "It is the only religion that Lifetime villagers have known. Some villagers may wish for you to pray at their bedside. Do not attempt do so, instead send for Father Daniel. He will be on hand if you need assistance."

Rebecca loitered at the building as the others continued their climb. She could see a multitude of fresh foliage behind it. Hellenic Temples, whatever their denomination, often had gardens, and she wondered briefly, if the Prayer House did too.

By the time she caught up with the others, they were approaching the tall, stone, spired building she had seen from the base of the hill. "This is the Town Hall," she heard Master Peter introduce, and he went on, stating that it contained both the infirmary and the council chambers. He eyed her warily as she rejoined the group, and her cheeks warmed, knowing that her curious loitering had not gone unnoticed. He said nothing though, and continued with the tour.

Behind the large wooden doors was a wide welcoming hall with a high ceiling. Light shone through the glass windows and onto the stone slabs at her feet. It was the only glass she had seen here unlike Mainstream that was fond of tall windows and ornamental mosaics. Instead, the Outlie's architecture seemed to rely heavily on wood; and in this large hall the most remarkable thing was the bare wooden beams that stretched across the room. You would never see such obvious evidence of building support like that in Mainstream where it was fashionable to have even electrical sockets hidden away, as if everything was a mysterious force of the gods. She found she quite liked the rustic charm of the building with its skeleton on display in a refreshing bout of architectural honesty.

A man bustled past them towards the council chambers, his head down, but Master Peter grabbed his arm and pulled him to face the group of nurses. "Good timing, son," he said.

Rebecca looked between the tanned, well-built, energetic young man with a scraggly beard and the pale, hard-edged father, but the only similarity she found was the delicate curve of their ears and the strong jawline that juxtaposed them.

"Medics, this is Councillor Matthew. We have two full-time councillors – Leah, being our other – and either can answer any questions you have about the village if I am unavailable."

Matthew nodded his greeting, which seemed to be the custom here. She had to clench her fists to stop herself from reaching for him. His eyes flickered across the nurses, taking them in, and in the brief moment they landed on her, she could see that they were the colour of the forest that enclosed the village. His smile didn't reach his eyes as he greeted them with an impersonal, "Welcome, Medics." He turned to his father, muttered something she couldn't hear, and then hurried away towards the council chambers without as much as a goodbye. She narrowed her eyes after him, wondering how he could get away with such brusqueness.

"Watch out for that one," Master Peter warned them, "he means well but he's a curious fellow. Very involved in the community. If he were to find out…" he trailed off, no doubt aware of their public setting, but Rebecca for one, understood his meaning regardless: his son was off-limits. "Let me introduce you to Councillor Leah," he continued. "I'm afraid I have prior engagements to attend to."

And with that Master Peter left them, just as tersely as he had greeted them.

Councillor Leah was small in stature with straight blonde hair that hung down past her shoulders. She curtsied upon seeing them like something out of a period drama. Rebecca heard Nate suppress a laugh behind her, clumsily turning his chuckle into a cough.

"Pleased to make your acquaintance, Medics," Leah greeted, her countenance perhaps warmer than that of her leader but still notably distant. "Allow me show you to your patients."

As soon as Leah opened the doors, Rebecca was assaulted with the strong smell of neglected patients. With dread, she noted that the small infirmary was full to capacity. There were a dozen straw pallets lined up on each side of the hall, pressed close to each other, with a sick person on each. There were a couple of patients closest to the door with other ailments but with no way to separate the contaminated, Rebecca wagered it wouldn't be long before they too were sick. The sound of coughing and vomiting filled the air.

"We've lost five patients to the sickness already," Leah whispered as she led them down the infirmary. "We only have one medic... Had," she corrected, with a suppressed sob. "He passed away last week. Young David was his Apprentice but he too has fallen ill." She guided them to the end of the hall where a fair-haired skinny boy, lay on a mat, obviously stricken with fever.

"David?" Leah asked him.

The boy groaned. His eyes opened and tried to focus on the group of nurses beside him before closing them again in exhaustion.

"These are the kind folk from Easton who are here to help with the sickness. Can you tell them your progress?"

After a moment, he breathed deeply and attempted to sit up. One of the nurses moved to help him. Rebecca picked up the wooden cup of water on the floor next to the boy but saw a house fly swimming on the surface and put it back down.

David struggled for words. "It is the fever that takes them. They cough, they are sick, and then... it becomes worse. We normally treat the fevering sickness with herbs but our usual solutions have had no effect." He stopped his explanation to cough into his elbow. The simple movement seemed to drain him as he slumped back down. The nurse still hovered beside him. "We heard," he struggled to say, "that the city of Easton has different medicine. Please. Please help us."

Leah looked from the sick boy to the nurses with pleading eyes. Rebecca followed her gaze from David's bedside to see the rest of her colleagues standing back, alarm crossing each of their faces as they considered the task ahead of them. Rebecca knew what they feared; it wasn't the sickness – likely no more complicated than the flu – no, it was the mention of 'Easton' that turned them hesitant; the reminder that they must complete this daunting task without so much as mentioning the outside world. How do they even have a medical conversation between themselves without using the word 'painkiller'?

Rebecca looked between their passive, anxious faces, and realised she would have to be the one to take that first step forward. She nodded to Councillor Leah, rolled up her sleeves, and then pulled a little pouch of medicine from her luggage.

"Okay," she said with determination, "let's begin."

Countless hours later, Rebecca allowed herself to take a break.

The nurses had been given sandwiches made by the villagers but Rebecca hadn't had the stomach to touch hers yet even though it was now approaching mid-afternoon. She stood on the steps outside and took a deep breath, relishing the clean air that had been sorely lacking inside. When she opened her eyes again, she noticed that the sun had shifted since her immersion and now shone from over the Prayer House and, like a sign, she followed it, sandwich in hand.

She didn't know the first thing about the religion here and it felt like it would be disrespectful to walk through the main entrance, under the image of the sun, when she didn't even know what it symbolised. So instead, she found a little wooden gate to the side of the building. She looked around, half-expecting to be caught out under Master Peter's reproachful glare, but there was no sign of him and the nearby villagers were going about their business unawares. She let the gate close behind her and followed the imprinted grass path round to the back of the Prayer House.

Once she rounded the building, she stopped in her tracks at the incredible view. This was the countryside that she had fantasised about when she first took the job; a garden lush in verdancy lay before her, full of bright flowers and buzzing wildlife, and over the foliage was an unobstructed view of green rolling hills that faded into the horizon. She closed her eyes and took a deep breath, filling her lungs with the scent of dirt and lavender.

She opened her eyes and noticed that she was standing on a paved area directly outside the back door. A few wooden stools were stacked in one corner and there were some seedlings growing in wooden crates against the wall. She wandered past the firepit towards the centre of the patio and gazed in wonder at the vine-wrapped arbour marking the entrance to the garden. A stone path stretched out before her, and step after step, she followed it.

The immediate ground either side of the path was marked into bays, not as regimented as vegetable patches, but still defined enough to indicate a dedicated gardener. The plants were also, to her knowledge, not all for practical purposes. The proud roses, the bright orange of montbretia, and the last of the summer blooms were grown for the sake of growth. They weren't needed, but it was obvious how much they were *wanted*. It may not have been as large or as glamorous as the Temple Gardens she'd seen in Mainstream but it felt authentic in a way that those formal city gardens never did.

The foliage behind the bays, she noted with delight, were allowed to grow freely, with wild flowers crowning the hedgerow like bridesmaid garlands. Birdsong filled the air and there was a hum of bees that Rebecca followed to a beehive, still busy even in September.

The stone path led to a natural pond covered in waterlilies and pondskaters with a single wooden bench at the side. It looked so peaceful and Rebecca yearned to be as close to nature as possible so she forwent the bench in favour of the dry, warm, grass. She sat cross-legged at the edge of the pond, just like she used to do as a child next to the lake at Athena Temple Gardens, and unwrapped the homemade sandwich from its cloth. The taste of proper bread – its full airy rise and the smell of flour – allowed a memory to resurface from long ago in her mother's kitchen. Back before the family fell apart there was a summer's day where her mother and her aunt had made bread, and Rebecca, being too young to be trusted, had sat at the kitchen table playing with her doll. She had forgotten that her family used to be more than one terse Solstice card a year.

Snap.

Rebecca jumped at the noise, nearly choking on her mouthful as she turned to see a large man attempting to crouch in the hedgerow, his face screwed up in a cringe and specks of greenery caught in his beard. It was so comical that instead of being frightened, she fought the urge to laugh out loud.

"Sorry!" the man said sheepishly. "I was gardening –" He gestured to the pile of weeds at his feet. "I didn't mean to disturb."

With a jolt, Rebecca realised who he was. The strong jaw, the council robes, the muscles that lay just beneath them. This was Councillor Matthew. She recognised him now from the glimpse she had caught that morning in the lobby. Peter had said his son was heavily involved with the community; she had assumed it was political like his father, but here Matthew was, literally getting his hands dirty.

"That's… okay," she said, not knowing if anything else was customary, and also not sure how much she ought to heed Master Peter's warning about staying away from his son.

Matthew smiled weakly and returned to pulling unwanted plants from the hedgerow.

Rebecca watched him for a moment with curiosity, until, with a blush, she realised she was staring, and pointedly returned to her lunch. She watched the fish swim aimlessly beside her; blissfully unaware of the complexities that lay outside their simple confinements.

Rebecca volunteered to take the first shift in the infirmary that evening. When her relief came, she walked down the main path helpfully lit by oil lamps until she arrived at the Inn.

The large hall was filled with chatter and laughter and well-lit by candlelight, though it took a few dozen candles to do so. She made her way to what she assumed was the bar: a long table lined with tankards and barrels where a very red-faced Nate was clearly taking advantage of the free drinks. She looked around and noted that the other nurses were nowhere to be seen and the villagers, although boisterous within their own groups, were giving Nate a wide berth.

"Hello, Nate," she said, her voice soft from the long day. "Have you eaten?"

He burped. "Aye, they got some pie and 'tatoes. And endless ale." He grinned. "This place is growing on me."

Rebecca rolled her eyes. "Maybe lay off the alcohol for a bit. You're working the next shift, remember?"

He huffed and waved her off. "Not for hours yet! Have a drink!"

"Maybe," she said, in a tone clearly meaning 'no,' "I'm going to order some food."

She left Nate to it and found the woman serving drinks.

"Medic Rebecca," she greeted cheerily. "Welcome! I'm Mary, Keeper of this Inn, along with my husband Jude," she said, pointing somewhere behind her, presumably to the kitchens. "Your belongings have been placed in your room, which is upstairs, second on the right. Now what can I get you to eat?"

Rebecca paused. She had assumed because of the lack of touch in Outlie culture and their natural distrust of outsiders that the Outliers were unfriendly, but this woman was welcoming even to a stranger, and had obviously made the effort to learn Rebecca's name. It was so different from the apathetic nature of most interactions in Mainstream; it always seemed hard to establish true connections in a place where your worth was immediately ascertained at a touch.

"Menu choices tonight are lamb pie or vegetable stew," Mary kindly prompted, "So what'll it be?"

"Stew, please," Rebecca said. As Mary walked away, Rebecca remembered her manners and managed to shout after her, "Thank you!"

Rebecca found a quiet corner and sat down at an empty table. Mary had given her a tankard of ale, which tasted earthier than any she'd had before, but also noticeably weaker. It took a few sips to adjust but once adjusted she easily drank her way down the pint.

When Mary returned with the stew, Rebecca meant to inquire

about the brewery or the chef but instead another question left her lips, "Keeper Mary? About the Prayer House garden... is there a gardener for it?"

"Oh, no, dear. It's recreational. Father Daniel has a couple of volunteers tend to it."

"Oh," Rebecca said. She had thought as much. She didn't know why she'd asked. Out of all the questions she had about this place, it was hardly the most pressing.

"Settling in okay then? Rumour is Easton is very different from here."

"Yes," Rebecca said cautiously. "It's very... different." She had to be careful so she stuck to something that would be true without need for explanation. "Bigger."

Mary turned up her nose at the notion. "Don't think I'd like to be anywhere bigger. How'd you know everyone otherwise?"

"You don't," Rebecca said. She shook her head, trying to dislodge the loneliness that had taken root. There was something built into the very structure of Mainstream that caused isolation; a million people around you but always with the constant reminder that you were no one without that *someone*. Sometimes it felt like everyone was scrambling around desperately for their soulmate just to use them as an escape; from loneliness, from work, from poverty. Despite how rare it was to be Bonded it still felt like you had failed at life if you had not. Rebecca shook her head again. It was dangerous to continue talking when she was feeling so melancholic; it must be the alcohol and her exhaustion that was letting her emotions flow so freely. Instead, she smiled weakly and thanked Mary for the dinner, returning to her solitude.

By the time she'd finished eating, Nate had stumbled up to the infirmary and the bar was emptying. There was no need for a bell, she realised; everyone in the village would know when the Inn closed.

She found her room, not even locked, just as Mary described it. The belongings she had been allowed to bring were still in their knapsack by the bed. She sat down on the bed experimentally. Straw mattress. Feather pillow.

She looked out of the single window. There was no glass, just a square cut into the clay and wooden shutters beside it. There were two torches marking the entrance to the village below her but beyond that, darkness. And the stars... more than she'd ever seen. The sky was much fuller than she had ever realised, with so many clusters of galaxies swirling together that they looked like clouds.

Rebecca fell into a deep sleep as soon as her head hit the pillow. That night she dreamt that the fish were in the sky, and the stars were in the lake.

Her first week at Petersville passed slowly, but day by day the patients showed signs of improvement. Apprentice David was making a speedy recovery now that they could treat the complications that were endangering him. With any luck he would take over the nurses' duties within another fortnight and they would be permitted to leave.

Rebecca had returned to the Prayer House garden every day but she hadn't seen Matthew there again; between her irregular shifts and his busy schedule, she hadn't expected to, but there was still a little spark of hope every time that she would. She knew she shouldn't speak to him because Master Peter would disapprove but she had barely seen Petersville's supposed leader since their arrival. She found she kept mentally rehearsing excuses to engage with Matthew: apologising for her previous awkwardness, complimenting him on the garden, asking him about the Council... anything. She kept seeing him around the village – him about to enter a meeting, or trading something on the other side of the marketplace – and yet she could never bring herself to go over to him and just talk, afraid he'd be as brusque with her as he was the first time they'd met.

She was walking back from her shift one day, exhausted, and looking forward to a long bath at the Inn to wash away the germs she still felt on her skin, when she saw Matthew outside the school. He was shepherding a dozen or so children, all no older than thirteen. He was jostling around with one of the older boys, and laughed when the child playfully slipped from his grasp. It was the first time she'd seen Matthew smile and it was oddly mesmerising. She hadn't fully realised she had stopped to watch until he turned towards her.

"Medic Rebecca," he greeted, letting go of the child immediately and straightening his posture. The children crowded around him while she awkwardly stood opposite them, unprepared to have a conversation.

"Councillor Matthew," she imitated. Although villagers here did have family names of sorts they didn't appear to use them after childhood: once they had a profession, it also became their formal name. She didn't think they were on a first name basis yet.

"Medic," one of the children spoke up. "Is it true you're from a giant building in the sky?"

"Wha…?" She stumbled over the start of her sentence but the girl was looking up at her with wide eyes, expecting an answer. "Where did you hear that?"

"Another outsider," the girl said, "the one with the beard." She giggled with a couple of other girls like they had an inside joke about Nate's beard. "Is it true?"

"No, I'm sorry," Rebecca replied. "I don't live in the sky."

"But he called it a sky-scrapper."

"Skyscraper?"

"Mmm-hmm."

Rebecca suppressed her instinct to roll her eyes; she was going to have some words with Nate later. "That's just what we call our buildings," she explained, and hoped it would suffice.

The girl looked disappointed.

"That's a strange word," Matthew commented. His forehead was creased, like he was actually contemplating the etymology.

Rebecca quickly changed the topic to distract him: "What's happening today then?"

One of the younger boys crossed his arms. "Don't you know?"

"Abel," Matthew scolded. "Medic Rebecca is new to our village. Easton might not have Friday playtime, isn't that right?" he asked her pointedly.

"Yes," she said, unsure, but playing along.

"Friday afternoon is for recreation," he explained to her. "Some children choose crafts, but naturally, the best kids," he said, ruffling the hair of one of the youngest with another bright smile, "choose to play football with me."

"Football?" she repeated, stunned. "You teach football?"

He smiled, ducking his head as if embarrassed. "It's a good break from meetings."

"I didn't know you had football here..." it seemed like such a Mainstream activity but she supposed kicking a ball was a universal pastime. "Where do you play?"

One of the kids started to sneer again but without even looking Matthew good-heartedly put his hand over the child's face and the kid squirmed away in disgust.

"There is a playing field at the base of the hill, furthest point from the gates."

"Near the Farmers' Quarter?"

He smiled. "You've been getting to know the place then?"

Before she could reply, an older boy in his early teens emerged from the school and threw a leather ball to Matthew, who caught it effortlessly.

"Duty calls," Matthew said as the kids cheered and ran towards the fields. "I'll, um," he trailed, his gaze torn between her and the kids who, in their eagerness, had already started to disappear down a nearby street. She wondered if he also felt nervous at being alone with her. "See you around," he said, then looked away and added, "I hope."

She blushed and averted her eyes. She barely managed a nod as he gave a small wave and began to chase after the children.

During the second week, the epidemic eased its grip on the village and the nurses began to disappear as some excuse or another called them back to the hospital. By the time their patients numbered half a dozen and none of them critical, it was only Rebecca and Nate left, with Apprentice David sufficiently recovered to cover the third shift. The patients didn't really need round-the-clock care anymore but while they had the staff it seemed sensible. Still, she knew eventually that the call would come for her; that Leah, or even Master Peter himself, would come through the infirmary doors one day soon and tell her to pack her bags. She thought of her single room in the loud houseshare in the crowded city and tried to make herself miss it, but no such feeling arose. She began to hope that maybe the hospital would forget about her, as they sometimes did in all their paperwork, and let her make the decision to return in her own time.

Nate, however, was all too eager to leave. She'd catch him sometimes, cursing under his breath about the smallest of things, like when they ran out of water and had to go to the well. He still hadn't adapted to the language either, still using "kronos" to describe things he didn't like and cursing using every Hellenic god there was, though it frequently got him curious looks. Unlike Nate, Rebecca was surprised by how well she had adapted in the last fortnight but she was still caught off-guard occasionally. Sunday, for instance.

On Sunday, she was browsing the crafts in the market when there was a sudden flurry of activity. Bemused, Rebecca watched as stallholders exchanged places and a steady stream of villagers began leaving the market and nearby buildings. Rebecca put down the garment she was holding and, out of curiosity, followed.

She rounded a bend and realised where they were all going. She knew she could have turned back, or made her way further up the hill, pretending that the infirmary was her destination all along, but she didn't. Instead she followed the crowd into the Prayer House.

She had purposefully not used the main entrance whenever she visited the gardens but buoyed by the worshippers she could finally cross the threshold. At first, it looked just as it did from the outside; like an old barn with wooden beams stretched across the ceiling. It was similar to the Town Hall in that regard; grand and full of light. Both were one of the few buildings that used glass windows instead of open air shutters, but here, they were mosaics of coloured glass that dappled the room in tinged light.

The villagers filed in and sat down on the pews and she was filled with a sudden anxiety: Were people assigned seats? Was it a great impropriety for her to be here? She stepped to the side, allowing everyone else to pass by her and remained at the back of the Prayer House, unsure as to what to do. As soon as she considered leaving, a new surge of villagers entered and she didn't dare go against them in case she caused a scene. Instead, she crept a little more into the shadows, hoping that they would forget her presence, but if the mutterings and turned heads in her direction were any indication, it would not be so easy.

The wall opened behind her and she jumped in surprise.

"Medic Rebecca!" Father Daniel greeted. "Glad you could make it."

She must have been lurking directly outside his office. So much for being inconspicuous.

"Take a seat," he said, gesturing to the rapidly filling pews. "Plenty of room."

Having been so openly invited, Rebecca now knew ducking out was an impossibility. She politely muttered her thanks and picked a seat as close to the door as possible and a good few yards away from everyone else.

When Father Daniel began preaching, it ought to have reminded her of being dragged to the Temple when she was a child, but it didn't. She remembered those regular Temple services as monotone and dull, failing to deliver on the expectation summoned by the incredible feasts and festivals that they lured people in with. But here, even at what she assumed was a regular service, the stories Father Daniel told were delivered with passionate conviction, and the hymns sung with reverence, and the morals strong. She could understand why the folk of Petersville took comfort in the belief of a singular almighty God rather than the dysfunctional mess that were its Hellenic counterparts. When she used to pray to Zeus, she thought he was more likely to laugh at her than appreciate her offering, but Father Daniel emphasised the benevolence of their God rather than his fierce power. She stayed for the entire Biblia service, and although by the end she did not believe, she had to admit that she was intrigued.

She stood with the rest of the congregation and followed them outside, nearly tripping over Matthew in the process.

He was in the doorway talking to a villager, and although he caught her eye and gave her a shy smile, he didn't make a move to talk to her. He and his counterpart were speaking in revered whispers and she didn't have the heart to interrupt.

Still, she felt her cheeks warm as she brushed past him.

Councillor Leah was standing outside. Rebecca gave Leah a friendly nod but was surprised when, instead of returning it, Leah came over to her as if Rebecca was the person she'd actually been waiting for.

"We normally break for lunch at this hour," Leah said. "Would you like to join us?"

"I..." Rebecca looked over Leah's shoulder. There were a number of folk Rebecca recognised from the turned heads at the start of the service, and now they were beckoning her to join. Was attending one service all it took for them to accept her? But before she even had time to think about it, Leah was already waving her friends over to introduce them to her. Their names were Ira and Abital, a husband and wife, and they too would be joining them for lunch. Leah led them, not down the hill to the Inn like Rebecca expected, but through several side streets, straight into the heart of the neighbourhood and into one of the clay houses.

"This is your home?" Rebecca asked, noting all the woollen throws and ornamental crafts that decorated in the simple room.

"Yes, for some time now," Leah said. "Welcome!"

Rebecca tried not to stare too obviously but it was her first time in a regular house here, having only travelled between the Inn at the bottom of the hill and the grand Town Hall at the top. Everything inside and out seemed to be made out of clay and there were only basic divides between rooms – no doors, just well-designed passageways – all on a single floor. It was through one of the doorways that Leah led them into the kitchen. A table with benches stretched the breath of the room over the stone floor and to the side was a lit grate being tended to by a man.

"This is my husband, Carpenter Joseph," Leah said as Joseph stood to greet them. He was shorter than most men with a full blond beard and an easy smile. From what little Rebecca knew of Leah, they seemed like a good fit; they mirrored each other in appearance and kindness if nothing more.

"He goes to the earlier service so he can cook for us," she explained, standing on tiptoes to kiss him on the cheek.

Joseph smiled indulgently at her.

"It's nice to meet you," Rebecca said with a nod as she knotted her fingers behind her back to resist the touch for Recognition.

There was a screech of wood on stone as Ira and Abital sat on the benches around the long table. Rebecca followed suit, still puzzled as to what she had done to deserve an invite, but they chatted around her in a way she hadn't yet experienced in the village; friendly and relaxed, rather than cautiously polite.

Joseph placed the food in the centre of the table – roasted meat, potatoes, vegetables, and bread – and encouraged them all to serve themselves. Rebecca waited until last and observed the others carefully so she could follow their customs.

"How did you find the service, Rebecca?" Abital asked. She was from a family of farmers, had long dark hair twisted in a braid, and was one of the few people Rebecca had seen in the village who wasn't entirely Caucasian. *Like Matthew*, her traitorous mind whispered, her thoughts always finding a way to circle back to him.

"You didn't seem familiar with the hymns."

"No, I think religious practices tend to differ between villages," Rebecca said smoothly. Her lies were becoming almost habitual by now. "But I enjoyed the service very much. It's kind of you to invite me to your gathering as well. Truthfully, I wasn't sure what I had done to deserve the invitation."

"Well, Leah speaks highly of you," Joseph said, "And we wanted to meet the newest member of our village. We don't get many newcomers."

"Oh. I don't know how long I'm staying for..." Rebecca murmured, and ducked her head with embarrassment.

"So tell us about yourself," Ira asked. He was a man so thin that his cheekbones stuck out like wings, but oddly it rather suited him. "What's Easton like?"

"Big," she said. It seemed to be the one word she kept coming back to. "And busy, but kind of empty... here, everyone seems to have family and close friends. I didn't really have that."

"Your family have passed?" Leah asked with a frown.

"No, that's not... they had a disagreement that separated them. One of my aunts married someone the others did not approve of," she said tactfully. In truth, it was a member of the Elite; the second son of a Bonded Pair. Some of the family clamoured after the riches it would bring, but to others, including Rebecca's mother, it felt like a betrayal.

"Some of them left... but, honestly, I don't know what happened to most of them."

There were frowns all around the table. "Every family has disagreements," Abital said, "but I can't imagine ever leaving the village because of it." There were murmurs of agreement.

"And you were content to live without your family?" Leah asked, incredulous.

"I never really thought about it. It was the way things were. I didn't question it, but I suppose... it is strange. And lonely. Definitely lonely."

28

Leah placed her hand over Rebecca's. Rebecca hadn't meant for the conversation to turn so personal and was deeply embarrassed by it but when she looked up she didn't see judgement on their faces, only understanding. Leah squeezed her hand. "Well, you have us now. No one's ever alone in Petersville."

"Cheers to that," Joseph said, and picked up the decanter of wine from the table. They held out their wooden cups and Rebecca imitated and drank with them.

They exchanged village gossip while they continued to eat and Rebecca observed them quietly. It never ceased to amaze her, the way they constantly touched each other, not for Recognition but out of friendship: Leah picking lint from Joseph's shoulder, or the animated gesticulation of Abital's hands casually brushing the others while talking. When Ira put a hand on Rebecca's back as a way of including her in a joke, she felt her pulse rise at the gesture. Touch here was so much more *sincere*.

As the wine flowed, they talked more freely despite Rebecca's presence, until they came to the subject of Master Peter.

"Can't blame him of course," Abital said.

There were murmurs of agreement.

"Why? What happened?" Rebecca asked.

Ira and Abital exchanged a look before turning to Leah.

Leah sighed and put down her drink. "We were told not to tell you. He didn't want the outsiders pitying him..."

"Master Peter's wife died from the sickness," Joseph filled in. "He had buried her ashes perhaps only a few hours before you arrived."

Rebecca frowned in sympathy. "I didn't know," she said, rapidly re-evaluating Peter and Matthew's behaviour over the last two weeks. Maybe Master Peter wasn't as naturally severe as he had first appeared; if he was hiding his grief then it would explain why he appeared so cold. It would also explain his recent absences. She thought back to Matthew's behaviour that first day too, how dismissive he had been of the nurses, and that moment in the gardens not long afterwards. Was he in pain then? Did he need someone to talk to and she had unconsciously snubbed him out of her own anxiety over what to say?

"Still," Abital said. "If Master Peter truly was unfit for duty, he could have asked Leah here to take over as Master."

Leah shook her head. "You forget that I've only been a Councillor for a year."

"Only because you were an Apprentice for five," Abital insisted. "You've done more service than Matthew."

"No," Leah said with emphasis. "Matthew is more senior."

"Why?" Abital asked. "Because he's Peter's son? That's crock and you know it. Matthew doesn't even want to be a Councillor, he just wants to spend all his time mucking around in the forest, what kind of –"

"That's enough," Joseph interrupted. "We have a guest." He stared pointedly at Rebecca who lowered her head at the attention.

"I apologise," Abital said, her voice more measured now. "Master Peter is a good man, and so is Matthew. I apologise for my words. I just think that Leah deserves more recognition for the good work she does. Master Peter ought to be taking advantage of her wisdom rather than pushing her to the sidelines just because he thinks she's a bit '*modern*,' like that's an insult."

"Abital," Leah warned.

"I'm done," Abital said, raising her hands.

Leah smiled softly at Abital, like it was an old argument they had, and Rebecca wondered what it was like to have friends that familiar.

"Master Peter is under pressure to succeed his line though," Ira commented. "Matthew is yet to be married and he is Peter's only child. Perhaps Peter believes that his legacy can instead be passed on through the Council."

"True," Joseph said. "The longer it takes for Matthew to find a partner..." he left the sentence hanging but the judgement Rebecca saw in their faces was enough to explain where he was heading.

She frowned at her plate, puzzled. She couldn't understand what the problem was. Matthew was in his mid-twenties, she hazarded, as was herself, yet they were already talking about him as if he were past his prime. But then, she reasoned, there were only a few hundred people in Petersville and as a Councillor, Matthew had no reason to leave the village; if he knew everyone here and did not love any of them then... yes, it seemed increasingly unlikely he would ever marry. Petersville did not engage in polyamory as many Settlers did in Mainstream. If his peers were settling into relationships then his chances of finding his own monogamous partner were becoming less and less with each passing year. She wondered suddenly if he had ever even been in love. As the conversation receded into background noise at this realisation, she felt a pang of deep empathy; Matthew must be as lonely as she was.

Rebecca was walking to the infirmary the next day when she heard a commotion in the council chambers. The shouts echoed through the hall and she saw some of her patients trying to surreptitiously eavesdrop from the doorway of the infirmary.

As she went to investigate, Rebecca spotted Leah standing outside the chambers, posted as a guard. "Leah," Rebecca greeted as she walked towards her. "What's going on?"

At this distance, the shouts were audible enough through the closed door for Rebecca to make out some of the words – "falsehoods about God" – and then, Nate's voice: "Oh, Zeus' tits!"

Rebecca cringed in dismay.

Leah said as if by rote, "Medic Nathaniel and Carpenter Joseph had a disagreement. It was brought in front of the Council."

"I should..."

Leah shook her head. "It's best to let them voice their anger."

"Not in this instance, trust me," Rebecca said, and made to push past her.

She was expecting more resistance but perhaps Leah knew on some level that Rebecca was right, or perhaps she simply wanted to be with her husband, but whatever the reason, she stepped aside and let Rebecca enter the chambers.

There were more people in the chambers than she expected. Carpenter Joseph had a handful of men in his corner while Nate stood his ground, alone, opposite. Master Peter stood between them, backed by a few council members. She wondered for a moment why Leah was excluded when so many of the other senior figures were there but when her eyes found Matthew's, standing behind his father's shoulder, her thoughts derailed entirely as he held her gaze.

All the men turned at her entrance and the argument dropped mid-sentence. Rebecca heard Leah close the thick wooden doors behind them.

"This is a private matter, Medic Rebecca," one of the men said with noticeable disdain. "Return to your work."

Master Peter raised his hand and the man was silenced. "She is permitted."

He looked as if he was about to object but Master Peter raised his hand again. "It will be useful to have a liaison who can understand Medic Nathaniel's culture."

Nate glared.

"Thank you," Rebecca said, and took a step toward Nate. "What happened?"

Joseph and Nate started shouting over each other again but amongst the insults flying between them she was able to discern what had happened. Nate had gone to the well for water and had struggled with the pump. He had cursed repeatedly and Joseph, frustrated with waiting, had confronted him and mentioned his language, to which Nate had snapped with some derogatory remark about monotheistic cultures. Words were exchanged, punches were thrown, and then the witnesses dragged them here in front of the council.

She could see the evidence of the fight now she was looking for it: a black eye blossoming on Joseph's face and a hunch that implied a well-placed kick, meanwhile Nate's pale complexion was scattered with fast-forming bruises. Even now they were inching towards each other, postures humming with eagerness for another fight.

"Oh my gods!" Nate exclaimed, not even bothering to hold back the plural. "You're all so bloody narrow-minded!"

Rebecca stepped towards him, saying his name in a warning tone.

"You come into *our* village," Joseph was saying, "and tell us *our* culture is wrong. You are our guest here!"

"Like I'd come to this shithole out of choice," Nate snarled, "with you rude, backwards, repressed Titans." He actually spat at Joseph's feet.

"Nate," Rebecca warned again, placing her hand on his arm. He shook her off without even looking.

"There he goes again! Speaking in the Devil's tongue!"

"Oh, I'll show you the Devil, you punk." And before Rebecca could so much as speak, Nate was aiming a fist at Joseph's face.

It connected.

But not with Joseph, she realised with delayed shock, but with Matthew. Before she'd had time to register it, he had stepped between them the moment the punch was thrown.

Matthew bent over as blood started pouring from his nose.

Rebecca swore and dashed towards him, elbowing Nate out of the way.

"Matthew, are you alright?" she asked, crouching beside him.

He glanced up and nodded but the tears in his eyes said otherwise. He was blinking them back stubbornly. She hadn't realised at the time but Master Peter must also have run towards them as he was now helping her pull Matthew to his feet.

Peter took his eyes off his son for a moment to glare at Nate. "You are expelled from Petersville, Medic Nathaniel. Pack your things. You have an hour."

Nate raised his hands. "Fine with me." And he stalked out of the hall.

"I'll deal with the rest of you in a minute," he said to the villagers. "Medic Rebecca, would you…?"

"Of course," she said, following his unspoken request. She ducked under Matthew's arm and led him out of the chambers. She tried to remain professional but this was the closest they had come to touching and even with layers of cloth between them she could feel his warmth radiating against her skin.

"Why did you do that?" she whispered to him as she sat him down on a chair at the far end of the infirmary, away from those still eavesdropping by the door. He was crying freely now. She knew it was instinctive from such an injury but she couldn't help but note that he didn't seem uncomfortable shedding tears in front of her.

"Carpenter Joseph is a good man," he said.

"That doesn't mean you should get between him and an angry Nate."

"Why not? It stopped the argument."

Rebecca didn't have an answer for that one. She put on a clean pair of cotton gloves and stemmed the bleeding with a cloth as she examined the damage.

"I'm going to have to set it."

Matthew grunted but looked up to her from his seat and gave her a confident nod.

"Want me to tell you when or –?"

"Just do it," he said through gritted teeth.

"Okay, deep breath through the mouth."

There was a thick crunch as Rebecca set the bones back to rights followed by a shout of pain from Matthew and then, "Mother… Holy… Fiddlesticks."

Rebecca burst out laughing before she could stop herself; Matthew obviously spent too much time controlling his language around children.

He glared up at her through his eyelashes. She tried to stifle her laughter with her other hand as she held onto his nose but she couldn't stop giggling. She was relieved when a smile emerged on his lips. She kept his gaze until her laughter faded and she had to

34

look away.

She taped his nose. "I've set a lot of bones," she said, "but that is, without a doubt, the most mild-mannered response I've ever had from doing so."

"What do folk normally say?" he asked. "Zeus' tits?" He chuckled. "Who the hell is Zeus and why do we care about her chest anyway?"

Rebecca knew she shouldn't laugh, shouldn't encourage him, but she couldn't help it.

"I don't know," she lied. "Nate says a lot of –" *(kronos)* "…nonsense," she self-corrected.

Matthew held her gaze. He didn't believe her; she could see it in his eyes.

They had only really spoken on two occasions and in both he had shown his curiosity. If she were to follow her attraction to him she realised she would have to keep lying to him and the thought unsettled her deeply.

She occupied the silence by cleaning the blood from his face.

"When I saw you in the gardens," he said eventually, "you were looking at the fish. This time of year the trout jump. Is Easton by a river?"

It took her a minute to connect the dots he had given her. "No, it isn't," she said. "I didn't know there was a river here."

Matthew's forehead crinkled in confusion. "Of course. It runs just west of the gates."

Rebecca put down the dirtied cloths and pulled off her gloves with more caution than it warranted, just to afford her time to think of a response. He'd been outside the gates. "I wasn't sure if… you left the village often," she said carefully.

"Some folk don't. Craftmakers need to sometimes. Traders. I trained as a builder initially so I got to know the forest."

This piece of information filled several missing pieces in her mind that she hadn't even realised were there. Firstly, it explained Matthew's unusual build; you didn't get such a muscular physique from sitting in meetings and playing football once a week. Secondly, it explained why Abital mentioned the forest while sharing her low opinion of him. But then, why did he change professions? Rebecca had already learned that it was rare among his people so this seemed highly unusual, but then, with a slow dawn of comprehension, she realised that she already knew the answer as to why: Master Peter wouldn't like his son roaming outside the gates when he knew of the dangers.

"I can show you where the trout are, if you like, sometime?" He said, his voice low and hopeful.

She looked down into his eyes and realised that he was asking her out. She shouldn't risk it. She should say no and return to her little room in London that he would never know existed and put this chapter of her life behind her. But there was a blush on his cheeks and he was looking at her so earnestly. She couldn't remember the last time anyone looked at her like she mattered, or the last time she felt her heart pound the way she did now.

"I would like that," she whispered.

Matthew met her the next evening outside the Town Hall. They hadn't arranged it but she was not surprised to see him there. No one seemed to formally arrange anything here; if you wanted to see someone in a village this small then you'd just go and see them. Rebecca had become so used to this way of life even in the couple of short weeks she had been here that she hadn't even noticed they hadn't set a date or place to meet. She had just assumed he would find her at the right time, and he did.

After the fight he had deemed his beard beyond saving and so was clean-shaven tonight, which only made his smile seem brighter. "I hope they're there," Matthew babbled excitedly as he led her down towards the gates. "I thought it might be a bit early so I went down and checked last night and I think I saw one but it was dark, I should have remembered a torch but I didn't have a guard and you can't have an open flame in the forest so…"

She was glad he was rambling because whereas his response to nerves seemed to be talking, hers was silence, especially here when she was so afraid of saying the wrong thing.

A chill went through the air and she shivered. In Mainstream society one would say 'Persephone will leave soon' to comment on the colder weather but she didn't know if Biblia had a similar explanation for the turning of seasons. Was their one god responsible for everything in nature? Rebecca had seen a child scolded the other day for taking "His name in vain." She supposed it was quite an offense when that god was also responsible for everything that kept them alive. She missed being able to blame any number of a dozen gods every time something went wrong: Hades, for those taken; Hermes, for trickery; Mnemosyne for forgetfulness, Kronos for chaos... the list was endless. She never believed a word of it, and maybe that was why she had also never met anyone in Mainstream who feared speaking against them.

This time the autumnal gale was enough to make her wrap her arms around herself. Dusk was already falling. "Quite a chill tonight, isn't there?" she ventured.

"Oh!" he exclaimed, as if he'd only just noticed. His councillor robes were longer and thicker than her cotton overalls. "Sorry, I didn't think. We'll be passing the Inn soon if you wish to get your coat."

"I don't have one here actually," she said. "I wasn't expecting to stay for this long."

His brow furrowed. "We'll have to fix that."

She thought he meant picking a coat up from the market tomorrow, or perhaps finding one of his own to lend her, but instead he reached for her hand and pulled her down a side street.

She trembled.

This was the first time she had touched him, skin to skin.

Even though she knew the odds and the horrendous consequences it would cause, there was still a little part of her, up until that moment, that was hoping they would Bond. She never truly believed she would find her soulmate – the odds being so astronomical – but every time she met someone she was attracted to there was always that little thought in the back of her head of 'what if?' and in Mainstream there wasn't the agonising wait to find out. But in the weeks since she met Matthew, that little seed had been allowed to grow, however unconscious, and now she couldn't help but feel the bruising weight of disappointment. She shook her head, reprimanding herself for her foolishness, using odds and probabilities as a comfort while she tried to focus on the warmth of his hand in hers; the simple touch that she had been devoid of since she left Mainstream. A brush of hands used to be so ordinary and so frequent that she had grown to hate it but now it was a comfort, especially coming from the man she had been so intrigued by for weeks. Here, touch wasn't a chore; it was used to show affection. She'd seen a young couple the day before; their fingers interlaced in a way that was so sensual, she began to think of it as a romantic gesture. She may not have Bonded at Matthew's touch but her feelings for him had grown nevertheless.

"Where are we going?" she asked when they'd taken enough turns through the maze of houses that she no longer knew which way was up. He was greeting everyone that they passed but didn't seem to notice the odd look people gave him when they noticed his company. He'd probably forgotten they were holding hands but she was too selfish to let go.

"Craftsmaker Joanna makes the best coats. It won't take a minute."

Before Rebecca could protest that she didn't think the hospital budget covered additional clothing, Matthew had come to a halt and knocked on a door. He finally let go of her hand with a blush and averted eyes. Her whole body seemed colder for the absence of it.

The door opened to a portly woman with two knitting needles in her hands and half a scarf falling from them. "Matthew! How lovely to see you. We've just finished supper I'm afraid, but –" She stopped abruptly when her eyes landed on Rebecca.

Rebecca shuffled her feet uncomfortably on the doorstep.

"Actually, Joanna, I was hoping I could source a new coat for Medic Rebecca here. The weather's turned."

At the prospect of a sale, Joanna dropped her hostility and her knitting and instead gasped in excitement, eyeing Rebecca up and down. "I think I have just the thing, Councillor. Wait right here."

She disappeared and through the open door Rebecca noticed that the interior looked much the same as Leah's house; all clay divides and woollen furnishings.

Matthew explained, "Joanna's husband is the Butcher. He gives Joanna and her guild the materials to craft with, though, as I understand it, the guild are a bit low on the ground at the moment."

Joanna came back, leather coat tucked under her arm, and told them, "Worst time of year for it as well, at the turn, but what are you going to do? We lost old Eve to the illness – before you got here mind," she added, presumably for Rebecca's benefit, "and she was our knitter. Ghastly task this," Joanna said, picking up the knitting once again and dropping it back with distaste, "and Lord knows I'm not the fastest. And then of course Selah has just had her first child–"

"I can knit," Rebecca interjected before she could stop herself. "If you need a hand making scarves or what-have-you for winter. I don't have anything to do in my free time and I enjoy it, so I could probably make a couple of items a week if you want. It would pay you back for the coat at the very least."

"Oh, bless you. Thank you," Joanna said with obvious relief. "I didn't realise you were staying for so long!"

Rebecca bit her lip, too overwhelmed by the implications of that statement to argue against it.

The leather coat was warm with its fur still attached and it was turning out to be a beautiful evening. Matthew was excitedly rambling about her new endeavour and the sun was beginning to set as they walked down to the gates. She thought they might have trouble but the guard just nodded his head and let them pass.

"I sometimes feel like I'm the only one here that likes going outside the gates," he admitted. "People fear it... I don't know why."

Rebecca knew exactly why; careful planning on the Master's behalf, no doubt subtly instilling a wariness of the outside from birth. "The wall provides a sense of safety," Rebecca said. "It's natural to fear what you don't know."

His face was concentrated once more and she assumed he would elaborate on her theory but instead his face relaxed, the topic forgotten. "Then they're missing out." He reached out to rub his fingers across a waxy leaf from a protruding bush. "I fell in love with the forest when I was working here. You never know what you'll see," he said in awe.

She wondered if, as happy with village life as he appeared to be, if he was also a little bored of it. She had a mental image of him standing on Oxford Street, just grinning in marvel at all people and the places, but then, she imagined all the strangers touching him for Recognition and the illusion was promptly shattered.

He led her through the woody undergrowth that emerged at a brook. By the fading light through the trees, she could see movement on the rocks. The whole river had borrowed the hue of red light from the setting sun. Rebecca gripped tightly onto Matthew's hand as to not to slip in the mud.

"How did you find out about this?" she whispered.

"I went off the map one day..." He caught her eye and smiled. "Father says I'm too curious for my own good but I wanted to know where Keeper Jude got his fish. Every year without fail he serves trout and I'd never seen them in the open river where we fetch water so I did my research and walked upstream until I found this. I should tell Jude they're back but..." he tailed off, a frown forming on his face.

"I understand. You don't want to be the one to give the death sentence."

"They haven't done anything wrong."

"Neither did the cow I'm wearing, or the chicken I had for

lunch."

Matthew shook his head. "They're inside the walls… it's different, somehow."

She squeezed his hand. "Thank you for showing me."

"You're welcome," he said, looking at her in that way that made her feel significant. "Rebecca," he sighed, like it was a benediction. "If you are staying, then I'd like to ask…" he looked towards the trout, the red on his cheeks highlighted even further by the sunset. "I would very much like to court you with the intention of marriage. If you are willing. If you can stay. I cannot leave my position here, otherwise I would offer…"

Urgently, she reached up and pulled him down for a kiss.

He gasped in surprise but returned it until every part of her body was singing in delight. He was laughing when he pulled away. "You're quite forward."

"You were the one talking about marriage!" she exclaimed.

He grinned. "Ah. I assume courting has different conventions in your culture then?"

"You could say that," she said, with a laugh.

He laughed again, resting his forehead against hers, and kissing her again chastely, like he couldn't resist.

"But we'll do things your way," she added.

"Is that a 'yes'? Are you staying?"

Rebecca reached up and traced his jaw with her fingers. His eyes were flickering over her face and she could see anticipation written in each movement. The truth was, every moment in Mainstream paled in comparison to this.

Her answer was an easy one. "Yes," she said, and kissed him again as the day gave way to night.

They began, as Matthew put it, "courting". He would meet her most evenings, either at the Town Hall, or would eat with her at the Inn. They took things slow at first, and even then, he was reluctant to show affection in front of others. She didn't know if this was how it was done here or if he was trying to keep them out of village gossip. Mostly, they would talk about their days, and as mundane as it should have been, Rebecca found herself relishing in it. She had never really had that experience as an adult of sharing her life with someone and it was comforting to know that someone cared if she had a bad day, or would laugh with her if she was having a good one.

Yet there was still a barrier between them, invisible and impenetrable. Often, his eyes would light up when she revealed something new about herself but then he would open his mouth to ask a further question, only to close down, and change the conversation entirely. It puzzled her. She had been warned of his curiosity, but now, when he had the opportunity to ask her anything he wanted, he hesitated. It was peculiar enough behaviour to unsettle her but she forcibly pushed it to the back of her mind, too afraid to disturb their fragile peace.

In their roles, both she and Matthew were more or less on call almost constantly, so sometimes she would expect to see him but hear from Keeper Mary that there was urgent business that evening, and if a patient took a turn for the worse or a serious accident happened in the village, Rebecca would not leave their bedside until they were stable. The first time that happened, Matthew visited the infirmary to make sure she had eaten and slept, but the second time, he actually stayed and told stories to the other patients until even Rebecca was smiling from it despite her exhaustion. From then on, he kept finding excuses to visit the infirmary.

It didn't go unnoticed. One day, about a month after she had first arrived in Petersville, she was practising stitching techniques with Apprentice David using scraps of leather when he said, apropos of nothing, "The village are talking. Are you and Councillor Matthew courting?"

She liked David; he had been training with the late Medic for going on three years and was now eager to pass on his knowledge of natural remedies. She had been sceptical at first but she had to concede that David was a gifted herbalist and the majority of common ailments seemed to respond to his concoctions. They worked well together, but until this moment, it hadn't occurred to her that they rarely talked about anything personal.

She hesitated, unsure how to respond. Matthew had been cautious with his affections in the fortnight they had been together but he hadn't outright told her that their relationship ought to be secret. Still, she didn't know if by answering David now, it would betray some kind of confidence.

"You did have courting in Easton, didn't you?" David teased.

She noted the past tense. They all seemed to assume she was staying but at some point she would actually have to tell the Mainstream authorities, her family, and even more dauntingly, appeal to Master Peter himself. Dread pooled in her stomach at the thought and solidified like concrete.

She marshalled her thoughts and turned to David. "Yes, I know what courting is. Matthew is a good man, if that's what you mean." She spotted his grip loosening on the leather, "Watch that you keep an even pressure."

David was silent for a minute as he remedied the problem and she thought the conversation might have been dropped.

"Matthew's probably just afraid to tell Master Peter," he said.

That makes two of us, she thought. "Why would that be?"

"You know… Master's wary of outsiders – sorry," he said, as if 'outsiders' was a derogatory term, "but Master will still see you as one. And Matthew's never shown interest before. In anyone. For a while we thought he might be…" his eyes flickered around the infirmary but all was still; their one patient soundly asleep – "otherwise inclined."

Rebecca smiled at his shyness. In Mainstream, because you could Bond with any gender it was also considered the norm to *date* any gender. If anything, it was monosexuals who received derogatory comments for being thought of as 'narrow-minded'. But, here, without the knowledge of soulmates and in a village so small, reproduction was perceived as the primary goal of a marriage and thus any slight inclination of homosexuality was discouraged. There was only one same-gender couple in the village as far as she knew and they tended the orchard on the outskirts, rarely to be seen socialising with the rest of the villagers. In truth, it baffled her.

"You know that's… okay, don't you?" she said cautiously.

David averted his eyes. "Not according to some."

"Then sod them."

David's eyes bulged comically at Rebecca's rare use of a curse word.

"Look," she explained, "some people just don't know any different. They think the way *they* are is the way that everyone is. But it does no good making yourself miserable for others' benefit. You ought to do what makes you happy in the long-term even if not everyone approves..." she shook her head; she was projecting too much onto him about her own issues. She'd give the kid one more push to accept himself and then she'd move on. "I courted someone of the same gender once," she said casually, "It's considered the norm in… in Easton."

David looked shocked, but then confused. "So you're not courting Matthew?"

"I…" she almost confirmed it, her heart beating in her chest at hearing the words together but then she paused with apprehension. "We need to talk to Master Peter," she reiterated, "before anything is decided."

That evening it was Harvest Festival at the Prayer House. Rebecca had half-heartedly considered attending as she knew Abital was bringing in goods from the Farmers' Quarter and there would be some friendly faces there, but when Matthew met her outside the Infirmary, she smiled and knew her plans were confirmed.

He grinned and held out his arm for her to take. He was wearing the purple councillor robes he saved for special occasions and he was clean-shaven, as had become his habit.

Cautiously, she took his arm. "If this is a public service we're attending, shouldn't we be discreet?"

He sighed. "Probably. But I'm rather tired of hiding away, aren't you?"

Before she could comment, he directed her into a nearby house – whose, she didn't know, as it was empty – and took down a dress from a wardrobe, handing it to her.

"Joanna wanted you to have this."

The kindness that the village showed her always managed to take her by surprise. Rebecca rubbed the material between her fingers; it was almost as soft as her clothes used to be in Mainstream, and she swayed on the spot, suddenly a little homesick.

His hands came out to steady her and she felt instantly grounded by the warmth that had become so familiar. "Are you okay?"

"Yes, sorry, it's just… very generous, and I'm... not used to it."

He laid his hands over hers and then pressed his lips against her forehead. She closed her eyes as she leaned into the touch. The spark of desire she'd had for him had grown over the last couple of weeks into a fire that flared every time he was near and kept her warm long after he had kissed her goodnight.

After the Festival, when the parents had taken the children home, Matthew and a few others offered to stay behind to help Father Daniel pack up the remaining food. It wasn't until Daniel was brewing the tea that she realised that there was an unspoken arrangement in place for further festivities. When the remaining congregation started towards the backdoor, Matthew took her hand and led her outside with the others. Although he'd sat beside her during the service, he hadn't begun to relax until the majority had departed, his father included.

He held her hand as the fire was lit, and didn't let go until tea was placed in their hands and a blanket thrown over their shoulders to ward off the encroaching cold.

"It's so lovely of you to join us, Rebecca," Father Daniel said as he took a seat by the fire. "I hear you're now living here permanently."

The whispered conversations of the others fell quiet as Daniel addressed the gossip that had no doubt been circling the village for weeks.

She looked to Matthew, who nodded, and then back to Daniel before confirming, "I hope to stay, yes. I just need to ask Master Peter for his blessing."

"You'd best make it sooner rather than later," Daniel advised, and Leah gave a hum of agreement from beside her. "Peter is a man who does not like surprises," he added with a meaningful look at the both of them.

Matthew lowered his head. "Tomorrow," he promised. "We'll talk to him tomorrow."

Daniel clapped his hands enthusiastically, cutting through their anxious thoughts. "Yes, of course, tomorrow," he declared. "The Lord has blessed us with a beautiful night, which, I believe, we ought to enjoy."

They sat around the fire until their cups were empty and their eyelids heavy. Their friends began to disappear, couple by couple, until Father Daniel excused himself to tidy away the crockery and Rebecca realised they were now alone by the fire, watching the embers glow red in the otherwise dark night.

She leaned into Matthew's embrace and felt the heat build in her chest even as the fire flickered at her feet. "I love it here," she whispered to the flames, but, she realised, that wasn't quite what she wanted to say. She loved Petersville because it made her feel loved, like she belonged, but if she was being honest with herself, she loved it here if only for one man.

She turned her head until she could see the fire paint his face from orange to red to colours she couldn't even name and knew that somewhere between his inquisitive mind and his bright smile, she had fallen in love with him.

She didn't know why her society had called this 'Settling'; the word that always implied giving up; second-best. If Bonding was perfection then she didn't want it; the imperfections she had with Matthew were all that she desired.

The following day, she resolved to speak to Matthew regarding her appeal to Master Peter but the council chambers were empty when she went to find him. She turned left towards the offices instead and upon hearing whispers, slowed her walk.

"Don't lie to me, son," Master Peter was saying, in a tone so terrifying that it halted Rebecca in her tracks. "There is not a heart in this village that hasn't seen you together. I never thought you'd sink that low for information, using the girl –"

"I'm not using her, Father! I haven't asked her anything!"

"You expect me to believe that? I catch you snooping around my offices *again* and now you're courting the only person in the village with outside knowledge?" He huffed derisively in disbelief. "You really think I'd believe that it's just a coincidence?"

Rebecca crept closer to Master Peter's office at the mention of her relationship with Matthew. The door was slightly ajar and she could see the two of them through the gap: Master Peter was red in the face, his frail body shaking with repressed anger, but Matthew was standing tall over him, not backing down from the older man.

"It *is* a coincidence!" Matthew shouted. "I was just here to search for missing papers."

"And the medic?"

"Her name's Rebecca. And I'm… I'm in love with her."

The words echoed and amplified in the room, buoying her heart even as anxiety twisted in her stomach, waiting to see what Master Peter would do. His face twitched and then crumpled. His hand came to rub over his face in that way that people tired of life do. He sighed, and then looked back up with a steel resolve. "You can't marry an outsider, Matthew. I won't allow it."

Matthew shook his head. He didn't even look surprised. He was silent for a moment, and just when Rebecca was thinking that it was over, that he wouldn't have the nerve to argue, he came out with the most brutal of blows: "Mother would have."

Master Peter physically recoiled, falling back against his table. "Don't you dare –"

"'Love is sacred, wherever you find it,' right? That's what she always said –"

"Matthew –"

"I will ask Rebecca to marry me, Father. Unless you can give me a legitimate reason why I shouldn't."

"She comes from a different culture," he scrambled to explain, "She doesn't understand our ways."

"Have you tried to get to know her?" Matthew defended. "Have you spoken more than three words to her since she arrived? She cares about the village, Father. She attends service and she knits for Joanna and she teaches David and she goes to the Prayer Garden every day –"

Peter held up his hand.

Matthew sagged. "Just tell me a reason. The real reason why you won't let me be happy."

Peter was quiet. Rebecca saw his lips move several times, as if about to speak, but no words came.

"You can't, can you?" Matthew said with frustrated tears lining his eyes. "You stop me from building, and you stop me from learning, and now you stop me from loving… and you never give me a reason for it."

They both stood in silence, seemingly exhausted from the argument. Rebecca was about to back away to give them their privacy, when she heard Peter's quiet words:

"I want you to be happy," he said.

Matthew shook his head dejectedly. "Then get to know the woman I want to marry."

Peter took a deep breath but then nodded firmly. "Fine. But, Matthew –" he said, just as Matthew was turning to leave, the hard edge returning to his voice, "that was your last warning. If I catch you in here again, I will disown you. You will spend the rest of your life locked inside the gates collecting the fertiliser for the farmers. Are we clear?"

"Yes, Master Peter," Matthew said, but when Master Peter turned his back, Matthew's eyes flickered towards the wood-panelled wall.

Rebecca feigned ignorance when Matthew found her at the Inn that evening. They were sat by the fire, Rebecca knitting while Matthew drank an unusual amount of ale.

After his third drink, he stood up and silently held out his hand. Rebecca put down her knitting and took it, not understanding why he was lighting a torch and leading her out of the Inn.

"Where are we going? People will talk –" she whispered. She knew how leaving together would look, and here, sex before marriage was highly discouraged.

"I've had enough of people's opinions today," he muttered. "Let them talk. I want to show you something."

He led her back up the Town Hall and nervously, she asked if they were going to see Peter, but Matthew shook his head and kept walking. He walked all the way around the building until they emerged at the back. He walked towards one of the three doors along the back of the Town Hall and took a large key out of his pocket. Most of the buildings weren't designed to have locks; if it was meant to be secure then it had a hidden doorway.

"What is this place?" she asked as they entered.

"My home," he said.

She watched in awe as he lit the brazier in the hall and his home came to life. Every stone surface was covered in rugs, even the walls, which made sense to use as insulation, but strangely there were no widows. Privacy for the Councillors, she assumed. He took her hand and led her down the hall. He turned into a doorway on the left and lit another brazier and a living area emerged from the darkness; kitchen, dining room, and living room all in one, with a noticeable door that she assumed was a pantry or bathroom. She noticed a bookcase at the far end which was interesting as she'd only seen a handful of books around the village, all of them handwritten.

"It's lovely," she said.

"The Councillor houses are. Leah and her husband will be moving next door soon, and my father lives on the other side."

"I never knew you lived here."

"We weren't meant to tell the outsiders."

Rebecca winced as she heard the resentment in Matthew's voice.

He lit a brazier at the end of the hall and led the way up the clay-moulded stairs. Only the grandest of buildings had staircases; most buildings were single storey and if they did have anything on a second storey then they used ladders or planks of wood jutting from the wall. The upstairs was a singular room that covered the entire spread of downstairs. It was panelled with wood, and the floor was wooden too, only adorned with the occasional rug instead of the dozens that littered downstairs. There were a couple of paintings, one of which she recognised as Artist Esther's work, but the others she didn't know. She smiled at the sight of the artwork in the otherwise simple room. Perhaps Matthew wouldn't be entirely shocked by Mainstream if he ever saw it, or at least their love for the arts.

The thought brought her swiftly back to the present. She looked to the large bed, actually on a frame unlike her bunk at the Inn, and nervously wondered: did Matthew bring her here to stay the night? Did he want to insult the traditions his father swore by so much as to not wait until marriage? Excitement bubbled in her chest at the same time guilt twisted in her stomach. When she understood Master Peter's stance, it was difficult to defy him in the way that Matthew seemed intent on doing.

Matthew shuffled nervously and took her hand without looking, but instead of leading her to his bed, he led her to the wooden chests to the side. He crouched down and lifted up both of the lids. The dark-polished wooden chest was filled with clothes, presumably his, but the lighter one was empty.

"I had Joseph craft it especially. The fish, you see –" he pointed to something carved on the lighter chest. She bent down to admire it, and gasped when she saw the incredible detail. There were intricate patterned borders but in the centre, a large trout jumped over rocks. She traced the raised wood with her fingertips.

"Matthew," she breathed, suddenly realising what this was. "Are you asking me to live with you?"

"I'm asking you to marry me," he said. "And, yes, abode with me, after, if you will… Closer to the infirmary. Good for emergencies and –"

She kissed him. "Yes," she said between breathless kisses, "Yes."

Master Peter called by the infirmary the next day and requested that Rebecca come to his office when the sun was at its highest. She wondered if Matthew had told him of their engagement and unknowing, dread followed her around all morning like a dogged shadow. When it was finally time, she left the infirmary and met Master Peter outside the chambers. He nodded his greeting but he didn't look like he meant it any more than he had on the first day. He stalked in the direction of his office and she followed obligingly, neither of them saying a word.

Her steps faltered as soon as she was through the door. From her vantage point the other day, she had not been able to see the large painting that hung opposite the patriarch's desk. A portrait of a young woman of Indian descent with a book splayed in her palms and a shy smile on her lips.

"Artist Esther's work," Master Peter said, noting her distraction.

"Who is it?" she asked, but she already suspected the answer. This was the missing piece of the puzzle that was Matthew; the mother that she never got to meet. It explained the skin darker than his father's, his unique passion for knowledge, and even that damn captivating smile.

"Elizabeth," Master Peter answered. "My late wife."

The name suited her, Rebecca could not help but muse. Intelligent. Fierce. Beautiful. It seemed incongruous that something as common as flu would take her.

"Take a seat, Medic Rebecca."

Startled from her thoughts, she did, feeling every bit like a nervous schoolchild. It seemed Master Peter did not want her asking any further questions about his late wife.

"My son informs me you are courting him and he insists I get to know you," he said with crossed arms and thinly veiled disgust. Rebecca prepared herself for the personal interrogation that was coming when he continued, "but what I think is much more pertinent is that we understand each other's cultures, particularly if you are going to inhabit Petersville for the foreseeable future. I propose we meet here at this time every week to discuss these matters. You can tell Matthew that we are 'getting to know each other' but of course given the subject matter of the things we are going to have to discuss, I must also request that our conversations remain private. I have many questions about Mainstream, and in return for your answers, I would like you to learn about our life here. Does that sound fair?"

Terrified, Rebecca nodded.

"Good. Then let us begin with a story."

She narrowed her eyes, sensing a trap, but she wasn't going to stop him; a story had to be better than the shouting match she had witnessed yesterday.

The story was this:

The hero of our story went to the Great War and fell in love.

He hadn't planned for it, neither of them had expected it, but in a time of war you didn't question the moments of happiness that you were given. The other man, the lover, had a family back home and a son who was too young to walk, but our hero only had the lover.

They served side by side, witnessed countless horrors, and under the cover of darkness they would kiss each other until the only nightmares they had were on the battlefield.

On another indistinguishable day, they were fighting in close range and our hero saw an enemy soldier targeting his lover. He didn't think twice. He aimed his rifle and pulled the trigger.

It wasn't until the battle was over and they ventured out from the trenches to claim their dead that they saw the enemy soldier, still somehow alive, stranded and lying in his own blood. The enemy looked up to our hero and his lover and did not have to beg for mercy as they could see it enough in his eyes. They called for the medic but camp was too far away and so they bent to carry the wounded soldier to safety.

But, then, as they were carrying the enemy, the lover's hand slipped and fell onto the enemy's bare skin.

They stopped in their tracks, transfixed, and our hero had to watch as the man he loved, and the soldier that had tried to kill the man he loved, joined souls.

"From what I hear," Master Peter said. "Spousal Depression is a cruelty in itself, but that is not the end of this story."

Our hero, unwilling to leave the side of his lover even as he Bonded to another, continued to carry the enemy soldier to their medic. It was a long and difficult journey, slowed even further by the weight of the lover's soul-transferred agony. It was as if our hero was carrying the burden of not one wounded soldier but two. But he would not leave them.

Eventually, they arrived at the medic's tent. A trail of blood followed them. The enemy soldier was now as pale as snow but the medic ran to the lover first, who was screaming in agony for his Soul who could no longer expend the energy. The lover begged the medic to help the enemy soldier but it was too late; the wounded man was dying; the light already fading from his eyes.

The lover fell to his knees with the body of his Soul in his arms.

He refused to let go, and soon followed the enemy into darkness.

Our hero watched as his lover, despite being in perfect health, breathed his last breath, not once thinking of his family back home, or looking to our hero who had loved him unreservedly.

"Soul break," Rebecca whispered. "After you Bond, when one of you dies, so does the other."

"Yes."

"So what happened to the hero of your tale? The man who lost his lover?"

"He returned home with a heavy heart and helped raise the child that his lover had left behind. He was not the only one from the Great War who had been torn apart by Souls. It was the greatest meeting of men in a long time. Before then, certainly before the Industrial Revolution, Souls were incredibly rare, but after the war many called for organisation to protect these new Bonded Pairs. Others, like my grandfather, took the opposite approach: to protect the innocent from tragedy."

"Grandfather? Your grandfather was the hero? Which means... the orphan child is your... father?" Rebecca asked.

He nodded. "Yes. My grandparents and many others like them made Petersville the large community it is today but there are families who have been here since before records began. The reason I told you this, is because if you stay, if you marry my son, you have to understand why we live this way. I need you to understand that the ancestors of this village wanted to protect their families from the destruction that Souls cause. This is not a fun little retreat, or whatever you think this is; this is an ideology that people have sacrificed for; to return to the simple life without the burden of knowledge. My father did this for me, and I have done it for Matthew, and if you are blessed with child, I expect you to do the same for them. The reason we do not tell our sons and daughters about soulmates is because we want to keep them safe. If they never know, they will never experience the agony of being abandoned, or

54

suffer the continual disappointment of the Search."

Rebecca understood. She had witnessed the difference in interactions here; how people touched out of love and not the selfish desire to Bond, how much they cared for the community they had built, how even the children seemed more carefree than their Mainstream counterparts. She could understand wanting to protect that. *She* wanted to protect that.

But she had the opportunity to choose that life, having known the alternative, and she realised that if Peter knew then he must also have made that decision at some point.

"But you know," Rebecca said, "and you didn't Search."

"It was my duty to stay. I was told when I relieved Grand Master Peter that the task would carry a great burden. Of course, in my ignorance, I thought he only spoke of the village, but when he passed me the papers that carried the truth I had already promised to serve our people. After elections, there is an overlap between Masters of four weeks, supposedly for further training but, of course, in reality, those weeks are spent battling Dissonance. By the time I stood before my people as their new leader, there could not be a single doubt in my mind."

"But weren't you curious about Mainstream? Even a little?"

"I had a duty."

"But –"

"It did not matter what I wanted," he said curtly.

Rebecca fell silent.

"Fine," she said, eventually, knowing without a doubt that Peter must have struggled with the revelation. She couldn't imagine the difficulty of hiding the deep depression Dissonance causes in a community as close as this and without even the option to leave, to explore, to calm the part of the mind that demands answers.

"But I was curious," he admitted after a long silence. "When your people arrived, I was concerned for my villagers, of course, but I also knew that this would be the closest I would get to having answers about the outside world. I observed you, and what I saw unsettled me. Your presence felt like static. Wound up like a string that is never pulled loose. The expectation you have of Bonding reads like stress in your muscles. I imagine you can't see it but as folk bereft of it, I can assure you that your anxiety is evident. I can't imagine what it must be like always hoping the next person you touch might be the one to complete you. You must carry a weight of disappointment for every touch that does not complete you."

Rebecca wrapped her arms around herself, a protective instinct to hide the wound that Master Peter had pried open with his sympathetic words. It took her awhile to speak again.

"Sorry, it's just… no one's really ever acknowledged the disappointment – the loneliness – like that before. We have our whole lives to accept the fact that it will probably never happen."

"'Never?'" Peter questioned. "I know the odds must be small –"

"They are. People like me – Settlers, they call us – we accept that, statistically speaking, it's not going to happen. We try to get on with our lives, even if, as you say, the burden never goes away."

"There are really so few that meet their soulmate?"

"Yes. There's probably only as many Bonded Pairs in Britain as there are people in the Farmer's Quarters here. Just over sixty. That's one hundred and twenty people Bonded out of fifty-six million."

"That is so... low," Peter whispered.

"The odds seem to get slimmer every year now," Rebecca explained. "There was a surge after the war, as you noted, and then with commercial travel… but as the population grows…" she shrugs.

"But that doesn't make any sense," Peter said, suddenly furious. "How can that be?!"

She held up her hands in a gesture of placation; Peter closed his eyes pained. When he reopened them, she continued.

"You need to think of it like this. Imagine the world is a room with six people. They will find their Pair in seconds. But then you add another ten and it takes a little longer. Well, just keep adding and adding and then add more rooms and more space and then more people besides. After a time, there are just too many people – too many places to look. It takes longer and longer. And then some stop looking and some just leave the room altogether. What you know is based on the world as it was sixty, seventy, years ago. Things have changed."

Rebecca saw the weight of this realisation drag his posture further into his chair. But still even as she pitied him, she found that she also envied his ignorance.

"But there's a difference between probable and possible. It can still happen," Rebecca said earnestly and he looked up. "Aren't you worried that one day it might? You can't identify Souls. You can't physically stop Bonding. One of your villagers could Bond with a trader, or an intruder, or with each other. You don't know for sure that one day Zeus won't gift this village with two Souls. Born here. Raised here. And they'll Bond here, in front of the innocents you're trying to protect, and those that Witness will perish, and even those that don't will suffer severe Dissonance because of it and forever carry the burden that you've tried so hard to relieve them of. It won't be like the old days when Bonding was treated like a miracle, an aberration, because I've seen it: on some level these people know they've been lied to. I see it in Matthew every day. Every glimpse of curiosity is stamped down upon. They *know* they have something to fear. And if they Witness, they will undoubtedly break. How are you not worried?"

Master Peter bowed his head. "There is not a day that goes by that I don't think about the possibility," he said gravely. The honesty was more than she expected. She was prepared to be scolded for questioning his ways but he treated her question as if it were almost welcome.

"One day," Rebecca said carefully, "at one of the Outlies somewhere in the world, it will happen. It's inevitable."

"Villages like ours secure the happiness of hundreds of thousands of people. Thousands of truly unburdened children. If a couple of people suffer from Witnessing then that might be a price worth paying."

"You've don't believe that," Rebecca said confidently. "You're just too far down this path to turn back. If the Outlies disbanded then the occupants would be forced into Mainstream anyway, and statistically, even more would be likely to perish from Witnessing."

"You speak like it's a certainty that my people will die upon Witnessing. But can't we prevent it? Isn't there anything I can do?"

Rebecca wondered how long he had wanted to ask these questions. With Grand Master Peter dead, and presumably all the founders, there was no one left in the village that shared the burden of his knowledge. The papers he was given could only hold limited information and must be severely outdated judging by his line of questioning. She just wished she had a better answer for him.

"No," she said. "Lifetimers don't have the time to process – to grieve, almost, for their missing Pair – that Mainstreamers spend their lives coming to terms with. That constant cycle of expectation and disappointment, that stress you said you could see in me when I first came here, it's condensed into such a short space of time and with such a strong impact that when they Witness the mind can't cope. If they've gone through Dissonance, or they've been integrated into Mainstream for long enough and been gradually introduced to the sight of Pairs then maybe it's possible but in every case of Outlier Witnesses so far, it has ended in suicide. They will find a way to end it. By whatever means necessary."

Rebecca went back to work and tried to push her conversation with Master Peter to the back of her mind. In return for the weekly meetings, he had given her permission to stay and to marry Matthew. It felt final now. She would have to use the postage stamps hidden in Master Peter's office to write to the hospital, and to her landlord, and also a member of her family, she supposed, but then she could stay here indefinitely. The thought didn't scare her exactly, but there was an anxiety crawling under her skin that she couldn't quite explain.

By the end of the day, her anxiety had grown and she went to find Matthew, only he wasn't in any of his usual haunts. So she ate supper at the Inn, alone, for the first time in weeks, and afterwards, lit a torch and made her way back up the hill towards his house.

There was no reply when she knocked. Worried, she pushed the door a little and became even more concerned when it gave way. Inside was pitch black. She kept her torch lit as she walked the corridor.

"Matthew?" she called. "It's me. Are you here?"

The silence pressed down around her. She peered into the kitchen but the light from the torch showed no sign of it having been recently used. She made her way up the stairs, dread building with every step.

She held her breath as she moved the torchlight around the bedroom, prepared to see nothing but an empty chest, or, worse, an unmoving body. But, no, there he was, huddled on the wooden floor, his knees drawn up, his back against the bed, eyes staring blankly ahead at the chest he had bought her. He looked strangely small. He did not seem to even notice her.

She lit the brazier, bathing the whole room in a startling orange glow, and extinguished her torch in the bucket beneath it. One of the windows was open, letting in the cold night air. She shivered and walked over to close it but when it creaked shut, she wished she hadn't; the absolute silence was worse than the cold.

She still had her back turned to him when he spoke, quiet and broken. "Why are you here?"

"I was worried about you; I hadn't seen you all day." She cautiously made her way towards him; unsure what had sparked this dark mood of his.

"No," he said, closing his eyes with what looked like great strain. "I mean, why are you *here*?"

As she looked at him, her confusion gave way to horror. He knew. Somehow, he knew. She felt like the floor had been taken out from beneath her; like she was freefalling through the wood and the stone all the way into the earth and beyond, molten and moving with the rocks. He *knew*.

His withdrawn behaviour suddenly clicked into place as Severe Dissonance. *How long had he been here suffering? What did he know? How did he find out? Did anyone else know?* The questions threatened to overwhelm her. He could take the entire village with him if he uttered a single word. But, selfishly, her largest concern was for herself. If Matthew knew about Mainstream then whatever they had would end. He would undoubtedly resent her for lying to him all these months and her new life would lie in tatters before it could even truly begin. Rebecca was almost afraid to question him, to confirm it, in case he confirmed her fears too. She could barely speak through the fear clogging her throat.

"You heard us," she said. It was the only explanation that made sense but if Matthew had indeed overheard her speak to Master Peter then that was *hours* ago. Dissonance was meant to be immediate and hard hitting. He should have left to Search, or screamed for answers, or followed the more troubling urge to eradicate himself from the equation entirely. If he was still here – quiet and meditative – then there must be a very good reason for it. Maybe he wanted to interrogate her, get all the information he could before he left or… she realised with heartbreak, he was here to say goodbye. Tears stung her eyes at the thought but she blinked them back as he gave the smallest of nods to confirm her suspicions; he had overheard their conversation.

She swallowed her grief. If he was going to leave then there was nothing she could do to stop him but she was a medical professional and she had to talk him through this, answer his questions, and ease his Dissonance any way she could. She took a deep breath, trying to push her own emotions aside, and carefully sat beside him on the floor.

He flinched as she drew closer and her heart broke at the rejection.

She stared at the carvings of the fish opposite them – once a clear and romantic gesture now shrouded in uncertainty – and collected herself the best she could. Then, she dared to answer his question. "I'm here because…" she trailed off, trying to dismiss her sullen thoughts. He didn't need to know the intricacies of her decision to stay here – of the loneliness that drove her here and the observations she had made since – he just wanted to understand *why*. "I *wanted* to be here," she stated. "I had the *choice*. I'd understand though if you…" She took a deep breath and let her head fall back against the mattress. "If you no longer do. You must feel the need to Search. If you have questions about Mainstream, I can –"

He shook his head vigorously. "I have many questions," he said with a broken laugh. "My whole life has been a lie," he said with a grimace. "And I'm not sure I even understand why." He took a deep breath and repeated sincerely, "I have *many* questions. But…" he trailed off to pick at his fingernails which were already bleeding from his vigorous attentions. "I don't understand how it could be true. How my *own father*," he spitted in anger, "could keep something so monumental from me. And how…" he broke off again and stared at Rebecca with a pained look of longing. "How there can be anything greater than my love for you. I even thought…" he said with another humourless laugh, "that we might be…" he hesitated, as if he could not say the word that was the crux of every prevarication in his life. He shook his head, and tried again, "I feel you so much in my heart, since the moment we met, that I hoped, if there truly were soulmates," he said the word with an odd inflexion, the notion still foreign on his tongue, "then we might be… then we *should* be... but I've been sat here for hours and as much as you're in my heart, you're not in my soul, are you?"

Rebecca shook her head, choking back tears. "Our minds would be almost as one. Souls share thoughts, feelings, even movements sometimes… You would know. You would have known straight away, from the moment we first touched in that alleyway..." she said, remembering her own unconscious disappointment in that pivotal moment. "They say it feels like the whole universe in your mind, ever expanding, reaching out in search of the other until you are entirely one… entirely consumed…" she shuddered unconsciously. Somewhere along the lines she had stopped wanting that for herself; the notion of merging souls with another now seemed unnatural; suffocating. "There is no mistaking something like that," she concluded uneasily.

"I thought as much." He thumped his head back against the hard edge of the bedframe, and then, heartbreakingly, he began to weep.

Rebecca wanted to reach out to comfort him but her medical training screamed at her not to. Dissonance was like an exposed nerve. You answered their questions – calmly and matter-of-factly – but you did not reach for Recognition until they initiated it. Touch in and of itself could be a trigger due to its cultural importance in Mainstream. And so, she suppressed her lover's instincts and sat back on her heels and watched helplessly as he cried.

"You're suffering from Dissonance," she informed him, in that calm tone that she had been schooled in. "Your mind is trying to comprehend all the differences, consequences, and opportunities of your newfound knowledge and it can be very overwhelming. You might feel angry, or lost, or confused, and I'm here to help talk you through it. Whatever you need."

Rebecca waited until his tears had subsided once again and then took a deep breath and finally broached the subject that he would need advice on most of all.

"A lot of people in your position feel the need to Search after the revelation. Searching is, uh, the act of purposefully meeting more people in the hopes that one of them is your soulmate. Many people in Mainstream do this as a way of life. We, uh," she said, swallowing her grief, "actually recommend it. Medically speaking. After Witnessing, or after… well, after receiving the burden. It's been proven to ease Dissonance. When you feel like you've tried to find your other half, it can put your mind at ease. If you want to, when you're ready, I can…" this time she failed to keep her tears at bay as a couple slip past the barrier of her eyelashes and roll down her cheeks. "I can help. Help you do that. It's usually done by integrating you into Mainstream, somewhere quiet at first, and we, uh, set you up with a Circle – which is like a, uh, Searching group – and a Dissonance counsellor, a Prayer House too if you want it... Whatever you need. Just tell me –"

Matthew shook his head again, viciously, with tears in his eyes, and teeth digging into his lips.

"Matthew," she said calmly. "You're going to have the urge to Search. If you haven't already experienced it then –"

He cried out, cutting her short. "I have," he confessed. "I've thought about it. I still *am* thinking about it. I can't –" he yelled suddenly, muffled by the movement of his head between his legs. "I can't *stop* thinking about it – who they are, what they look like, where they are, if they're looking for me... And I don't know why –" he admitted, his tear-streaked face finally emerging from his cocoon. "Because I *love* you," he said, looking at her with desperate, teary eyes, "and I'd never normally think to leave you, except that –" Rebecca forced down her own tears at his words even as they tore her apart. "What if they're out there, somewhere, looking for me, and I... I'm just hiding away here? Never to be found?" He shook his head. "It seems like the utmost cruelty to know that they exist – or *did* exist, I suppose..." he frowned as this thought occurred to him and looked to Rebecca for confirmation, "You wouldn't even know if they had died, would you?"

Rebecca shook her head. It was the plot of many Shakespeare tragedies.

He grunted, his frown still firmly affixed, as he continued "– to know that they exist – or *existed* – and not even know what they look like," he finished. "It's madness. It must drive people to madness."

"It does, sometimes, if you let it." Rebecca sighed sadly, having witnessed first-hand many results of such madness in the emergency room – lovesick teens with cut wrists, broken bones in the desperate pursuit of Searching, lonely romantics with the dead look in their eyes – the knowledge was known to drive many to madness. "But in Mainstream, people have their whole lives to come to terms with the odds of Bonding and decide what they want to do with the knowledge but you –"

"I know what I want," he interrupted with certainty. "I want to stay."

"Matthew –"

"No, listen. I *am* curious. I have thought about it. But I keep coming back to the same thing; I wouldn't leave – I wouldn't *Search* – because it would mean losing you. No matter how great the promised happiness is if I found my soulmate, I doubt it would erase the pain of leaving you to find it. And if that's not 'medically recommended' then quite frankly, I don't give a damn, because I'm not leaving you; not for anything."

Rebecca's heart soared at the declaration. She could scarcely believe it. He was still early in his Dissonance and could yet change his mind, but the fact that he was thinking of her mere hours into this revelation made her want to believe that maybe they could come out of this the other side. He wasn't even blaming her for the secrecy. Not yet, at least.

"But you had the choice your whole life," he concluded, "And that's what I don't understand. Why are you here? Why did you even come here at all when you could have had… that?"

She sighed, wondering how to explain her decision. She knew that if she had never come here then Matthew would have spent his life alone, and if her life had continued along the same trajectory, she might have ended up the same way, but she didn't know that going in. She had only spent a month in Petersville but already she had found a happiness she didn't know she could have.

"I came here because I was lonely," she whispered, like a confession. "In Mainstream, loneliness is like a disease that you can't shake. Everyone is Searching so hard for that one person that they don't make time for anybody else, sometimes they even trample over the ones they love to get there," she said, thinking of her own fractured family. "And Souls are so revered that there's this hierarchy almost, a huge gap between those that have Bonded and everyone else. It's the foundation for so much of society that I didn't even realise there was another way to be. But this life… where everyone is on an even keel, where neighbours look out for each other, where the joy is in the work completed and friends made… it's simpler. Healthier, probably. And I'm staying because I've found where I belong. My family. That's more important to me than trying to find my soulmate."

"I like it too," he whispered with a smile lilting his lips. His eyes searched hers with familiar curiosity. "Did you ever try to find him?"

"Or her," she corrected absently. Your soulmate could be of any gender; she knew she was being pedantic but she didn't want to mislead him by not correcting inaccuracies. "No," she answered vehemently and then, "Well, I mean to say that I wasn't a Dedicated Searcher. There are some folk who really do try. They travel and meet as many people as they can, try to increase the odds… but in general, we just get on. It's just our society works very differently because of the…" she tried to find a way of explaining in a way that he would understand but she kept coming back to her conversation with Peter. It really was the best word for it. "Burden," she finished solemnly. "There's more touch because that's what makes souls Bond. Every time there's an exchange, we ensure our hands brush and whereas here you greet with a nod or a wave, in Mainstream, there's this gesture you do to passing strangers –"

"Show me?" he asked urgently. There it was; the burning curiosity behind the darkness of his eyes. She knew he would eventually ask, but she didn't think it would be so soon. And now he was finally giving her the opportunity, she couldn't resist fanning his curiosity and seeing how the fire spread.

"Okay," she said. She held up her right hand and tucked her ring and little fingers underneath her thumb so her first and middle fingers protruded out together like a salute. "Like this."

He mirrored the move, although the gesture wasn't as tight as hers.

"Almost," she said, "but you don't want people getting tangled up, so you need to keep your other fingers far out of the way."

He adjusted it.

"Okay, and keep those two fingers that are sticking out really close together. It's more polite... don't ask me why."

His Recognition gesture was near perfect now.

"Good, okay, so then we just both move to touch our fingertips together. Often because you're walking past, it's just a touch at hip-height, you just turn the hand at your side outwards a little, towards them, and they do the same."

Matthew's forehead furrowed as he tried out the movement.

It was strange having to explain the custom to someone. It was something that you saw adults doing when you were a kid and mimicked in the playground until you hit puberty and started doing it for real. She remembered the first time she reached out in Recognition to a stranger. She must have been about eleven. She hadn't had the guts to do it when she was walking past but later Rebecca had seen the stranger eating a sandwich on a bench and purposefully strode towards her and held out two fingers. Painfully childish now that she looked back on it but everyone had an embarrassing early Recognition story and perhaps she was just giving Matthew his.

Rebecca tried again. "Because we're sitting down, we can just raise our hands towards each other like this." She turned towards him and held out her hand like she would for a handshake, though with her two fingers prominent.

Cautiously, he mirrored her, until their fingertips brushed each other. She closed her eyes at the sensation. She hadn't realised how much she had wanted to do this with him until now. She knew you could Bond at any touch of bare skin but because this was the most traditional way of doing so there was something inherently romantic about it to her. Their hands hovered for a moment mid-air, tips trembling with the effort of staying still. She opened her eyes to see the curious expression on his face fall at the same time he dropped his hand.

"You do that with strangers?" he asked.

"It feels intimate, I know, but in Mainstream, touch is desensitised. Sometimes hundreds of people touch you every day. You have to think nothing of it or you'd become overwhelmed."

He shuddered. "I can't imagine that".

"Many people don't like it," Rebecca said softly. "You can wear a thick black band, it symbolises that you don't want to be touched. If we integrate you into Mainstream that's how…" she trailed off at Matthew's pointed glare, remembering his insistence that they not leave the village.

For a moment, they were silent. Sensing his willingness to touch again she picked up the hand that had fallen in his lap and laced her fingers through his, gently encouraging a change of topic. "I know you are having a difficult time with your father... Is that why you were in his office? I heard you argue yesterday, I thought perhaps that you might have been there to make amends."

"You…?" He shook his head. "I'm sorry you had to see that. I was villainous towards him yesterday, I shouldn't have said those things. He's my father, I –" He stopped, and rubbed his hands over his chin where his beard used to be. "But, yes, since we lost mother, father has been worse than usual. He rarely leaves his office but never tells me why. We had always argued but when we lost mother it was like we lost our buffer. Now we can't seem to have a conversation without raising our voices. So I've been avoiding him. That's why I didn't tell folk about us because I knew…" He narrowed his eyes. "I just knew he would disapprove."

"He gave us his blessing today," she whispered. "But I guess you heard."

"Yes," he said with a small smile. "If you still want to…"

"I do. If you do."

"Of course."

"Okay."

They fell into silence again, Matthew's fingers moving to trace over her fourth finger. They wore wedding bands on fingers here, rather than on wrists. "In any case," Matthew said. "It had gotten to the stage where I knew he was hiding something big about what lay beyond the boundary. He'd banned me from asking about it and I was no longer a builder so I couldn't look for myself but... I knew there would be a hidden room in his office. And when he caught me in there yesterday, I watched him to see where his eyes went."

"You wanted to get caught."

"I wouldn't know where else to look otherwise. It probably would have taken me several trips to locate it and each visit was a risk. So, yes, I wanted to get caught."

Rebecca smiled to herself. "That's really smart."

"That's one word for it."

She shuffled closer towards him.

"What did you find?" she asked seriously, knowing that while she was having a civil conversation with Peter over lunch, Matthew must have been only yards away, behind a closed door, processing such life-altering news alone.

He looked to their joined hands. "A lot I didn't understand," he said, "numbers and machines and things locked even further away, but then I heard you two and it made sense. All the secrets and the lies... everything made sense. I assume the squares I found were to contact the outside world?"

He described what they looked like and she smiled when she realised what he was trying to explain. "Postage stamps. They're used to send letters to... well, anyone in the world, really."

"Of course," he laughed.

"What?"

"The etymology. *Post-* and *-age*. Latin. French. The act of posting."

Rebecca laughed and shook her head. "Where do you learn these things?"

"It was a hobby of mine when I was a child, so my mother had a book made for me for my thirteenth birthday. It's still on my bookshelf, I believe."

Rebecca smiled. She never did have a good look at those books downstairs.

"Father didn't approve though. I think a lot of the words were Greek in origin… that's the birthplace of your religion, isn't it? It was in the documents I found. I thought it had a lot of reach in language considering its lack of influence everywhere else but that explains it."

"You're handling this surprisingly well," Rebecca couldn't help but observe.

Matthew laughed, and this time Rebecca could hear the madness lining it. "I've been sat here since midday. I've had time to pretend I'm handling it well."

Rebecca reached for his shoulder and turned him to make him face her. "I mean it," she said. "Most people suffering Dissonance this severe would have left by now, or had a psychotic break, or at least gotten mad –"

"Oh, I got mad," he said, and pointed behind him. She didn't know what she was meant to be looking at until she noticed the absence of a picture, and instead, on the floor in the corner, the smithereens that were once canvas. "Father got me that upon my appointment as Councillor. I couldn't bear to see it hanging in our home."

She bit her lip, finally broaching her fears. "If you're angry with him, you should be angry with me too."

"No, you were forced to lie," he said with certainty. "But if he had told me from the start…"

"You heard his story," Rebecca said with a shake of her head. "He did it to protect you."

"I wanted the choice! Like you had, like he had, like everybody else apparently has… He's lied to me, every single day of my life. I don't know if I'll be able to look him in the eye again."

"If he knows that you know," she said warily, "he'll make you leave to protect the others."

"I know." He frowned. "That's why we're not going to tell him. I love Petersville, I know you do too. If we just pretend that we know nothing… we can stay."

"Then you'll have to act like nothing's changed."

He nodded gravely and his voice dropped to a tremor. "I can do that. I can do that."

Matthew put on a brave face as they planned their wedding, but Rebecca could see the evidence every day as he battled with severe Dissonance.

Some days he could barely get out of bed in the mornings yet alone go about his duties as Councillor but somehow he managed to hide his deep depression from the villagers. Perhaps the timing of his discovery was a blessing in disguise because any stress the villagers saw in him could easily be attributed to the wedding, and his diminished smile simply hidden beneath his reclaimed beard. Being in love to some extent disguised the anguish beneath, for which Rebecca was grateful.

This was the illness that the hospital had warned them about before coming to the Outlie but she had never before seen it first-hand. Matthew's mind was visibly struggling to process the difference between his life here and the life that lay outside these walls. His depression was accompanied by an unshakeable sense of unease, a wariness of others, and a dangerous distrust of reality. All too often she would find him frozen in the middle of a routine task: one evening, she came home to see the dirty dishes abandoned and him curled up on the cold stone floor having a panic attack. There were many panic attacks the first few days. All the thousand small things that were made different with the truth stockpiled until everything was in doubt. When his initial shock wore off, anger took its place; anger solely squared at his own father who Matthew blamed for keeping the truth a secret. She knew it could take years to overcome Dissonance – for the Lifetimer to adapt healthily to the change – and that was only with specialist counselling and Mainstream support. They had neither of those things in Petersville.

With a shudder she tried to push away the possibility that Matthew might spend his whole life suffering the effects of the knowledge.

They used the wedding as a distraction; both pouring every free minute into preparations with the knowledge that the sooner they could inhabit together, the more she could support him through his Dissonance.

When she posted the necessary letters to Mainstream, she wrote to her mother and never even received a response. It didn't hurt her as much as she thought it would, perhaps because family now meant something more to her than blood. Meanwhile the villagers seemed so happy that Matthew had at last found love that they abandoned any previous reservations they had about her status as an outsider. By Matthew's side, Rebecca found herself involved in the community more than ever and was pleasantly surprised to find that sometimes she would have visitors to the infirmary that came, not to find aid, but to find her.

Leah helped her navigate the village to find the tailor and jeweller and someone who could make bouquets. It was difficult to find blooms now autumn was definitely in sway but the village was resourceful. It would differ greatly from any wedding she had been to before but Matthew seemed happy to include a few of her own cultural traditions such as a feast beforehand and a few select phrases to use during the ceremony.

The night before the wedding, Rebecca retired to the Inn and bathed in her room. She could see the white gown hanging on the back of the door and a nervous bubble of excitement caught in her throat. This was it, she knew. It had happened so fast, barely over a month since she had first stepped foot in Petersville, but it felt so right, marrying Matthew. She was still smiling when Leah arrived to cut her hair. Leah bounced around her, excitedly chattering about the wedding. Rebecca closed her eyes and let it wash over her, too content to even speak. This would be her last night alone, but she also knew, since coming to this village that she had never truly been alone at all.

Their wedding ceremony took place on a clear day in mid-October in the Prayer House gardens, just as the perennial trees were turning ochre and shredding their leaves. She walked down an aisle made from fallen leaves and a natural avenue formed between the many guests, using the wooden stools that she had noticed on her very first day here. Two of Matthew's students acted as her flower girls, scattering some of the yarrow flowers the women had picked the day before, while Leah took the position of looking after them as they ran ahead in their twirling red dresses.

A gentle nudge from Master Peter set her down the aisle. Peter had become a point of contention between them because although Matthew's relationship with his father had deteriorated, Rebecca had only been brought closer to him with their regular meetings and shared understanding. She recognised the lengths to which Master Peter had gone to protect his son and he seemed relieved that he finally had someone with which to share the burden. After their initial meeting, Peter's hostility had dropped dramatically, until his curiosity and his kindness outweighed his distrust. And when she was asked to choose someone to give her away, she could think of no one else whose opinion mattered more.

They turned the corner, arm in arm, until she walked under the evergreen arbour and down the path that she had fallen in love with on her first visit. Smiling faces supported her from either side and at the end of the avenue was the most beautiful sight; Matthew, with the afternoon sun behind him standing by the lake where she first spoke to him. The man who, even after finding out the truth and knowing that there was a perfect happiness waiting for him somewhere in the world, still chose her. He was given the choice that Master Peter feared, and still chose Petersville. Today they were making the promise that that would always be the case.

They exchanged their vows, her eyes never leaving his. The irises that used to be the depth of forests, now looked like they too had changed with the seasons, reflecting a beautiful ochre between the pigments of green. He was smiling that wide happy smile that she loved from first sight, red leaves fell from the sky to land at her feet, and she knew that this was it; this was happiness.

*

It was two weeks after their wedding when Master Peter turned up on their doorstep. It was late enough in the evening that Rebecca was already dressed in her nightrobes.

"I'm here to see my son," was his only explanation as he walked past her into their home. "I need to talk to you both."

She led him into the living room and then climbed the stairs to their bedroom to find her husband. Matthew was slouched against the wall where the broken painting used to hang, chipping away at a wooden carving with a small knife, with flyaway shavings caught in his beard. This area of the house had become a little workshop of his; every day he was experimenting with something new, like he just couldn't sit still anymore.

"What's he doing here?" Matthew asked, not looking up as he kept carefully discarding wood.

"Probably to find out why you haven't been talking to him," she said.

Matthew's hand slipped and he grunted as blood started pouring from the gash on his first finger. Rebecca picked up a cloth and walked over to him, pressing it to the wound. Matthew gritted his teeth as it continued to bleed.

"You should wash that," Rebecca advised, "some of the chippings might have –"

"Do you think I should tell him?" Matthew asked. "That I know?"

She sighed. "It's not my place to say. If you think it's for the best." Her weekly meetings with Peter had become threaded with tension ever since Matthew found out the truth. She loved Peter but had begrudgingly become the buffer between them; an exhausting role given Peter's scrutiny and Matthew's anger. The web of lies was weighing heavily on her and as much as she wished the burden away, she couldn't deny that if Peter knew that the secret had spread, he would be well within his rights to ask them to leave.

Matthew banged his head against the wall behind him, and then, seemingly resolved, he stood up, bloody cloth still wrapped around his hand.

They made it back downstairs to find Peter pacing the living room. He stopped upon seeing them and his eyes flickered down to Matthew's hand. "Oh, what have you done now?" he chided, stepping back into his fatherly role.

"It's nothing," Matthew said, childishly trying to hide it behind his back. Rebecca's reminded of the fight in the Council Chambers when Matthew refused to let his father see him cry. It must be an age-old routine between them. Matthew made no move to sit down as he asked pointedly, "Why are you here, Father?"

Master Peter straightened, as if remembering his purpose, but then strangely he turned away to face the bookshelves instead. "At first, I thought your distant behaviour was because of our disagreement," Peter said. "Or because of wedding preparations, your honeymoon... but it's not just distance. Distance, I could understand," Peter said. He walked towards the bookcase and traced his fingers over the hand-bound books. Rebecca closed her eyes in dread as she realised where this was heading. "But it wasn't just distance. Matthew, when you met your wife you were the happiest that I have ever seen you and on your wedding day I imagined that the smile would never leave your face, but... I watched. I know my son, and you have not been my son for weeks now." His fingers landed upon the book that Matthew's mother had given him on etymology. He pulled it out, and flicked through it, pausing every now and then. The silence was unbearable; the anticipation for what was to come. Rebecca exchanged a look with her husband who looked equally as anxious. She slipped her hand into his as Peter finally put the book down and turned back towards them, but his eyes did not go to his son, but to her.

"I know what Dissonance looks like."

It was an accusation, plain and simple. She took a deep breath, ready to explain, when Matthew beat her to it.

"Rebecca didn't tell me," he said. "I found out."

Peter's attention snapped back to his son. "It's true then. You know. How?"

"It doesn't matter," Matthew said dismissively.

"It does if others can –"

"They won't," Matthew stated firmly.

There was a terrible silence as the two men stared at each other. Then, Peter shuddered, and his shoulders sagged. Unable to bear the sight, Rebecca reached out for him but he pulled away before she could connect.

"We're staying," she said. "Aren't we Matthew?"

Matthew nodded solemnly.

Peter gave a hollow chuckle. "No, you're not. You can't live a lie your whole life and go back to it as if nothing has changed –"

"You did," Rebecca interrupted before she could stop herself.

"I had a *duty*."

At Peter's harsh words and fierce glare, she was silenced. This wasn't her argument; this was about what Matthew would choose to do.

"Maybe I have a duty too," Matthew uttered after a moment of tense silence, "to this village, to you. I don't want to leave, Father."

"But you *will*," Peter insisted, but this time there was emotion laced between the venom of his words. "I ought to ask you to leave now before you taint the village with your knowledge. If any of the others were to find out… but I can't. I can't banish my only son. Please understand."

"I understand. I'll keep the secret, Father."

Peter continued, as if he didn't even hear his son and dragged a hand across his face. "Perhaps. But someday you will leave, and the change will destroy you."

Matthew shook his head, tears in his voice. "How can you be so sure?"

Peter stepped forward, his hands cradling Matthew's face. "Because you're my son. I know you. You've always followed your curiosity, even when it has gotten you hurt." His eyes flickered down to the reddened rag around Matthew's hand, still clutched in Rebecca's grasp. "But please," he begged, resting his forehead against his son's, "just this once. Don't leave. Don't investigate. Stay, and we'll get you through this. It'll be hard, and you'll be fighting against your instincts every step of the way, but please. Please don't leave."

Matthew was crying freely now. He dropped Rebecca's hand to embrace his father. "I won't, Father. I promise you, we won't leave."

They kept their oath for five years; years that passed quickly, in peacefulness and happiness; in the clicking of knitting needles and in the soothing making of herbal medicine. Matthew's collection of hobbies grew until half of the top room was covered in his crafts but for all his restlessness, he appeared to be content, and even his relationship with his father began to heal with time. Life was slow and uneventful without modern technology and Rebecca found herself calming to the slower pace. Steadily, the loneliness she carried from Mainstream began to fill with love and acceptance. Here, without soulmates, without the hierarchy and the poisonous ideals that came with it, she finally felt like she belonged...

And then, Rebecca fell pregnant.

She knew it instinctively long before the symptoms manifested because she would find herself watching the children play. When she had first arrived, she thought that it was freedom she saw in their play, but watching now, she could see the caution these children had even now. Every time she saw the goalkeeper flinch away from the ball, or see a young child nervous to try a new game, she started thinking... could the children sense the repression around them? Were they raised to be afraid, but unknowing of what? It had been so long since she'd been outside Petersville that she'd forgotten how other children played. But the thoughts taunted her, night and day, until Master Peter's words that were meant to convince her so long ago, started to haunt her.

The reason we do not tell our sons and daughters about soulmates is because we want to keep them safe. If they never know, they will never experience the agony of being abandoned, or suffer the continual disappointment of the Search.

Rebecca knew that if she raised her child here then it would be safe, yes, but she would also be limiting its options; taking away its right to choose the kind of love that they would want. What if the child wanted to Search? By staying here, she would be denying their child the chance to find guaranteed lifelong happiness. Mainstream meant exposing the child to the loneliness that she herself had only just escaped but at least the world there wasn't a lie. She started wondering which fantasy was healthier after all; the belief that your soulmate would solve all your problems or the eradication of any such beliefs entirely. She remembered how difficult it was keeping the truth from Matthew and wondered: could she lie to her own child for the rest of her life? Could she live with making such a major decision for her unborn child?

This was the moral limit in her mind that she hadn't realised was there until she crossed it; she was fine making the choice to Settle as an adult and she could pretend that there was no choice to make to keep the villagers safe but she would not take away the chance to Bond from her child. If they left before the child was born then it should be able to adapt to Mainstream like any other child... any later and it was risky, just as it was going to be a risk for Matthew if he chose to leave with her.

The second morning when she felt the sickness and had not yet bled she knew for certain that her body was no longer hers alone. Matthew already had his suspicions, she knew, and she would not be able to hide her condition for much longer.

That evening she could find no excuse not to have the discussion with him.

After another bout of nausea, she sat on their sofa, and rested her head in her hands in mental preparation for the difficult conversation to come.

Matthew came to console her with a hand on her back and a tankard of water. "I know you say you're not sick but –"

"I'm pregnant," she blurted. "Matty, I'm pregnant."

His face shifted into a number of expressions in moments: shock, joy, worry… but settled on confusion. "And this is not… good news?"

"I…" Rebecca started, and then trailed off. She didn't know how to have this discussion.

"I thought we both wanted children, Becky. What is it?"

She smiled, both at the rarely used endearment, and at the memory of that conversation long ago. Children were an assumed part of marriage here but Matthew had, quite awkwardly, early in their marriage, asked if she wanted that for herself. "I do. I really do want the child, but…" She took a deep breath and just as she was about to make her declaration, he beat her to it:

"You don't want to have it here."

She closed her eyes to stem the tears that wanted to escape and moved her head: yes.

Matthew shakily came to sit beside her on the sofa.

"You want to move back to Mainstream," he stated.

She nodded again.

Matthew let out a long sigh and stared straight ahead. She followed his eyes to the bookcase with the various ornaments he'd crafted since the revelation perched atop it.

"Why?" he asked eventually.

"I have to give our child the choice. I can't let her believe this is the only way she can live. What if she doesn't want that? I can't do that to her. And I can't lie to her my whole life."

"Her?"

Rebecca clamped her mouth shut. She hadn't even realised the pronoun. Why was she so certain the child she was carrying was a girl? She shook her head, "She, it, whatever. Matthew, I can't do it, but I don't expect you to come with me –"

"Of course I'm coming with you," Matthew interjected but then his face clouded over with doubt. "Unless... you don't want me to?"

"No, no," she insisted, putting her hands over his in reassurance. "You are my family, of course I want you with me, but please understand that it needs to be your choice to leave here. This is your home. We'd be leaving your father alone and your entire life behind. I can't guarantee your safety if we leave for Mainstream; the society there is so different in words I can't even explain. You handled Dissonance so well last time it makes me think you'd really be okay, especially if we take it slow at first, but if you Witness..." she broke off, unable to even complete the thought. With a deep breath she forced herself to continue. "But that's like worrying you'll be hit by lightning. It's so, so unlikely, even if we did move to the city. I've lived there all my life and no one I know has ever Witnessed. It's highly improbable you'd ever even *see* a Bonded Pair, yet alone see a Bond forming but it's not *im*possible and if you do... if you *do...*" she shook her head, her voice breaking.

Matthew gave a wry smile. "Then I'll stay at home with the baby. Won't meet many people that way."

Rebecca still couldn't believe after all these years how Matthew took everything in stride. "You understand what could happen to you? Aren't you worried? Even a little?"

Matthew turned towards her, clasping her hands in his. "You know best, Becky. If you think our child is better raised in Mainstream then I support you. We'll work out the rest. And, as you say, the odds of me Witnessing are minimal. Like being struck by lightning."

"But people still get struck," Rebecca murmured. "Matthew, if anything happened to you because I made you leave here, I'd never forgive myself."

"I will be fine," Matthew said quietly. "Whatever happens, we're doing it for our child. And you're right; I don't know if I could deny her the opportunity either." One hand moved from hers to rest over her belly. "We have to go, for her sake."

But there was a sparkle in his eye that she recognised and hadn't seen for a very long time; Matthew was curious for himself too.

They began tentatively preparing for the move; trading away items they would no longer need and not acquiring anything new. Their home became sparser and sparser until the only thing in their bedroom, bar the mattress on the floor, was the carved chest Matthew had given her that was too sentimental for her to trade away. They would have to leave it behind though, all the same, too heavy to carry through the woodlands.

Rebecca had sent various letters using the stolen postage stamps and snuck over to the hidden collection point one evening. The hospital in London had offered her re-employment. Ideally, she would have introduced Matthew to Mainstream slowly, not by heading straight back into the chaotic city, but she needed a job, especially if she was going to be supporting Matthew and their child as well. She could apply for a transfer once she arrived, she assured herself. She had also arranged an apartment that was located near to a Prayer House with a good adaptation programme. She had even contacted the Outlie Affairs department of the Pair Bond Service who assured her that they would provide transport from the Outlie and help them with Dissonance counselling and other adaptation needs as soon as they were on the outside.

After a month, just as winter was giving way to spring, they were ready to leave. They had written to the Outlie department again to confirm the date of their departure. The only thing left to do was to break the news to Peter. Aside from the fact he was Matthew's father, he needed to know as the leader of the village so that he could prepare a story to give to their inquiring neighbours.

"I can't do it," Matthew said, pacing the bare stone floor of their living room, the rugs long since given away.

"You have to, Matty," she insisted. "If it comes from me, he won't believe it was your choice."

"But I can't do it. He's going to hate us. We'll never see him again, for crying out loud! He's the only family we have. I can't –" He broke off with a groan, rubbing his calloused hands over his face. He'd spent a lot of time in the woods recently. "We promised him."

She knew the importance they placed on oaths in the village. A promise was a promise. "Then stay," she said gravely.

He groaned again in frustration. "I can't do that either!"

Rebecca stood in front of him and held his hands, preventing his pacing. "So what do you want to do?"

His face crumpled. "I don't know. Can we lie? Say someone kidnapped us?"

She raised an eyebrow.

He sighed. "You're right. Of course you're right, that would just make things worse. Can we… write a letter? Sneak out in the middle of the night?" He must have seen the look on her face because then he shook his head. "You're right. It's the coward's way out, but can we take it anyway?" he asked, looking at her with hopeful eyes.

"You don't want to say goodbye to your own father?"

"Of course I want to, but it's not going to be a goodbye, it's going to be a shouting match. I'd much rather remember him as he was than witness what we'll do to him." He looked back at her with those same sad eyes. "I really am a terrible person, aren't I?"

She couldn't have him think that of himself. She cradled his face in her hands and assured him, "You're trusting me with Mainstream, I'll trust you with Petersville. However you want to handle it is fine by me."

Matthew nodded. He had decided. "We'll write a letter."

They left the following night. Noah would be posted on the Gates and he had a reputation for shirking his duty to see his friends. They struggled to write the letter, and Matthew nearly changed his mind a dozen times, but eventually their apology and explanation was written. It was past midnight and Matthew was checking the house for anything they might have forgotten to pack while Rebecca, who had all-hours access to the Town Hall, left the letter on Master Peter's desk.

They took only a backpack of belongings each with a couple of larger sentimental items cradled in their hands. They made their trip the long way round, down the fields and around the edge of the village. It was a bitterly cold February night and they could only see by the light of the near-full moon. When they made it to the Gates, Matthew had a plan to divert Noah, but as it was, he was already nowhere to be seen.

"Something this difficult shouldn't be so easy," Matthew mused.

"It's your last chance if you –" she began, but he shook his head.

"Let's do it," he said.

He took her hand, and together they left Petersville behind them.

By the time they approached the road, every muscle was aching from carrying their belongings through the dark forest. When Rebecca glimpsed the sight of tyres on the road, she grasped Matthew's hand. She knew the Outlie Affairs department must be experienced in what they do, but she was still nervous. "Remember when I explained to you about Mainstream transport?"

His eyes lit up, tiredness forgotten. "Automobiles? We're going to use an automobile?"

He rushed towards the road before she could stop him. She ran after him as fast as she could while carrying luggage.

She almost laughed at the sight that greeted her, because next to the beat-up old car was the same man that delivered her to the village over five years ago.

"Chris?" she greeted. "Chris Thompson?"

"Rebecca! I was wondering if it was going to be you," he said with a wide smile. "I heard rumours…" he trailed off when he noticed Matthew studying the car intently. "This is the guy then?"

Matthew straightened and gave the quickest introduction she'd ever seen him give before he started barrelling Chris with questions about the car. "How does it work? What's under there? What's that made of?"

Rebecca shook her head at his behaviour. "You don't have to indulge him," Rebecca told Chris.

Chris shrugged. "Makes a change from the usual pick-ups," he said, and started answering Matthew's dozen questions. She knew that Chris must usually tend to Outliers in a lot worst state but it seemed that Matthew's curiosity was currently outweighing everything else. It wouldn't stay that way; the differences would soon stack up until Dissonance overwhelmed him again, but right now, as she watched him dance around the car with an ecstatic grin, she thought it might be worth it.

She hadn't really considered her own feelings towards returning to Mainstream, too preoccupied with the practicalities and worrying about Matthew, but seeing him so enthusiastic about the change had her reflecting on her own reaction. Was she excited to be returning? When she first came to Petersville five years ago she had felt alienated by Mainstream society and had blamed it for her loneliness. Petersville had offered her family, and a place to belong, and she would miss the friends she had made there, but would she miss Petersville itself? The way it stood rooted in the past, the caution that she still heeded with every word, and its simple ways? Over the years, she had had her doubts. Sometimes she had lain awake at night, craving a sugary drink, or straining her ears for the sound of traffic, or wanting to do something as simple as buying a banana or going to the movies. Mainstream, in contrast, seemed filled with possibilities. Thousands of small things she never appreciated before, but this time, with Matthew at her side, there was hope building in her chest that she might find enjoyment from it too, and their child... their child would have the whole world to choose from. She hoped that this time Mainstream would not feel so isolating; now that she knew happiness, she hoped that she could dismiss society's insistence that she wasn't complete without a Bond.

Matthew stared out of the window the whole way into the city, constantly asking questions. She was exhausted but his cheery spirit kept her awake; sleepily watching him marvel at the world that she had detested so much. It truly felt like she was seeing the world for the first time through his eyes.

As the brick and stone houses grew closer and closer together, he grew silent, and then he asked quietly, "This is all one settlement?"

"Yes, but there's communities within it. You get to know your little area. It's probably best not to think about the rest for now. We'll get you settled in, and remember, there's no pressure to even leave the house if you don't want to."

He nodded, but there was trepidation in it. "There's people outside even now…" he said, as he looked back out of the window. "There's so many people…"

"I know, it can be scary," Rebecca began.

"No, I mean… no one will know who we are," he said with a soft smile. "I didn't really believe it was possible."

She smiled. Of course, after a lifetime with everyone knowing everything about him, especially being the Master's son, he would be optimistic about the anonymity that came with a fresh start.

Matthew's new fascination, as the car slowed in the traffic, seemed to be the architecture. He gaped at the pillared stone buildings and the marble statues. He kept asking her for the names of the depicted figures but after a while he got the hint, "And they're all gods? How do you keep track of them all?"

"Honestly, most people don't. Only the devout know all the stories. Here, my favourite Temple is coming up," she said, pulling him towards her side of the backseat. "It's Athena Temple."

It was a towering presence in the dark, lit by the spotlights in front of it, casting giant shadows of its pillars into the woods around it.

"Most Temples have gardens, and this one has a lake and woods and lots of small formal gardens with shrines. It will be near our house actually. I'll have to take you there sometime."

"I'd like that," he smiled, but it didn't reach his eyes, and she knew that beneath all of his optimism, some small knot was beginning to unravel.

When they arrived at the flat, Matthew took the key from Chris's proffered hand before Rebecca could. He lifted the key into the light of the streetlamp and studied it, small and intricate as it was. "Fascinating," he murmured, and then together, they set off down the small paved avenue to the house.

He paused at the doorway to study the mosaic beneath them. It was just red and black brick squares in an octagonal pattern. Hundreds of people had probably crossed it without even looking but Rebecca found herself pausing too; it had been a long time since she had seen a tile mosaic.

"City is an unusual choice –" Chris was babbling behind them. "Most Lifetimers prefer starting out in the countryside, you know how it is. Everything alright chaps?"

"Fine," Matthew muttered, breaking his gaze from the mosaic.

She saw his eyes briefly take in the ornamental pillars on either side of the door with their peeling white paint, but he didn't comment, and opened the front door.

"So this is the communal hallway," Chris continued. "You can pick up your post from the lockers there – that's the little key on your keyring there – but otherwise I imagine you can stick to the second floor." He crossed the cheap vinyl mosaic-imitation that perhaps used to depict an oceanic theme but was now just a dull grey. Matthew's eyes were still on the light switch that Chris had turned on without looking. They followed him upstairs, Matthew trailing behind, fascinated by everything.

They entered the apartment and while Matthew was taking in every detail, Rebecca knew the things to check for and darted around the rooms, letting Chris show her the appliances.

"I imagine you'll want to get settled," Chris said, "so let me just show you and Matthew the adaptation pack. Where has he gotten to anyway?"

Rebecca followed the flickering light to the living room where he was turning a lamp on and off, watching the filament light up. Of course. Petersville didn't have electricity. It must look like magic to him. She couldn't wait to see his face when she introduced him to radio and TV and all the cultural milestones she had grown up with.

"Right," Chris said. "Matthew, if you'd just like to join us a minute–"

Matthew seemed to shake himself out of it and cautiously sat on the sofa where Rebecca was. It was softer than what he was used to; he kept fidgeting.

Chris spread out the contents of the adaptation pack on the table, "Firstly, here are your documents. We've given you Rebecca's surname, Brighton, since you're married. Most importantly, here are our contact details, if you need help at any time... I'm sure Rebecca here will show you how the telephone works, or you can pop in, whatever is easier for you. Ah! Speaking of going out, here," he said, pulling out a thick rubber black wristband, "is your bracelet. It signifies that you don't want to be touched for Recognition. There's no shame in wearing it, plenty of people with non-Hellenic beliefs wear one, and even some Settlers and Non-Trads are beginning to, so keep it nice and visible and most folk will know not to touch you, alright?"

Matthew nodded, and slipped the bracelet onto his wrist where a Hellenic wedding band would normally sit.

"Rebecca tells me you're Biblical. There's a Prayer House just down the road but bear in mind there are many different denominations so if it's not quite right we can try another. There's five Biblia Prayer Houses in London and hopefully one will be the right fit. There's a park nearby that you might like to visit when you're ready. It's important not to push yourself. No one expects you to adapt overnight. You seem to be handling things very well so far but there's no shame in needing time. A psychiatrist will be here tomorrow morning for an initial assessment and then we'll plan your counselling schedule from there. You're going to be just fine, Matthew," Chris said with a practised smile. His eyes flickered to Rebecca. "All the information you need should be in the pack, but as I say, if you need anything, just–" He mimed making a telephone call.

Rebecca escorted Chris to the door, and when she closed it, the world seemed very small and quiet again. Matthew was still sat on the sofa, staring ahead at the wall that evidenced years of previous owners.

"Are you okay?"

When Matthew didn't respond, she sat beside him again, until, eventually, he turned his head into her shoulder and cried.

*

It was when they came home from the hospital with a little girl bundled up between them that Matthew first suggested he get a job.

"I'm going crazy, just sat by myself all day, and I don't know how we're affording all of this –"

"I have savings, I told you, and maternity leave. Don't worry. We'll be okay."

He let it drop, and he was easy to distract with their beautiful daughter. They named her after Matthew's late mother, Elizabeth, and above her cot was placed a guardian angel that Matthew had carved for her back in Petersville.

Rebecca returned to work and Matthew seemed to be content as a househusband. She would return from work to find him lifting Elizabeth in the air and her gurgling in delight. But he was restless even now, she knew. When he mentioned his desire to work again, she suggested he help out at the Prayer House and for a while that was all he needed, until Father Jackson's brother offered him a job at an office.

"I've been adapting well, Becky, and he said it would be mostly paperwork, I wouldn't see that many people."

After a while, he had her convinced. He was a curious man who was turning the house upside down trying to entertain himself, and on a practical level, she couldn't deny that their funds were beginning to dwindle. When he came back from his first day at work, she knew she had made the right choice in supporting him. He spent the evening grinning and playing with Elizabeth until their stomachs were aching with laughter.

Her family was happy, and it was all that she'd ever wanted.

*

Waking up feels like falling asleep. It is slow, and muddled, and heavy. It takes Rebecca a moment to replace the memories of the Outlie with the reality of Mainstream and to correct the years in her mind; it's 1992, a full decade after she met Matthew. The mental picture of a happy family shatters like glass and the remnants of red leaves at their wedding melt into a red river.

A heavy weight settles in her stomach. She looks over the empty side of the bed to Matthew's alarm clock that informs her it's past ten in the morning. She hopes that the Meyers took Lizzie to nursery on time. She hopes that she ate breakfast without complaint.

Rebecca needs to tell Master Peter about his son passing but she knows she is no longer welcome in Petersville. They never returned after they left, too afraid to face the consequences of their actions.

She lies awake, counting her regrets, as if finding the first mistake would unravel the past and set her life back to rights. Was her mistake letting Matthew take the office job? If he never left the house, or at least their neighbourhood, he never would have Witnessed the Bond. Maybe they never should have left Petersville at all, least of all for London. His relapse into Dissonance after leaving the Outlie had been difficult as he had tried to comprehend the new reality of Mainstream. Matthew had a lot of counselling and support from his Prayer House, and some small part of Rebecca had hoped that maybe after all this time, if he Witnessed, it wouldn't break him.

She numbly follows through her morning routine until she reaches the bathroom door. Her hand hovers over the door handle, but she can't do it. She can't stand in the same tub where he died. Everything in this house has been touched by him; there are memories in everything from the toaster to the pen on the bedside table. She crams herself into the small ensuite they rarely used and washes using the sink. She scrubs her skin until it's as red as the bathroom skirting board but she still feels his blood on her hands.

Rebecca remembers the way to the Outlie like she never forgot. Maybe she knew on some level that she would one day have to return. She looks up at the wooden fence of Petersville to see countless rooftops of clay housing for the first time in over three years. It doesn't seem right that it's a bright sunny day and that she can hear children playing and distant folk music coming from the Inn. Life carries on, as it always does.

The guard lets her through after signing the visitor's agreement and she begins the long trek up to the Town Hall. Her old neighbours titter as she passes. She pretends that she cannot hear Abital gossip to her friends and cannot feel the curious gaze of Father Daniel but the disapproving whispers and averted eyes follow her and she feels every single one.

She enters the Chambers and asks the Apprentice if she can see Master Peter, hoping that their leader is still the man with whom she is acquainted. She recognises the Apprentice as one of her flower girls who used to be in Matthew's Friday afternoon football class but she cannot remember her name. The Apprentice takes down her name and then, flustered, scuttles off to find Councillor Leah.

Rebecca peers into the infirmary while she waits, wanting to see David running the place smoothly. She likes to think that she trained him well and she realises that he may even have an Apprentice of his own by now. But, David isn't there. Instead there is a stranger tending to the patients.

Gingerly, Rebecca steps into the room, causing the woman to look up.

"Can I help you?" the woman asks.

The peculiarity of being the one answering that question instead of asking it makes Rebecca stumble for a minute. Then she says, "I'm looking for Medic David."

"Oh, didn't you hear? I'm from Charleston. He exchanged places with me a year or so ago."

"He moved to Charleston?" Rebecca gasps. It was the village that Petersville traded with; the halfway point between here and the fictional Easton. "Why?" she asks with dread. Did he find a lover? Was he banished for it?

"His husband is Charlestive," she says plainly.

Rebecca breathes a sigh of relief. David left by choice, then. And got married. There's a small smile on her face at the thought.

The woman drops her voice to a conspiratory whisper, "My town are much more progressive about these things, you know."

"Yes, I –" Rebecca stops short at the feel of someone standing behind her. She turns to see Councillor Leah. Pale. Straight-backed. Eyes averted.

"Leah –" Rebecca steps forward in an attempt at greeting but Leah steps back.

"Master Peter is currently negotiating with the Farmers but will be returning shortly. I suggest that you wait in the Chambers until he is available. There is food and drink prepared, please help yourself." Her voice is empty but the eyes that blink away from Rebecca are full of unshed tears.

Rebecca doesn't blame her for her coldness. When they left, they said goodbye to no one, not even their closest friends, of whom, Leah was the closest. Rebecca crosses the hallway back into the Chambers and isn't surprised when Leah doesn't stay to talk.

Belatedly Rebecca realises that she hasn't eaten anything in the last twenty-four hours and forces herself to chew a bread roll. She picks at the bread and wonders if they are still made by Baker Tom.

"– not allowed!" Master Peter bellows as the Chamber doors fly open. Rebecca stands at the abrupt noise. He marches towards Rebecca, his cloth robes billowing in the breeze. When he reaches her, he turns to Councillor Leah hovering behind him. "She," he says, finger pointed at Rebecca, "is banished from this community for committing the highest of crimes. She broke her oath and took my son with her. Do you not understand the simple rules of banishment, Leah? Medic Rebecca is not allowed within the walls of this village."

"She said it was important, Master Peter," Leah says meekly.

Master Peter purses his lips. "Leave us," he orders her, "and tell that useless boy on the gates that he should seek an apprenticeship elsewhere." Leah leaves with her head down.

"Follow me," he snaps at Rebecca and leads her into his private office. The same room where he had told her the war story years ago, the one that, to this day he didn't know Matthew had overheard. It seemed only like an added cruelty to tell Peter he was the one that gave his son Dissonance, however indirectly.

Peter crosses his arms and stares down at her. He's lost more hair since last she saw him and he is worryingly thin. She wonders if he'll be stepping down soon and that's why he was being so hard on Leah, his likely successor. "Quite some nerve you have coming back here, and without my son and grandchild at that."

"Trust me, I don't want to be here," she bites. For a moment, it's like nothing's changed. It's like it's five years ago and they're still arguing about Matthew. The red-hot coals of anger are almost welcome to the raw grief that burns her insides.

"Spit it out then. Got another one on the way? What is it?"

Rebecca looks up into his defiant eyes, at the determined slant of his shoulders, and she immediately loses her strength. She cannot tell this man that his son is dead. She looks to the ground.

"Oh," he says.

Her head snaps up at his voice, needing to match the exclamation with an expression, and it's exactly what she thought. He's looking at her differently now. He's looking at her like he knows it's something bad.

"Peter…" she begins, and sees his face weather slowly with hers.

"No," he says. Like it's that simple. Like one word will stop the truth.

She doesn't realise she is crying until her tongue licks salty water from her lips. If tears are escaping, it will not be long before other things start emerging from the ashes. She needs to do this fast. Tell him before she can't speak anymore. "Yesterday. Found him in the bathtub. Knife straight to the… the heart. He… Just…" she swallows her nerves and tries again. "He died."

The silence is deafening. She looks up through blurry eyes to see the word forming on his lips. *Suicide*, he wants to say, but neither of them will speak it. It's such an ugly word for such a good man.

"He died," Master Peter repeats. His eyes dart around the room like he's trying to make sense of it; like he'll find an explanation hidden in this room. "He's dead?" He shakes his head, and when his eyes meet hers once again, his gaze has hardened into burning rock. His voice is slow and weighted, "What did you do to him?"

The whisper is as harsh as a knife's edge and it cuts straight through her. Her voice cracks with the pain of it, "I did nothing."

"I told you this would happen, I told you!" Master Peter slams his fist into a wall. The clay crumbles. Rebecca can see blood on his knuckles. "I told you if you took him this would happen. You *oathbreaker*," he spits, and she knows it's the strongest curse he has. "You promised me you would keep him safe…" He is whimpering now, one bloody hand cradling his face.

"I thought I could," she croaks. "He handled Dissonance so well the first time, I thought… And it was his choice to leave, he didn't have to go with me, you know that, but he –"

"It wasn't a choice!" Master Peter shouts. "It never was! He

92

never would have left you. You killed him when you took him away from here. You destroyed every happiness he ever had."

His voice had fallen back to a whisper and Rebecca responds in kind, "That's not true. He loved Lizzie."

"Lizzie?" he repeats quietly. "Elizabeth? You named your child after…?" His eyes flicker to the painting of his late wife and then his gaze returns harsher than ever. "He could have loved her here. I could have met my own grandchild."

"I wasn't going to raise my daughter in a community that fosters lies."

Master Peter slams his fist into the wall again.

Rebecca cringes at his inflicted injuries. "Please, Peter, don't –"

"Don't call me that," he says. "We are no longer family. We ceased being family the moment you broke my wishes and forced my son to leave..." his voice fades. He sounds exhausted. "The moment you both left me."

It hits her the way he intended it to; a sharp stab to tear at old wounds. They both know the hardest part for them was leaving Matthew's father alone. He had no other family. Over time, Rebecca had become close enough to Peter to consider him as her own father, and so when they left, they left him with no one at all.

"You're a medic," he continues, "you knew the likelihood of a Lifetime Outlier adapting to Mainstream and yet you still did it out of your own selfish –"

"I did it for Elizabeth. And I'd do it again."

He stares at her and she holds his gaze, unafraid.

"Peter," she tries again. "Matthew was doing fine –"

Master Peter huffs a sarcastic laugh. "Of course, because 'fine' people end up floating in –"

"No. He was fine. Happy. His Dissonance was bad at first but it was fading. He saw a counsellor every week to help with adaptation and the Prayer House was always on hand. And Lizzie was helping, I think, he saw how good Mainstream was for her, and he got a job in an office."

Master Peter looks horrified.

"Yes, an office. I made sure it was somewhere small, something safe, nearby, but he wanted a job to help pay for things and he was curious about technology." The explanation seems to curb Master Peter's retaliation, so Rebecca continues, "They'd never seen anyone so happy to answer a phone before. Every day was something new and he loved that. And then they promoted him and he started going along to meetings and I told him not to feel pressured, that he should make sure he's ready, but he was doing so well..." Rebecca forces herself to stop rambling but the words are pouring out uncontrollably with her tears. "He ended up... in the bathtub," she says, in lieu of saying the dreadful word, "because he was at a meeting when someone Bonded. He Witnessed it, Peter, there's no coming back from that. You know that. There's nothing I could have done."

"No," Master Peter says again. "No."

She hears the word echo in her mind and like a knife cutting strings, she begins to feel it: the spinning scraping of daggers against her charred stomach, the tight clenching of her heart, the acid building in her throat... it all wants to escape. She falls to the dusty ground exhausted with self-contained grief and anger and pain. Arms wrap around her as she falls and they cradle each other in the Council Chambers until their tears run dry.

When Rebecca returns from Petersville, still tear-stained and exhausted from telling Master Peter the news, she picks up her daughter from nursery.

A deep-seated loneliness has begun to encroach on her, one that she recognises from her years in Mainstream before meeting Matthew, and she needs to see her daughter, and hold her again in her arms. Part of Rebecca is naïve enough to believe that as long as she never lets her daughter go, she won't encounter the same fate as Matthew. Logically, she knows that Lizzie should be safe regardless having been raised completely outside the Outlie but a mother's fear does not listen to logic. It is fear that governs her actions, the same fear that motivated the founders of Petersville to hide away from the world. If it wasn't for Lizzie and the sacrifices that they made to give her the opportunities of Mainstream, Rebecca thinks she would return to Petersville, where there is at least the illusion of safety. In Mainstream, there is no such comfort. It is full of strangers that could tear their life apart at any time without warning, and she knows, undoubtedly, that she will spend her entire life afraid for her daughter.

"It was an all-day tantrum," the carer complains as she pushes Lizzie into Rebecca's arms. Lizzie looks up at her mother with wide eyes, and they continue to take in their fill of each other as the carer bustles about, muttering under her breath as she locks up for the evening.

Lizzie is unusually quiet on the drive home, probably exhausted from crying for so long. She is still awake though, and staring at the back of the car seat in front of her. They haven't said a single word to each other, Rebecca realises. She never wanted to be that kind of mother.

Rebecca makes a detour to her favourite park. It's in the grounds of Athena Temple but has a play park for Lizzie and plenty of wildlife in the gardens. She worries they will come home before the workmen have repaired the damage to the hallway and bathroom. She unbuckles Lizzie from the back of the car and carries the sleepy toddler out of the car park. She pretends that her hands are too full with Lizzie to reach out in Recognition to passers-by but as she walks her mind stretches and she wonders about Matthew's true soul, somewhere out there, brushing hands looking for him and never knowing that their quest is futile.

About halfway down the main path, Lizzie seems to understand where they are and squirms until Rebecca acquiesces and lets her down. Lizzie walks several steps herself before wobbling and falling on her rear. Lizzie frowns as if not understanding her failure and struggles to stand up once more. She falls again and looks back to Rebecca. Her eyes are wide and her brown wavy hair is swept by the breeze to reveal the button ears that are reminiscent of Matthew's. Lizzie didn't inherit his smile though. Rebecca already misses it. If Matthew was here, he would have swept Lizzie off the ground and onto his shoulders. She would giggle in delight, pulling at his hair, and directing him as if he was a horse. "Giddy-up," Matthew would joke.

Rebecca waits until Lizzie holds her arms out towards her. Rebecca responds to her silent request and bends down so that she can hold Lizzie's little hands in hers and they can take the small steps together. It keeps her hands busy and they manage to avoid every stranger on the short walk to the lake. As soon as Lizzie sees their destination, she tries to get free but Rebecca keeps a firm hold on her until they sit in their usual place by the lakeside and Lizzie is cradled in Rebecca's lap. They watch the fish for a while. Rebecca pulls Lizzie back every time she gets too close to the water.

Lizzie will get hungry soon. They will have to go home and find something to eat. And then there will be something else they need to do. And then something else.

"Sad," Lizzie says, as she plays with the grass.

"Yes, it's sad," Rebecca agrees, although she doesn't know if Lizzie is talking about herself or her mother or the blades of grass. "We will miss your daddy very much. Did anyone tell you what happened?"

Lizzie looks up at that, always wide-eyed, always curious like her father. "No," she says and shakes her head; she does not yet realise that the word and action can be independent.

"Daddy was sick, so the angels took him," Rebecca explains.

Lizzie knows about angels. Matthew used to tell her Biblical stories at bedtime and she seemed to enjoy them more than any other story.

"Where?" Lizzie asks.

"Far away."

"We visit?"

"We can't, sweetheart. We can never see him again."

"Forever?"

Rebecca nods sadly, and Lizzie frowns. Rebecca's not entirely sure if her daughter truly understands the concept of 'forever' as the last time she used it, it was about a broken toy.

"The angels are going to take good care of him for us."

Lizzie scrunches her nose up at Rebecca. She has never seen her mother cry before. Rebecca bends over and buries her face in her daughter's hair to hide the tears. She breathes in the familiar smell and holds on tight until Lizzie becomes bored and Rebecca has to let Lizzie wiggle out of her grasp.

"I'll keep you safe," Rebecca promises to Lizzie.

Her daughter is not listening; she has found a snail and is talking gibberish to it as she moves it towards another snail.

"We'll move to a new house," Rebecca continues. "Somewhere small, quiet, away from…" She looks up and sees strangers all around her, any of which could be her soulmate, or even her daughter's. A single touch could break them.

"Away from danger. No one else. Just me and you, Lizzie, I promise. Just me and you."

Lizzie lets go of the two snail shells. "Just me and you," she repeats.

FIVE REASONS WHY NOW IS A GREAT TIME TO START SEARCHING FOR YOUR SOULMATE

*The odds may be six hundred thousand to one but here's five good reasons why now is the best time to reach out in **Recognition** everywhere you can…*

1. You're more likely to Bond now than at any other time in recent history.

Despite our ever increasing population, the odds of finding your soulmate are actually on the up. Pre-20th century, unless Zeus was feeling particularly generous and placed your soulmate in the same village it was unlikely you would ever have the opportunity to meet them but now due to the ease of long distance travel and our increasingly inter-sectionalised society you can meet more people than ever before meaning it's statistically more likely that one of them will be the *right* one.

2. The majority of companies now offer FWTs.

Many companies have adopted the UN's guidelines for Fair Work Transfers to accommodate Distance Searching but be sure to check with your company before applying. Ensure you know the length of contract, language limitations, pay rate conversion and any job alterations before accepting. FWTs have made Searching further afield much easier and affordable than before and as of last year 37% of all Pairs were international.

3. Not in work? Studying can up your odds too.

It's a well-known fact that you are more likely to find your soulmate under the age of thirty than you are over thirty but do you know *why* that is? Studies show that you meet proportionally more people in your youth due to attending large contact-based events such as festivals, gigs, and clubbing, but it's attending university that tops the list. With an average of twenty thousand students, additional social events, part-time jobs, and academic conferences, all often away from home, it's not surprising that the biggest chance of meeting your soulmate comes from going to university.

4. There are more Bonding Circles and Conventions than ever before.

Whether you skip along to a meet at the local once in a while or attend the biggest UK convention in Birmingham every year, there are plenty of Searchers up and down the country that are finding new ways to meet people. Organised Circles are becoming increasingly popular - it's admin-heavy and so incurs a small fee but ensures that you don't waste time by touching the same person twice. There is much less stigma around conventions then there was only a few years ago and it shows in the figures. Last year, UK ABC (Annual Bonding Convention, Birmingham NEC) boasted a new Pair, as did the ISRC (International Souls Recognition Convention, Los Angeles) just last month.

5. It's good for you! Searching is proven to help those suffering from Witness Recovery and Depression.

Optimism is an inherent part of Searching and just knowing you've gone out there and tried your best can be beneficial to your mental health. Those who have Witnessed a Bond are often motivated to search for their own Pair afterwards and a recent study by Her Majesty's Pair Bond Service suggests that even those who fall into Witness Depression due to low self-esteem or other mitigating factors often circle back round to Witness Motivation. A number of mental health charities advise Searching as a form of therapy, so there's no reason not to give it a try!

*to find your nearest **Searching Circle** or for more information please visit **searching.org.uk** or call **0800 SEARCH***

Ed

"*Slowly even at winter's edge / the feelings come back in their shapes / and colours – conflicting – they come back / they are changed.*"
— Adrienne Rich

The dream goes like this – he will turn a corner, open a door, jump from a forty-storey building, and somehow always end up here; the footpath laid before him as it was that day. The vision has every detail painted in vibrancy; lucid, in a way none of his other dreams are, as if he completes another brush stroke of the horizon every time he recalls the memory. The same bird song, the same light breeze, the same lake at the base of the hill reflecting the hazy morning light, dew still clinging to the grass, fog lingering in the valley, like the world hung in balance, *waiting*.

And the same hand held in his.

It's a few days after Solstice and they're wrapped up warm to ward off the crisp December air. Ed can feel his own breath tickling against his chin, the warm exhale returned to him by the embrace of the university scarf around his neck. His husband wears a thick parka, the fur of the hood settling around his shoulders as he looks out towards the lake as if enchanted.

They never speak in his dreams. In reality, they were talking while they walked this path; about mundanities of life, about their future, about a dozen insignificant things that were to become even more insignificant. But in the dream, there are no words shared between them.

He can feel the cold of Simon's fingertips in his palm and knows what is predetermined to happen as a shadow appears on the horizon.

Please, he begs silently to Simon, to the dream. *Please not again.*

Simon is wearing fingerless gloves; a Searcher tradition, but also a practical one. Maybe they just happened to be the pair he chose before they left the house that morning, maybe he thought the grey fabric suited the blue parka, maybe they were already in the coat pocket or were lying expectantly on the top of the cabinet... a tiny, unthinking, decision that would change everything.

He feels Simon's hand break from his as the path narrows and the shadow approaches. That's all that she ever is, the stranger; a shadow. Every other detail is picture perfect except for her, who shall always remain a stranger, no matter how many times he revisits this memory.

He wants to tear Simon away, wants to scream, wants to go back to their home, back to the cabinet where Simon took those damn gloves and take them from him. But he's tried all this before and the dream never allows him to change so much as a single detail. And so Ed watches, helpless, as the shadow reaches out and with the barest touch against his husband's fingertips, engulfs him with an impossible light.

Ed wakes gasping; a scream caught in his throat, sweat dripping from his skin, lungs aching as they struggle to contract and relax. He blinks in an attempt to adjust to the absence of light. He sits hunched over in his bed, disorientated, as fragments of reality start piecing themselves back together.

He reaches over blindly for the towel beside his bed, and with shaking hands, numbly begins to wipe away the worst of the residue, but the memory still sticks to his skin as uncomfortable as the sweat on his brow had been. He leans forward, focuses on his laboured breathing, and exchanges the towel for the glass of water, sipping at it until he can delude himself into thinking that he's okay.

A different bed, a different house, a different time.

Five years even, and yet, it still haunts him. The water, the towel, the bedsheets that never stay clean for long. A routine.

4am. He wonders if it's worth going back to sleep; if he can afford not to.

He sighs and hates how close it sounds to a whimper.

Sometimes when he is too weak, too tired, to push it away, the ghost of Simon's arms come to rest around him, soothing him back to sleep. "Shhh," he used to whisper when Ed had had nightmares, rubbing his hands down goose-pimpled arms and pressing his lips to Ed's temple, "it's just a dream," he'd say, "and dreams got nothing on reality."

How right he was. Ed would endure that nightmare a thousand

times over if only that's all it was.

Edwin Hart stifles a yawn as he reaches for his mug of coffee only to discover that it's long since gone cold.

"Naturally," he mutters, as he places the celebratory Golden Jubilee mug back on the long-faded coaster.

A sad sight, but perhaps not quite as sad as the view outside his office window; another indistinguishable grey day of the new millennium, drizzle clinging to the third-storey window and low-hanging clouds cloaking the city of London even at midday. The dullness outside is so consuming that it takes hold of his office too. The unremarkable square space with its simple furniture can no longer be brightened by the single overhead light and glare of the computer screen, too easily overpowered by the dark clouds around them. On days like this it was easy to see why people thought so little of a civil service career when this was the height of success: a grey office in a grey city with only a name plaque on the door to show for your sixteen years of service.

Sixteen years. And most of those had been spent at this exact desk, never once shuffled from department to department as many of his colleagues had been. Ed's been the Primary Tester for the Pair Bonding Service for going on ten years. Testing is an analytical job composed of monitoring intuition tests and synchronized brain waves in new Pairs. It serves the dual purpose of providing new Pairs with the legally required Soulmate Certificate while providing Her Majesty's government with crucial research on this phenomenon. It's a perfectly good job but after ten years everything is rote by this point; he knows every possible combination of acceptable responses from new Pairs, he knows the location of even the most obscure paperwork, he knows the cafeteria menu week by repetitive week, and as of last month, he even knows the culprit responsible for stealing his post-it notes.

The routine means it's all too easy for the lines between now and *then* to blur and for Simon's name to appear on the Soulmate

Certificate before him.

Ed's pen pauses, mid-signature. He grits his teeth and glares at the printed text until the letters of his ex-husband's name are scattered back across the certificate where they belong. The angry ink blot serves to remind him of his grievous error as his hand flicks to finish his signature, a little firmer than it had started out.

Ed sighs, a frequent habit of his, as if he can physically exhale the grief still lodged inside him, and reaches for the next file, doing his best to dismiss the sudden weight of the wedding band around his wrist.

His movements falter at the sound of a siren.

He battles the unusual stirrings of curiosity for a good two minutes, carrying on with his work, until he hears the familiar chanting of protestors amongst the sirens and realises that he's been straining to pick out words from the muffled voices and consequently not reading the file at all.

"Oh for crying out loud," he mutters, flipping the file shut, more annoyed with himself for caring than for the actual disturbance. He extracts himself from the desk and strides the two steps it takes to get to the window, opening it a crack until he can hear the protestors chant and see the handmade signs they hold and come to the inevitable conclusion that they're here about the new legislation.

Ed grunts, unsurprised.

His mind strays back to Simon. He wonders if the news about giving financial support to low-income Pairs has reached his new home in Australia. A memory surfaces of Simon vehemently explaining what it was like to grow up counting pennies and cutting out coupons and sharing a bedroom with three older brothers, all of whom were working before they left school. He wonders if Simon still cares for the struggles that used to be his own now that he belongs to someone else, some*where* else.

Ed shakes his head, dislodging the memory. He walks away from the window and back to his desk where his reassuring routine awaits him.

By the end of the working day, Ed is more than eager to accept a colleague's offer for a drink, especially as Kevin Li normally distances himself as far away from politics as it was possible to get while still being a civil servant and was therefore unlikely to bring about unwelcome reminders of Simon.

They end up at the local pub; it's a little rough around the edges but it has an open fireplace which is nice in winter and a stack of well-thumbed playing cards that are handy when stuck with dull company. It's not until they're paying for their drinks and Kevin drops a handful of change, sending coins skittering across the alcohol-sticky bar, that Ed realises something isn't quite right.

Kevin is a man of endless energy and today is no exception but instead of him bursting with smiles and enthusiasm, he seems to be vibrating with nerves instead. His hands are still shaking as he attempts to rescue a penny from the underside of a beer mat.

Ed scrutinises his friend as he helps pick up the fallen coins and place them in the impatient hands of the bartender.

Kevin used to be a Searcher – that's how he ended up in England in the first place, hopping between jobs across the globe on Fair Work Transfers in order to meet as many people as possible – but he's been here for two years now on what was originally a six month contract and apart from the occasional visit to see his family in Hong Kong, he doesn't seem in a hurry to relocate. His girlfriend probably has something to do with it. Ed is still baffled how Kevin Li, the naïve and optimistic Searcher, ended up falling in love with the hard-edged statistician Penny Morgan, but stranger still is that she happened to fall for him too.

Kevin swipes his long fringe out of his face and readjusts his square glasses, but no amount of fidgeting can disguise his nerves.

"You alright?" Ed asks as they make their way to their usual table by the window.

"Yeah…" Kevin says, but now they're sitting down, he's picking at his cuticles and Ed believes him even less.

"Did you see the protestors earlier?" Ed asks, somehow broaching the topic that he'd been so eager to avoid. He takes a sip of his ale and finds that it still tastes of the cheap soap suds used to wash the glass. "Don't know if you can see them from Reports but the disturbance might be big enough to make the news tonight. A hundred or so of them, all protesting this new loan scheme like they've got nothing better to do –"

"I need to ask you something."

Ed pauses, glass halfway to his lips. Kevin's interruptions do not usually carry so much weight. Ed slowly lowers his pint.

"Or, tell you something," Kevin amends, wringing his hands. "Both, I suppose."

"Right." Ed links his fingers together and leans across the table like he would if he were interviewing a particularly difficult Pair. "What is it?"

Kevin finally looks up but his wide brown eyes seem to flicker around the room, looking anywhere but straight across at him. "I…" He visibly swallows. His hands are wrung tight enough for the skin to pale around the knuckles. "You can't be mad."

Ed thins his lips, knowing that whatever follows that statement will inevitably do just that. He takes a steadying breath and purposefully relaxes his shoulders the best he can. "Okay."

"I mean it," Kevin says, a finger escaping the confines of his twisted hands to point at Ed against the beer glass. His eyes nearly have the courage to meet Ed's but they fall just shy. "You're not to get all…" he flounders for the word, finger absently trailing through the condensation before settling on, "judgey."

"I don't –" Ed begins to protest but Kevin's glare cuts him short. "Fine," he says, raising his hands in surrender. "I will not get 'all judgey,'" he imitates with only a smidgen of mockery at his younger colleague. "Just spit it out already."

"Okay," Kevin breathes, more exhale than word.

The silence stretches on for long enough that Ed starts to think that Kevin has lost his nerve. He watches intently, looking for clues in the sweat on his brow. The tension is broken by the sudden gust of wind and laughter as the door swings open and a large group of young people make their way to the bar. No one Ed recognises, not unsurprising in a city this big, and he's also entirely unsurprised that none of them come over for Recognition given the awkward stiltedness they are probably projecting.

He turns his attention back to Kevin who must have been building his courage while Ed was distracted because he suddenly blurts out the absurd words: "I'm going to ask Penny to marry me."

This declaration stalls Ed; his hand paused halfway towards his warming pint. He looks across to his drinking partner who looks just about ready to flee.

"Right," he says numbly. "Right."

"I know you think marriage is stupid," Kevin says in a rush, "and it doesn't mean she won't eventually leave me, or whatever you're going to say, and I know it seems like it's too soon –"

"It's been two months!" Ed exclaims, finally having found something to say.

"Three!"

Ed gapes at this perfectly illustrative example of immaturity. "Oh, I'm sorry, *three*. Kevin, you're too young to understand –"

Kevin throws his hands in the air. "See, this is why I made you promise! I knew you'd do this. I'm not *too young*. I'm nearly thirty! I know what I'm doing!"

"I don't mean young like that – although, you are – I just mean that you're inexperienced. This is your first relationship; you can't just go rushing in like that. Three months ago you were going to Circles and Bonding conventions and planning a trip to goddamn Reykjavik to meet your soulmate and now you're... what? Marrying for a green card?"

There's a fire in Kevin's eyes like Ed's never seen as he folds his arms and glares across the table. "That's not why I'm doing it and you know it. I love Penny. I want to spend my life with her. It's what I want."

"It's what you want *now*, it doesn't mean it's what you'll want for always. You can't know anything for sure after such a short amount of time." He leans back against the creaking chair in utter disbelief, as if the situation might make more sense from further away. When it doesn't, he shakes his head and gets back to the matter at hand. "I should have known that you'd take all your goddamn romanticism with you when you decided to Settle. You're still full of all these naïve fantasies of love but real life isn't like that Kevin –"

"You think I don't know –?" he seems to cut himself short as if there's much more to that sentence than Ed is permitted to hear. "I know," he rectifies. "I *know*. I know marriage takes work. But if it's right, it's right. Just because I'm not all bitter and cynical about love doesn't mean that I'm naïve."

"Okay, fine," Ed concedes. "But you know that just because you Settle doesn't mean you have to get married, right? Penny doesn't strike me as the mortgage and children type of woman anyway."

"And how would you know?" Kevin snaps with more spine that Ed thought he possessed. "You think I'd be here, asking you to be my best man, if I wasn't sure it was what she wanted? We're serious about this, man, and I know you hate weddings and stuff because of what happened with… you know," he trails off awkwardly, "but I at least thought you'd want us to be happy."

Ed stares down at his drink, ashamed. "Best man?"

"Yeah," Kevin sighs, the fight going out of him, as he slumps against the chair. "Of course. You're the reason why we met, remember?"

He remembers. Ed and Penny were on the same internship programme at PBS and had worked alongside each other for years before Kevin appeared on the scene. They'd been no more than colleagues at first but when Simon had left she'd become something akin to a friend. Penny was a Settler but had never *settled*, presumably no one ever having piqued her interest enough to do so. As for Kevin, Ed had met him about two years ago, when he had turned up at Ed's office, completely lost, with a stack of mismatched paperwork and a quivering lip, and Ed couldn't help but take pity on the newly transferred administrator. Penny and Kevin couldn't be more different from each other and it probably would have never crossed his mind to introduce them if they hadn't both happened to work in the same building and turned up simultaneously to sit with him one lunchtime. It was hardly as instrumental as Kevin is making it out to be. It was happenstance; one that resulted in him being in the middle of far too many Searcher-vs-Settler debates for his liking.

"You would've met eventually," Ed reasons.

Kevin shakes his head. "I don't know about that. I don't know if she'd even have given me the time of day if you hadn't been there. It was fate, man. You pushed this woman in my path and it changed my entire life."

"Fate," Ed repeats in a monotone, as sceptical as the notion warrants.

Kevin waves his hand in Ed's direction, dismissing him as he leans back, dejected. "See, you're doing it again. *Judgey.*"

"Kev —"

"No, man, forget it," he says, grabbing his coat. "If you're not going to support us then don't bother. I don't know what I was thinking; asking you to care about anyone but yourself."

Kevin leaves, his drink untouched, and it takes Ed longer than he'd like to admit to do the same.

Between the persistence of the protestors at work and his fallout with Kevin, Ed's week has been difficult to say the least, and the last thing he needed was to be cajoled into a blind date at the end of it.

There are several ways Ed would have preferred to spend his Friday evening than sitting morosely at a candlelit Italian restaurant in Soho waiting for his date to arrive. They may not be particularly glamorous alternatives; in fact, one would simply be lying on his bed staring at his ceiling until he was tired enough to sleep, but all are distinctly preferable to meeting a stranger for dinner.

But he had owed his colleague, Chris Thompson, a favour because of a case involving an Outlier a few months ago and apparently one awkward dinner date was all he had wanted in exchange. Now his date is ten minutes late, however, and the servers are looking at him with pity, Ed is wondering if ought to have argued otherwise.

He considers how long it's polite to wait as he re-reads the laminated menu. Twenty minutes? Half an hour? He has no idea. He hasn't been on a first date since his twenties and he's never previously agreed to one without knowing the person beforehand. His eyes flicker between his watch and the doorway every time he thinks it's not too obvious to do so as the minutes tick past ever more slowly. He pulls at the sleeves of his blazer and the shirt cuffs sticking out from beneath it, wondering if he can remember the last time he had been caught in such an awkward position.

The edges start to blur again and for a minute he's convinced that he's seen these same plastic tealight holders and frayed red tablecovers before; that it's the same Italian restaurant he took Simon to for their anniversary, years beforehand. It's near impossible, places closing and re-opening and re-branding constantly in the capital, but for a moment, he can see it; him, sat in this exact chair seven years ago, with no idea of what the future would hold. He wonders if he would make the same choices if he lived it over again. It's a thought that plagues him, that bleeds into the quiet of an empty, dark, house, when he's too tired to keep it at bay: *If I knew he would leave, would I have loved him anyway?*

The answer is always, irrevocably, *yes.*

Simon fades from his vision, reality encroaching again with the jarring sound of cutlery cutting against crockery. Who is he to lecture Kevin about love, when he would make the same self-destructive choice every time? Kevin may be making a mistake marrying so soon but Ed has no right to tell him not to.

He checks the time again. Fifteen minutes late. His hands are shaking as he reaches for the glass of water.

Holy Zeus, his first date since Simon and he gets stood up; it's so bloody typical he can't even find it within himself to be angry. Perhaps his date saw him and fled; saw his lifeless, greying hair, his thick-lensed glasses, and 'divorce' written across his face, and ran for the hills. He wouldn't blame her.

He digs into his trouser pocket and pulls out his Nokia just in time to avoid another pitying glance of a passing waiter. He's still not used to having a mobile phone but if it serves any purpose it's in calling his colleague to tell him that the wonderful woman he promised didn't even have the gall to show up. In retrospect, it was extraordinarily stupid to agree to this in any case without asking for details first. All Chris disclosed is that they'd have 'lots in common' but Ed doesn't know if that means another divorcee or a fellow employee of the Pair Bond Service. He doesn't even know what she looks like for godsake, all Chris gave him was the name –

"Rebecca. Rebecca Brighton."

Ed strains his neck as he turns to find the source of the words and sees a small, meek woman standing behind the board with the maître in a long, unremarkable, brown dress.

"I'm here to meet…" but she trails off when her gaze meet his. Her eyes grow wide; the very picture of a deer in the headlights.

Ed swallows his nerves. Is it possible that this woman wants to be here even less than he does? More to the point, *how* is that possible given that he was practically strong-armed here? Then he follows Rebecca's panicked look to the window behind her and sees an ever-enthusiastic Chris Thompson giving her a thumbs up. Ed swears under his breath. By the looks of it, his date was very literally strong-armed here.

Ed narrows his eyes when he sees someone in the shadow behind Chris, a pre-teen girl from the looks of it. Mousy hair, chunky jumper, a petulant look on her face, though her curious eyes are squinting through the window looking straight at him. Ed looks away, uncomfortable under such scrutiny. He thought Chris's kids were older than that but Ed's been so anti-social these last few years it's entirely possible he's mistaken. Unless the child was Rebecca's? He narrows his eyes to get a closer look but Chris and the child disappear from sight before he can start speculating.

In their stead, his date approaches, led by the maître. As she gets closer, Ed sees that his first assessment of her had been correct; she looks terrified; visibly shaking as she grips the chair to pull it out.

Ed remembers his manners and stands up with his hand outstretched in Recognition but he falters midway when he notices the thick black band around her wrist. No Recognition then. She's clearly not interested in greeting him at all as she busies herself with sitting down, and Ed, feeling embarrassed and at least three types of awkward, withdraws his hand and sits back down to find that Rebecca has already hidden herself behind the menu without so much as an apology for her tardiness.

He puffs out a breath, wondering how on earth this date actually managed to get worse when it was already at dire.

Despite his best efforts, his eyes fall to her wrist again. Why is she wearing a black band? The possibilities race through Ed's mind – Is she a dedicated Settler? Is it due to her religion? Is she somehow connected to an Outlie? – If she knows Chris then the latter would make the most sense but there are a hundred reasons why people don't want to be touched for Recognition and he still has enough wits about him to know it is rude to ask. Instead, he looks at what else he can see around the rectangular menu that hides her face. Her plain dress looks homemade now that he's closer, made out of some sort of simple material, and her dishwater hair is tied up in a messy bun, but he's in no position to judge her clothing given that his shirt hasn't seen an iron since Simon was here.

He shakes his head to dispel the thought of Simon before he can take hold. She couldn't be more different than him in looks alone – a woman, for starters, with skin as white as a crumpled Kleenex and long tangled hair, whereas Simon would never let his thick hair grow longer than half an inch before going to Billy's for a trim.

They couldn't be more different, he reassures himself.

"So…" Ed starts, buckling under the unbearable silence. "How'd you know Chris?"

This safe bit of small talk seems to have the opposite effect than what he had intended; she practically jumps at being spoken to and then turns rigid like a statue; nothing but complete silence behind the menu barrier.

Ed decides to persevere. "I know Chris from PBS," he says. "The Pair Bond Service?"

Still no response.

Ed raps his fingertips against the tablecloth, risking another glance towards his companion, before trying again. "I'm the Primary Tester there. It's my job to officiate new Bonds, collect research, monitor unusual cases sometimes… it's mostly just sitting behind a computer pressing buttons. And paperwork. A lot of paperwork. But I like it. What do you do?"

Nothing, apparently, if her continued silence is anything to go by.

He stares.

She stays silent.

He has no idea what to do. He has no idea how even ended up on a date given that he has no intention for this to actually progress anywhere. What's the point in dating if he doesn't want to marry? What's the point in any of it?

It's a favour, he reminds himself, it's just a favour for a colleague; all he has to do is get through it.

"Okay," Ed says decisively, a plan having formed in his mind.

He reaches over and tugs the menu out of her hands. She makes a little squeak in surprise as her pale face appears before him.

"Neither of us want to be here," he surmises, "so how's this for a deal? We get starters and a drink, enough to convince our mutual friend that we both successfully navigated a social engagement without disaster, and then we leave. Thirty minutes tops. We don't even have to speak to each other."

For a moment longer, she is silent, and he begins to fear he has overstepped or assumed too much but now he can see her hazel eyes, he's not so sure. It just looks like she's... processing. And that's fine too. He thinks she might also be younger than he thought at first glance. Mid-thirties at most.

"Okay," she says. "Mediterranean salad. Appletizer."

Ed breathes a sigh of relief. "Okay. Okay. Good."

Ed thinks he used to be quite good at dating but it's been so long he can't quite be sure. Meeting Simon had been an accident, dating him a logical progression, and then marrying was just a consequence of falling in love. It was, in retrospect, easy.

Ed had met Simon at a Post-Grad Science Department Mixer. Ed had been picking apart the finger sandwiches with suspicion, wondering when he'd become desperate enough to attend a school social, when a petite postgraduate with buzzed hair and a fitted blazer stood beside him by the buffet table and touched his hand in Recognition.

Simon had such a charming smile that Ed forgot how to speak for a minute and when he'd regained his mental faculties he'd rather wished he hadn't when he said, "Finger sandwiches, huh? They must be out of toe sandwiches again."

He cringed, expecting Simon to turn away with disdain, but then he heard him laughing and opened his eyes to see him ungracefully snorting into his palm.

"That is the worst joke that I have *ever* heard," he said between chuckles.

Ed huffed, relieved. "You clearly haven't heard the one about the explosion at the cheese factory then."

"Oh?"

Simon was a microbiologist whose doctoral study Ed didn't understand but he happily pretended to for the rest of the evening when their jokes segued into academia. The hall was emptying and he was just drumming up the courage to ask Simon out when he beat him to the punch.

"Call me," he said, like it was just that easy.

"I didn't know you were dating!"

Ed winces as Penny's loud declaration comes skittering across the PBS cafeteria come Monday lunchtime, turning a few heads in its wake. He looks up from his curdling carbonara to see his triumphant colleague dropping her lunch tray in front of him with a clatter, swinging her legs round the bench to join him before he can protest the matter. He feels undeniably trapped.

"I'm not 'dating,'" Ed insists. "It was *a* date. Singular. Past tense. It means nothing."

Penny raises an eyebrow and crosses her arms. Ed's known her for long enough to recognise that pose of determination. In a distant part of his mind, he resigns himself to the knowledge that his entire lunch hour is now going to be taken up with invasive personal questions.

Penelope Morgan has worked for the Pair Bond Service for as long as he has but she works as statistician, meaning that she's about as much fun as any mathematician but with the added bonus that she's the most critical, pessimistic, and stubborn person that he's ever had the misfortune to meet. She's in her mid-thirties, a few years Ed's junior, proudly Welsh, and models her auburn hair short and severe enough to cut down anyone that tries to get too close.

"Look," Ed pre-empts her, "I'm sure you've been saving some anecdotes for this occasion, and I'd love to hear them, but it really was just a one-time thing. I'm not dating."

Her expression changes into one of curiosity, which, Ed has learnt, is even worse than the folded arms of determination. "Funny how you're so quick to defend. It's been, what? Five years? And if you're still a Settler…"

"Of course I'm still –" he jumps in but then cuts himself short when he notes her disbelieving expression. "Probably," he amends, "I'm *probably* still a Settler. I'm just saying that it was a disaster, I was forced there, and it certainly doesn't mean I'm ready to date so put away that list of suggestions I know you have. It's not happening."

Penny looks put out enough to imply that she did actually have a list of possible suitors. He needs to find some colleagues that actually stay out of his business, between her, Kevin, and now the blind date Chris orchestrated, he feels like his entire life is being micromanaged.

"Fine," she says, starting to pick at her food. "But it would be good for you to get back out there, you know. I think you're ready. You're looking less –" she waves her hand at him as if there's some physical sign of depression that he's visibly shrugged off "– you know."

"Sure," he says with only the slightest hint of condescension.

"Right," she continues oblivious. "And it's not like you have to marry anyone, or get yourself into some crazy complicated situation, you can, just, you know, *have some fun*."

"Fun," Ed repeats, like the word is a foreign concept.

Penny glares. "Don't pretend like you don't get my meaning, you get my meaning."

Ed hides his smile behind his mug of coffee.

"But, Ed," she says, reaching out to lay her hand companionably over his. "You're smart. Kevin's inevitably going to try and talk you into Searching or some bullshit, but you know this is the only sensible option, right? As much as it sucks – and trust me, dating *sucks* – Settling is way better than any other option. Statistically speaking finding your soulmate is like... six hundred thousand to one. Well, a little less, actually," she says with a scrunched nose, probably trying to remember the figures. "I think it's currently about six hundred and *nineteen* thousand to one... but my point is this," she says, reigning herself back in with a shake of the head. "Don't let anyone put any stupid ideas in your head. Godknows this place is full of romantic, naïve, lunatics –" she cuts off as a known Searcher walks by and gives her a dirty look.

Penny rolls her eyes as if she's used to it and continues her speech between bites of her food, talking about Ed's deepest insecurities as casually as one would about the weather. "Whatever. So you're probably thinking you can't do this whole Settling thing again, right? After Simon?"

Ed nods, cautiously.

"Right. Ten years together is a long time, I get that, even if I don't *get* that. But, I'll tell you this: the reason why I kept going back out there when I was single? Date after disastrous date?"

Ed looks across at her, intently; genuinely needing to know the answer.

"Because when you have a good one, it makes it all worth it."

Ed's shoulders sag. He wasn't sure what magical words he was expecting to hear to make him motivated to Settle again but apparently they weren't it. Perhaps it's the unsettling thought of sitting in an identical restaurant, date after date, stretching indeterminately into the future, just waiting for one not to be totally horrendous. It doesn't seem like a good enough pay off.

"You've probably forgotten what it feels like," Penny infers from his sullen silence. "The excitement… that feeling…" she trails off, a warm and shy smile on her face as she flutters her fingers over her stomach. Butterflies. "It makes it all worth it."

Ed smiles adoringly at the sight; he's not sure if he's ever seen her looking so soft, so happy. "You feel like that?" he prompts. "With Kevin?"

She scoffs, but it's not as harsh sounding as her usual displays of dismissal. "Yeah, I do. And it did. Make it all worth it, I mean."

Ed nods, a smile still lining his lips. He's been so wrapped up in his own mind these past few years, he thinks he may have missed the subtle ways Penny has changed since her and Kevin finally found what was underneath their vitriol for each other. There's a brightness in her eyes now that almost reminds Ed of Bonded Pairs. She's lighter in a way than she was before, like a huge weight has been lifted off her shoulders. She smiles more, she's kinder… still in a very Penny way, of course, but Ed knows that three months ago,

Penny would not have had the patience to have this conversation with him. Before, she would have mocked him, and ignored his feelings, and forced him to go on date after date even if he was completely unwilling. Love has made her become a better version of herself, he thinks.

Some of his thoughts must show on his face because she scowls across at him. "You're doing it, aren't you? Having sappy romantic thoughts about Bonding or some shit. I thought you were on my side, man."

Ed waves it off, knowing that Penny would only grow more incensed if she knew it was herself in his thoughts. "No, no, I was thinking about the work I've got to do this afternoon."

She frowns. "You're not going to the consultation? I thought all senior management had to go."

Ed rubs his eyes, tilting his glasses up towards his hairline. In everything, he'd forgotten about the department-wide meeting about the new legislation, but he's also entirely uninterested. "The new loan scheme won't affect me. Not in Testing."

She raises an eyebrow. "You seem mighty confident about that."

"There a reason why I shouldn't be?"

"Not that I know of, but nothing's ever certain in government, you know that." She glances at the cafeteria clock and then winces. "Urgh, I've got to go. Finance have got me helping with some of the figures for this afternoon. Say 'hi' to Kevin for me if you see him," she says as she stands, but then hesitates, "that is, if you guys are talking this week."

She's walking away before Ed can defend himself. He looks back at his cold food and when he looks up again both Penny and Kevin are standing in the doorway, her hand in his, lips pressed against his cheek in goodbye, a soft smile on his face.

Ed looks away, something akin to guilt pooling in his gut.

After he met Simon, he couldn't stop thinking about him.

Ed would be in a lecture, taking notes, when out of nowhere

Simon's charming smile would appear in his mind and the sentence he had been writing would slip away entirely; irrelevant, unimportant. The thought of Simon was so utterly distracting that in the twenty two hours it took Ed to actually call the number scribbled on graph paper, he had become embarrassingly desperate. He didn't know what he'd do if the number turned out to be faked or if Simon had lost interest.

Then, somehow, he called, and managed to string some words together that resulted in the promise of a date.

They had arranged a visit to a museum but there was a torrential downpour as they were cutting through Athena Gardens and so their actual first date was sitting cross-legged on a dirty bandstand sharing some hot fresh chips. They never even made it to the museum, having talked on that empty concrete octagon until past closing time.

"So, why Bonding Science?" Simon asked, between a chip and a swig of coke. "You Witness or something?"

Ed snorted, though the sound was lost in the rain around them. "No, I'm not that much of a cliché."

"But there's gotta be a reason, right?" he asked, the can clinking back against the concrete between their crossed legs. "Not many Bonding students are Settlers. So what is it?"

"A Settler, huh?" Ed mused over a chip. "Never thought of myself that way."

"Well, you are on a date. Right?" Simon asked teasingly, pointing between them. "This is date?"

"It's a date."

"Right. So you're a Settler."

Ed huffed. "I'm not sure if it's that clear cut."

"Aw man," Simon said with a cringe, leaning back on his hands. "Don't tell me you're a Waiter. If you're one of those people that date but are always off fantasying about The One then whatever but that's not my kinda –"

"No, that's not it," Ed interjected, reaching out to place his hand over Simon's. It took Simon's eyes flickering down to the contact for Ed to realise that it was oddly intimate for a first date and as a blush spread across his cheeks, Ed reluctantly took his hand back. "I'm here. Entirely. And happy to be. I just... never thought much about what I wanted. I figured it would all just come together when I met the right person, whether they be my soulmate or..." he trailed off, unable to look Simon in his eyes. "Or otherwise."

The air between them became charged like the thunderstorm around them and with tense shoulders Ed waited for it to break.

"Yeah, I get that." Simon took another swig of coke; the can between them casually shared. "So," he said, pulling Ed's gaze back, "if you've finished avoiding the question..."

"I was not avoiding the question."

Simon gave him a look that said he wasn't so easily convinced.

"Fine. I..." Ed trailed off, looking back out into sodden park. "I didn't Witness," he confirmed, "but my parents come from money and know people in the Elite, so you know, we'd go to functions and –"

Ed broke off when he realised that there was a lilt to Simon's lips like he wanted to laugh. Simon was distinctly working class and probably suppressing the urge to mock Ed for his rather privileged upbringing. As the smile exploded into a laugh, Ed cussed him out and threw a chip at him, which he elegantly ducked. Simon laughed again.

"If you're just going to mock me –"

Simon crossed his heart. "Nothing but compassion here, my friend. Go on, you were telling me about how hard it was growing up with such riches and privileges."

Ed shook his head in amusement and continued. "Well, it meant that we went to parties. Symposiums. Feasts. Award shows. You know, Elite parties."

"I really don't," Simon deadpanned.

"Okay," Ed huffed. "Well, the Elite is mostly made up of Bonded Pairs, their families, and other Arts royalty, it's all very... formal and Hellenic and very, very, cliquey. Kids, especially kids that aren't born from a Pair, get largely ignored. 'Be seen and not heard.' All that nonsense. So I'd just... watch. I had nothing else to do; I was an only child and I wasn't fawned over like those from Pairs. I was practically invisible. So I went from room to room, observing, and even as a kid I could tell, you know, who was Bonded and who was not. Once, at a charity feast, I watched this elderly Pair the whole night and they said not a single word to each other."

"Well, that's depressing."

"Not to me. Not to a kid whose parents were constantly arguing. It was... serene. And I guess I just wanted to understand how they could do it; communicating without saying a word, loving each other unconditionally and forever. I wanted to know how that was possible."

"Oh, I see," Simon said, with emphasised realisation. "It's a tragic divorce backstory!" He shook his head. "I should have known."

"Oh, like your tragic adoption backstory is any less cliché."

Simon gaped, and for a moment, Ed thought he had gone a step too far before Simon grinned and it turned into a food fight. When the pigeons swooped down to pick up the remains, they were wrapped up in each other under the bandstand and the playfighting turned to kisses almost without thought. There was a lightness in his chest like at any moment he could take flight.

Ed finds Kevin at the end of the day, just as he's packing up to leave.

"Oh, hey," Kevin says, stilted and awkward, darting glances at the office cubicles around him for eavesdroppers but it's just turned five and no one loves admin enough to stay one minute after they're paid to.

"Hi, Kevin."

"You weren't at the meeting earlier."

"No, I was... busy."

"You should've been there, man, it looks like it's going to be fucking brutal. I heard Science might have their budget *halved* –"

"Listen, Kevin," Ed says, cutting him short. "I wanted to apologise."

Kevin keeps tidying his desk, eyes averted as he shakes his head with a laugh. "A full week later, well done."

Ed taps his fingers against the cubicle divide. "Well, I can be a bit slow on the uptake. Or maybe…" he says, finally looking back up at Kevin, "people just move faster than I would. That isn't to say that they are necessarily wrong."

Kevin stops shuffling his papers for a fraction of a second and Ed knows that he got his meaning.

"I shouldn't have taken my bitterness about marriage out on you," Ed says. "I know you're doing what you think is best and I'm in no position to judge your decisions."

Kevin raises an eyebrow, as if he doesn't believe for a minute that Ed can be non-judgemental.

"I mean it, Kev. You've got nothing but my full support."

This time, he actually puts down the stack of papers. "You mean that? For real?"

Ed can't quite bring himself to say 'for real' but he nods, solemnly, and hopes it gets the point across. "And if you'd still have me, I'd be honoured to be your Best Man."

There's a flurry of movement and before Ed can even process what's happened there is a fully grown man wrapped around his waist more in approximation of a rugby tackle than a hug.

Ed laughs, winded.

Kevin backs away, probably as embarrassed by the display of affection as Ed is. "What changed your mind, man?"

Ed smiles wryly, remembering the soft private smile that Penny let slip while they were talking earlier that day. "I don't know, it's just… It's just nice to see you both happy, I suppose."

Ed shakes his head. It's all become far too sentimental for his liking and it looks very much like Kevin is considering another hug so before he can action it Ed clears his throat and slaps a hand on his friend's arm, backing out of further conversation.

"Have a good evening, Kev."

"Yeah, man," he hears from behind him. "You too."

The pigeons squawk and shuffle around him as Ed makes his way down the damp avenue towards the bandstand where he had fallen in love with Simon all those years ago. Sometimes he needs to see where it happened, to touch some tangible reminder of their shared life, just to reassure himself that the ten years he spent with Simon were real and not imagined.

A raggedy pigeon limps past him, looking as forlorn as Ed feels, with several askew feathers and a stub for a foot. He follows its path with his eyes as the bird hops off the pavement and into the rain-soaked grass before ducking beneath an ironcast gate and into the playground.

He looks up from the bird, expecting to see the playground deserted given that dusk is falling on a rainy day, but he stops in his tracks when he realises that there is a child there; one that he recognises.

It's the kid that was trailing behind Chris on that awful date in the Italian last week. The girl is sat on the swings, alone, in overly long school trousers and scruffy black shoes, an oversized coat around her shoulders and a school bag at her feet, sodden through by the drizzle. She's hunched in on herself, frowning down at the ground as she kicks at it, the swing only moving incrementally instead of with its full playful purpose.

He scans the gardens, hoping to see an adult nearby, but there's only a handful of after-work joggers and dog-walkers; no one that looks like they're accompanying the girl. It's not his problem, he assures himself, and she's old enough to take care of herself. But the gardens are big, and it's getting dark, and there's too many reports of missing children in the world for him to just walk away.

"You're such a pushover," he mutters to himself in disbelief, even as he turns off his path and towards the playground.

Ed has no idea how to go about this and doesn't want to scare the child so he keeps his distance and calls out to her from the far side of railings, "Hey! You okay there, kid? It's getting dark. Shouldn't you be getting home?"

He sounds like his father he realises with revulsion.

The child jumps and her eyes snap up and there's a moment where she's clearly deciding if Ed poses a danger or not. He tries to make himself look as non-threatening as possible but he realises, by extension, that it probably only serves to make him look *more* threatening.

But before he can say anything more, her eyes widen with recognition.

Ed's widen with fear.

"You're that guy my mum dated," she accuses before Ed can think to retreat.

Ed opens his mouth to defend himself but gets distracted by the fact that the kid is apparently Rebecca's, not Chris's, as he'd previously assumed. Now he's looking for it he can see the similarities: her skin is a shade darker than her mother's but her light-brown hair – bushy and tangled and long – is near-identical.

"Oh pur-lease," she says, dragging the word out dramatically like teenagers were prone to do, "don't look so surprised. It was the first time Mum had been on a date. *Ever.* Of course I was going to remember you, even if you are crazy boring."

"'Boring?'" Ed is asking before he can stop himself. "She said I was 'boring'?"

"No," she says with disgust. "*I* said that you were boring. You were wearing a suit."

"It was a date," he defends. "Lots of people wear suits to dates. It's what you're supposed to wear. Suits are nice."

"Suits are *boring*."

Ed starts to argue back before he catches himself and realises that he's somehow been roped into an extremely juvenile conversation about fashion with an adolescent girl. He shakes himself out of it and opens the gate to the playground so he can walk over to the swings. "Okay, well, does your mother know you're here? It's getting dark."

"So you've said," she rebuts in a deadpan. "What's it to you? You don't know me."

"I... suppose I don't," Ed acquiesces. "But I'm sure your mother's worried." He watches her scuff the ground, uninterested, and feels at an utter loss before he remembers the weight in his pocket. "Here," he says, getting her attention. "I have a mobile phone." He digs out his Nokia and offers it to her. "If you want to call home?"

"Okay, *genius*," she says sarcastically, head tilted to the side as if patronising him. He wonders where kids pick up all these little quirks. From TV, he supposes. "I'm twelve and three-quarters. I can clearly take myself home if I wanted. So why would I want to call home if I clearly *didn't want to be at home*?"

She's got him there. He takes a deep breath, pockets the phone, and wonders when kids got so bloody mouthy. Well, two can play at that game. He crosses his arms, leaning against the side of the swings. "I don't know, kid, you tell me. Why don't you want to go home?"

The kid rolls her eyes. "My name's Lizzie, you know. 'Kid' makes me sound like an eight year old boy."

"Okay, *Lizzie*," he reiterates, "why don't you want to go home?"

She kicks off from the ground, setting herself in motion before grinding her peeling shoes into the tarmac and halting the movement. He has a feeling that she's deciding if he can be trusted.

"If you tell me," he adds, "I won't call your mother."

He's bluffing. He doesn't have Rebecca's number. But Lizzie doesn't know that.

She seems to mull this over, kicking back and forth on the swing, until eventually she comes to a stop and looks over at him, eyes narrowed. "We're in a fight."

"Huh," he says, and lowers himself into the unoccupied swing next to her. The contraption groans with the added weight. He wonders if Lizzie posed the statement as a test – if he's meant to take Rebecca's side or something – but he's genuinely curious so instead he asks, "And why's that?"

"Urgh," Lizzie grunts, digging her toes into the tarmac and looking away. "She's just crazy. Which you obviously know because you ended that date in like… record time. Thanks, by the way, it meant she got back before Chris could make me watch *another* episode of *Frasier*, so silver linings and all that."

"You're welcome?" Ed says, confused.

"Yeah, whatever, so she's just super strict. Doesn't let me do *anything*. Especially at this new school because it's huge, right? And, I dunno, she's just paranoid. So I'm meant to come straight back home every day, no afterschool clubs, or parties, or *anything*. And I got invited to go see *Harry Potter*, right? With Katie. Who Mum knows. She's like… my best friend. But then Mum's like, 'who else is going?' and because I'm super honest – which totally should have been the takeaway here – I tell her that Katie's boyfriend, Craig, is going and maybe some of his friends, because it's her thirteenth birthday, so it's a big thing, you know?"

Ed nods, even though he's not entirely sure if he's managed to keep track of who's who in this teenage drama.

"And then Mum suddenly starts going off on one. She's like, 'we talked about this, new people, be careful, blah blah blah' and I'm like 'yeah, Mum, we talked about this when I was like, eight, but things change you know? I'm not a kid anymore and all my friends are dating and stuff and I've never even kissed a boy or Recognised anyone or whatever because she's *psychotic* and won't even let me leave the damn house."

Ed waits for a second, checking that she's actually done this time, before releasing a thoughtful hum.

"Urgh," Lizzie grunts again. "You're going to take her side, aren't you?"

"No?" Ed hazards, still attempting to process the lightning-speed story.

Lizzie stills, and looks across at him curiously. He's not sure if he's ever had the full attention of a child on him before but it's unsettling; like she can somehow see past all the walls that he's erected around himself and see the messed up person inside. "You're weird," she surmises after a moment.

It sounds oddly like a compliment so he decides to take it as one. "Thank you."

Lizzie huffs and Ed looks away to watch the streetlights as they flicker to pink on the pavement ahead of them.

"Your mum probably has her reasons though," he says. He doesn't know what they are but he remembers seeing the black band around her wrist at the Italian restaurant and that often symbolises complications.

Lizzie rolls her eyes. "Yeah, she's got her reasons alright," she says with amusement, or with mockery, he can't tell, but it definitely raises more questions than answers. "But, I'm not her, you know?" she continues, "I actually want to go out and *meet people*." Then she seems to reconsider and adds, "Well, some people. Someone special maybe. I don't like most people but some people might be alright. I don't know though, do I? Unless she lets me *meet* them."

Ed hums again, contemplatively. "You've got a point there," he says, thinking back on Penny's conversation that afternoon; perhaps he *should* date more just to see what's actually out there.

He pushes his toes against the tarmac and sets himself into a slow, steady, motion on the swing beside her. For a moment, he feels as if he's also twelve years old, not just at the ridiculousness of swinging from a piece of plastic, but because he's back to having silly thoughts about love that he feels entirely too inadequate to pursue. He wonders if many people feel that way having come out of long relationships or long periods of solitude; realising that there's this whole messy, complicated world out there that they haven't had to battle through since their first inexperienced steps into adulthood. The landscape has changed since he was young. The terminology.

The baggage that piles up over the years. It all adds up to make the concept of intentionally trying to meet new people again incredibly overwhelming.

"I think Mum's worried I'm going to be a Searcher," Lizzie muses conversationally, as if by using the swings as intended they were now permitted to speak as equals. "I was reading this book about it, that's all, so maybe she's worried I'll meet someone *too* special, you know? And disappear on her."

"Maybe," he says, but he's distracted, still selfishly caught up in his own thoughts. "But I don't think it's wrong if you want to Search though. It's good to... consider all the options. Sometimes it's good to question what you've been taught to believe." He clamps his mouth shut upon realising he's basically telling the kid to ignore her own mother, which is probably not advisable, and grounds his swing to a halt. "Not that you should... I mean, you should listen to your mother."

Lizzie snorts. "You're *so* weird."

"Yeah," Ed sighs in defeat, "I guess I am."

Lizzie narrows her eyes, scrutinising him again. "What about you?" she says, rocking her heels on the ground. "You're old. You must have met people before Mum, right? Are you married or something? You look like you should be married."

"Because I wear a suit?" he recalls with a teasing smile.

"Yeah," she says with a laugh. "Because you wear a suit. Married people are boring, everyone knows that."

He shakes his head with a laugh. "Unbelievable," he mutters.

"So, are you? Married?"

His smile falters and he looks down at his conjoined hands, resting in his lap. "Yeah," he says eventually, looking past Lizzie's plaited brown hair to see the bandstand shrouded in shadows behind her, "Yeah, I was married."

He had brought Simon back to the bandstand one day in late summer, just as the leaves were starting to turn golden, and knelt down on one knee. Simon raised an eyebrow as if to say, 'Really? You're doing this? The cheesiest proposal in history?' but then his lips quirked to the side, and he knew he had him. *Until our souls complete.*

It had been a couple of years since their first date at the same location; their studies now both behind them and their careers well underway.

After his Master's degree in Bonding Science two years ago, Ed had managed to secure an internship at the Pair Bond Service shortly followed by an entry admin job in Reports. It meant he could stay in London while Simon worked on his doctorate. Between the salary at PBS and his generous family inheritance, Ed was able to afford a good townhouse in the city and after a couple of months of skirting around the issue, Simon turned up one day with a suitcase and an expression that brooked no arguments.

That year, Simon's thesis had been accepted and Ed had attended Simon's graduation just as summer was breaking and hollered loud enough when his name was called that several professors turned to stare at him. Ed had felt flustered until he caught Simon's eye as he was coming off stage and saw that he was biting his lip in an attempt not to laugh. It made all the embarrassment worth it, and Ed was fairly sure, it was in that moment that he decided he wanted to marry him.

A few weeks later and Simon had found a well-paid job at a private lab and Ed was training in-house at PBS to be a Tester. Things were good and steady and Ed knew it was the right time to cement their relationship for the future and propose marriage. It took him the entire summer to find the courage but when Simon said 'yes' it was as if there had never been any doubt.

It may have been the happiest day of his life as they stood on that bandstand in Athena Gardens; their future stretched out before them like it was nothing to fear.

"I think I want to get married one day," Lizzie says, dragging him from his thoughts as they walk through the streets.

He'd given her a very edited version of his life with Simon and she'd seemed so interested, eyes wide with curiosity, that she didn't even put up a fight when he got up from the creaking swing and started to walk her home. His story had been frequently interrupted with her off-hand directions – "the south exit's quicker" – and her incessant questioning about Bonding which was as endearing as it was tiresome. He apparently doesn't mind the routine questions about his tragic tale when they're coming from a place of genuine curiosity.

He's about to ask why she's so keen on marriage given her seemingly conflicting interest in Bonding when she effectively answers him, "Weddings look like fun."

Ed gives a one-armed shrug, trying to push away the memories of his own service. "They're okay if you like that sort of thing. Have you ever been to one?"

She snorts, shakes her head. "Like Mum would ever."

It's the first opening he's really been given to uncover further information about his mysterious date but it seems highly inappropriate to interrogate Rebecca's daughter for information, no matter how much he's tempted.

Lizzie looks across at him though and rolls her eyes. "Mum was married, ages ago. Wears the ring still, like you wear that band," she nods across at the thin golden Hellenic wedding band around his wrist. "Kinda sad."

He stumbles as they cross the street, so distracted with processing that information. Another divorcee? Or widow? And a ring; not a bracelet. That could mean she was Biblic. He hadn't even noticed the ring on the date, preoccupied as he was with her black band of solitude.

Lizzie is kicking at fallen leaves as she walks and he realises that he hasn't said anything for a good two minutes, wrapped in his own thoughts, only jolted out of it by the touch of a passing stranger for Recognition. He could ask further questions but the child looks uncomfortable enough so he decides to return to their previous conversation instead. "It's been a while since I've been to a wedding but I think my friends are about to get engaged."

Lizzie turns back to him, her gaze having been trailing the stranger that just passed, but now she looks to Ed with wide eyes and a bright smile. "Really? That's exciting!"

Is it? Ed wonders. "They seem happy."

Lizzie frowns and tilts her head as if disapproving of his response but then they're walking down a narrow alley, resembling a muddy footpath more than a proper road, caged in by small bungalows on one side and a tall wire fence on the other.

"Is there a park or something here?" he asks, trying to make shapes out of the darkness.

"It's St. Martin's playing field, behind the Prayer House on Hadley Road."

"Right," Ed says, having no idea what that meant. He'd moved back into the city after Simon had left, into a characterless townhouse in the suburbs similar to the one he had first bought and shared with Simon after university, but he'd rarely had reason to stray from his path from home to work to pub. He knew they'd been walking for about fifteen minutes and he had recognised a corner shop a street or two ago that tells him he can't be more than a couple of miles from his own home, a borough or two perhaps, but he certainly never knew there was a Prayer House so close to him.

Lizzie stops a couple of doors down to rummage in her backpack for a key and Ed takes a moment to look at the place. Two windows, one floor, and a garden that is no more than a cracked paving slab and a rusted chair folded up against the stippled wall. It's small; perhaps even smaller than Simon's family home in Croydon; the six of them packed into the two-bed, one-bathroom household like sardines. At least there were presumably only the two of them living in this bungalow.

"We've been here for a few years now," Lizzie says, as she finds the key. "I think our old house was bigger, but Naomi – that's

Mum's counsellor – thought we should move, so, we moved."

Before Lizzie can get her key in the door, it opens before her, casting the pitiful garden in an orange haze from the light inside.

"Lizzie!" Rebecca cries. "I thought I heard you, oh thank God –" her mumblings continue but Ed can't hear them as they are pressed into the collar of Lizzie's thick coat as the girl is swallowed by the arms of her mother and an impossible amount of wool. Ed looks away, awkwardly, and steps a little further into the shadows.

Rebecca pulls her daughter out to arm's reach, the woollen blanket around her shoulders brushing against Lizzie too. She studies her briefly, up and down, as if checking for injuries, and then all at once, a storm crosses her face. "Where the hell have you been?!" she exclaims. "Do you know how worried I've been? It's nearly seven o'clock Elizabeth! Do you know all the terrible things I've been imagining? Were you out with friends? A boy? What were you doing that was so important that you could worry your mother like this? Do you know what could have happened? You're to walk straight from school to home on the path we agreed. I don't care if you're mad at me, you *come home*. You hear me? Elizabeth Brighton," she scorns, "you listen when I'm talking to you, what are you even –?"

And then she follows Lizzie's embarrassed gaze to find Ed lingering beside her and Ed no longer knows which of them are more embarrassed by the situation.

Rebecca flushes a bright crimson and pulls Lizzie closer, ushering her behind her and towards the door.

"But Mum –" Lizzie protests. "He's cool. He works for PBS!"

This little detail sets Rebecca's face as hard as a stone. "Enough," she demands, and Lizzie silences immediately. "Eat your dinner and do your homework. You'll make your excuses later. Inside. Now."

Lizzie grunts, and her eyes flicker over to Ed as if to say 'thank you' and 'sorry' all at once, before she squeezes past her mother into the open doorway and out of sight.

Rebecca pushes the front door closed as soon as her daughter's behind it, the message loud and clear. It casts them both suddenly in darkness; the only light from the windows and the streetlamps. Her long tangled hair seems tinted red in the light. For a minute, they both do nothing but stare at each other across the tiny patio.

"So," Ed starts, "you can speak."

Rebecca glares and folds her arms. Defensive. Furious. "What the hell are you doing here?"

Hell, not Hades, he manages to interpret. Biblic, for sure. He sees the ring this time too. He swallows his nerves; it's been a while since he's had to face the wrath of a mother. Simon's mother was likely the last and she had hated him. "I saw her in the Gardens. I thought it best –"

"You thought it best?" she mimics, incredulous, "You know nothing about us!"

"She was alone! It was getting dark! What was I meant to do?"

"So you thought it was *best* to pick her up and fill her head with all sorts of ideas –"

"What? What ideas? I had no ulterior –"

"Bonding! Searching! All that nonsense!"

"Nonsense?"

"– instead of calling her mother?"

"She didn't want to –" Ed breaks off in frustration and runs his hand through his thinning hair before turning back to her, hands propped on hips, determined to defend his actions. "You *do* know she was there because she didn't want to go home, right? She's feeling..." he raises his hands, trying to think of the appropriate word. "Trapped. Confused. I don't know. I thought I could help, and I'm sorry if that was wrong, okay, but I really think you need to talk to her. She seems unhappy and could do with being given a bit of space to work stuff out. She's a teenager, you know? Sometimes they need to... *explore* a little."

Rebecca's scowl deepens even further. "I know my own daughter," she says coldly. "How dare you come here and tell me I don't know what's best for her. You don't know us."

Ed raises his hands in defence. "You're right, I don't," he acquiesces. "So, why don't you tell me what I'm clearly not understanding here? Why can't she –?"

"It's meant to just be the two of us," she interrupts, though it seems more for her benefit than for his. "Lizzie knows this. Agreed to this. It's safer. She knows other people –" she says with a not too subtle glare at Ed "– are dangerous."

"*All* people? Rebecca, it's not like she's hanging out with hardened criminals. She just wants to go to a little girl's birthday party. She wants to, I don't know, do whatever twelve-year-olds do. What's so wrong with that?"

Rebecca toes the ground with her slippers, in a motion very reminiscent of her daughter scuffing her shoes at the playground. "You don't understand. You can't." And it's said in a tone that implies that she is not planning on making him understand any time soon. And why would she explain? He's practically a stranger. The odds of them running into each other again are minimal in a city this big, even if they do have a corner shop in common.

"You're right," he sighs in defeat. "I can't."

She looks up at this, though her gaze is fixed somewhere over his shoulder. Neither of them are fond of eye contact it seems.

"And I suppose," he adds, "I don't have to."

Her jaw clenches and she nods. It's as good of a dismissal as any.

"Okay then," he says with finality, looking down to the ground. "Sorry to have bothered you."

He turns and starts making his way back through the darkness.

"Ed!" Lizzie cries.

He turns back to see her running out of the doorway, textbook in hand. Rebecca holds her back with a firm hand and something muttered into her ear. She seems to sag against her mother, the fight gone out of her. In the dim light, he can see Lizzie's wide eyes staring at him and they seem sad; defeated.

134

He raises his hand in goodbye and turns away before he can see them doing the same.

Ed returns to work the next day, to the same comforting routine to which he has become accustomed; even the protestors outside are starting to dwindle, the news fading into normality, and now he's made amends with Kevin his lunchtime routine has returned to normal too. There's an edge of nervousness to Kevin that reminds Ed of the summer before he proposed to Simon but Penny seems to attribute Kevin's stress to his reassignment to the new legislation taskforce and Kevin is more than willing to play along, complaining about financial records and budgeting decisions.

It's almost comforting to be sandwiched between them in the cafeteria, caught between their familiar bickering, as if it can drown out his argument with Rebecca that's been playing on a loop in his head since they parted ways.

I know my own daughter. How dare you come here and tell me I don't know what's best for her.

He had never felt the urge to step in before but he'd felt Lizzie's frustration like it was his own and supposed he had argued like it was too; without any tact or thought to Rebecca's own position. The resigned look Lizzie had given him before he walked away haunts him, edging in on his thoughts the same way Simon frequently does. Snippets of their conversations keep remerging in quiet moments; his mind still trying to piece together the puzzle of the Brightons even though he's determined not to care.

In his weakest moments he picks up the office phone ready to dial Chris's extension but he always talks himself out of it, whether out of guilt for prying or out of stubborn determination to let it go.

You don't know us, Rebecca had said, almost an exact mimicry of her daughter in the playground not an hour before and Ed can't help but wonder what it was that made the Brightons so afraid of being known.

Kevin asks Penny to marry him that Friday night, over a dinner or some sort, and naturally she agrees. Come Saturday, Ed finds himself at an engagement party at a cocktail bar in Southwark. It's not their usual type of bar but he supposes the occasion warrants it. While his friends enjoy the novelty of overpriced drinks amongst C-list celebrities, it only serves to remind Ed of his youth and the mimicry of sophistication he used to carry out.

It's uncomfortable enough that he finds himself amongst the smokers on the balcony, nursing his whiskey concoction as he looks out onto the river at the passing boats and the twinkling lights. He wonders briefly if there's someone standing on the other side of the Thames, looking out over the river, feeling just as melancholic.

"Yo, my man," Kevin slurs, stumbling his way towards Ed. "There you are." His hand clamps down on Ed's shoulder and he wonders if it's more for balance than for any display of solidarity. "Want you to meet someone."

Ed bites his tongue, having had his fill of new people for the foreseeable future after the disaster with the Brightons, but his shoulders relax a little when he sees who is in Kevin's shadow.

"Ed, this is Jasmine Wallace, she's going to be Penny's maid of honour."

Ed chuckles. He wonders how drunk Kevin must be to not realise that they already know each other. "Jazz," he greets, reaching out for an informal handshake. "Good to see you outside the basement."

"Oh, haha," she says as she takes the proffered hand. Jasmine works for the Science department – a mortician first and foremost – and is quite possibly the only person in the building more cynical about life than Penny. She's a large Indian woman with a shaved head and noticeable piercings but this is the first time he's seen her in a dress, or, for that matter, in anything other than her eccentrically decorated lab coat.

"Oh good, you know each other!" Kevin exclaims gleefully. "Look, Penny and I are hoping to get this sorted in a couple of months so we're gonna need your help planning some stuff. Now, we were just talking venue –"

"A couple of months?" Ed baulks.

"Yeah I know," Kevin says, "it's gonna be crazy, but what's the point in waiting, right? So, venue –"

He expects Jasmine to back him up on this, to tell Kevin that it's crazy to get married, yet alone try to organise a wedding in a matter of months. Jasmine's Non-Trad after all, if there's anyone that's going to be cynical about this, it's her, but he looks across to see a genuine smile on her face as she nods in response to Kevin's rambling.

Exciting, Lizzie had said.

He watches Kevin gesticulate and Jasmine laugh and at all the bright eyes surrounding them and wonders if it's not just the buzz of a Saturday night and the second glass of whiskey that causes a hopeful bubble to rise in his chest.

He should have known that the peace would not last for long. Monday morning finds Kevin marching into Ed's office and slamming the door behind him loudly enough to make Ed wince. He didn't sleep well last night, having been trapped in the field again with Simon, and it's considerably unfair to be expected to deal with Kevin at 9am before he's had the chance for another dose of caffeine and to plough through the hundred memos about the new legislation. Ed groans, rubbing at his temples in an attempt to abate the oncoming headache.

When he looks up again, Kevin is pacing the three steps it takes to cross the width of his office, angry enough that heat seems to roll off him in waves.

Ed leans back in his chair with his arms folded, resigned for the long-haul. "Okay. What happened?"

"Penny!"

Ed waves his hand as if to say both *obviously* and *go on*.

Kevin sees the gesture and rolls his eyes. "We had an argument."

Ed raises an eyebrow and gives much the same gesture as that was hardly an improvement.

"Okay, okay," Kevin says, dropping himself into the chair opposite Ed's desk. "I know we argue all the time but that's just us... you know, being us. It's never like this."

"What did she say?"

Kevin makes a sound of disgust. "What *didn't* she say?" He bites his lip and shakes his head, as if refusing to give the words power. "I forget sometimes, you know, all the things she used to say about people like me. I forgot how mean she could be. But she fucking hates Searchers, man."

Ed frowns in sympathy. "I don't think that's true."

"You didn't hear the things she said."

"Okay, then walk me through it," Ed says, and absently wonders when on earth he became a counsellor; first for Lizzie, and now for Kevin.

Kevin looks surprised at the offer but apparently not enough to miss the given opportunity as he leans back in his chair and starts explaining, "So we're talking about the wedding, right? And I say that obviously, as an ex-Searcher – and given my family of very proud and traditional Searchers – that I want ''til my soul completes –'"

"Ah," Ed says, suddenly knowing where this is going. "And she wanted ''til death do us part.'"

Kevin shrugs. "Of course she did because she's a fucking idiot. Never mind it's not at all true, I mean, look at –" he waves his hand at Ed and then seems to decide better of it and lowers his hand. "Sorry, I just mean... She's a proud Settler and I get that's a thing they do but it's not realistic, is it? If one of us Bonds then we leave, that's just... how it works."

"Right," Ed says, swallowing the sudden lump in his throat. He pushes Simon as far from his thoughts as he can.

"And it's not just that, it's what it *means*. She doesn't seem to care how important it is to me. She doesn't know how hard it was... the sacrifices I made..."

138

Ed narrows his eyes as Kevin seems to get lost in his thoughts, and he's reminded of the argument they'd had in the pub last week when Kevin had first mentioned getting married.

You think I don't know –?

He had cut himself short as if there was a lot more to his story than Ed was permitted to hear. It reminds him so suddenly of the similar words Rebecca had said to him outside her house, days ago now, that his breath catches on the memory.

You don't understand. You can't.

There are some experiences you can't understand unless you've lived them. He sees the sorrow on Kevin's face and wonders if it's been there the whole time beneath his outward enthusiasm; if Ed's really been wrapped up with his own grief for so long that he's never thought to see behind the mask.

Ed taps his fingers against the desk, caught in a moment of indecision; on one hand he could mind his own business, on the other, he could offer to listen. Decided, he takes a deep breath, and broaches the topic. "What was Searching like? Tell me, I want to understand."

Kevin shakes his head, like he doesn't believe him, and why would he? He's never been receptive before.

"I'm serious, Kev," he says, inching forward in his chair. "Tell me what it's like."

Kevin exhales, still eying Ed suspiciously, but must find something earnest in his expression because he soon visibly backs down and asks, "Have you ever had that feeling that someone is the *one*? Like a celebrity crush, or, like, someone you see every day but you never get to Recognise?"

Ed shakes his head. He's never been much of a romantic.

"Okay, well, that's what all the romance novels make it out to be right? And it's what most new Searchers think too. That it's going to be that easy. That you can, I don't know, sense your soulmate or some shit; that it'll be like a fairy-tale. So anyways I'm doing this admin job in New York, really boring stuff, but it's my first Distance

Search, I'm eighteen, and I'm full of these stupid romantic notions that I'm just gonna, I don't know, *stumble* across my soulmate like they do in the movies. I get coffee from the same place every day and I make sure to brush fingertips when I'm getting my coffee, you know, as you do, and after a month or so I think I've touched everyone there for Recognition except..." he sighs. "Except for this one girl. There's this chef out back, I can always just see her through the open kitchen door, making pastries or whatever it is that she does, and she's the most beautiful girl I've ever seen in my life," Kevin smiles shyly at the memory. "I got butterflies every time I saw her. She started waving hello to me in the morning. I picked up her name from the other staff, you know, because they'd talk, and I knew all sorts of little details about her, but I never had an excuse to Recognise her. It went on for months and months... and I built up this whole story in my head of how it was *our story*; us, dancing around each other, until finally we would touch and –" Kevin closes his eyes with a wide smile.

"You thought this girl was your soulmate?"

"I was *convinced* of it. And so one day I walk in, maybe a few minutes earlier than usual, I don't know, but for whatever reason she's behind the counter and I jump at the chance. She's already leaving for the back but I call her name and she turns around, surprised, and I flounder because there's this whole... space between us and I have no idea how to bridge it, or how to make this seem cool or casual, so I panic, and I just tell her something like, 'Hi, I'm a Searcher, I have this feeling about you, please can I –?'"

Kevin cringes at the recollection and Ed winces in sympathy. "And how did that go?"

"About as well as you'd expect. She accepted. We touched. And there was... nothing. And I felt like the biggest loser on the planet. I never returned to the café again. And I definitely never thought about Searching like that again."

"I'm sorry," Ed says, unsure of what else to say.

Kevin shrugs. "I can't imagine what would've happened if that was it, honestly. Wouldn't have met Penny, that's for sure." The name of his fiancée seems to remind him of the purpose of his story and he says, "But that's the problem. Everyone thinks Searching is easy but it's not. It was crushing that first time. I was so disappointed, I cried for days. I felt like I'd been sold this lie, you know? I thought about quitting, about going back home, but then I went to my Circle meeting and this older guy, Martez, also a Dedicated Distancer, tells me about his first disappointment. It's something all serious Searchers go through, that moment when you realise what you've been sold is the dream, and the reality is… harder. Much harder. Searching is going out, over and over again, and coming home empty handed. It's meeting all these amazing people, finding all these amazing opportunities, and always having to walk away at the end of it. It takes guts, man, more than anyone ever realises."

Ed solemnly nods. It takes courage to meet people, but even more, he imagines, to walk away.

"People called me naïve for being a Searcher," Kevin says, and Ed swallows the guilt knowing he was among them, "but I was anything but in the end. I chose to do it because I thought it was the right thing to do. Because I knew there was something perfect out there and I wanted to strive for it. That's not *cowardly*." From his inflection, Ed assumes this was one of the names Penny must have called him last night. "It's honest."

Kevin clears his throat and continues, "That was my whole life and I left it all behind for Penny because for the first time something felt more right than Searching and now she just… dismisses it, like it doesn't even matter."

"I'm sure that's not true, Kev, she loves you."

Kevin snorts. "Love is *messy*. What's that old poem? Bonding is lightning; *divine, a spectacle,* but love is fire…"

"…*can burn you, consume you, leave you,*" Ed mutters along with Kevin, and then clears his throat, embarrassed. Poetry is Searcher fodder; he didn't even realise he knew the words. It's not entirely wrong though; love is common and unpredictable, Bonding is rare but certain.

"Yeah," Kevin says, slowly and deliberately, as if he read some meaning into the words. "I'm going to fix this." He stands, palm purposefully clasping Ed's shoulder this time as he says a very sincere thank you. Ed thinks it might be the first time in a long time that anyone's truly meant it.

When Ed finally reaches the end of Monday morning's memos it is nearly five o'clock and something has become very apparent: the new legislation is a nightmare. It has ramifications that Ed hadn't even considered, such as how on earth the government would go about funding such an endeavour. He had assumed that the money would come straight from the taxpayers; it was a glorified loan, after all, built on a similar model to that for students; a little boost to give disadvantaged Pairs a foot up the ladder, to be repaid once their Bond had solidified and they'd acquired a stable income. He hadn't considered the possibility that the Pair Bonding Service would be footing the bill itself but it looks very much like that is the case. PBS has the same budget but with an entire new *department* to support, yet alone the loans themselves. He now understands why Kevin was assigned to the taskforce purely for admin and why every one of his colleagues seem to be treading carefully as if the very floors are made of glass. Every department budget has been halved with immediate effect. Testing is relatively safe as a Certificate is a legal requirement for new Pairs but outreach programmes such as Outlie Affairs and Family Relations and other 'non-essential' services are likely to be dissolved entirely. People are going to lose their jobs.

Ed realises his hands are shaking over the keyboard. He has a routine. Civil service is meant to be a stable job and PBS has never changed this dramatically, not once in the decade that he has sat behind this desk. He has a *routine*. He swallows on a dry throat, clenches his hand purposefully, once, twice, until he forces the shaking to stop.

Why does everything have to change at once? A date, a wedding, his job. It's too much. He's not ready.

Ed gets an unexpected visitor on Tuesday in the form of Rebecca Brighton. It's just gone midday and he's leaving the Testing chambers with the Pair's file under his arm when he sees her sitting on the bench outside. The sight of her, sat curled into her oversized jumper, pale and ragged, in the pristine hallway of Testing is so surreal, so out of place, that it makes him pause and re-evaluate whether or not the entire day has been an incredibly lucid dream.

She startles when she sees him, jumping from the bench, clutching her handbag to her chest like a physical barrier. "Edwin," she greets, sounding surprised, which is laughable given that she's the one that sought him out.

"Rebecca," he says, puzzled. "What are you doing here?"

"I had…" she trails off, seemingly to think of a better tact, "Chris told me where you were. I'll explain. I want to explain."

It's not an apology for what happened, Ed notes, but Kevin's sarcastic – *a full week later, well done* – comes back to him nonetheless.

Ed sighs, annoyed at the lack of resolve he seems to have around the Brightons. He'd never expected to see her again and he wonders, if she's here, if that means he's been on her mind as much as she's been on his.

"Okay," he says, waving his hand. "Lead the way."

They go to a café a few doors down; one of the independent coffee shops that claim to be 'authentic' but also have faux-leather seats and very uniform looking pastries. It is, however, the nearest.

Rebecca hardly seems comfortable *en route* but considering she looks uncomfortable everywhere except her own front porch, he doesn't concern himself too much with the fact. He can't help but notice that she practically darts out of the way every time someone gets even remotely near, which in central London, is quite the feat.

He finds himself unconsciously protecting her, putting himself between her and the rest of the world when he can, accepting the passing touches for Recognition on her behalf.

They take a corner table and he's unsurprised when Rebecca chooses the seat with her back to the wall, looking out warily at the rest of the clientele, her milky tea cradled in her hands.

Ed sips his bitter coffee and shifts in his seat, feeling the wicker creak beneath him.

When she talks, she talks to the tea. "I know Chris because he runs the Outlie support group here."

He realises belatedly that she was answering the first question he had asked of her on their date. It feels like a lifetime ago.

She glances up, meets his eyes for a fraction of a second. "I go. Every Tuesday. At PBS. I have a personal counsellor too, Naomi, I don't know if you know her... "

Ed shakes his head.

"No," she says, thoughtfully, "I suppose you wouldn't, she's not technically an employee like Chris is, she's freelance or something. But she's nice. I don't know what I'd do without her. It's been almost ten years since but..."

"You're an Outlier," Ed concludes.

"Yes. I mean... no, not entirely. My husband was a Lifetimer."

Past tense. Ed nods. Lizzie's father, presumably. Dead? Or as good as? He drinks his coffee and pretends that he doesn't have a thousand questions he wants to ask. It's his job to interrogate subjects and it goes against his every instinct to sit there, being shown tiny glimpses of her secrets, and not to *push*.

"I lived at the Outlie with him for a few years then we moved to Mainstream before Lizzie was born to give her..." she laughs bitterly, and Ed wonders what joke he's missing out on before she continues, "We moved to give her more choices, more opportunities, but now I am so afraid of giving them to her that..." she looks down at her hands, something like shame darkening her features. "I wonder, sometimes, if we may as well have stayed."

Ed doesn't know what to say, and Rebecca seems lost in her thoughts, so he says the only thing that comes to mind. "I don't think it was a mistake."

Her eyes snap up to his, more curious than anything else, and he realises that he has no authority of which to make this statement; he doesn't know what happened in the past or what trials she goes through every day. Despite their trying interactions and the glimpses of their life that he has seen, the truth is that he barely knows her at all.

"I'm sorry," he says, his cheeks warming with embarrassment. "I don't mean to presume... or to say... I just –" he breaks off and sees a gaggle of school children pass the window, presumably having snuck out during lunch break, and he suddenly knows why he said what he said with such conviction. "Lizzie strikes me as a very curious child. I can't imagine her being raised behind a wall," he tilts his head to the side, and re-evaluates, remembering how they'd met, "Can't imagine she'd stay put, quite frankly."

A wistful smile briefly crosses Rebecca's face but it's gone before it can take hold. "Just like her father," she says.

Rebecca seems lost in her memories again. Ed lets her remain there for a few moments as he takes another sip and contemplates his next move. He could veer away from this difficult discussion, ask after Chris or the meeting, or if he really wanted to play it safe, make chit-chat about the décor of the café, but this is the closest he's ever come to seeing behind the curtain, to actually getting to know this woman, and it's more tempting than it has any right to be.

He puts down the coffee cup, decided. "What happened to her father?"

Rebecca swallows in discomfort, fingers clasped around the teacup tight enough to shatter, and for a minute Ed thinks he's made a terrible mistake.

"You don't have to tell me," Ed says. "I don't have to –"

Her eyes meet his. He wonders if she's remembering the argument outside her house too.

You don't understand. You can't.

You're right, I can't. And I suppose, I don't have to.

They're at a precipice; could fall either way. Walk away after this brief apology, never to cross paths again, or step into the unknown together.

She takes a shaky first sip of her tea, the moment stretching, time slowing, more than Ed thought was possible. Her index finger circles the rim of the cup and a front tooth emerges to bite at her lower lip.

He's about to apologise again, to change the topic of conversation, when she finally looks across at him with determination.

"He Witnessed," she says. "Barely three years into Mainstream adaptation. I wasn't there. I was working. Lizzie was at nursery, thank God, and I came home to find him…"

She doesn't need to finish the sentence for him to know how that story ends. A Lifetimer Witnessing. There's only one way that story ends. No wonder she wears the black band, no wonder she's so wary of others, no wonder she lost her temper when she'd found out Ed had been talking to her daughter about Bonding of all things. He cringes at the memory; a Bond had killed Rebecca's husband, of course she was terrified of the same thing happening to her daughter.

"That's why you're so afraid for Lizzie," he surmises.

She nods meekly. "She was raised entirely in Mainstream. I know everyone says she ought to be fine if she Witnessed – the counsellors and the group and the experts – but I… I have a feeling that it's going to take her from me. Somehow, someday. She's going to leave me and I can't…"

She chokes on a sob, the sleeve of her jumper coming up to hide her face and wipe her tears away. Ed's reaching over before he can think better of it, placing his hand over hers on the teacup.

Her eyes widen as she looks across at him.

The black band. He'd forgotten. Within seconds, he'd forgotten. Their first touch, even, they could have Bonded. *Fuck.* "Sorry, I –" he moves to retreat but her other hand falls from her face to lay over his on the table, cementing the touch between them.

Her guardedness falls. She looks so grateful. Tears slip from her eyes without any resistance. He wonders how long it's been since anyone but her daughter has held her hand. "Thank you," she whispers.

Ed holds her gaze and nods sincerely. "Any time."

They talk for longer than either of them are used to, time slipping well past Ed's allocated lunch break. He finds out about Rebecca's job as a home carer, the Prayer House they attend at the weekend, and then, onto Lizzie's school.

"There used to be a Biblic secondary school as well that catered to Outlie descendants," Rebecca explains during another cup of tea. "Lizzie went for her first year, it was an hour away but it had a mini-bus service to eliminate public transport which was great. It was still relatively small and had Biblic services in the morning, minimal touch and everything you'd expect, lots of support, but it closed last year. Didn't have the funding it needed anymore. Hundreds of Outlie kids just... having to be mainstreamed. It was in the news for a while, I don't know if you heard it?"

Ed shakes his head.

"I try to keep tabs on Lizzie's old school friends, to give her encouragement, try to make her feel less like she's facing this alone, but some of the stories I hear I can't share with her."

Ed frowns. He can't imagine but he's fairly certain he doesn't want to. "So Lizzie's now at a state school?" He asks with concern. He vaguely remembers the uniform from when he saw her in the park but can't put a name to the school. "How does that work?"

She shrugs. "They do the best they can. They put the Biblic kids in the same class so it tends to be a smaller size than the rest which is good, they're excused from assemblies and other large gatherings, and there's a Dissonance counsellor on hand, Alex – contracted by PBS, I think – but most of the staff aren't trained, and the rest of the kids... well, some of them don't understand. I got a letter the other day from the headmaster. They want to put a black band on her and the rest of the Outlie kids to make them easily identifiable, 'in case of emergency' they say... but I know my daughter. She hates anyone that tries to put her in a box. Besides, those kids get bullied enough without marking them as clear targets." She clutches at her own black band while she says this, worrying it between her fingers. He wonders if she resents hers a little too.

"But she's doing okay there so far?"

Rebecca shrugs. "She seems to be handling it but now she's seen how big the world is I think she's eager to chase after it all at once and no amount of me warning her of the dangers is going to stop her. It doesn't help that she's so smart. She's outstripping everyone in that class of hers. She knows it too. She does her homework in five minutes flat, her weekends are spent obsessively researching whatever has taken her fancy that week, and her teachers say she spends the entire school day daydreaming, bored out of her mind. I think soon we're going to have to choose whether we let her join the advanced classes with the other gifted children which would mean Mainstreaming her entirely, or if I force her to stay in the Biblic classes, safe, but never to reach her potential."

"I think I know what she'd choose," Ed says wryly.

"Me too, that's why I haven't asked her; I'm too afraid of the answer."

Ed discloses his past more naturally, and more honestly, with her than with anyone else, and it's not just to balance the playing field after her revelations but because Rebecca's patient understanding makes him want to confess to things that have been tucked away and out of sight for years. They talk for two hours until Ed has to leave for a Test that afternoon, and even then, he does so regretfully. He shrugs on his coat and they walk out into the drizzle, hovering outside the door as moisture beads on her impermeable jumper.

"Let me walk you," Ed says, even though he doesn't have time and they both know it.

She shakes her head. "I have to," she swallows, "take the bus." It looks like the very thought frightens her terribly, although she must do it every week to get to the support group.

"Right," he says. "Well, thank you for seeing me. It's been nice, I'm glad you –"

"I really am sorry," she blurts out. "For what I said that night. You were looking out for my daughter and I..." she looks down at her lace-ups, scuffing them at the ground in a way that's become oddly endearing to him. "You didn't have to help, but you did." She looks up at him, her gaze steadier than it ever has been as they both huddle together in the wet city air. "Thank you."

A foreign warmth blooms in his chest. It's so unexpected that it knocks him outside of reality for a moment. He wants to apologise in return but he can't gather the words to express the sentiment. He sees her lips move, sees her reach out to touch his arm in goodbye, and he knows his lips move in response but he couldn't say what words leave his mouth. He stands there, frozen, as she gives a shy wave and walks away down the street until she disappears into the crowd. The warmth still lingers in his chest and he wonders, with trepidation, if it could possibly mean what he remembers it meaning.

After they were married, Ed and Simon had bought a house in the countryside an hour's train journey from the city. It was a large cottage with four bedrooms and they were both looking forward to filling it with new tiny people. They'd both always wanted children and they were excited to start a family now they had the means to raise them.

One winter's day soon after Solstice on their fourth year in the house, they'd left their completed adoption pack on the kitchen table to wander the footpath that led out of the village Temple gardens. It went on for miles, over hills and fields and a great lake, and everything was covered in a thin layer of morning dew. They held hands as they walked; warmth stirring in his chest despite the cold of his fingers. Ed kept imagining what it would be like soon with a toddler swinging between them while an older child ran down to the lake to play on the hanging tyre. It was no longer a fantasy but a real tangible future.

But then, with just a touch of fingertips, it was stolen from him.

The Bond was so bright that it blinded him, so divine that it awed him, and the entire world seemed to fall into revered silence around them. As Simon's soul merged with another, it cracked Ed's heart wide open until he could feel the cold wind sweeping inside of him, numbing the love that was.

For countless days, Ed swore and cried and broke crockery in frustration but at the end of it, all he felt was the cold. His whirlwind of anger had solidified to ice. He would find himself sat on the sofa they had both bought together, staring at the empty walls and the abandoned adoption brochures and not feel a damn thing.

He's long forgotten how to feel anything but cold.

Penny stops by his office later that afternoon. "Hey, there you are," she says, letting herself in. "Where've you been all afternoon?"

"Had lunch out," Ed says, busying himself with files. "It ran late."

He actually hears Penny stopping in her tracks. He looks up when she's been quiet for an uncharacteristic amount of time.

"You?" she asks with disbelief. "Had lunch... out?"

Ed realises too late that he's opened Pandora's box instead of shutting down this conversation as he'd intended.

"Ed," she says, now openly suspicious. "Not once in five years have you *gone out for lunch*. You're the cafeteria's most ardent fan. You've sat in the same seat, every lunchtime, eating the same crappy pasta every Tuesday, probably for as long as I've known you." She stares down at him in disbelief. "What the actual fuck?"

Ed suddenly regrets spending the last few years being so unbelievably predictable. "Am I not allowed to break my routine every now and then? Maybe I felt like some fresh air."

Penny folds her arms. "It's raining."

"Even still."

Penny shakes her head with a laugh. "Unbelievable," she mutters, but then, louder, "Fine, keep your secrets."

Ed tries to keep the surprise off his face; old Penny would not have let that go.

"I just came to say 'thanks' for whatever you said to Kevin yesterday. He storms off to see you first thing in the morning and then by the time we get home he's all *zen*. All understanding, and open, and communicative, and I don't know how on earth he got that from you but… whatever, we sorted it out, and I guess we've got you to thank, so… thanks."

Ed counts this as the third genuine thank you he's received in as many days and he still doesn't know how to handle them. He thins his lips, and nods, and thinks that's the end of it until Penny settles in the chair opposite and pulls out a wedding magazine with determination.

"We need to talk colours."

Ed isn't quite sure how to progress things with Rebecca. The only friends he has are his colleagues and that was only a culmination of time and common ground, but with Rebecca he's not quite sure where to begin. She'd given him her home phone number at the café yesterday and gawked a little as he'd typed it – slow and clumsily – into his mobile phone, but the last time he had had this much trepidation over whether or not to call, it was Simon's voice at the other end of the line. He doesn't know if he can just call for a chat, or if he needs an excuse to do so, or how long he's even meant to leave before calling.

He keeps his mobile out on his desk all day and then finds when he's microwaving a pizza in his kitchen that evening that it's found its way onto the worktop too.

When his home phone rings two bites into the pizza he immediately jumps at it, heart racing, television forgotten, as he does his best to convince himself that it's only Penny or Kevin – or, godforbid, a member of his family – calling.

He picks up the receiver and clears his throat. "Ed Hart residence."

"Ed? I'm sorry to disturb you –"

He knows that voice. He falls back onto the arm of the sofa, reeling. She called *him*.

"Don't be sorry," Ed says in a rush, and then cringes at how desperate he sounds. "I mean, I wasn't doing anything." That was worse. "I mean to say that I was eating... not that you were disturbing..." he clears his throat again and decides to abandon this disastrous thread entirely. "How are you?"

He has a feeling that she's smiling, although he can't prove this theory. "I'm good, and thank you again for today. I just... might have a favour to ask."

Ed closes his eyes and wills himself to calm down. "A favour?" he asks, in an attempt at nonchalance.

"I know it's probably too much, and you can decline of course, I haven't even told Lizzie I was going to ask so you're under absolutely no obligation."

"Okay..." Ed says, his curiosity piqued at the mention of her daughter. "What can I do for you?"

Rebecca sighs. "Your conversation with her last week apparently sparked a new obsession about Searching? Bonding? All that. I think she knew I'd disapprove because she didn't tell me," she says sadly. "But I was tidying her room after we had coffee and I found a dozen library books and a notebook full of ideas. I think she's working on a little project and I figure if anyone knows about Bonds, it's you."

Ed nods, though she can't see it. "You're supporting this then?"

He hears her deliberation shortly followed an unrelated muffled conversation in the background, something about school. He smiles at the domesticity of it, and with a sudden intensity, misses the children he never had with Simon; a burning ache for a path not taken.

"Sorry about that," Rebecca says, bringing him out of his

thoughts. "Lizzie had a question. But where was I? Supporting it. Right. Yes, I am. Matthew and I came to Mainstream so that she could have this choice, so she could do this exploring, and I think you're right in saying there's no use in hiding her away, so from now on, I am... supportive," she sounds terrified as she says it but there's a determination to the words too.

"Even if she decides to be a Searcher?"

"Even then."

Ed smiles. "Lizzie's lucky to have you."

There's a moment of silence in which Ed likes to imagine Rebecca is smiling again.

"So, what do you say?" Rebecca asks. "Can you come round after work tomorrow? Help her with this project of hers?"

"I'd love to."

If it's possible, the Brighton's house seems even smaller from the inside; the one thing that the two-bed bungalow has going for it is that it looks lived in unlike Ed's over-sized, over-empty townhouse. Every inch of the living room is covered in clutter. Rebecca walks through it confidently, as if she doesn't see how just how narrow the path she walks is, while Ed is busy trying not to knock magazines from shelves with elbows and stepping on unfinished knitting with his shoes. It seems busy, lived in, like a home should be; there's muffled music playing from across the room and the faint smell of candles and laundry detergent.

"Do you want tea or anything?" Rebecca asks. "Oh, watch the –"

Ed rights himself just as he was about to walk into a clothes horse.

"Sorry it's such a mess. Lizzie's just through –" she points across the living room to one of the two closed doors on the other side, presumably the bedrooms, as the kitchen and bathroom are to his immediate left. "Good thing she's playing that music of hers so loudly," she says, as they cross the living room, "Otherwise she would have tackled you by now. Are you sure you don't want a cup of tea? I really am thankful you're here, you know. And you must stay for dinner, it's the least I can do."

Before Ed can respond, Rebecca has knocked on the door and pushed it open. If Ed thought the rest of the house was chaotic it's got nothing on Lizzie's bedroom; he doubts there's a single space unoccupied by a book or a poster or a cassette tape in the entire room; even her narrow bed has been co-opted as a desk. There's a tape player blasting out an old Pink Floyd record but it can barely be seen through the clutter atop the chest of drawers. Lizzie sits cross-legged on the floor, back against the edge of the bed, literally surrounded by splayed textbooks. He has to remind himself that she is *twelve* and not twenty, the age he was when he'd found himself in similar positions but with beer cans propped between books instead of stacks of Lego.

She immediately lights up when she sees him, nearly tripping over a glass of squash in her haste to stand up. "Ed!"

"Careful!" Rebecca admonishes but her voice is tired enough to imply that it is a regular hazard in this house.

Ed raises his hand in approximation of a wave. "Hey, Lizzie, how's it going?"

"Mum said you were coming by! Come on, I want to show what I'm working on –" she reaches out and drags Ed towards the landscape of library books. He does his best not to step on any splayed pages, though he's sure he fails as he lands, ungracefully, against the bedframe. He's pretty sure he hears a snigger that does not belong to Lizzie as he rights himself. He looks up to see Rebecca facing away from him, turning down the music, and when she turns back, her face is neutral. "Don't make too much of a mess, try not to ask him too many inappropriate questions, dinner in half an hour."

"Okay, okay," Lizzie says, but Ed doubts she even heard what her mother said as she's too busy piling books atop Ed's lap.

He picks through them as Lizzie starts monologuing about her research and Rebecca leaves them, the door left ajar so that if he tilts his head, he can see her through the living room into the kitchen.

After ten minutes of Lizzie detailing what seems like a very eclectic mix of information that she's gathered with no focus or goal in mind, he leans forward and flips through the stacks in case he's missed something. "These are all science textbooks," he observes.

"No, they're not," she says, utterly offended, and points them out, "That one's law, and that one's international politics, these two are history, and this whole stack is social sciences so that hardly counts as *actual* science. It's broad." And then she scrunches her face up at them, face filled with doubt. "Wait. Do you think it's not broad enough?" she looks genuinely concerned that the dozen textbooks she's made notes on aren't sufficient for her home project.

"Well, that all depends on what you want to learn," he says diplomatically. "I recognise most of these from my university days actually, but... have you thought that there might be another way to find out about Searching other than reading about –" he picks up the nearest open textbook and reads the chapter heading, "*Post-War Bonding Documentation in the West –*" he can't help but pull a face. "Okay, see, I do that for a living and I still think that's incredibly dull. What do you actually want to know?"

Lizzie shrugs. "Everything."

"Everything," Ed says, mulling it over.

"Yeah. The mythology and history of Bonds, how Bonding *actually* works – like the neural pathways and stuff – what happens to Bonds over time, the things that people do *because* of Bonds – everything from Searching to religion to Outlies to legislation – what it actually feels like. Everything."

"Okay, that's... broad," he agrees. "I can tell you a little about all of those. Uh, the Greek myth you likely already know –"

Lizzie nods her head enthusiastically. "Four arms, four legs, two faces."

"Right. So the history... you know about the big ones? Searchers like Elizabeth I? Souls like Patroclus and Achilles, Ferdinand and Isabella...?"

Lizzie waves him off before he can get any further. Of course.

These were likely covered in the school curriculum. "I'm curious though," Lizzie says, and Ed finds himself just as intrigued by her questioning. "There seems to be some debate about the first documented Pair."

"Ah, yes, that's because it depends how you define 'documented,'" Ed explains. "The mythology of twinned Souls are embedded into nearly every culture on Earth. It's in oral stories of tribes and written in records during the expansion of the Roman Empire. It's referenced in the Upanishads and the Bible and the Scrolls that the Temples preach. It can be heard in ancient music and song. It's evidenced by dual-mummified bodies in Ancient Egypt and the use of light in Renaissance paintings. Some even say the divine act of Bonding is depicted on cave walls. So the debate really is: when does legend become history? How can we verify ancient stories through our modern lens?"

Lizzie seems to ponder this, and then asks, "When do *you* believe it started?"

Ed sighs. He hasn't had to give thought to this question since he was in education himself but he's interested to note that his answer hasn't changed one whit in all this time. "I believe that it stretches back as far as humanity does," he says. "Far beyond Ancient Greece as the Temples would have us believe. I believe that we've always had the ability to Bond."

Lizzie frowns. "Do you believe in evolution?"

"Yes, of course –"

"Then how can you believe that? Apes don't have the ability. No other animal has the ability –"

"It's exactly *because* of evolution that I believe it. Our brain structure changed somewhere along the line and formed the emomery. It's arguably the thing that makes humans *human* and certainly the thing that makes Bonding feasible."

"How long ago was that?"

Ed racks his mind, attempting to recall the numerous conversations he had had with Simon on the matter. This was where

their scientific fields collided so he ought to be able to remember...
"Approximately one and a half million years ago," he states, having
stumbled across the right memory. "Speaking of the emomery, how
familiar are you with Dr Vest's work on artificial stimulation?"

She digs around for a paper. It's the transcript of his interview
with Oxford University. A good one, from what he remembers. Also,
fairly advanced.

"You understood this?" he asks, intrigued, as this was at least
university level neuroscience.

Lizzie looks shy enough for him to wager it was above her
understanding even before she bashfully admits as much.

"Right," he says, and scans the document to remind himself of
the main arguments. Comparative brain scans between pre-Bonded
and post-Bonded individuals showed new activity in the emomery –
the centre of the brain between the temporal and parietal lobes – thus
confirming it as the location where the Bond forms and remains
active. The question is: if we find a way to artificially stimulate the
emomery instead of relying on Instant Touch Recognition what
would happen?

"It says here that Dr Vest works at PBS," Lizzie states while he
reads. "Is that true? Do you know him?"

"Yeah," Ed says distractedly. "Idris – Dr Vest – is Jasmine's
partner," and then realises that won't mean a thing to the girl and
clarifies, "he's Head of Science."

"Is he still working on...?"

"Artificial stimulation? Yes."

"What do you think will happen if he succeeds?"

Ed reads over Idris's words and they echo his own sentiments –

*I haven't met a Bonding scientist who doesn't have a theory about
what would happen if we stimulated the emomery without ITR,
because although we know that Bonding is triggered by touch we
still don't know why that is. For decades we've analysed skin cells,
hair follicles, everything we could think of, to see if they're capable*

of interpreting DNA or anything else telling, and we've still come up empty handed. We have no proven explanation for why touch triggers the emomery and forms a Bond with a particular individual, only thousands of theories, so what would happen if it's triggered without touch? How would the emomery know who to Bond with? The optimistic answer, of course, is that it finds your Pair – a shortcut, of sorts. But there are some in my field that think nothing would happen. That if we found another method other than touch, it would not work – or worse, think it a failure and commit Soul Break having tried to Bond and failed.

Idris is right to say that everyone has a theory. Ed probably has the most cynical view out of his colleagues though. "I think it is folly to try," he says. "I've witnessed ITR. It's… well, I see why people call it divine. I don't think we'll ever succeed in creating a Bond otherwise."

"What did it look like?" Lizzie asks with wide eyes.

Her curiosity seemingly knows no bounds. He closes his eyes and sees the field lay before him. The light. *Blinding.* How do you describe something so moving yet so intangible? Science could never accurately describe the sensation. Poetry, though. *"Breathing life; like starlight on a desolate planet."*

"Huh?"

He got lost, and lost Lizzie in the process.

He shakes his head and asks, "You've been going to textbooks for all this information?"

Lizzie nods. "What else is there?"

"Music, art, poetry."

"Poetry?" Lizzie sneers. "That's posh stuff, Elite stuff –" and then she breaks off with a look of wonder and realisation. *"Searcher* stuff."

"Well, not exclusively but –"

Lizzie is already scrambling over the book piles for, unbelievably, more books. This one is extracted from underneath her bed; a tatty poetry anthology, Biblic in origin from the looks of it and thus unlikely to actually give her the information she's looking for, but curiously it's one of the few he's seen that actually looks to be her own rather than borrowed from a library.

"If you want to know what a Bond feels like," Ed continues as Lizzie scans the index with eagerness, "then poetry is probably the closest you'll get. I had an entire module on it even as a Bonding Science student. I might be able to dig around at home, see if I've still got any of the books –"

Lizzie's eyes light up. "Seriously?"

"Seriously," he nods. "As long as it's okay with your mum."

Lizzie grins like he's just handed her the entire universe.

"So, what I don't get –" Lizzie asks before slurping up a mouthful of spaghetti, still chewing it as she continues, "is why some places give soulmates special treatment and others don't."

"Lizzie," Rebecca scolds with familiar exhaustion, "you shouldn't talk with your mouth full."

Lizzie swallows, and then looks at Ed across the table, continuing as if the interruption never happened. "Why is that?"

Ed shrugs and twists some pasta around his fork. "Dependent on culture, mostly. History. In some cultures, Bonds are seen as almost godlike and Pairs are literally worshipped. Even some Hellenic factions believe that Souls are literally picked by the gods, that's why the Elite, as we call them, have such standing here because their lifestyles are more or less funded by the Temples. Pairs aren't officially given any special treatment in the UK, not by the state, but by the people, the religion, the media… it's a different matter."

"They are now though," Lizzie says. "The new loan system for Pairs… isn't that like special treatment?"

Ed hums thoughtfully; he hadn't considered it that way. "Well, no, not really. It would be, I suppose, if we were *giving* them money rather than loaning it, and to all Pairs rather than just the ones in need. It's just a system to give those at the bottom of the ladder a step up, no different from other benefit schemes designed to help the working classes."

"But it *is* different," Rebecca says suddenly, turning her attention towards Ed. "Because it's only available to a select few. They say they're helping the working classes but in reality they're only helping a tiny, decimal, percentage of already privileged people."

Ed shook his head. "Not all Pairs are privileged. People used to slip through the cracks. Pairs from working class backgrounds, or international Pairs, or non-Hellenic Pairs; those who didn't get the support they needed from the Temples because they're not seen as being as desirable, godlike, pure."

"I understand that and it's awful that the Elite can be so unwelcoming but the state is getting more and more involved with Bonded affairs and I'm worried that they're neglecting other –"

"For a good reason," Ed interjects. "Pairs need our support."

Rebecca scoffs and looks at him with barely concealed anger. "They shouldn't be a *priority*. There's always going to be people that fall through the cracks in the system. But instead of addressing the underlying problem of discrimination by the Elite – or, hell, even the fact that they're afforded such privileges in the first place – Parliament's just putting a plaster over the easiest wound to treat. Loans aren't going to fix a damn thing and you know it."

Ed can feel Lizzie cautiously looking between them as they challenge each other across the table. He forces himself to break the stare and pick up his fork again, scraping bolognaise around the edges of the bowl. "Simon left for Australia," he confesses. "When he Bonded. He was from a large working class family and his soulmate was international; an Iranian woman, here on a work visa. They welcome any Pairs in Australia, you know that? They have much more advanced Soul rights there than we do. They recognise how good soulmates are for the Arts, for the Temples, for the economy... so, I conducted their Test, I gave them their soulmate certificate, and the very next day they flew to the other side of the world. The man I'd seen every day of my life for near ten years, just gone like that." He shakes his head, trying to dislodge the grief that has taken residence. "Simon's mother used to despise me but now we write to each other every year at Solstice as if we can delude ourselves into thinking that he's just... on holiday or something. I don't know. I doubt he writes to her at all."

He's staring into his pasta bowl, the edges of it blurring with unshed tears. He blinks them away and feels a flush of embarrassment on his cheeks.

It's Lizzie that speaks first, leaning across the table towards him. "You think he would have stayed in the country if he could have." It's not a question; Lizzie's too smart for that.

Ed nods. "Simon loved his brothers, and the city, and the snow. If he didn't stay for me or his mother... his brothers should have been enough to sway the Bond. But," Ed swallows. "He left anyway, because he felt like he had no other choice."

He feels Rebecca curl her hand against his and he clings to the warmth that it brings. "I understand that," she says. "I'm not saying people like Simon shouldn't be supported when they're going through a Bond, of course they should be, but I can't help but worry that it's the beginning of a slippery slope; that by allocating more resources to Pairs, more people are going to be forgotten, neglected, than Pairs ever were. They're such a small number but the people that they affect – like me, like yourself – are so much greater, and I worry that they will be forgotten."

He looks across at her, squeezes her hand, and thinks of Lizzie and the necessary support that she has already lost. "I understand that too."

The tightness in his chest eases as he exhales, breathing easy for the first time since he uttered Simon's name, with her warm hand encased in his and the mutual understanding firm and steady between them.

Sudden, random, unexpected, inexplicable; the awe of the Bonding was as indescribable as the insurmountable pain afterwards. Years of life shared together, abandoned in a split second.

Ed watched until he couldn't anymore. He clenched his fist in anger and walked straight into the nearest pub and drank until he couldn't stand straight, yet alone think straight. He probably wept. He doesn't remember. He just knows he lost three hours sometime between Witnessing and coming home, his heart in tatters and his mind scrambled, to find them both packing things in boxes.

"Goddammit, just talk to me would you?" he shouted after Simon. "After all we've been through, this is it? You're just going to leave? Don't you care about *anything*? This is our house. Our life. Fine! You don't care about me," he said, his voice cracking on nearly every word, "but don't you care about your family? Your job? You have a life here, Simon. With me."

Simon finally looked at him but Ed could tell from his eyes that it was no longer just his husband staring back. It was a new being; one he only knew half of. Simon was glowing outwardly with the fullness of the Bond but when Ed looked into his eyes he saw nothing at all. He knew, academically, it was only because the Bond was so new. Simon was well within the recesses of his mind, getting to know his Pair in the most direct way he could, but it didn't matter how deep in his mind he was, it was still further than Ed could go.

"I'm sorry for your pain," Simon said eventually.

And that was it. He wasn't sorry for leaving, only that the action caused pain.

Ed hid himself in the kitchen and drank every bottle in the house. He cried more in those initial hours than in his entire lifetime. He broke every belonging Simon left behind in frustration. He *hated* him for what he had done.

When Monday morning rolled round, Ed brushed the smell of alcohol from his breath and let the coldness settle within him. After two days of insurmountable pain he could feel it no longer; it had become a constant ache behind his ribs; a coldness wrapped around his heart where Simon used to be.

He drove to work and was handed a dozen casefiles with a

pitying frown. Of course they all knew. Simon's last name was his last name and he was due to be Tested that day. A colleague offered to take it but there was part of Ed that just had to see it for himself and hold the quantifiable proof in his hands; a piece of paper that would in one fell swoop divorce him and announce Simon's Bond to another.

Ed had stood behind the glass window of the Testing chamber, pressing buttons as he always did, and if a part of Simon realised it was his voice over the intercom, he didn't show it. Simon was completely in his own world, or rather, a shared world; one that no longer included him.

The first week back at work was the hardest. Every day he would come crawling home to the house that he had bought with Simon and drink until he could fall asleep. He would snap at anyone who dared speak to him at work until even the interns knew to avoid him.

That weekend he rose with a hangover and reached blindly for the bottle beside him. He didn't know what it tasted of but he felt the burn at the back of his throat and it was so welcome. There wasn't much that cut through the coldness that had taken hold.

The doorbell felt like a siren in his head. He groaned and cursed all the gods he could name but the visitor was insistent and after the third ring he thought it was less painful to get out of bed and tell the person to go away than be subjected to the persistent noise.

"What?!" he snapped when he opened the door.

"Er..." the woman said, looking down at Ed with a raised eyebrow.

He followed her gaze: skewwhiff dressing gown, boxers, stained t-shirt. He probably smelled strongly of alcohol. He couldn't remember the last time he shaved. Distantly he knew that this equated to a mess but he didn't much care. "What do you want?" he asked, leaning against the doorframe as he doubted his ability to stand for a moment longer.

"I'm Penny. Penny Morgan. From Stats?"

Ed rubbed his eyes and looked at the woman on his doorstep

again. He did know her. Through the blurry memories of this week, he remembered that she was one of the people who tried talking to him at work. About moving house. But it was the weekend. Why was she here?

"My mother lives out this way," she continued. "Nice houses. Anyway, since I was passing I thought I'd do my duty and check that you're still alive."

Ed furrowed his brow.

"Have you eaten?" she asked.

"I just woke up."

"Right," she said. "You realise it's nearly 6'o'clock. In the evening."

Ed ran his fingers through his stubble.

She sighed. "Fine," she said, and then pushed past him into the house. "You're lucky my mother always gives me leftovers."

She made him eat and gave him a drink other than alcohol, and after a while, Ed could see a little clearer. She sat down at the opposite end of the dining room table that now seemed far too long in a house that seemed far too big.

"I was serious about what I said in the canteen, you know. We're really going to have to find you a new place," she said, wrinkling her nose in disgust. "And get you out of the countryside. Urgh. I don't know how you stand it here."

"Me neither," Ed muttered towards his empty plate. Was this one actually his? Or had they bought that set of crockery together? He couldn't remember.

"You realise you've got Spousal Depression, right? It's like Witness Depression but with the added bonus of getting dumped."

Ed looked up and over to the woman examining her painted nails at the other end of the table.

"Yes…" Ed said slowly. "That makes sense."

"PBS should have offered you counselling."

"They did," he said. He remembered one of the faces on Monday had been from the Family Relations department. "But I refused."

"That was stupid."

"Probably," Ed conceded.

Penny smiled at that. She seemed to have a strange sense of humour. "Alright then, you'll have to make do with the one psychology module I took in first year. Firstly, get yourself out of this nightmare of a living situation. Secondly, deal with your feelings. Thirdly, sit down and decide what you want to do next."

"That's it?" he asked.

"Yeah, that's it."

It's been five years but he wonders if he may finally be on the final part of Penny's three-point plan: trying to work out what he wants. Ed has fallen into an undefined pattern with Rebecca; one of coffee dates and home dinners and evening phone calls, and he begins to wonder if there not ought to be a name to this relationship – a label to ensure understanding – but he can't possibly think of what that might be.

It starts gnawing at his mind, becoming as insistent and intrusive as his memories of Simon; questions of what he *wants* almost as unwelcome, as terrifying, as the reoccurring night terrors that still plague his unconscious mind.

It's the weekend and Rebecca has invited Ed around for lunch after the weekly service at the Prayer House. Such invitations always imply her place, not his, and he thinks it has more to do with the fact his house is not a home rather than the fact that she doesn't want to leave the safety of hers. The house he'd bought in the city after Simon left is transient; a place of mourning; as grey and empty as his mind has been for the last few years. It may as well be a tomb for all its coldness. So, he goes for lunch at Rebecca's and when Lizzie becomes buried under the stacks of poetry he'd given her, Rebecca suggests that they leave her to it and go for a walk.

Athena Gardens feels different with someone by his side. He doubts that he has walked these paths with anything but a heavy heart for the last few years and the company is pleasant. The trees are becoming bare, the fallen leaves decomposing with the rain that has become all too frequent, and the breeze is cold enough for one of Rebecca's hand-knitted hats to be protecting his ears.

Conversation can sometimes stall without Lizzie as a buffer but the silence isn't as uncomfortable as it used to be. They still haven't put a name to what they mean to each other but if Rebecca's gloved hand sometimes slips into his when they're walking then he doesn't pull away. Her black band sometimes hides between the long sleeves of her coat and her thick gloves but when strangers approach he finds himself standing between them; protecting her from Recognition as if it was instinctual for him to do so.

They talk about work, about school, and when they've walked far enough from home for it to feel private, about their lost husbands.

"I remember our first visit to this Garden," Rebecca says. "Matthew saw it out the car window when we first arrived but it took a year, maybe more, for us to come this far away from home. We went early morning. Lizzie woke us up with her crying and the sun was just rising. It was summer. I remember because it was so early – can't have been long past five o'clock – and I cradled Lizzie in my arms and took Matthew's hand and we finally ventured all this way. It was Lizzie's first visit too, come to think of it."

"What did he make of it?"

Rebecca smiles sadly. "He used to be the gardener at Petersville, used to know the fields too, so I don't think the park was as interesting to him as all the features." She runs her fingertips over the stone granite of a statue as they pass it. They had wandered into a Prayer Garden – Apollo's Shrine – he reads on the plaque; a small sheltered space for prayer. "He found it all very extravagant, I think, fascinating but... full of riches that I don't think he thought quite justified the cause. Then, I showed him the Temple," she laughs, and looks up through the trees where they can see the pediment of Athena Temple, the whole thing decked out in its royal colours presumably for an upcoming celebration.

"Simon wasn't one for it either," Ed muses. "Thought it was all a bit much. He was Hellenic though, beneath it all. His family were ex-Searchers – Waiters, I suppose we call them now, Settled in theory but still hoping for completion – and so they were raised to believe in Bonding as a divine act. We had our wedding in a Temple, not as grand as this one, of course, just the one in our village, not five minutes from our old house. It was beautiful, surrounded by fields, you could hear the birds sing..." he trails off, so lost in the memory that he can almost feel the sun on his skin as he had that day.

"Are your friends Kevin and...?"

"Penny," Ed fills in.

"Penny," she amends. "Are they planning to have their wedding in a Temple? I know you said he was a Searcher, so I presume Hellenic, but I don't know if you've said about her?"

Ed furrows his brow in thought as they circle out of the Prayer Garden and turn into the formal gardens instead; rows upon rows of bare stems coming from the ground. "Actually, Kevin's agnostic from what I know. As for Penny, I don't think she believes in anything but, then again, she plays her cards pretty close to her chest so it's anyone's guess. In any case, they booked Hermes Temple on Lavelle Street. It's nice. I went to see it with them and Jasmine last week. Good sized hall."

She smiles and it looks almost teasing, as if she wants to comment on the fact that what makes a good wedding in Ed's mind is a 'good sized hall'. He's practically minded and doesn't see the problem with that but he takes her unspoken jab at his personality anyway with a self-depreciating shake of the head.

He looks across at her, wondering if he's meant to invite her. They've been friends for a month or so now but there's always been an undercurrent beneath that – one of interest or curiosity or possibility – and even while they hover in this strange sort of undefined space, he wonders if he's meant to be thinking as far ahead as spending Winter Solstice with her or as far as Penny and

Kevin's wedding in the Spring. It's daunting. He doesn't know quite how to go about this task of rearranging his future that in the last five years had become nothing but blank space.

"It's strange, isn't it?" Ed muses. "I never thought I'd have to think about such things again."

"Weddings?"

Ed gives a one-armed shrug and looks at the path before them. "Any of it. I'm not quite sure how to go about it to be honest."

She's quiet for long enough that he begins to think she did not pick up on his wider meaning, on his unspoken apology for not being able to process whatever it is that stirs between them, but then he looks across and sees her brow furrowed in thought and remembers that it sometimes takes her a while to find the words. He lets her take the time, listening to their synchronised footsteps down the aisles of the formal garden. Rose stems with nothing but thorns.

"I think it changes things when you've lost someone like we have," she says finally. "You can't help but worry that those you care about are making the same mistake. Your grief taints everything good in this world. Sometimes it's hard to see past it."

Ed smiles sadly. She's a woman of few words at times but when she does speak it's with wisdom that Ed knows better than to envy. This could be the end of the conversation if he let it but there's also an unspoken question between the lines; one that's asking him to talk about his own grief. He never speaks of the depression that has accompanied him for years; he doubts the word has even been spoken since that day Penny accosted him in the dining room of his old house.

Penny was always succinct; to the point, even brutally so, but Rebecca was patient and understanding, in the way that only someone who has suffered the same fate knew how to be. The Gardens were deserted around them; a steady drizzle in the air as they turned back into the open park.

A calm settles on his shoulders, decided. "Yes," he admits, as soft as the dew. "It's hard. I had..." he swallows, takes a moment to find the courage between the birdsong and the condensation on his collar. "Spousal depression. For years, I… couldn't see anything past the day's end. I still have these dreams. At night. Of the moment when he left. I live it time and time again, like I just can't escape it. It always takes me some time to adjust afterwards. I wake and I feel so disorientated. Unable to untangle my thoughts. But the sad truth is that I feel like that all the time, to a lesser extent perhaps, but I still feel just as lost. Every change, every decision I have to make, terrifies me."

Rebecca looks across and up to him with wide, sympathetic eyes. He has to look away; the sight too full of meaning for him to process.

"I understand," she says after a time, and he genuinely believes that she does. "I'm not sure if I know what I want either. I sometimes feel like I'm just stumbling around in the dark hoping to find the answer."

Ed closes his eyes; feels the sting behind his eyelids. *Yes, that's exactly what it feels like.*

"Sometimes it takes a while, I think, to know, and I don't think that's a bad thing. Like your friends. You said it took them years to see what was right in front of them."

Ed chuckles, though it's still fraught with emotion.

"They have a saying in the Outlie group – *Time is what you make it* – and I think that's true. When Lizzie was growing up, I put so much pressure on myself to keep going forward, to keep strong for her, that I know it's taking me a long time to recover but it's *my* time, I'm not on anybody else's schedule, and neither should you. It takes however long it takes."

Ed feels the sting of tears again at her patient understanding and almost unconsciously lets his hand slip into hers as his tears begin to fall with the rain.

Penny and Kevin are working on the guest list when Ed joins them for lunch, fighting over a single pen and a piece of paper that already looks highly edited.

"– okay but we can only have forty guests so why does your entire extended family have to make up half of them?" Penny is saying, pointing at a scrawl. "I mean, do you even know this Joyce?"

"Well, no, but you can't invite Chen and then not invite his wife."

Penny flicks the paper at him again. "Then why are we inviting Chen? He's… what? A second cousin to you?"

"Yeah, but he has to come because he's bringing Eric."

"And Eric is…?"

Kevin looks at her with disbelief, and perhaps also a little condensation. "My brother."

"Right," Penny says, looking as guilty as perhaps she ought to.

Ed picks at his moussaka, debating whether or not to weigh in. "Why does it have to be forty? I thought the hall was big enough for sixty or so."

Jasmine chooses that moment to appear with a coffee and offers an explanation as she joins them, "It is, except now we're eating there too, and once they've set up the tables there's only room for forty. Including us," she says, pointing at the four of them sat at the table.

"Oh," Ed says, and decides not to ask why the reception plans have changed yet again because he didn't have the entire afternoon to listen to the explanation. "So, uh," he hesitates, absently separating vegetables with the prongs of his fork, "there'd be no room for, uh, extra guests?"

He feels their gazes on him more than anything else; an intense scrutiny that's normally reserved for Lizzie and her textbooks.

He risks a glance when the silence becomes too uncomfortable. While Penny and Kevin are still exchanging a look of disbelief, Jasmine's looking straight at him. "You got yourself a date, Hart?"

Ed clenches his jaw, already regretting opening himself up for this conversation. "Not exactly. Look, it doesn't matter –" and he's about to ask them to forget it when he remembers just how *excited*

Lizzie had been over the concept of a wedding. He can't quite imagine gussing up for one now and leaving them at home. Lizzie would be devastated. "But if you have two seats spare, I'd appreciate it."

"Two?" That got Penny's attention; her eyes wide and fixed on Ed. "Her kid too?"

Jasmine raises an eyebrow in disbelief. "You hate children."

"I didn't even know she *had* a kid," Kevin says. "You've barely told us a thing about this mystery woman you're seeing."

"I don't hate children," Ed defends, "and I'm not hiding her away from you or anything, I just –"

"Then you should introduce us," Penny says brusquely. "If she's going to come, then she should meet us. Right?" she says to Kevin, who nods in agreement.

"Right," Ed says, already wincing at the idea of telling Rebecca that not only has he invited her and her daughter to a large gathering but she also has to spend an evening in the company of his loudmouthed friends before she's afforded the privilege. "I'll... run it past her."

Despite his fears, the meeting isn't as disastrous as it quite possibly could have been. The next Saturday while Lizzie is at a birthday party (and Rebecca tearing her hair out because of it) Ed picks her up and walks her to a nearby café where they meet Penny and Kevin for lunch.

Rebecca is understandably quiet at first but a few minutes into wedding talk she begins to pitch in with details of her own, of the difference between Mainstream Hellenic and Outlie Biblic traditions, and Penny, sensing the opening door, eagerly asks every one of the dozen questions that Ed has been too polite to ask.

Rebecca is patient as always in answering them and artfully skirts around answers that she's not comfortable giving and by the end of it she seems to have struck up a camaraderie with the sharp-tongued woman.

By the time they've finished talking bridesmaids and dresses and flower arrangements, Penny turns to Kevin for a brief silent conversation and then turns back to Rebecca. "You should come. We'd like you to be there. Your daughter too."

Ed looks across at Rebecca and notes the sudden panic on her face. He wants to tell her that she doesn't have to accept. But she knows this. What he really wants to do is let her know that she's not alone in this. He lowers his hand atop hers on the table and gives it a gentle squeeze. He doesn't care what their companions read into the action; doesn't care what it might symbolise to the outside world. He does it because she turns to him with a soft smile and he knows she understood.

"Thank you," she says. "I'm honoured, and we would love to."

Lizzie is so excited when she finds out that she's going to a wedding that she actually abandons her mountain of books to jump up from the sofa and scream excitedly.

Rebecca scolds her good-naturedly; the smile tugging at her lips displacing any actual attempt at discipline as her daughter untangles herself from her research to tackle her in a hug. Rebecca laughs at the assault, wrapping her arms around her daughter and closing her eyes as if holding on to the memory just as tight. Ed can't help but laugh along with them, one that gets caught in his throat when Lizzie turns and pulls him into a hug too.

"Thank you, thank you, thank you," she mutters into his chest.

Ed is so stunned by the show of affection that he can only bring his hands up to tap her back cautiously and look over the child's shoulder to share a look of disbelief and awe with Rebecca. She only smiles, as if she knew it was inevitable.

When the days and night turn colder it's harder not to think about Simon. When the frost first touches the lampposts, when Ed wraps the same scarf around his neck, and the low sun is cloaked in fog over the banks of the Thames, it's hard to not think of that day when

Simon left.

While the people around him start preparing for Solstice – conversations steadily turning from wedding planning to present planning, fairy lights flickering to life throughout the city, and familiar songs being played from tinny radios on every corner – Ed prepares himself for a relapse. He's felt lighter lately, as if the ice around his heart was beginning to thaw, but he knows it cannot last. He'll grit his teeth through Solstice Day with his family as he does every year and then he'll return to a cold empty house and the new year will loom before him with its certainty of continued nothingness and he will feel more alone, more isolated, than ever before.

He wants to believe it will be different this year – that it will somehow be *easier* with Rebecca around – but it feels a little too much like false hope.

Rebecca has to work a few days before Solstice and instead of relying on Chris to look after Lizzie, it's Ed that gets the call instead. He decides to take Lizzie into the city to look at the lights on Oxford Street. She rarely gets the chance to go somewhere so busy, so populated, but Rebecca has begun to relax her rules, especially where Ed is concerned, and Lizzie seems happier for it. She keeps pointing out things in shop windows and asking questions and tugging on Ed's hand to drag him into shops. He doesn't mind it, really, and it's also a good opportunity for him to gather some ideas about presents. He hasn't explicitly discussed the upcoming festivities with Rebecca. He knows that their Biblic denomination still celebrate Solstice but in a different manner and with a different importance placed onto it – something about God providing light in darkness – and although he'll be away for the day it still feels right to buy them a little something so they know he's thinking of them.

He could just buy Lizzie a book voucher or some poetry or music to support her very keen interests but it's Rebecca that he's really stuck on. He's so out of practice that he can't even puzzle out what he's *meant* to do, yet alone what he'll actually do. So, he follows

Lizzie from store to store, absently looking at mass-manufactured trinkets and wondering if any of them could be sufficient.

They're wandering through a department store when Lizzie stops suddenly in front of him and Ed nearly walks into the back of her.

"Lizzie? What –?"

Then he turns and sees what she's looking at: a long turquoise dress with floral lacing around the hem. It's nice. Formal. It would look good on her actually, just the right colour to complement her skin tone.

"It's beautiful," Lizzie whispers, stepping towards it as if enchanted. They're on the second floor – the clothes in this corner all belonging to some designer or another – and he can anticipate Lizzie's crestfallen face even before she reaches out for the price tag. It's on sale but even then still likely to be out of her price range. He watches her frown, her shoulders slump, and the tag fall from her hand, resigned. He can tell by how she schools her face into one of nonchalance that she's had practice at this; she doesn't pout or protest like some children do when they're denied things, she just steps away with a one-armed shrug; the light extinguished from her eyes as if it was never there. He realises suddenly that this is the exact expression she had had that first night on their porch when he had walked away from them. *Resignation.* He couldn't place it before but now his heart aches at the sight.

He reaches for the tag before he can stop himself. It's a good price and a small enough size to fit Lizzie, who already has quite a tall frame for someone her age. "Try it on," he says, lifting the hanger from its rail and holding it out towards her.

She shakes her head sadly.

"You need something for the wedding, don't you? And I owe you a birthday present," he says, as she'd turned thirteen not long after he'd met her. "Try it on."

She cautiously reaches out and runs her fingertips over the fabric, and then she looks up at him, eyes wide and hopeful. "Seriously?"

"Seriously," he says with an indulgent smile.

He walks her over to the changing room by the sale rack where a young woman takes her under her wing. "I'll be right out here if you need anything," Ed reassures her, and as soon as she's disappeared into the rooms he digs out his mobile phone and calls Rebecca's landline. He's half-expecting her to still be at work but he's relieved when she does pick up; he doesn't want to cross a line without her blessing. "I want to buy Lizzie a dress for the wedding, is that alright?" He browses the sale rack as he talks in case there's anything else Lizzie should try on. "I don't want to overstep but she found one she loved –"

"You don't have to do that," Rebecca begins to protest. "I can –"

"No, no," Ed says, already knowing that Rebecca is offering to pay with money she doesn't have. "I want to. But I wanted to make sure it was okay. I didn't want her to come home with a big bag of shopping and you to have a thousand questions."

He pauses when he sees a navy floor-length dress as Rebecca teases him on exactly how much he's planning to buy. It's a size or two too big for Lizzie but for some reason he doesn't move on from it. They say their goodbyes after Rebecca's given him her blessing and he pockets his phone so he can pull out the dress to see it fully: capped sleeves, thick silky material, beautifully long.

He's so distracted by the dress that it's not until the young woman from the changing room is nearly at his shoulder that he actually looks up. "Sir? Your daughter's asking for you."

It takes a while for him to process the situation. Daughter. Changing room. Lizzie. "She's not my… I mean, I'm not the father. I'm…" *What exactly? What exactly was he to her?* He closes his eyes in embarrassment, completely flustered by this simple question. "I'm… I'm with her, yes." The simplest answer.

The poor saleswoman looks almost as embarrassed as Ed feels as she stares at her black polished shoes. "My apologises, sir, it's just that she wants to show you."

Ed fumbles the navy dress onto the nearest hook and follows the woman into the hallway of the changing room where Lizzie is nervously shifting in front of the mirror. He's smiling before he even realises he is. On the one hand, she looks ridiculous; her mousy hair in its unravelling braid and her mismatched threadbare socks bunched around her ankles with an elegant ball gown between them, on the other, it hardly matters. There's a cautious smile on her face, twisted with disbelief and amusement, as if she's seen herself in the mirror and knows exactly how strange it looks but that she's elected not to care. They both look at each other for a moment; both perched on the edge of laughter and something much more profound.

But then her head ducks, touching the fabric with wonder, and when she looks back up, her smile stops being self-deprecating and breaks into one that's simply full of joy. "Can I?" she asks. "Please?"

His answer is, of course, yes.

He can't remember when he was given his first piece of formal wear; it's possible that he'd had them since infancy. It was a necessity in the social circles his parents frequented; occasion after occasion that called for the latest formal fashion. He's grown to despise the feeling of pressed cotton against his skin and the pinch of a tie around his neck. He finds it suffocating. In some ironic twist of fate, it was always Simon that was the smart dresser by choice, and Ed, when left to his own devices – as he has been for the last few years – was simply in the habit of disguising a wrinkled shirt with a blazer.

He wonders though, if his opinion may differ if he hadn't been dressed up and paraded around quite so much as a child. If he could appreciate the finer things if they had never been a given, as Simon did.

He picks up the navy dress once more, sees its simple material and elegance, and knows that there is definitely someone in his life that will appreciate it.

Lizzie walks out of the changing rooms just as he's taking it off the rack. "For your mum," he says, holding it up to her. "For

Solstice. What do you think?"

And the grin across her face makes something akin to pride take residence in his chest.

He accompanies Rebecca and Lizzie to the Prayer House the Sunday before Solstice. It's the first time he's been extended the honour and he's intrigued to go to a Biblic service. He's never been particularly religious; it was Simon that wanted the Temple wedding and Simon who would sometimes just wake up and want to pray. Ed's never had the urge, and can't imagine he ever will, but he's never minded the concept and aside from adjusting to a different religious practice, the act of supporting without believing is much the same.

He approaches the Brighton's house laden down with the gifts he's hoping to place under the Candelabra before they leave for the service, as he himself will be leaving for Surrey the following day, but when he opens the door, the mood is far from festive. He cuts his greeting short as he senses the tension even before he sees them hunched over the kitchen table and hears the associated murmurs. Rebecca looks up with an apologetic smile and he drops the armful of presents by the door as he makes his way over.

"Hey," he greets softly, placing a comforting palm on Lizzie's back as he walks past her to take a chair beside Rebecca. "What's going on?"

Rebecca sighs. Lizzie looks up briefly from her folded arms, looking thoroughly put out; her cheeks red and wisps of hair falling over her face.

He looks between them, searching for an explanation, and finds it when Rebecca hands him a printed letter with the school's familiar branding across the top. "What's this?" he asks, even as he skims the letter and some of the words begin to put the story together.

"As of next term, Lizzie's being mainstreamed," Rebecca summarises. "It's out of our hands."

Ed's grip on the letter loosens, sending it fluttering to the table.

"They lost their funding for Biblic students," Rebecca explains.

"They say they'll still keep the counsellor but the special classes, assemblies... that's all going to go."

"I'll be okay, Mum," Lizzie says, though her puffy face says otherwise.

Rebecca reaches across, squeezes her hand. "I know you will be, sweetheart. Because you're strong. But you shouldn't have to do this alone."

"Neither should you," Lizzie says.

Ed furrows his brow, looking between them. There's more here than he's privy to; he can tell by the guilt in Rebecca's eyes matched with the earnest look of her daughter.

"Rebecca?" he pries.

She looks away.

"Tell him, Mum," Lizzie says. "He'll find out eventually anyway."

"I don't want you to worry," is the first thing Rebecca says, which immediately *makes him worry*. He inches forward on his seat, reaching forward to tuck away the strand of hair that obscures his view of Rebecca's face. His fingers brush against her cheek and her eyelids flutter close at the touch.

"Rebecca?" he tries again.

"I'm no longer seeing Naomi," she says.

"Your counsellor? Why?"

"I'm not a Lifetimer," she says simply, her eyes locked somewhere over his shoulder. He wonders if she is reciting someone else's words to him. "I've been in Mainstream most of my life. Matthew passed away ten years ago now. I don't need the support like others do. The focus has to be on those that could suffer Dissonance, I know this. It was lucky that I had her for as long as I did really."

"Naomi..." Ed says, thinking out loud as he tries to recall a conversation they had a long time ago. "She was contracted by PBS." *Job cuts*, he remembers. He didn't bother to find out who because it wasn't him; wasn't his department. *You stupid, stupid*

178

man, he berates himself. "I'm sorry," he says, overcome with guilt. "I knew they were cutting budgets, I just didn't think…"

"They're making Pairs a priority," Rebecca shrugs. "We know this. They're the Pair Bonding Service after all. It was only a matter of time before they outsourced everything else."

"But they can't just do that," Ed protests. "They can't just cut off your support. For both of you. Just like that. Expect you to make do."

"They gave us the numbers of some charities," Rebecca says.

They're both far too calm about this for his liking. He's reminded of Lizzie's look of defeat in the department store, and outside her house that first night; it's as if they constantly just expect things to be taken from them. "What about the protestors?" he starts. "There were people outside my office daily. It was headline news. It was…" and then he realises. It's Solstice. That means all that commotion was *months* ago, and all the protests just died away while he was – what? Off playing happy families? Ed runs his hands through his hair in frustration. How could he have let himself get distracted? He worked for the very organisation that was now stripping away support for the people he cared about. He could have done something.

"Ed," he hears, and looks up to see Rebecca placing her hand over his. "Don't worry. We'll be okay. Lizzie still has her counsellor at school. I still have the support group that Chris runs. We have the Prayer House."

Lizzie kicks him good-naturedly under the table. "And we have you."

"Right," Ed says, with a suppressed chuckle that is neither a laugh nor a sob. "Right."

For the first time, Solstice is tainted with a different shade of regret as Ed sits at a long table in a dining room in Surrey with family members that are more like acquaintances, somehow feeling more alone, more isolated, than he normally would. He escapes when he can and uses his mobile phone to call the Brightons from the relative sanctuary of his childhood bedroom. When he hears Lizzie's shriek of joy at the CD player she'd found under the Candelabra, even through the static of the bad connection, it is easily the best part of the day. He sits on the thick coverlet draped over the single bed, staring at the bare walls, marvelling that this room can somehow hold more meaning and memory despite the thirty years of distance than his current house in London.

The melancholy doesn't last for long though, not when Rebecca whispers, "you shouldn't have," in reverence as she holds the dress in her hands. They talk for a while longer; so soft that it feels like sharing secrets. Rebecca tells him about the Prayer House service, and Lizzie playing with her presents, and then she quietly apologises that they forgot to give Ed his presents before he left, "With everything that happened... it slipped our minds, I'm sorry. But please know that we haven't forgotten you, you're very important to us. To us both." A warmth blossoms in his chest at the admission, so sudden that it takes him a moment longer than it should to reassure her that it can wait.

"I'll see you when I get back tomorrow," he says like a promise, and even after he's said his goodbyes, he's astounded to note that the warmth still lingers, all through the feast and the port and the politics, it lingers.

He doesn't return home, not really, not until he steps through Rebecca's door and finds himself tackled into a hug by Lizzie. He laughs, almost getting used to Lizzie's always erratic and exaggerated expressions of emotion, and clasps his hands around her back, lifting her a little in his arms just to hear her squeal.

"You survived your family then?" Rebecca interjects as Lizzie untangles herself, and then surprises him by inching him into a hug of her own. Ed attempts to mask his surprise but it's difficult because even after all this time Rebecca was still wary of touch; although they held hands from time to time, and other such chaste

180

gestures, it was rarely initiated by her. He brings a cautious hand to her back, holding her in place for as long as he dares. His eyelids flutter closed against his will as he feels warmth surrounding him; her long hair tickling his collar and her fingers pressed against the small of his back. Tears prick his eyes but not for the usual reasons this time of year brings.

He doesn't remember the last time he was held.

He reluctantly lets her go and remembers that before there had been her in his arms, there had been a question. "I survived," he says. "Barely. Happy to be home."

She smiles, her hand briefly falling into his as she steps back; the gentle squeeze of her hand in his saying more than words ever could.

Rebecca gives him a hand-knitted hat, and it's lovely, and thoughtful, and far more than he expected, but it's Lizzie's Solstice present that takes him most by surprise.

She's so nervous when she approaches with an envelope in her hands that he almost wants to tell her not to worry about it but there's also a fierce determination in her eyes that warns him not to discourage her. So he cradles his cup of tea at the kitchen table and waits for her to find the courage.

Then, she squares her shoulders, and holds up the plain envelope to him with a single red ribbon wrapped around it. "I wrote you a poem."

The breath catches in Ed's throat. Two months ago, Lizzie had scoffed at the very idea, dismissing poems as 'posh stuff' clearly not meant for her, and now, instead of say, writing him an essay or drawing him a picture or bestowing him a book, all of which would have been arguably more in character, she offers her words to him, like a priest would a prayer to a god.

"I wanted to have a go," she explains. "I don't know if I'm any good. I've been writing a few to practice but I... wanted you to have this one."

Ed shakes his head in disbelief as he takes the envelope from her proffered hand. He's fairly certain Lizzie could turn her hand to any field or practice and be extremely proficient and so it's more the implied meaning of the gesture that has him rattling his mind for something to say rather than platitudes for the work. "Thank you," he settles on after a moment, sincerely. "That's very thoughtful."

He exchanges a quick glance with Rebecca, but she gives a minute shrug, as if to say she doesn't know the contents of the envelope either.

He carefully removes the folded lined paper inside, torn from a school notebook by the looks of it, and unfolds it to see words neatly written atop it in blue ink, as if she's taken extra care to ensure the words are legible. The first thing he notices is the shape of the poem. It's not rigorously structured like the majority of school poetry is; it's not written in couplets, or clearly segmented into stanzas, it's not even uniform in terms of line length. He also highly doubts that Lizzie would concede to something as rudimentary as rhyme.

He looks across the paper to Lizzie, hoping that she sees the pride in his eyes born from the fact that she stubbornly remains unconventional in all things. It's one of the things that endears her most to him.

And then, he begins to read.

It's good. It would be unbelievably good, if he did not know the child that penned it.

"It's about Athena Gardens," Lizzie says unnecessarily, almost bouncing on her toes with impatience.

"Yes, I see that," he replies, distractedly, still reading and re-reading a few of the lines. Sure, it was outwardly about Athena Gardens, but it was more about chance meetings, about paths crossing, memories inlaid with every step. It was beautiful, and unnerving, and incredibly insightful for a young teen.

He drops the pages onto the kitchen table and pulls Lizzie into a hug as he hears Rebecca practically scramble for the abandoned poem. "Thank you," he says again, though the words are gruff with unspoken emotion. "It's wonderful."

"So it's okay?" she asks, pulling out of his grasp, returning to her standard academic mindset in which the merit of the poem is the only thing of importance, personal significance forgotten.

He pushes down his own emotions to match her intellectual scrutiny and clears his throat just to be sure. "Lizzie," he says seriously, placing his hands on her shoulders, forcing eye contact so he'll know she'll actually believe him, "It's good. It reads like you've been writing poetry for years, not a month. And I'm not just saying this, okay? I think you've really got something here. You could be a poet if you wanted."

Her eyes that had been shining brightly suddenly close down. He wonders what it is he said wrong when she says, "I'm an Outlie descendent. I can't be a poet."

He tightens his grip on her shoulders. "Yes, you can."

"I'm not one of *them* – I'm not an Elite kid, I'm not Hellenic, I'm not even going to be a Searcher I don't think. I can't be –"

"Yes, you can," he says through gritted teeth because he is sick and tired of seeing that weary look of resignation on her face, over and over again, like it was normal to expect rejection. He is brimming with barely contained anger at the world for having convinced a brilliant thirteen-year-old girl that she can't be anything she wants to be. "Yes," he says firmly, "you can."

The fire is back in her eyes at these words, her shoulders set straight, and he only has a moment to wonder at the fact he was the one that put that confidence back in her, where it deserves to live, before the screech of a wooden chair on linoleum breaks their gaze.

"I'm sorry, I –" Rebecca is saying, standing up, tears rolling down her cheek as the poem falls from her hands to the table. "I have to –"

And then she's scurrying across the living room to her bedroom and Ed feels the weight of guilt twist in his stomach.

The door closes and it leaves a terrible silence in its wake.

Ed turns back to Lizzie, who's hurriedly reclaiming her poem, stretching across the table to grab at the paper. "It was me," she's muttering, "It was too much, I shouldn't have –"

Ed clasps his hand over hers, stilling the movement. "It wasn't you, Lizzie," he says with certainty, "It wasn't the poem," he says, though, less certain of it than the first statement. "You did nothing wrong. I just overstepped, okay? That's why she's upset. It's my fault, not yours."

Lizzie looks to him, confused, but it would undoubtedly only confuse her further if he tried to explain the complications of adult relationships when children are involved, especially when the relationship in question was already a complication in itself.

He sighs. "Why don't you find me the rest of the poetry you've been working on while I talk to your mother? Then we can talk about it after?"

She casts one sorrowful glance to the closed door before turning back to Ed with a sure nod. "Okay. It will take me awhile to find all of them anyway."

He smiles at her subtle blessing to take his time as she turns to rummage through the stacks of books around the house.

Ed knocks softly on the door before twisting the handle and opening it into the darkened room. He's never been in Rebecca's bedroom before but the blinds are closed and all he can see is simple furniture and a worn pink coverlet over the single bed. It's easily the tidiest room in the house; her room of solitude, no doubt. He lets his eyes adjust to the darkness before following the sounds of Rebecca's muffled cries to her silhouette by the window.

"I'm sorry," she's saying between sobs, the sleeve of her cardigan rubbing across her face as if to catch the falling tears and mucus.

"No, I am," he says softly, and cautiously lays his hand over her turned shoulder. She shudders at the touch, and he's about to retreat with an apology when her delicate fingers clasp over his. Her tears fall unimpeded. "I shouldn't have overstepped," he says. "It's Lizzie's future I'm influencing, I understand the importance of that –

Her breath catches and she twists to see him, their joined hands falling from her shoulder. "You think that's why I'm upset?"

He frowns. He can't think why else it would be, unless she truly was upset over Lizzie writing poetry but he thought they'd gotten past her restriction on Lizzie's learning.

"That's not –" she begins, but breaks off with another sob, hand coming to rub at her face again. "I'm sorry, I don't normally –" and then, "I don't want you to see me like this. Weak. I'm not weak. I'm fine."

"I know," Ed whispers. "I know you're strong." He steps forward, tries to lower her hands from her face so he can see her eyes and try to work out what monumental thing he must have overlooked. "But I'm here. I want to help. Please tell me what's going on. Is it the poem?"

She shakes her head.

"Lizzie?"

A vicious shake of her head this time.

"And it's definitely not because I overstepped?"

She looks up at him with an expression of disbelief, but there's something wry beneath it, as if she's also disbelieving in herself.

He furrows his brow, still holding her gaze and trying to tease out some meaning from her tear-clouded eyes. His hand is still cupping her cheek; her hand trapped between them, his thumb absently stroking across her skin. They're close; much closer than they normally allow themselves to be, and she's looking at him with an expression he still can't decipher. She closes her eyes, her face turning incrementally towards his touch.

"Hey," he whispers, moving his other hand to her neck and gently raising her eyes to his again. "Whatever it is, it's okay, we'll be okay."

Her face crumples and he has no idea how to read it until, between one blink of the eye and the next, her lips are on his.

The touch is so foreign, so soft and uncertain, that Ed feels suspended in time, as if the very world is holding its breath in anticipation. He feels every particle between them – her slight exhale against his mouth, the salt from dried tears in the crevices of her upper lip, her loose hair tickling against the palm that he still rests on her cheek, the scratch from her cardigan where her arm brushes against his bare skin, the wet tear caught between her face and his – every point of contact between them heightened.

It can't be more than a few seconds of contact; no more than a few cautious, delicate, slight movements between them, when Rebecca is pulling away again. Her hand comes to cover her face, but this time, not to wipe away tears, but to hide her mouth. "Sorry, I –" she begins, but doesn't finish. She wraps her arms around herself; looks anywhere but at him.

Ed stands there, still frozen in time, utterly incapable of decoding what just transpired between them.

"I shouldn't have done that," she says.

Ed opens his mouth, can feel the movement, but there's no words even forming in his mind, yet alone daring to come out. He doesn't know if he's sorry for it. He doesn't know what his beating heart is trying to tell him.

"I…" he manages, inelegantly. "I have to think."

And this time, it's him that runs from the room, from the house, and he's marching past the corner shop three streets over when he realises that he never got to see the rest of Lizzie's poetry.

The next couple of days pass in a blur. He's not actively avoiding Rebecca but there's always a shortfall of staff between Solstice and New Year and Ed routinely works every day between them to account for it – and to ensure he rises from bed, which is not guaranteed during the winter months – the fact that he doesn't pick up the phone to call is a different matter. It's not that he hasn't thought about it – he has to the point of distraction – it's just that every time he imagines dialling her number, he can't possibly imagine what happens afterwards. He doesn't know what words could take them back to the place where they were before the kiss; not sure if there are the words, or if, more terrifyingly, if he wants there to be.

He replays the scene in his mind over and over again but he still can't puzzle out what was going through her mind. Ed had thought they'd gotten pretty good at communication after their rocky start; he'd opened up to her about Simon and his depression, and likewise, she'd told him about Matthew and her experience as an Outlier. They've shared their very deepest thoughts with one another, so why was it now impossible to pick up the phone and just *talk*?

Ed works that weekend, doing some extra hours in Reports, and it's blissfully quiet, just him and Radio 2 and an entire room of non-judgemental filing cabinets, until he hears the office door open adjacent to the store he's in. He pauses mid-movement, praying that whoever it is will turn around and leave again having retrieved whatever it was that they needed, but before he can consider the childish possibility of hiding, Jasmine walks into the store holding up some tupperware as an offering.

"Figured you probably forgot to eat."

It's 2pm. Ed did in fact forget about lunch. He glances through the plastic of the box to see Jasmine's famous homemade Indian samosas and probably a rice dish the other side of it and his stomach rumbles. He sighs in defeat, abandons the file, and begins to extract himself from the mountain of paperwork he has accumulated around him.

"Thanks, Jazz. What are you doing here anyway?"

She gives a one-armed shrug. "Had a project to check up on."

But Ed checks his wristwatch for the date and has another suspicion as to why she's here. "So Penny didn't send you?"

"She's still in Hong Kong, how could she?" she asks with a wry smile.

Ed sighs, and takes the proffered tupperware. "I'm fine," he says, in an attempt to ward off any incoming conversation about his wellbeing. He pries off the lid, mouth watering at the smell of spices, and leans against a desk as he digs in with the fork provided. And, oddly, as he says it, he realises that he means it. He's been so preoccupied with thoughts of Rebecca that his mind hasn't sat still long enough for the depression to set in. He doesn't know if it's necessarily *better* but it's a different kind of torture at least.

He grunts after the first bite, pointing down at the food with his fork. "This is really good, Jazz, thank you. How was your Solstice?"

She raises an eyebrow as if to say she notices his clumsy attempt to change the conversation but luckily for him, she doesn't comment on it as she comes over to perch on the desk across from him. She shrugs. "I don't celebrate it –"

"Oh, sorry, yes, of course, I –"

"But Idris and Indigo do," she interjects before he can make a total fool of himself. "And so I was subjected to all five of their siblings for an entire day. Not exactly how I'd choose to spend the longest night of the year but there you are."

Ed huffs. He can imagine that would be difficult for Jasmine; a Non-Trad to be with a Searcher family for the most religious holiday of the year. "Do you do it every year? With Idris' family, I mean?"

"No," she says, kicking out her legs in front of her. "First time actually. I know we've been together for donkey's years but it's hard for them to see us as anything more than friends, you know? So I'm not normally invited to family things."

"But you and Idris are practically married. You're inseparable. You look after Indigo together."

"Sure, except we're not married, we *are* inseparable – as in, not Bonded – and it's not like I've adopted Indie, he's just my best friend's kid brother, you know, it's just how it worked out."

Ed shakes his head, occupies himself with eating. "That's nonsense. I get that you two don't fit the standard model of a relationship and maybe that's confusing to some people but anyone can see what you two mean to each other. You're family. I don't see the need to make it any more complicated than that."

Ed nearly chokes, mid-swallow, when he hears his own words and realises how closely her situation mirrors his. Jasmine and Idris are partners, but in the non-traditional, non-romantic sense of the word. They live together, they raise a child together, and they look at each other as if the other hung the moon.

Holy Zeus. Is *that* what he wants with Rebecca? A Non-Trad arrangement? Is that what they've been doing? Is that what Rebecca thinks this *is*?

"You alright there, Hart?" Jasmine asks with concern, as he struggles to breathe in more ways than one.

He holds up his hand to show that he's okay, even as his mind races so fast he almost feels sick. "Just…re-evaluating."

A look of understanding crosses Jasmine's face and he wonders if he and Rebecca have really been that transparent. "Hmm… yeah, see I *did* wonder what was going on between you and the Outlie girl."

"That makes two of us," Ed mutters, and he puts the food aside, too nauseated to be interested whatsoever. "She kissed me," he confesses.

"And it changed things?" Jasmine hazards.

"Apparently so. I don't know what we were, but it… complicates things somehow, muddies the water, in a way nothing else has."

Jasmine shrugs. "I get that. Kissing has connotations, you know? Makes you think of the whole big," she makes an arc with her hands, "trad narrative – sex, marriage, babies, all that – in a way that other non-sexual acts of intimacy might not."

Ed looks at her with bulging eyes; the way she talks about relationships as if there's *facts*, as if terms like 'non-sexual acts of intimacy' actually hold meaning; it's like she's somehow uncovered a handbook on interpersonal relationships that he's just too close-minded to possess.

"You're new to this," Jasmine says, clearly taking pity on him. "It's hard to dismantle boxes if you don't know they're there, but just know you can if you want to, yeah? A kiss doesn't have to mean all that if you don't want it to. You can build a relationship that works for everyone involved, labels and societal expectations be darned."

Ed stares at his shoes. He feels incredibly naïve for assuming the kiss meant she wanted a romantic relationship even though she's never so much as indicated otherwise. "Presumably though, working that out requires talking to her?"

"Might be a good start, yeah," she says dryly, standing up to collect her abandoned tupperware from beside Ed.

Ed sighs, and runs his hands through his greasy hair as Jasmine makes a move to leave. "And working out what I want, I suppose that comes into it too?"

"Well, I didn't say it was easy," she says, and squeezes his shoulder in a show of support. She's almost out the door when she turns back, a thoughtful expression on her face. "It might help, if you're unsure, to think in broad terms about the future. When you close your eyes at night, where do you see yourself? What's the future that you dream of?" She shrugs. "I know it sounds sappy, but that's how I figured out my mess. Might help with yours too."

He nods, attempts to smile, and watches her leave; he doesn't have the heart to tell her that he's never once dreamed of a future since Simon Bonded. Not even with Rebecca.

He's back in the field. Cold. Path. Gloves. Lake. The shadow approaches. Simon's hand breaks from his, but then... a shift; a change in perspective like never before. *He* becomes Simon, or Simon becomes him, he's not quite sure, but it's his hand that reaches towards the shadow, begging for a touch, for completion. Reaching into the unknown, hoping, hoping...

Ed wakes gasping, arm stretched out in front of him. There is no light blinding him this time; only darkness. He feels hyper aware of it. An absence he can't explain, in his mind, in his soul. A nothingness. But a different nothingness than the one that has dogged him all these years; somehow sharper, more concentrated, almost tangible. He focuses on reality; recalls his outstretched fingers and curls them into a fist. His thoughts remain muddled and surreal, still carrying the remnants of sleep, as he forcibly returns his arm to his side.

He tries to return to his routine – reaches for the water, for the towel, checks the time – but the dream has effectively disrupted any sense of normality he was clinging to. The dream never changes. When he finds himself on that path, it always ends the same way. Except this time, *this* time, it didn't, and he stares at his fingers atop the bedsheets, wondering, under the illusion of safety that the dead of night brings, what that could possibly mean.

"Thought I might find you here."

Ed sighs, wondering if Penny had put the entire PBS staff on suicide watch while she was out of the country, and looks up from his desk to see Chris standing in the doorway to his office a couple of days before New Year's.

Chris seems to take Ed's irritated silence as an invitation and waltzes over the threshold, coming to sit down in the chair opposite without so much as a greeting.

Ed closes the file he was working on. "It's my office, Chris. Why wouldn't I be here?"

"It's Tuesday," he responds like it's an answer in itself.

It takes Ed a moment to work out why that means anything and then feels like an imbecile when he gets there. His jaw clenches and his eyes close in guilt; he ought to have seen this coming. "The Outlie support group meets on a Tuesday," Ed concludes. "You've just seen Rebecca."

"That I have," Chris says, lounging back in the chair with his usual saunter. "Seems that you haven't recently though. Odd, seeing as you two seem to have had a standing lunch date for the last couple of months. And don't think I haven't heard the rumours. I've heard the rumours."

"It's not like that."

"Like what?" Chris teases.

Ed glares at the smug look on his colleague's face as if he can remove it by sheer force of will.

Chris doesn't budge.

Ed bites his cheek, suppressing his annoyance, and pretends to busy himself with the files in front of him. "Why are you here, Chris?" And then, a moment later, when he finds the courage to ask, "Is Rebecca okay?"

Chris clicks his tongue, and it's enough of a deliberation to snap Ed to attention, files forgotten on the desk. "I wouldn't say so, no."

Fear lodges in his throat. How long has it been since he spoke to her? Three days? Four? He resists the ridiculous urge to jump to his feet and run across the city of London to find her and see that she was okay with his own two eyes. "What happened?" he asks instead, tightly, with urgency.

Chris shrugs. "You tell me."

Ed runs his hands through his hair in frustration. "It's complicated. And I'm under no obligation to explain it to you."

"Okay, *buddy*," Chris says, leaning forward, dropping his casual act and turning into a force to be reckoned with within a matter of seconds. "Here's how it is: Rebecca is a friend, as well as a client. I care about what happens to her, and to Lizzie. You and I both know that they ain't got much support right now, but you've become something to her, and I don't care what you're calling it, or what in Hades happened between you two over Solstice, but you gotta recognise that you have a responsibility here; that you have an impact on their lives. So, no, you don't have to tell me anything, but I sure as Zeus hope you know what you're doing because I may not be here to pick up the pieces this time, not the way things are headed."

Ed averts his eyes, guiltily. He knows the PBS cuts affected the Outlie Relations department most of all; he's witnessed first-hand the devastation it's caused to the Brightons. Chris could very well lose his job too in the following months.

"Look, buddy, I'm not telling you what to do, but the way she was this morning? It was like we were back at square one and that's a sight no counsellor wants to see. I'm not saying that you're to blame, I'm just saying that something's changed for her, and if you know what it is, then maybe it's a good idea to fix it, alright?"

Ed nods numbly, and a few minutes later, Chris retreats. He tries not to let it show but the burden of Chris' words falls heavy on Ed's shoulders. He knows the Brightons are rapidly losing support and now is absolutely the worst time to duck out, but he knows, if he came back now to hold them steady through the changes, then he wouldn't be moving any time soon, and that thought terrifies him.

In the end, the worry wins out. Barely an hour after Chris had visited, Ed pulls out his mobile phone from his desk drawer and dials their home number. It goes to voicemail.

He tries her number twice more that hour but it's not until four thirty that someone finally picks up.

"Hello?"

It's Lizzie's voice, not Rebecca's, and it's unexpected enough that Ed has to rapidly adjust the words he'd been carefully rehearsing for the entire afternoon.

"Lizzie," he starts. "It's Ed. Is your mum there?"

"Oh," she says, and either he's imagining it or there's a bite to her voice now, as if three days of silence were enough to erase all the trust they'd built over months. It felt as if they were back to their first terse conversation in the park. "Mum can't come to the phone right now."

Ed clenches his fist by his side, suppressing and displacing the immense worry that that sentence brings. "Why? Is she alright?"

Lizzie sighs and he's not imagining it; that's the kind of exasperated sigh she'd given him when they'd first met, as if it was far too much effort to explain herself to such a simpleton. "Obviously not. Go away."

"Lizzie –" he begs, even as her words cut deep; deeper than Ed knew they could go. "I'm sorry. I just want to talk to her –"

"Well, she doesn't want to talk to you, so –"

"Okay, okay," Ed mutters, attempting to control his breathing. "Okay, I understand. Can you just pass a message onto her please? Tell her I'm just thinking, okay? I'm not gone. If you still need me I'm here, for both of you. I've just… got a lot in my head, and I need to get a few things straight, but I'm not leaving because of what happened, okay? Please. Will you tell her?"

The sigh again. "Fine."

"Okay, thank you, and Lizzie –"

But she hangs up before he can ask after her.

Chris is right to put the blame on him, he realises. He'd been telling himself the silence was mutual – she hadn't called either after all – but there's an imbalance here. She was the one that opened up, and he was the one that walked away. It's his responsibility to right things.

Penny and Kevin come back from Hong Kong just before New Year's and insist on throwing a party to which Ed is naturally dragged along to. It's busy, and loud, and full of people half his age, but it makes a change to bring in the new year with friends and there's something almost exciting in meeting new people that he wouldn't otherwise meet. He can't help but think it would be all the more enjoyable with the addition of two familiar faces though.

He escapes to the first floor sometime after ten o'clock, turning his mobile phone over and over in his hands. Surely just the fact that he misses them proves that they ought to be together? That he wants to be a family? But every time his finger hovers over the little plastic green button, something stops him, and he thinks that that's probably some kind of sign too. He never used to be one to shy from commitment – he was the one that proposed to Simon, and who first raised the topic of children with him – and so he knows that there's something stopping him this time, something bigger than practical

194

questions. Doubt, perhaps, that he's not in love and whether he would want this *without* love. Or perhaps, something even bigger, even scarier, so big that he feels – even in the week that has passed since the thought first occurred to him – that he can still only approach the edges of understanding.

He's doing another rotation of the hallway when one of the doors open and a couple of giggling, and most likely intoxicated, people spill out. Some aspects about houseparties apparently haven't changed since his youth. His mouth quirks in amusement as they stumble past him smelling of sex and alcohol and he politely averts his eyes; pocketing his phone once more. He thinks he's alone again until he hears the click of a door and sees another man leaving the room with an array of empty bottles dangling from between his fingers. They share a nod of acknowledgement and Ed doesn't think anything of it until a second later when he feels the stranger's fingers brushing against his

Ed inhales sharply, his hand pulling away on instinct. Flashbacks of the dream – of him reaching, reaching, instead of Simon – coming back to him. His eyes squeeze shut as he desperately scrambles to find reality again.

"Oh, sorry dude, I thought you were –" the man is saying, as he continues to move past. "My mistake."

"No," Ed says, and surprises both of them by reaching out and circling his fingers around the stranger's wrist. "No, sorry, you just caught me by surprise. Thank you for Recognising me."

The man smiles, and it's rather dazzling, and even if he is at least ten years Ed's junior and a Bond likely impossible with such a considerable gap, it was still nice to be sought out. People have touched Ed for Recognition since Simon, of course they have – in formal meetings and in hurried fingers on the street and in supermarket aisles – it's habitual when passing someone of a similar age, and he's probably unconsciously Recognised a dozen new people at the party tonight, but he cannot honestly remember the last time a stranger went out their way to do so.

Ed hadn't even realised that the touch had been missing from his life but he supposes he hasn't been particularly social since Simon left and perhaps it showed; if he appeared to strangers as closed off, as *unwilling* – as perhaps he had been – then no wonder no one had approached him for Recognition.

He realises he's still holding the gaze of the younger man and forces himself to look away.

"Good luck in your Search," the man says.

Routine. There's a routine for this. "Yes," Ed says. "In yours also."

And he watches, completely dumbfounded, as the stranger walks away, not realising the thoughts he has sent unravelling in his wake.

A few days into the new year, Ed gets a phone call from Lizzie's school, which is as unnerving as it is unexpected. He's barely sat down at his desk Tuesday morning when his mobile phone rings loudly enough to sound from his satchel.

When he sees the school's name on the screen, he almost doesn't believe it, and for one even more unbelievable moment, almost doesn't answer it.

"Ed Hart."

"Yes, hello, it's Mrs Vickers from Cassandra High. We've been trying to contact Ms Brighton for a few minutes but –"

"Is everything okay?"

"Elizabeth had a panic attack in assembly. Well, we think that's what it was. At first we thought it was Dissonance, and it might be? Honestly we're not sure. She's still here in the office, recovering, and we thought –"

"Wait, slow down," Ed says, as he shifts to the edge of his chair. "You *don't know* if it's Dissonance? Shouldn't her counsellor be there? Er…" he rattles his mind, trying to remember, it must have been a month since the name last crossed his lips. "Alex! Where's Alex?"

"Oh," she says awkwardly, "Mr Hart, you should have received a letter. Or rather, Ms Brighton should have. Alex had to be let go at the start of this term."

"No, no, that was the classes, the assemblies, but Lizzie still had the counsellor –"

"You must be mistaken, Mr Hart. There was a late amendment, perhaps only a week or so before term, did you not get the letter?"

"No, I didn't."

"Okay," she says awkwardly. "Well, Lizzie's here now if you want to talk to her –"

And then there's a flurry of static and Ed knows he's being passed over to Lizzie before he can object any further.

It's a small, shaking voice that greets him between sniffles and the sound breaks his heart. "Ed?" she asks.

His eyes flutter closed in guilt, in regret, in sheer pain that somewhere across the city Lizzie had to go through this alone. "Hey," he whispers, cradling the phone like a lifeline. "It's me. Are you okay?"

There's another shaky inhale and Ed strains his ears until he's sure of it: she's not breathing right. Ten minutes, the teacher had said. She's been this way for ten minutes. Why didn't they call the school nurse? An ambulance even? She's an Outlie child and they haven't even established if this is an episode of Dissonance? A small part of him knows he's being ridiculous – Lizzie's lived in Mainstream all her life and despite being raised Biblic it's hardly likely that she would suffer Dissonance severe enough to cause injury – but Rebecca's concerns have clearly become ingrained into his own.

"Okay," he says with determination, pushing down his own frustration so he can focus on Lizzie. "It sounds like you're having a panic attack and I'm going to help you through it okay? But first – and I'm really sorry – but we need to check that this isn't Dissonance. Did anything happen at assembly that might have triggered you? Anything to do with Bonding or Searching? Anything that felt jarring to your brain, like nails on a chalkboard?" he presses when there's still silence. "What do you remember?"

Another shaky inhale. "It wasn't Dissonance. I was... reading my poetry. I won a... thing. Had to read. In front of school."

"That was very brave of you," Ed says in his calmest voice although he's anything but. "That must have been scary, huh?"

He hears Lizzie's nod more than he hears her quiet admission.

He tries to tame his protective instincts now he knows she's not in immediate danger and coaches her through the breathing and focusing exercises he learnt to cope with his night terrors. It feels like an eternity before he hears steady breathing on the other end of the line.

"Okay," he says finally, "Are your fingers and toes still tingly?"

"Yeah, and my legs. I don't know if I can stand."

"That's okay, it'll pass, but if there's something sugary there it will help. Is there squash? Some biscuits?"

He pinches the bridge of his nose as Lizzie relays this to the teacher; the anger rising in him once more that he even has to do so. There should be someone there for her.

"I still feel sick though," she says. And he wonders what it means that she followed his instructions before even questioning them; he thought he lost all progress he made with her but perhaps not.

"Then try just taking a few sips of the squash," he says softly. "Trust me, it will help."

"Okay," she says firmly, and he can imagine the set of her shoulders as clearly as if he saw it only yesterday.

"How are you feeling?" he asks after some time has passed.

There's a pause on the line, one without the background noise of squash and biscuits and teachers' gossip, and he wonders what's going on. And then, Lizzie whispers like it's a secret to be ashamed of, "I want to go home."

"Okay," he says, grabbing the satchel he realises he had packed. "Okay, pass me back to your teacher, I'm coming to get you."

Lizzie's cheeks are still rubbed raw and her eyes still shining when he arrives in the school office thirty minutes later, having practically run out of work and onto the nearest bus. Her usual defiance is nowhere to be found as she shuffles uncomfortably from foot to foot as Ed talks to the teacher. She tells them they've yet to contact Ms Brighton – Rebecca – but they'll keep trying and Ed makes a mental note to buy Rebecca a mobile phone.

Lizzie's uncharacteristically quiet on the way home, avoiding not only Ed, but also everyone they pass on the street; her eyes fixed on the ground without their usual curiosity. Her arms are wrapped around her stomach as if putting another physical barrier between her and the rest of the world. He doesn't know if she's just tired from the panic attack or if there's something else at play here but he knows enough not to push for answers as they take the familiar shortcut through Athena Gardens.

He waits for her to break the silence, and it's just when they're passing the bandstand and the park where they first met, that she finally does. "This doesn't mean I've forgiven you."

Ed nods. That's fair. "Okay, I understand. You know that I never meant to hurt you though, right? Either of you?"

"Yeah," she says, scuffing the ground with her tatty school shoes. "So you've said. Doesn't mean you didn't though. You just disappeared."

He swallows his guilt. "I know."

A couple passes them. Ed holds out his hand, touches, and moves on. It's only Lizzie's scrutiny that makes him realise he even reached out for Recognition. It's become habitual lately. But, he realises, it wasn't when he was last with them; it used to be passive in their company – a result from standing as the barrier between them and the rest of the world – but he doubts he has ever actually *initiated* a touch for Recognition in her presence.

"Why did you do that?" she asks.

Ed stumbles, trying to find words to describe the complexity of motivations for the act, some of which he doesn't even know for himself yet, and fails.

"I thought you liked Mum," she adds.

"I do," he says, immediately defensive, before thinking better of it, "Sort of. It's complicated, Lizzie. And just because I want to Recognise, doesn't mean I don't like your mum. One doesn't negate the other."

"So you're a Waiter?"

Ed is so unprepared for this question that he nearly trips over his own two feet. He remembers Simon accusing him of the same thing years ago.

If you're one of those people that date but are always off fantasying about The One then whatever but –

"No," he says firmly before Lizzie can get the wrong idea, "I wouldn't do that to your mum."

The idea was never overly distasteful to him in the way that it was to Simon. Plenty of people find that compromise between Searching and Settling – Chris and his wife among them – but now he knows what it feels like when it actually happens – the devastation a Bond leaves behind when there's already love involved – he can't imagine ever purposefully making that choice and potentially hurting Rebecca in the same way.

"Then what?" she challenges, daggers in her eyes as she looks up at him.

He looks away in shame. "Truthfully Lizzie, that's what I don't know. That's why I thought I'd stay away until I figured it out."

"That's stupid. You can't just run away and make decisions about relationships by yourself and then come back and say what it is that *you* want. That's not how that works. You're both meant to get a say. Like, did you even ask Mum what she wanted before you disappeared? No. Because you don't fucking care."

"Lizzie," he scolds, but if he's honest, his anger is mostly directed at himself.

"Don't you dare tell me that it's complicated, or that I'm too young to understand, because I *understand*," she snaps, and it's so

200

reminiscent of Kevin when Ed challenged him about Penny that it gives him pause. "I know you've both been through stuff but that doesn't mean you get to run away when things get hard."

She stops in her tracks, and then, before he can stop her, she's spinning on her heel and marching back the way they came.

"Lizzie? What are you doing?"

She visibly swallows her nerves but her shoulders are set and her eyes are looking straight ahead with her usual defiance and he knows better than to try to stop her.

"I'm going back to school," she says. "I am going to go back to class and I am going to look those bullies straight in the eye because I am a Brighton and *I* am not a fucking coward."

The accusation that Ed *is* a coward goes unsaid but Ed is too busy being proud to be overly offended by it. He chases after her, struggling to match her pace despite his wider gait.

"They say I'm doing it wrong, that people like me can't write poetry but if that was true, I wouldn't have won the regional competition, would I?"

"It was a *regional* competition?" Ed says in awe. When Lizzie said she had won something, he had just assumed it was a school prize, not a district-wide honour.

Lizzie rolls her eyes in that way she does. "Yeah, keep up. Got some book tokens. Gonna be published in an anthology. But then I had to..." the fight goes out of her just briefly, her pace slowing ever so slightly at the memory. "They presented me the tokens in assembly. Said it was an honour for the school. And because it was a short poem, Headmaster said I should read it out loud... but, I wasn't ready. Wasn't prepared." She shakes her head, pushes on. "Next time I'll be ready. And the next time Gail Simmons and her cronies laugh at me, the next time Jason Martin says 'only Searchers can write poetry', and Ingrid Tate calls me Outlie scum... well, I'll have a fucking poem for them too."

Ed grins. He can't help it. How is this the same girl he picked up from school, shaking and defeated, not half an hour ago? This girl is made from fire. The Brightons know how to recover from a knockback, he'll give them that. His chest swells with pride, but he can't say the words – can't step in as the father only to let them down again. They deserve better. But he can say one thing with the utmost certainty, "Your mum is going to be so proud of you."

"Yeah?" she asks, eyes shining, as if there was a single doubt.

"Yeah," he repeats with a soft smile. "You're going to prove to these kids that no one is *supposed* to be anything and you're not going to let their immense stupidity, nor anyone else's, get in your fucking way. That's amazingly courageous, Lizzie. Of course she's going to be proud of you."

Lizzie nods determined, the biggest smile stretching across her face, even as her eyes still shine with her tears. "Yeah," she repeats firmly. "Yeah, I'm gonna show them."

Ed arrives back at work after a harrowing conversation with Rebecca to find an entire inquisition in his office, constituting most of the wedding party and then some. When they see him in the doorway, they all start talking over each other as if they can't decide who has more right to shout at him. Finally, Penny wins out as Ed drops his satchel, exhausted, by the door and shrugs out of his coat. "Where on earth have you been?" she practically shrieks.

"Personal emergency," he says. It's barely midday. They all skip out on work sometimes during the day – it's a big enough building to do so without raising suspicion – so he's not sure why he's under quite so much scrutiny.

"Personal emergency?" she repeats in disbelief, more huff than actual words.

Kevin steps forward, hand on Ed's elbow, concern lining his brow. "You alright man? It's just… not like you to miss work."

"It is like him to skip out without telling anybody though."

Ed doesn't have to look up to know it's Chris speaking – the only one who was likely to know what actually transpired between him and Rebecca – and he barely gets a look in when Chris pushes past him and out the door, knocking his shoulder hard enough to hurt.

Ed winces, too emotionally drained from the morning to fight it.

"You had a Test this morning," Jasmine says. "At ten o'clock."

Ed swears under his breath. He'd forgotten.

"We've been trying to call you," she says.

His mobile phone was probably still at the bottom of his satchel, forgotten since the call from the school. He shakes his head, and he must look distraught enough that Jasmine ushers the other colleagues to disperse, leaving just the four of them in his office.

"We got Ariston to cover you," Penny says. "He's in the Testing chambers right now with them. But, seriously Ed, it's not like you to miss work. You alright?"

Ed shakes his head, a hysterical laugh wanting to escape from between his lips. *Alright?* He was a thousand things before *alright*. But he looks up, at three matching faces of concern looking at him, and wonders when, during all of his anger and solitude, he managed to acquire friends. "No," he says honestly, because it's what they deserve. "I got a call from Lizzie's school. She's alright now but... I had to deal with it."

"I thought you guys were...?" Penny begins, but clearly none of them know how to finish that sentence as it hangs between them incomplete. "I mean, why you?" she tries again. "Where was Rebecca?"

Ed sighs and walks past them to his desk, happy for the familiar sight and some semblance of routine as he falls into the chair behind it. "She was working. They couldn't get a hold of her. So... they called me. It's fine," he says to ward off their concerned stares and the questions likely to follow. "I mean, it's not *fine*. They lost all the Outlie support at that school practically overnight, including her counsellor, that I didn't know about, and apparently, having talked to Rebecca just now, she didn't know either. Lizzie didn't want us to worry," Ed scoffs. "Typical Brighton bravado there. But it meant when something happened this morning there was no one there for her and I'm just so –" his fist clenches again, unclenches, trying to control his anger. "They keep having everything taken away from them. And if I leave…" he shakes his head, dispelling the thought, not even sure where it came from. He closes his eyes, remembers Lizzie's look of resigned acceptance that first time when he tried to leave, how much worse it would be now they know what it's like to be a family. "I don't want to be another disappointment in their lives. Another thing they lose. But…" he sighs, he's not strong enough to finish the thought; too devastating to voice.

"You're not sure if you can stay either," Jasmine infers.

It's slightly kinder than the words he had in his own head and he nods with gritted teeth, begrudgingly accepting them as the truth.

"You can't make yourself love them if you don't," Penny says, perching on the desk beside him. "You can't just stay out of some twisted sense of duty."

"I know," Ed whispers to his hands, and then, a little stronger; "I know."

A moment of silence falls over them; Ed still caught in his introspection as they look down upon him. Then, the moment breaks, and Kevin clasps his hand on Ed's shoulder. "We'll leave you be, yeah?"

Ed nods his thanks as his friends depart.

"But next time," Penny says from the door, "send a goddamn memo if you're going to disappear, alright?"

That evening, Ed sees an elderly Bonded Pair on his walk home.

They are strolling through Athena Temple Gardens and the aura is noticeable even without the awed glances of strangers around them. Ed finds himself stopping in the street and watching like the rest of the gawping passers-by as if he too is unaccustomed to the sight.

Ed has been the primary Tester in the UK for twelve years but he doesn't recognise this Pair. They must have been Bonded in excess of forty years, he assumes, going by their complete silence and perfect coordination. Ed has worked with newly Bonded Pairs for so long that it's customary for him to see them in their experimental state, when they are still testing their boundaries and in the midst of merging their lives together. After about a year, they tend to be comfortably Bonded, after ten years, they usually speak in synchronised speech, but after thirty, their communication is mostly silent, having reached full understanding of each other, just like that Pair he had observed at a Feast as a child.

This Pair walk without any awareness of what is around them, completely in their own minds. No pain, no suffering, nothing but each other's love. It's truly remarkable.

He watches until they turn a corner out of sight and Ed snaps back to himself. His mind has been so busy lately – full of questions he hadn't dared ask himself – but at the sight of a Pair, he feels as enchanted, as peaceful, as he did when he was a child.

That night he doesn't need to dream to remember because he returns to the memory by choice. He lies in bed and closes his eyes. He remembers walking the field – path, gloves, lake – but this time, he doesn't feel the cold seeping into his bones, he doesn't feel the dread building at what is to come; instead, he feels at peace, as if this were all meant to be. This time it is not a shadow on the horizon that approaches, but a person, a real person, who was about to make someone's life complete. The light doesn't blind him anymore. He can see the way Simon's eyes turn wide with wonder and the way the wrinkles around his eyes seem to dissipate; old worries smoothed away with a single touch. Ed basks in the glow, in the beauty of the miracle, feeling utterly at peace, and it's not until he opens his eyes to his own reality that he realises that he is smiling.

Ed asks Rebecca to meet him that weekend and she's gracious enough to accept. They meet in Athena Gardens despite the bitter January cold, as if the forthcoming conversation feels too big to be contained between four walls.

He sits on the bench they agreed on, the one beside the bandstand and the park where he'd first met Lizzie, and waits. It's a frosty day, the landscape tinted white, and there's the promise of snow in the air. He's wrapped up warm; thick parka, university scarf, fingerless gloves and the woollen hat that Rebecca had knitted him for Solstice. He sees that she's similarly dressed when she approaches, wearing at least one jumper beneath her worn raincoat. They'd been so occupied worrying over Lizzie's wellbeing in the five minutes they'd seen each other a few days ago that he hadn't had the chance to really take her in. He missed her.

He stands to his feet but then pauses, no longer knowing what greeting is appropriate. They'd been cautiously polite under the watchful eye of the teachers when they'd met at school and the time before that was the fateful kiss.

And so they hover, in this undefined space, and awkwardly exchange greetings before sitting down on the frozen wooden bench with as much space between them as it allows.

"Thank you for meeting me," Ed begins. "I apologise it took so much time."

Rebecca smiles softly and he wonders what's so funny before she reminds him of her support group's motto, *"Time is what you make it. It took as long as it took. If you could have been here sooner, you would have."*

He nods, still amazed at her patience and understanding, even after all this time.

"I only wish you had told me that's what you were doing. You said you had to think. I didn't realise you meant about all of it. I thought we were on the same page. But, we weren't were we? When I kissed you, you realised that we weren't."

Ed swallows, and nods. "I panicked. I'm sorry. I shouldn't have run. It's just that... I didn't know which way was up. I still don't think I even understand why you were crying that day. You never said, and I was too afraid to ask."

Rebecca shakes her head with a wince, as if disappointed with herself. "Because I saw how much you loved Lizzie, how much she loved you, and I wanted it so much – that big family picture; for her to have a father again – that it hurt to see it and know that it wouldn't last. I think I knew, on some level, that your hesitance ran deeper than I could go; that you'd eventually leave. I didn't understand what it was, but I felt it. And I did the only thing I could think to do to make you stay. I thought, if you loved me too, if I offered you the life that you nearly had with Simon – a family – then maybe you would stay. So, I kissed you."

He nods. That makes sense and he doesn't blame her for it in the slightest.

She looks away, over to the empty roundabout where a few stray leaves have been blown. "I wasn't thinking straight," she continues. "It was selfish. And I ended up pushing you away, making you leave in the exact way I was so afraid you'd do. But I just…" her eyes are closed, and if he's not mistaken, he thinks he sees a tear fall down the cheek furthest from him. "I wanted to be selfish, for once, I just… wanted."

There's an admission there between the lines that both of them are too afraid to draw attention to.

"Thank you, for explaining," he says, and barely resists bridging the distance between them to comfort her. "I think if anyone's entitled to give into temptation now and then, it's you. But you didn't push me away. Even the kiss, it wasn't… unwelcome, exactly, it just… complicated matters. I'm sorry if you've been blaming yourself this whole time. I ought to have stayed. To have told you at least that much. But I'm a coward, and it's always easier to run than to stay."

"You're not running now though."

His mouth twists somewhere between a smile and a wince. "Depends on your definition."

Rebecca takes a deep breath beside him, preparing herself no doubt for the rejection that's to come. He doesn't want her to get the wrong idea so before he can think better of it he's reaching across and placing his hand atop hers.

Her eyes snap to his; expectant, hopeful.

"I like you, I like Lizzie, I like being part of this family. I want to be involved in your lives, if you'll let me, but I also…" he breaks off with a shake of his head. He must have gone over the words a hundred times but now they all leave him and he has no idea where to start. "I think Witnessing was so tied to losing my husband that for a long time, I couldn't see past it – all there was in that memory was my own pain – but now I remember, and I can see what everyone else sees. I realise that underneath all that pain, that I felt *jealous*; that I wanted it for myself. Because, Rebecca," he says earnestly with a wondrous sigh, "it was the most *extraordinary* thing. It was like waking up in the middle of the night to a thunderstorm, or walking through a deserted city at sunrise, or standing on the edge of a cliff and seeing nothing but water as far as the eye can see. The world felt *tangible*, but dreamlike, like you've stepped out from yourself to see the world as it truly is. And I wondered, if Bonding looks like that from the outside then what must it be like on the inside? It must be the most magnificent thing. And I feel like I would be doing a disservice to myself if I didn't at least try to have that."

She looks at him with watery eyes and an unsure smile, but with understanding. "You want to Search."

Ed nods earnestly, placing another hand between them. "I want to Search."

She nods, but there's defeat in her eyes; an expression he's far too sick of seeing.

"But," he says, bolstered by the way she looks straight back up to him, "I don't want to lose my family." *You are my family*, goes unspoken, but he knows that she hears it regardless. "And I want us to try and think of a way to make that possible. I don't want be a Waiter – I won't Settle with you while still looking; to create the possibility that I leave you so suddenly, without no one, like Simon did to me – but I also don't want to give this up entirely. If there's a way to balance both my life here and my Search that won't hurt you, then I will do it, but I also understand if it's not what you want. It must be hard for you to think of Searching at all, yet alone be involved with someone who actively wants that. If we can't resolve this then I understand, but I desperately want to try."

He's practically shaking after his declaration and does his best to focus on the warmth of their joined hands and on the fact that she has yet to pull away.

He doesn't know how much time passes but it feels like an eternity as he holds his breath waiting for her response.

Eventually, she looks back to him, determined in a way that reminds him so much of her daughter. "I want to try."

"Okay," he says, a cautious smile spreading across his face. He squeezes the hand between his. "Okay."

They stay on that bench for hours working out the details; long enough that the snow begins to fall and cling to Rebecca's loose hair.

"I think I want to do Distance Searching," Ed admits. "Meet as many people as I can. But it doesn't have to be for long, or even right away. I can start small. I'll do the Circles in London. Then maybe weekends away in other cities."

"So how would that work if you got a placement abroad?"

"I'd take short placements. Make sure they have holidays. Come back every Solstice, write to Lizzie every birthday, call you every time I'm the other side of the globe wondering what on earth I'm doing."

She laughs. "I can do that."

"Keep me grounded," he says. My anchor. My home.

"And if you actually do Bond?" she asks.

"Come on, Rebecca, you know the odds –"

"I know them," she says curtly. "And yet we've both been affected by them. I need to know you have a plan for if it happens."

He sighs deeply. "I suppose that depends. Would you be able to stand the sight of me?"

"I don't know," she whispers, in what sounds like a moment of raw honesty. She could be referring to Dissonance, or her own personal feelings, or, more likely, both. "I like to believe I could."

"Good. Because I like to believe that we'd stay, that my Pair wouldn't cut you out of my life entirely. That's been known to happen after all."

"Are you *sure* you're okay with this?" Ed urges. "I know you and Lizzie don't have much in the way of support right now, and if you need me here, I'll stay."

Rebecca smiles wryly. "I would never ask you to do that. We're okay, I promise. And I know from experience that if your heart is telling you to do something, you have to listen to it, however painful it may be. It wasn't an easy decision for us to leave Petersville for Lizzie but we did it because we felt it was the right thing to do. I would never have forgiven myself if we stayed there, squandered the chance Lizzie had to explore, to be herself, and I imagine, that you will never forgive yourself if you don't give yourself the opportunity to Search."

"So that's a yes?"

She nudges him playfully. "Yes, it's a yes. I support you in this, wholeheartedly."

He rests his head against hers, presses a kiss to her temple, so full of gratitude that it's truly overwhelming.

They walk home – and as they've decided, now also *his* home – hand in hand, just as the Temple empties after the evening service. They walk down the path towards the masses, Ed standing firmly between Rebecca and the worshippers, and as he protects her, he reaches out for every single one of the passing strangers, giddy with the thought that any of them could be the *one*. The potential sets a flicker of hope stirring in his chest.

Penny and Kevin get married on a beautiful afternoon in early Spring, a day with clear blue skies and a breeze that feels warmer than any in recent memory. Ed leaves the cab and holds the door open for his companions.

"Wow," Lizzie says as soon as she gets a glimpse of the Community Temple. And then, "Is that Apollo?"

Ed ought to have seen this coming. Lizzie's recent obsession is Hellenic gods, brought on by the need to subvert the poetic stereotypes that she's been shackled with. She's been having great fun playing with the reader's expectations, by, for example, writing about the gods' mundanities rather than their glory.

Rebecca sighs good-naturedly as she trails after her daughter who's already talking a thousand miles per hour about Apollo's various exploits. He leaves them to it while he enters the Temple to find Jasmine and discover the state of affairs. Kevin seemed okay last night at the stag party but Ed's not taking any chances.

He knocks on the door to the groom's chambers but it's wrenched open before he can so much as rap his knuckles against the wood.

"Ed!" He's swept into a one-armed hug by the groom. "I'm so glad you're here."

"Where else would I be?"

The question goes unanswered as Kevin thrusts two different bow ties at him. "Jasmine says one of these is more black than the other but I've been staring at them for five minutes and I honestly don't see the difference."

Ed sighs tiredly and holds them up to the light. "It's this one," he says, passing the right one back to him. "It's midnight, not coal."

Kevin looks at him in awe, and then down at the bow tie, and then back to Ed. "Did I mention how glad I am that you're here?"

Ed chuckles. "You did."

Penny is beautiful in her gown and Kevin honestly looks like he stops breathing when he first sees her, until she makes her way down the aisle of the cella towards him and he breaks into the widest grin that Ed's ever seen. Ed glances at Lizzie beside him and sees that she's watching as if enchanted, eyes wide and curious. Both the Brightons are holding up considerably well under the circumstances; it helps that Rebecca already knew a number of the attendees, including Chris, and that her black band is visible enough on her bare arm that no one mistakenly reaches for her in Recognition. As for Lizzie, she seems to be too excited to let the new experience faze her. She's never been to a wedding before, and never been in a Temple for so long, nor, he imagines, been treated to a Hellenic feast before. The way her eyes bulge when the food is served is almost comical.

Ed gently brushes a kiss against Rebecca's knuckles as he rises to give the Best Man's speech. It's been a couple of months since they made their arrangement and it's going well; they've built an affectionate friendship, a stable household for Lizzie, and he gets to travel – gets to Search – and then come back home to them. It's pretty ideal, and when he sees Rebecca's sad smile from time to time, he's learnt the ways to soothe away the furrow on her brow.

"Let me start," he says to the crowded Temple, "by emphasising how important a changed mind can be."

He tells the story of Kevin giving up Searching, makes the jab that perhaps he just transferred the urge to Ed, and how proud he is that both of them had the conviction to know what they wanted, "because sometimes it's not easy to admit to love."

His eyes fall to Rebecca as he says this; words he has yet spoken, afraid of their misinterpretation, but that he aches for her to hear nonetheless.

"It takes courage to question what you think you know," he says with a nod to Lizzie. "To question our beliefs, to look inside ourselves and recognise that the unknown isn't always something to be afraid of – that it might actually hold possibilities more exciting and more fulfilling than we could ever imagine…" A tension hangs between the three of them; imperceptible; time stretched thin again, full of said possibilities. He looks away, back to his friends, and to the dozens of people here to support them. "Penny and Kevin are here today because they made the difficult decision to look inwards and make the conscious effort to change. May we forever strive to do the same." He raises his glass, "To the happy couple!"

"To the happy couple!"

July 1945
Paterson, New Jersey

Monsieur Jack Kerouac:

I am sorry that we could not rescue a final meeting from our departure. I'm writing in the hope of reaching you before your voyage.

I understand that you were openly conscious that we were not the same *comme amis*. I have known it, and respected this change, in a way. But perhaps I should explain, for I have felt myself mostly responsible for it. We are of different kinds, as you have said, and I acknowledge it more fully now than before, because at one time I was fearful of this difference, perhaps ashamed of it. But when I Bond, I do not wish to escape to myself, I wish to escape <u>from</u> myself. I can't stand my own mind. I wish to obliterate my consciousness and my knowledge of independent existence. I am no child of nature, I am ugly and imperfect to myself, and I cannot through poetry or romantic visions exalt myself to such glory. Who I am? Who do I seek?

Mon cher, if I overreach for my missing soul, then it is only because I crave their healing touch so much. Do we not all wish to be perfect? Complete? There are those towns that tell their occupants nothing of their lost soul. Oh I wish I was given such merciful ignorance. I am sick of this damned life! Always searching, never to find.

Well, these last years have been the nearest to fulfilment of my earthly desires, at least, and I thank you for the gift. You were right, I suppose, in keeping your distance. I was too intent on self-fulfilment. I overtaxed my own patience even more than I did yours, possibly. I wonder if you comprehend the meanings which I can't explain. At any rate, if you are able to understand me, I ask your tolerance; if not, I plead for your forgiveness.

When we meet again, I promise you that we will meet again as brothers in comedy, a tragedy, what you will, but brothers. Until then, write me a story, my angel. Let us pass the time while we wait for our lost souls to arrive.

Allen.

Lizzie & Rewan

"We two, how long we were fool'd... We have circled and circled till we have arrived home again, we two,"

- Walt Whitman

It is a warm April evening and Elizabeth Brighton is still studying in the university library. She hunches over the desk in her woollen dress and long cardigan, hair tied back loosely with an elastic band, tapping the biro poised between her bitten fingernails against the spread of a book in a futile attempt to stay focused. She keeps circling back to the premise of her doctoral research; the line in one of Allen Ginsberg's letters, *My fantasies and phrases have gotten so lovingly mixed up in yours, Jack.* It's what made Lizzie realise that the Beat Generation could only be studied in relation to each other. Ginsberg is the nucleus of her research and although his work can stand alone, it is by recognising shared language and mythology that further meanings can be uncovered.

She is checking a reference to Biblical mythology when a line comes unbidden to her: *Consider, you who pursue me, whether I may not in unknown ways be looking upon you...* it is Walt Whitman; one of Ginsberg's major influences.

Everything seems connected. Everything keeps circling. (*A Vision*, Yeats.) Other people's words keep building in her mind until she is deafened by it.

"Ah!" Lizzie exclaims as her mobile phone rings obnoxiously loud in the quiet library.

She clamours for the phone, heart beating wildly in her chest as she searches the stacks for angry librarians. She forgot to turn her phone back to silent after the telephone interview earlier that day and doesn't want to face the wrath of the librarians for her mistake. Thankfully, this floor of the library still seems deserted. She looks down at the screen and immediately relaxes at the name on the screen.

"Hey, Ed," she greets, cradling the phone under her chin as she continues chasing a reference on the laptop screen in front of her.

"Hey," he greets, "I'm not disturbing you, am I?"

"No, I was just about to head home," she lies smoothly. "What's up?"

"Home? Where are you? Rebecca's?"

"No, gods no, if I visit Mum tonight she won't let me leave again – you know how she gets – I'm just finishing up some work at uni then I'll head back to mine, get some takeaway or something –"

"Oh," he says. "But it's Monday. I thought you said the results were tonight."

Lizzie's fingers pause on the keyboard in front of her as she diverts her entire attention into sounding as casual as possible when she answers, "Yeah, they are. But I won't hear for a while yet. Look," she says, before Ed can jump in and insist that she spend the evening with company, "this must be costing you a fortune calling like this from abroad. Why don't I message you when I know the results?"

Ed sighs and even through the static across the Atlantic, Lizzie recognises it as the type of sigh that means he's weighing up if it's worth arguing with her or not.

"Fine," he finally acquiesces. "But promise me you won't work yourself into a state over this. Whatever the result, know that I'm proud of you for getting this far, okay?"

Lizzie shakes her head with a smile. "You're such a sap," she says because she daren't say anything serious and risk breaking her facade of indifference. "I'll message you tonight. Using Wi-Fi. Like anyone with a shred of common sense would do when they're calling long distance," she can't help but tease. "Good luck at the conference."

Lizzie pockets her phone and closes her laptop. Now that Ed has reminded her of the real life events she was trying her utmost to ignore there is no hope in Ginsberg's voice returning to her. She packs up her books and shoulders her bag and makes her way out of the library.

Ed's probably right in saying that she shouldn't be alone tonight but she'd feel suffocated under the watchful eyes of her mother, and while Ed's still in Canada, she doesn't have much more of a choice unless she cajoles her supervisor or her agent into spending time with her, which is laughably pathetic.

It's not that she *wants* to be in this situation either. She's always aspired to have plenty of people in her life, of having a family, it just... hasn't happened. Somehow she can never seem to get people to stay.

She remembers the first time she felt this way; she was at nursery school and they were asked to draw a picture of their family and friends. Lizzie had slaved over a picture of her mother but when she looked up, she noticed that everyone else had a whole array of people on their paper. She looked back to her drawing, saw the expanse of white space and suddenly felt the desperate need to fill it. The feeling has never left her since.

Instead, she clings to her research and to her poetry as if one day she will find enough words to fill the void.

The streets of London are unusually busy for a weekday evening as she walks back from the chippy. She places her headphones over her long hair; a tool for both blocking out the world and for avoiding unnecessary social interaction, and listens to the cheeriest song she can find on her MP3 player. She tries, as usual, to cross the street when people approach but sometimes there's no avoiding it and she has to allow strangers to touch for Recognition. It's a social necessity that has always made her uncomfortable but more from the fact it requires touching strangers rather than because she might Bond.

She can't imagine being Bonded, truthfully. The complications alone terrify her; the potential of triggering an episode of Dissonance or Depression in her mum would be enough but she also just can't imagine being Bonded with someone equally as dysfunctional as her. Ed says that's how it works, through similar brainwaves or something. Her head is already busy enough, jumping between a hundred different open threads on a simple walk home, that she can't imagine the presence of a whole other person forced upon her.

Lizzie is lost in her thoughts as she walks the familiar path from the takeaway to her flat. She almost makes it home without incident until she emerges from the staircase on the fifth floor to find her neighbour blocking her path.

Cat Lady is outside her front door, leaning against the brick wall and exhaling smoke into the already polluted city. She is effectively blocking half of the fifth floor external passageway. Lizzie pauses and gauges if it is possible to squeeze past her and into the comfort of her own house, three doors down, but Lizzie isn't exactly small herself.

Cat Lady turns towards her with glazed eyes. Lizzie curses the rustling of the plastic bag in the breeze for giving her away. They hold their ground like an old fashioned gun draw before they both seem to remember that they are British. Reluctantly Lizzie pulls her headphones away from what was quite a rousing chorus and says, "Good evening. Nice night, isn't it?"

Cat Lady nods but says nothing. Her eyes have gained clarity and stay trained on Lizzie as she takes another drag of her cigarette. Lizzie inches closer, hoping to slip past before the awkwardness turns into conversation.

Truthfully, Cat Lady is what Lizzie fears her mum is becoming when Ed is away: alone, reclusive, slowly turning mad with loneliness. Her mum would probably be just fine if she had ever actually succeeded in making connections outside their tiny little family, but she *hasn't*, and so when Ed is away and Lizzie is busy, she just sits there... all alone. Lizzie recognises that she is also dangerously close to taking the same path if she keeps failing to source some permanent attachments of her own. Cat Lady smells of urine and cheap smokes; her greying hair tangled like furballs. Lizzie briefly entertains a bizarre Kafka-esque narrative where Cat Lady is slowly turning into one of her cats, no longer even capable of speech, and one day Lizzie would notice that she hadn't seen her in a while and open her neighbour's door to find four dead cats inside instead of three.

Lizzie is surprised, therefore, when Cat Lady speaks quite clearly and matter-of-factly: "You're Elizabeth Brighton."

Lizzie stops her approach. "Er, yes, I am."

There is always a concern nowadays that people will recognise her, not just as a semi-permanent feature at one of London's arts universities, but increasingly as a poet in her own right. She wouldn't have pegged Cat Lady from the Council Estate as a fan of the Arts though. Cat Lady pauses, conducting a nod-stare-smoke routine. Lizzie twists the handles of the plastic bag in her hands.

"Anyway, I gotta –" Lizzie says, holding up the takeaway as an explanation.

Cat Lady nods but doesn't make a move to allow her to pass. In fact, now that Cat Lady is turned towards her, she takes up even more of the passageway. "Saw your name in the paper."

"Right." Of course she did, and probably not in the best light. The papers are, by and large, owned by the Elite, who resent someone like her meddling in divine arts when it should be reserved for someone like their poster boy, Rewan Pentaghast. Lizzie should probably say something more but all she can think about is how her dinner is getting cold. She fights the urge to push her way through to the safety of her home. She forces herself to remain calm and polite as she shuffles from foot to foot, clutching at the key in the pocket of her jumper-dress. "So, I should –"

"I've never met a poet."

Cat Lady sounds judgemental and Lizzie wonders just what exactly it said in that paper she read.

"Right. Well, now you have. Hello." Lizzie waves. She read someone do that in a romance novel before, but in real life, it just feels ridiculous.

"I thought it was tonight."

"I'm sorry, what was tonight?"

"The Smitherson Prize."

Lizzie's breath catches, not having dared say the words out loud herself. Her fingers clench around the handles of the plastic bag so tightly that she can feel four crescent shapes being dug into her palm. It's a full moon tonight, she thinks as an aside, Rewan Pentaghast is probably sitting in his penthouse writing about the moon goddess as Lizzie hovers here on this housing block passageway, staving off a panic attack, caught between a bag of congealing grease and a lady who named her cats after hobbits.

"Yes, the results are announced tonight," Lizzie says, "but the presentation isn't until the weekend. Please excuse me, I must –"

"I should let you go," Cat Lady says but contradicts her statement by not moving a goddamned inch. "I didn't realise that Pentaghast fellow was so handsome but they had a picture in the paper. Favourite to win, isn't he?"

Lizzie forces her clenched fist to relax but her facial expression is rather more difficult to control. Lizzie speaks carefully, attempting to banish all emotion from her voice, "So I hear."

Cat Lady nods and finally breaks her gaze to stub the cigarette out on the low brick wall. "Such a handsome fellow," she repeats "Any chance he'll be coming round this way?"

Lizzie closes her eyes and bites out, "Not bloody likely, no."

This has all become quite enough. Lizzie walks forward with as much confidence as she can muster and barges past Cat Lady with a perfunctory, "Excuse me please."

Lizzie doesn't look back as she makes it to her doorway, fumbles with the keys, and then, finally, closes the door behind her. She dumps the takeaway bag on the kitchen table and takes the vodka bottle from the top of the fridge. Only the dregs remain. She tilts the glass bottle upwards and drinks it in one gulp, closing her eyes at the comforting warmth that instantly spreads throughout. She focuses on her breathing just like Ed taught her until the panic has receded.

The Smitherson may be the most prestigious award she's been nominated for to date but it makes no difference; if the Elite are making the decision then she isn't going to win. The nomination was a token acknowledgment of her existence but the Board could never actually award it to her without starting a debate about 'traditional values' that the Arts world is definitely not ready to have.

Her collection *StillBeat* is a textual intervention of the timeless work of the Beat Generation and its continued relevance to human experience, particularly examining the darker side of Searching; the rejection of other love and the deep loneliness that the act can instil. The Board will definitely not consider it as 'worthy' as the other submissions, all of whom are written by known Temple Poets, including the new Poet Oracle, Rewan Pentaghast, whose collection *Eternity* is fourteen sonnets inspired by his parents' Bond.

Eternity is utterly unoriginal in Lizzie's mind but the Board will still fawn over it if the last handful of awards this season are anything to go by. Pentaghast is one of them after all. If his status as a child of Pair didn't confirm it, then the acceptance of Poet Oracle certainly did. The Temples now have a firm hold over him for the next ten years, which means she can expect to see uninspired collection after uninspired collection winning out over her own work for the foreseeable future.

It irks her. The Elite act like the Arts wouldn't exist without them facilitating it. They don't much like that Lizzie is still stubbornly pursuing it without their approval, and without Temple training, loudly and publicly enough to cause them trouble too. This is why she fell in love with Ginsberg and the Beat Generation in the first place, because their refusal to write like they were told to write had started a whole movement; a movement that pressured the publishing industry to change. They had changed so much but still couldn't penetrate the upper circles of the Elite. Ginsberg's honest words about the human experience were not deemed 'worthy' enough by the Temples to be considered for the many awards that the Elite covet, and now, sixty years later, nothing had changed; her poetry can be printed, can become known and respected in certain circles, but it will never be considered highbrow enough to get recognition from the Arts world at large. It wouldn't bother her except that the awards she's excluded from are the only way to make a decent living as a poet. If she won the Smitherson, for instance, she wouldn't have to think about bills for a whole year, especially considering the worldwide attention it would bring to her work. The point is though, that she won't, not while Pairs and Priests are in charge of the decision.

She pulls her mobile phone out from her pocket. Carol, her agent, said she would call with the news before eight. There's still over an hour to go before then. She's going to lose, she knows this, but it doesn't mean that she doesn't want desperately to win.

Lizzie sighs and switches on the television to a sitcom loud enough to drown out everything else. She sits in front of the syndicated laughter, picking at her lukewarm dinner, wishing with every minute that she had something more to drink.

*

The grounds of Athena Temple are quiet this evening. Rewan Pentaghast walks along the gravel path of the Prayer Garden until he stands before Apollo's Shrine. He breathes in the familiar, comforting scent of the tall pine trees that line the garden, separating it from the rest of the grounds. There is a full moon gaining brightness with the waning sunlight and it causes the grass to take on an ethereal aura.

Unlike the Athena Temple itself that holds regular services and celebrations, Apollo's Shrine can perhaps only accommodate three men width-ways, intended for private prayer and contemplation.

Rewan climbs the three stone steps of the Shrine and jumps in surprise when a large figure emerges from the shadows. When the light falls across the jovial face of Priest Helo however, Rewan immediately calms.

The Priest smiles as he brushes dirt from his robes. He must have been kneeling in prayer. He speaks softly, with remnants of his Irish heritage lilting his words, "My apologies, Rewan, I didn't mean to startle you."

"Priest Helo," he greets. "It's late. I didn't expect you to still be here."

"Not usually, but Apollonia is this Sunday and I've been preparing," Priest Helo explains. "Thank you again for offering a poem for the occasion. Are you still able to attend in person? I understand it's the day after –"

"It shouldn't be a problem," Rewan interrupts.

Priest Helo looks taken aback by his unusual abruptness. It's thrown their exchange off-kilter. Rewan sways slightly on the spot, unsure how to remedy the situation.

"I'll leave you in peace then, shall I?" Priest Helo says, indicating the Shrine around them.

Rewan nods his thanks, but doesn't trust himself to speak again. He watches the Priest disappear into the encroaching night.

It's darker in the Shrine, cast with shadows, but Rewan came prepared. He pulls a tealight from his pocket and attempts to brush away any dirt on the altar before placing the solitary candle below Apollo and lighting it with a match. It catches. The flame flickers in the draught that cuts across the open walls either side of him; it causes the shadows to stretch across the pillars of the Shrine and onto the grass outside.

He hitches his tailored trousers to kneel on the stone surface. He braces himself on his hands and touches his head to the floor, causing his dark curls to part and fall over his face. He breathes slowly a couple of times, and then he rises, having collected his thoughts. His knees already ache against the cold stone.

He closes his eyes and begins the traditional recital, "Almighty Zeus," Rewan's deep voice is magnified by the stone then immediately taken by the wind. "Fair ruler and father of all, hear my prayer," he continues. "Giver of Souls, keep me patient in my Searching. I pray that you take pity and lead me to the lost one to bind our souls once more."

Rewan takes a moment to gather his thoughts before adding a personal prayer, "I thank the Muses for aiding me in my creative path. I am assured that you will have chosen a just winner tonight, but I ask that, win or lose, your spirits will guide me and keep me true."

He wants to say more. The anxiety over tonight's promised announcement is clawing at his throat, but the words will not come, because for the first time, he doubts that he will win. He cannot explain why tonight is different. He has been rewarded with many similar prestigious awards, and at twenty-four he has already been bestowed the honour of Poet Oracle – the youngest ever to be granted the national Arts post – and so he should have no reason to believe that the Smitherson won't also be awarded to him but for some reason… he doubts it, and he is tremendously afraid of what will happen if his doubts come to fruition. He does not pray for success; only that whatever happens, the gods stay beside him.

Rewan opens his eyes to see the candle burning strong in front of him where before it had been flickering. Perhaps the gods have heard his prayer.

He stands, brushing the dust from his trousers, and blows out the candle. He blinks, adjusting to the darkness as he leaves the shadow of the Shrine. He can feel the warm tealight cooling, changing states in his palm, as he walks back home under the watchful gaze of Artemis and her full moon.

The apartment seems even larger and lonelier than the state in which he'd left it. Rewan turns on the light to the main room and hears the pleasant clicking of his brogues across the wooden floor before he hangs up his keys and toes off his shoes. He pads across the large room to switch on the music player before the silence can encroach, choosing some soothing jazz on a low volume. He takes his time selecting a bottle of red wine from the rack. Then he pulls down a wine glass, briefly wondering if the other eleven have ever been used, and retreats to his favourite armchair, placing the wine and glass beside him. He sinks into the comfort of the green velvet chair and takes a refreshing sip of wine. For a moment, he can relax, but then he opens his eyes to see his mobile phone sitting on the sofa opposite and it taunts him in its silence. It is half past seven. His agent, Hector, said he would call with news before eight.

After five minutes of this torture, Rewan leaves his wine, turns off the music, and makes his way to the black grand piano, leaving the silent phone far behind. The window is still open beside the piano and the faint chatter and scent of spices from the Michelin starred restaurant opposite drift into the stillness of the apartment. He is appeased by the sight of the city lights reflected in the gloss of the piano as he sits and tinkers with the keys.

He could lose himself like this. His black clothes merge with the soft edges of the night into nothingness. He imagines himself as the piano keys: white face, black hair, white hands, black sleeves, contrasting; just as the structured beauty of music does to his chaotic state of mind.

Moonlight Sonata is rote by this point and comforting in its familiarity. He feels every note in its creation through the sinking of fingers as they push down keys and in the shifting of feet on pedals. He closes his eyes as the rising base notes meet the melody; the left hand dancing towards the right but never quite meeting. He wonders if he has ever been so close to his soulmate; if they keep crossing paths at the wrong moment, always too far away to touch.

He spends much of his time daydreaming about what it will be like; loving someone with the knowledge that they will never leave you. The perfect person always by your side; able to sense when you need comfort and give it straight to your heart. To become one soul, communicating mostly through emotions, with no secrets or misunderstandings between you. Together, for eternity, never to be abandoned. It's not just the happily ever after that Rewan craves, it's the divine act of Bonding itself. His parents brushed hands at a classical concert when they Bonded. They said it was like seeing every corner of the universe; a moment in which everything was connected. Rewan cannot wait to have this perfect moment for himself, and he has faith that Zeus will give it to him as long as he remains true. His soulmate could be anyone; man or woman, older or younger, British or the other side of the world. He knows that the outside won't matter at all when they share a soul, but when he closes his eyes and imagines the life-changing moment, he always pictures a woman of great intelligence and wit, their eyes locked to each other as they see the universe together.

An incorrect note cuts across his fantasy. His fingers jump away from the keys. He has not been concentrating.

If Rewan has to stand in his parents' townhouse in two hours' time, surrounded by the judgemental ranks of the Elite, having lost the prize, it will be a humiliation to the family. His parents own the biggest media conglomerate in the country; they're one of the most prominent and respected Souls around, a cornerstone of the Elite, but even their newspapers may not be able to spin a story able to cover the embarrassment of their son, Poet Oracle, losing such an important competition.

He focuses back on the music and plays the familiar piece in the dark to an audience of potted plants until it is no longer distraction enough. He lifts his fingers from the keys and looks back to the inactive phone. The silence suddenly seems vast. Not even the sounds of the street below can penetrate the force field he has built around himself and the weight of the impending news. It is seven forty-five. He thinks, perhaps, he ought to pour himself another glass of wine.

*

Lizzie tells herself not to get wound up but it's the only way her body knows how to cope with the anxiety. She fidgets and she paces and so far she's managed to stave off a panic attack but with every second that the phone remains silent, it becomes a little harder to ignore the pounding of her heart.

When the call finally comes, it sends her into such a panic that she just stares at the phone dumbly for a good few seconds until her brain kicks in with instructions on how to answer it.

Lizzie mutes the television and accepts the call.

What greets her is a high-pitched screech. And, then, between the excited squeaking, Lizzie makes out the words: "You won, you won, *you won!*"

Lizzie actually drops the phone in shock, like a scripted move from the sitcom still mutely playing out. She wipes her hands slick with sweat on her woollen dress and picks up the phone again, shaking –

"– did you hear me?" Carol asks.

"I heard you," she replies numbly, though, she's not actually sure if she believes it. "I... won?" The words don't sound right in her mouth. Slow to form; heavy, and muddled. She tries again, "I actually... won?" There's a bubble of hope blooming in her chest but she can't let herself give into it; things don't ever work out like this. "But, the Oracle shouldn't he have...?"

Carol isn't hearing her concerns; she's still relaying the same news with every variation of words possible. Winning the Smitherson Prize means a lot of money, world-wide recognition, and almost certainly a steep increase of sales. It means that this time next month, Lizzie might be able to buy a dinner fancier than the chippy.

Carol's compliments start to filter through the noise, about how much the board loved the work, and Lizzie can't help the elation bubbling up through her. Her face splits into a grin so wide she has to stuff her fist inside her mouth so she doesn't make involuntary squeaking noises.

Lizzie throws the phone aside as soon as Carol hangs up and jumps up and down in excitement, finally letting the sounds of joy escape her lips to fill the empty apartment up with her happiness. "I won," she says to herself again. It's starting to feel real; the words solidifying. "I actually won."

Once she's expended her energy, she falls back down onto her sofa with a grin, dreamingly staring up at the mouldy ceiling.

She's still blissfully zoned out when the phone rings again. She doesn't even need to look at the caller recognition to know it's her mum.

"Well?"

Lizzie can barely keep the smile off her face as she answers, "Your daughter is a Smitherson Prize Winning poet."

Her mum starts squeaking and rambling in a way Lizzie recognises as a good thing. Lizzie doesn't catch a word, too busy laughing with the sheer joy of it. She manages to hang up eventually, with the promise to visit tomorrow to celebrate. She then sends a message to Ed, knowing he'll call back as soon as he gets a spare moment at the conference. She grins the entire time, imagining his reaction. He'd always been so supportive of her poetry and knows there's not going to be a single person at the International Bonding Centre that hasn't heard about her success by morning.

It's as she's putting the phone back on the table that the bubble finally breaks, when she realises that those are the only people she has to tell. Her heart sinks with loneliness. There are three people in this world that care, and she's grateful for each of them, but there's still a big yearning space to fill.

*

Rewan is back in his favourite armchair and has drunk a good half bottle of wine when his home phone finally rings at exactly eight-oh-three. He stares at Hector's name flashing on the screen and carefully puts down his glass on the coffee table.

The phone is heavy in his hand as he answers it, "Hello?"

He knows from the second of silence on the other end that it is not good news.

"Mate, it's Hec. I'll cut straight to it, shall I? You got second. Brighton won."

Rewan feels his heart shrink with every other muscle in his body as it retreats.

He chokes out, "Brighton? Elizabeth Brighton?"

He knew if he lost, it would be to her. He thought the nomination was a fluke at first because he hadn't heard of her, so he went out and bought everything she'd ever published, and… she was good. So good that he wondered why on earth he hadn't heard of her – that is, until he read her bio and understood exactly why. He knows it should take away the sting of losing, a little, knowing that at least he lost to someone like her, someone who is completely original, and in need of recognition. But it still hurts; the failure raw and biting.

"Yeah that's the one, the Outlie girl with her collection 'bout the Beat Gen. Panel were totally gaga for the research from the sounds of it, which I guess yours... Well, anyways, the decision is complete kronos. The Elite are gonna shit themselves when they find out. They *loved* you, don't doubt it for a sec Rew, I'll send you the statement soon as poss but they definitely said it was 'heartfelt' and 'strong' and –"

"What did they say about *StillBeat*?"

"Brighton's collection? Eh, who knows. 'Refreshing,' I think? 'Innovative.' Y'know, the kinda talk that means they got a boner for the brains –"

Rewan pulls a grimace. Hector constantly walks the fine line between vulgar and humorous and often loses.

"– but they're too emotionally constipated to deal with your *Eternity*. Fucking academics. Shoulda been judged by poets, not professors. It's an Elite award after all, don't know what they were thinking with the reshuffle. Different panel, mate, and you woulda won."

Rewan shakes his head. "There's nothing to be done."

Hector huffs and continues ranting but Rewan feels a weight lift from his shoulders. It is finally as empty inside his head as the apartment. He feels hollowed out, but peaceful, now that he knows the result. The gods have chosen a worthy winner, but his parents… they will not see that at all. Neither will the Elite as a whole.

"You still got the presentation ceremony next weekend," Hector says. "Try to write a good acceptance speech for second place, yeah? Don't sound bitter or privileged or condescending –"

"When have I ever –?"

"The Reed-Whittal speech, Rew."

Rewan cringes at the memory, "Oh."

"And remember to congratulate Brighton and all. Send it to me by Thursday so we can make any changes. Not taking a date, I assume?"

"Not unless I Bond over the next week, no."

Hector chuckles. It wasn't meant to be funny but Hector, a polysettler with two partners and a serious girlfriend, scoffs at Rewan's celibacy while he patiently Searches for his soulmate. Children of the Elite are expected to be Dedicated Searchers, to expand their Search abroad, and to do anything they can to stay 'pure'. It suits Rewan just fine but he knows that others in his position struggle to meet these expectations – his acquaintance, Arcadius, for instance, cannot abide by the Elite's rules; he refuses to follow the expected path and his reputation has suffered dearly for it. Losing a poetry competition seems trivial compared to the many 'indiscretions' Arcadius has been scorned for, but he will still suffer for it, he knows.

"And I'll trust you to get a suit sorted. Nothing too fancy, okay? I'll send over the details tomorrow along with the statement."

"Thank you, Hector."

"No worries. And, kid?"

"Yes?"

"You're still the best poet in the country, the Oracle even. Don't let this one setback get to you, okay? Different panel, I tell you. Different panel."

"Thank you, Hector. Good night."

Rewan hangs up and sits with the phone in his hands, allowing himself a moment to process the defeat. Then, he straightens his back with determination, downs the remainder of his wine, and makes his way to the party.

*

When Lizzie opens her laptop, she is hoping that the news might have brought out the fan or two that Carol insists she has. There are no new emails, and she doesn't do social media, so she ends browsing the Arts pages of online newspapers. The first headline is enough to knock any remaining positivity out from her –

SMITHERSON SHOCKER!
POET ORACLE PENTAGHAST DENIED WIN.

She genuinely has to get to the third paragraph before her name is mentioned: "Pentaghast was knocked from the top-spot by newcomer Elizabeth Brighton. A working-class, mixed-raced poet with Outlie origins. Brighton's poetry, inspired by her academic research, focuses on distinctly non-Hellenic themes, and does indeed seem like an unusual choice for the Board..."

Newcomer?! Everything else she's heard time and time again but 'newcomer' in particular irks her seeing as it's entirely false. She's older than he is even! Admittedly, only by a year or two, but still… she's been writing poetry just as long as Pentaghast has, and if their quibble is that *StillBeat* is her first full collection, as opposed to pamphlets, then that's only because it was difficult to find a publisher whereas Pentaghast has had his unoriginal poetry churned out by the press since he was twelve-years-old. Pentaghast may have been crowned the youngest ever Poet Oracle a few months ago but that's only because his parents are Bonded and have enough sway in the Elite to make it so. It's Elite bias, plain and simple, and she tries to tell herself that as she reads article after article, but soon it becomes clear that her achievement is just a footnote, an aberration, in this man's life.

It seems that winning the Smitherson has stoked the media's apathy towards her into a roaring fire of hatred. She can barely bring herself to read the harsh comments about her sandwiched in between the love for Rewan Pentaghast. Her dreams of recognition shatter and become a nightmare of the wrong kind of fame instead. She wonders if she will forever be known as the poet that denied the Poet Oracle his prize, even though the choice wasn't hers to make.

She hears a commotion outside, and with dread, rises from the sofa. She creeps over to the single window and pulls back the netting to peer outside.

There are a couple of news vans parked on the street with cameramen filming the weeds and journalists prodding at the intercom. How do they even know where she lives? What if more show up? At university? At her mum's house?!

This is how she has the panic attack, in the end, hunched against the cold radiator under the draughty window on a spring evening, wondering how the best thing to ever happen to her so quickly turned into the worst thing.

*

Rewan stands by the mantelpiece at the side of the andron in his parents London townhouse, trying to avoid the pitying looks of the guests. He should be the centre of attention, the jewel in the Elite's crown, but with one failure, he's been pushed aside. Everyone in this room is talking about him, and if they aren't talking about him, then they are thinking about talking about him.

His parents' house is even grander than his own and this isn't even their primary property. One wall is made entirely of glass panels, showing the impressive courtyard in the centre of the house where a few guests are wandering the paths. The other walls are plain white, designed to be easily decorated to suit each feast, festival, or symposium held in the hall. Tonight, they host twisted streamers of purple and gold; the colours are meant to be the royal colours of celebration. Ornamental pillars reach up towards the tall marbled ceiling from which chandeliers trickle back down. The only music on this occasion comes from the grand piano by the glass; it's the same model that Rewan has in his own apartment not a ten minute walk from here. He wonders if anyone would miss him from his own party if he left.

"This is a sad sight," comments a familiar voice.

Rewan ceases surveying the room and looks to his right to see none other than the journalist, Elena Morenzo raising her eyebrows at his self-pitying behaviour. He chuckles despite himself; Elena may be the only person to even speak to him tonight.

Elena's never been made to feel welcome here. She's the girlfriend of Arcadius Harchester for one – a man known for his 'dalliances' of various kinds – but Elena is outspoken enough to have built her own reputation alongside it. Normally someone of her standing wouldn't be invited to Elite events but she earns her place by writing up the social columns for various papers – documenting the Elite's symposiums, charity feasts, and Arts events – glorifying the very institution that she resents, and for that the Elite tolerate her.

Rewan *likes* Elena, like he likes Arcadius, but he was told some years ago to keep his distance. *You don't want to be associated with those kinds of people*, his parents had said – and whether they meant 'polysettlers' or 'atheists' he still didn't know – *it makes the wrong impression.* So much so, that the Elite often referred to Archie and others like him as being 'disgraced' – a word they coined because they could not say 'disowned.' But on the rare occasion that Rewan could rationalise talking to a member of their party, it always felt pleasantly refreshing from the standard Elite fair. Invigorating. Dangerous.

Elena's long, dark hair falls over her shoulder as she rolls a cigarette between her fingers. "It sucks, I know. But this isn't helping. You, standing here, feeling sorry for yourself."

He sighs at having been caught out. "So what would help?"

She looks up from her cigarette with a smirk. "Besides burning this whole institution to the ground?"

"Besides that."

She shrugs. "You win the next one."

Rewan laughs humourlessly. "Right. Like it's that easy."

"It will be," she says off-handedly. "The Smitherson Board was changed last minute so the Elite did not have the control they normally have over it. They won't let it happen again. And so, you

234

will win the next Elite award, a dozen more after that, and then you will win back your place in here too," she says, with a nod indicating the scornful faces around them. "If you want it, that is," she adds, examining him with curiosity out the corner of her eye. He wants to interpret her interest as camaraderie – an invitation into their guild if he chooses to abandon tradition – but he knows it more likely stems from her journalistic nature to pry out a good story. Friendship is always just an illusion here, after all.

"I…" Rewan begins to defend, but the words fall flat on his tongue. He used to think he belonged here – he fit their values, their customs, and besides, it was the only world he knew – but one failure had made him an outsider, and the people who he had considered acquaintances have not spoken a single word to him this evening, too busy protecting their own reputation. Did he really want to spend his life trying to win back their respect? "I'm not sure if I have an alternative," he says in the end. The Elite are gatekeepers of the Arts, and if he was to have a career, he needed them, regardless of his personal feelings about the situation. "They named me the Poet Oracle."

She looks disappointed by his response, but doesn't comment on it, perching the rolled cigarette between her glossed red lips and shrugging. "Then you best get used to evenings like this one. You want a smoke?" she asks, offering the one she just rolled.

"I don't smoke, but thank you."

"You really are dull," Elena says, with a teasing smile, taking the cigarette back between her perfectly polished fingernails. "You don't do drugs, you don't smoke, you're hardly even drinking, so the question remains: how exactly do you survive these things?"

"I just keep praying it will end," he replies, half-serious.

She chuckles, but it breaks into a sigh as she sees Archie leave for the courtyard with a suspiciously thick cigarette in his hands. "If you'll excuse me," she says, "I have to give Archie another lesson in subtlety."

Rewan watches her leave for the courtyard. He sees the stares and hears the whispers that follow her and understands for the first time what it feels like to be the subject of the Elite's disapproval.

*

Lizzie walks into the lecture hall on Tuesday morning to see flowers on her desk and thirteen English undergraduates gossiping about them.

Lizzie takes a deep breath and reassures herself that the garish array of bright lilies, gerbera, and carnations on the desk are probably a mandatory token of congratulations from the English Department and absolutely nothing to panic about.

"Who are they from?" Front Row Girl asks. "Rewan Pentaghast?"

Her hand falters above the attached envelope. Oh gods, what will she do if they are from him? A new spread of possibilities open in her mind at the suggestion; a vast and terrifying array of potential complicated situations that she would fail to handle gracefully. She feels herself flush with embarrassment.

She forces her body to relax as she picks up the card swiftly, pretending for the sake of her class that this is a casual affair that happens every day. She's already had plenty of practice feigning calm since the announcement yesterday, but in truth, she doesn't know how to deal with the sudden attention; there is a pack of journalists outside her house, her phone has been constantly ringing, and she hit 'snooze' three times this morning, utterly dreading facing the manic onslaught of the university. It's not that she's not happy with winning the Smitherson Prize but so far it's not doing wonders for her social anxiety. More than anything right now, she just wishes there was a handbook for 'sudden fame' with a chapter on 'receiving flowers' to give her some kind of guidance in etiquette.

She breathes a sigh of relief when she flicks open the card to see familiar handwriting. It's from Elijah, her supervisor. *Oh, thank the gods*.

Lizzie realises she has yet to dispel her student's question. "It's from my supervisor," Lizzie tells them, "Congratulating me."

"On the Smitherson prize?" Front Row Girl pipes up again. "Congrats. I heard you won."

The rest of the class murmur and Lizzie is now as red as the carnations in front of her. She quickly diverts their attention away from herself and onto the planned lecture.

"I saw the best minds of my generation destroyed by madness!" Lizzie excitedly recites from memory. "Starving. Hysterical. Naked. Dragging themselves through the negro streets at dawn, looking for an angry fix. Angelheaded hipsters, burning for the ancient heavenly connection to the starry dynamo in the machinery of night! Who – poverty, and tatters, and hollow-eyed, and high! – sat up smoking, in the supernatural darkness…"

Lizzie opens her eyes to see bright yellow flowers below her (*below her?!*) and comes out of her reading with a sudden bout of embarrassment. During her recital of *Howl* to the class she has somehow ended up standing on the plastic chair behind the desk, arms raised to the ceiling like an amateur Shakespearean performer.

She may have underestimated just how excited she was over the prize. There can be no other possible explanation for such uncharacteristic chair dramatics.

She shakily steps down from her stage. The thirteen undergraduates are staring back at her. If it's possible, the students look as uncomfortable as Lizzie feels; they exchange surreptitious glances with each other in an attempt to work out if their lecturer intended such dramatics, and if so, whether it is to be laughed at or pitied. Lizzie coughs and adjusts the pashmina around her shoulders to cover any lingering awkwardness.

Context. She's fairly certain there had been some context here.

"So Ginsberg's *Howl* is about such madness," she says, hoping that at least a couple of students will write off her eccentric display as an intentional demonstration. "It depicts the desperation of these men, who, let's remember, were only in their twenties when they came to fame, much the same age as most of you," Lizzie says, resisting adding 'and me' being only a few years older than her students. "The writings of the Beat Generation capture the attitudes that were circling around post-War America in the late 40s and 50s. Some of the historical context you've highlighted as," she ticks the students' earlier answers off on her fingers as she lists: "The growth of Outlies, the emergence of the Elite, censorship including the restrictions on books that were thought improper, the increasing popularity of Biblical religions in the U.S., and of course the Great Search that was kick-started by Jack Kerouac in *On The Road*. The Beat Generation were concerned with breaking such boundaries."

Okay, that sounds about right. Lizzie is back (cautiously avoiding the eyes of her students but back), and most importantly, not standing on a chair. She takes a breath, allowing the scratch of pens and click of keyboards to cease before continuing.

"So with the historical context in mind, have a look again at that first line of *Howl*: 'I saw the best minds of my generation destroyed by madness.' Do you think Ginsberg is referring to a specific type of 'madness' here? And what is it?"

Lizzie is happy to accept almost every answer for this and as the discussion continues Lizzie has a line of Pentaghast come unbidden into her mind: *to find that the gods had cursed them with exquisite madness*. It's a decent line, she admits, although it's from an older collection, not *Eternity*. She found the fourteen poems inspired by Pentaghast's Bonded parents nauseatingly fluffy; full of drivel about the romance of Searching and, that awful line, *refractions of your being, reflected in eternal light*, stolen from his mother. Pathetic. If that line ever sneaks into her subconscious, she'll be damned.

"Bonding?"

For a worrying moment, Lizzie is afraid that she has been speaking her thoughts out loud, but she tunes back into the students' discussion to realise they are still debating over Ginsberg's 'madness'.

Lizzie is about to politely encourage Front Row Girl to expand her horizons when Back Row Man makes her job a lot easier by making a derisive snort.

"You don't agree?" Lizzie prompts him.

Back Row Man shrugs. "They're desperate for any sort of connection, not just their soulmate."

Lizzie is slightly disappointed. Anyone who had read *Howl* could have come to that conclusion. He can do better, she knows it.

"Okay, and why do you say that?"

Back Row Man raises his head from where it was propped by his hands and says, "'Who wandered around and around at midnight in the railroad yard wondering where to go.'" It's a perfect quote, recited from memory. He shrugs again, attempting to look bored by the whole affair. "The Beats were poor, and sad, and lonely, and would chase any high: be it sex or drugs or crime or visions, or, I suppose, *Bonding*," he says, the word dripping with disdain "They just didn't want to be forced to open an antique store."

A small laugh escapes from Lizzie's lips but judging by the silence no one else got his joke. It's not a line of *Howl* usually made light of – *who cut their wrists three times successively unsuccessfully, gave up and were forced to open antique stores where they thought they were growing old and cried* – and yet it's one of Lizzie's favourites as it says so much about what the Beat Generation considered the inadequacy of Settling; how they romanticised Searching to the exclusion of everything else. Kerouac even broke into several Outlies to meet more people and left a trail of Dissonance in his wake. It wasn't until twenty years later that Kerouac realised how fruitless his Search was and fell into a deep pit of depression; accepting that he would likely never Bond but also unable to Settle having fought so long against it.

"I don't think that's true," Front Row Girl jumps in, glaring with defiance at Back Row Man. "Why can't it just be about Searching? It's like Rewan Pentaghast says in *Eternity* –"

Lizzie fights the urge to roll her eyes. Of course she has a

Pentaghast fangirl in her class. She can see the pale pink cover of *Eternity* sandwiched between the neat stack of coursebooks on her desk.

Lizzie glances around the room while Front Row Girl natters away and is dismayed to see the pink of *Eternity* on another desk, and sticking out of a rucksack, and on a spare chair... pink, pink, pink... everywhere.

By the time class ends, Lizzie's earlier enthusiasm has dissipated, replaced with a simmering pink rage.

Come lunchtime, Lizzie sneaks into her supervisor's office with its big windows and colourful modern oil paintings and makes herself at home at the spare desk, slouching in the chair with her feet on the desk as her phone connects her with Ed Hart, an entire ocean away.

It's not until Ed answers, sleepily, that she remembers the time difference. It must be 6am where he is. "Shit, sorry, I woke you –"

But he's already talking over her concerns, "Nonsense, nonsense. I'm here." As he always is, even if he's away, even if him and Mum are on rocky terms, he's never once missed a call from Lizzie. "What's wrong?"

"Who said anything's wrong?" Lizzie deflects, but even if she had managed to hide her hurt tone at the start of the conversation, it's no use now as her eyes land upon the Arts pages splayed across her supervisor's desk and the black and white portrait of Rewan Pentaghast blown up across them, staring back at her. She'd read that one this morning. The one that said she had 'no formal training' despite having more qualifications to her name than her competitor. What they *meant* was that she hadn't trained at a Temple.

"Do me a favour," she says instead, "and don't pick up a paper this morning. Or turn on the news. Or go on the internet. Even better, just don't bother getting up today, like I wish I hadn't."

"Oh, Lizzie," he says, voice full of sympathy that makes tears sting her eyes. "That bad?"

"I took the most prestigious poetry prize away from their poster boy, of course it's that bad. I don't know what I was expecting, of course they're going to blame the panel and paint me as the villain instead of admitting that, just possibly, their precious Rewan Pentaghast isn't the most brilliant poet of the twenty-first century. Not that I am," she hastens to add. "I'm not saying I'm better, I just –" she pinches the bridge of her nose, trying to calm herself down. "He's no more experienced than I am, not really, not if it weren't for the Temples declaring him as a conduit to the gods. I'm the one doing a PhD in Poetry let's remember but they keep making it sound like I just stuck some words together and won by blind luck.

"And I know, I know," she continues before he can jump in with well-meaning platitudes. "They've always hated me because of who I am and what I write and that's just how it is. I know that. I get that. But even the tabloids are spinning it like there's some sort of big rivalry between us just because we both happened to write about Searching or Bonding or whatever. I've never even met the guy."

"Well…" Ed hedges.

Lizzie grits her teeth in response. "What?"

"Well, I can see where they're coming from, that's all. You've both been nominated for the same awards three times this season, it's just that he won the previous two."

"How do you know that?" Lizzie asks. "*I* don't even know that."

"I do keep tabs on you, you know."

"Whatever," Lizzie says with a shake of her head and the smallest of smiles on her lips. "It doesn't matter what I do, what awards I win, the papers will always love him because he's Elite's Most Eligible, and hate me because I'm anything but. It's fine."

Ed sighs, and it sounds more tired than even 6am warrants. "You're allowed to want recognition, Lizzie."

Lizzie sags in the chair, tilting her head back to the ceiling with eyes closed, blinking back tears. Ed only has one setting and that setting is *Sincere*. Sometimes though, it's really what she needs to hear.

"Yeah," she whispers, "I won. And I guess it would be nice if someone… if… urgh!" she exclaims, kicking at the carpet. "I know that this sounds stupid and petty and naïve but I thought that maybe things would turn around with this; that maybe the Elite would finally recognise poetry about human experience to be just as important to the Arts as the traditional stuff the Temple poets churn out; that they'd, I don't know, invite me into their stupid private club as an actual recognised poet and we'd have a chance to change things, but instead, they've just used it to ostracise me even more."

"You don't mean that, Lizzie," he says softly. "You've never wanted an invitation to the Elite; you've just wanted them to come out and meet you halfway, as well they should."

She sighs. He's right, as always. "I know. But I'm starting to think that's never going to happen. I don't know what to do."

"You do what you've always done," Ed says. "You persevere."

Lizzie ends the call but she still feels unsettled and overwhelmed, her emotions simmering under the surface, dangerously close to erupting.

*

Rewan emerges from his cocoon of sleep sometime after midday. After the party last night, he had turned off every communications device in his house and he has no intention of facing the world today either. It's only the call of basic bodily functions that causes him to rise eventually and shuffle down the corridor towards the bathroom. And then, once he's up, he figures he may as well have coffee.

By early evening, Rewan realises that there isn't all that much to do at home without technology. He had a shower, got changed into some old jeans and a faded Camiro Temple t-shirt, and now stands in what he optimistically once called his 'writing room'. It was nestled in these four velvet red walls that he wrote the majority of *Eternity*. It is a deliberately sparse room; one window, one chair, one desk, and behind it, a painting of the Muses. It didn't feel cliché at the time but now he thinks the only thing that would make it worse would be a typewriter and an overflowing wastepaper basket.

The doorbell rings, the sound long and harsh.

Rewan jars. As much as he longs for it to be a friendly face – a brash Arcadius or a talkative Elena to distract him from his thoughts – he knows he has not failed spectacularly enough to warrant a housecall from the ostracised Elites. No. The doorbell signals the arrival of one of two people: his agent or his parents. Both of whom have a spare key, so there's very little point in ignoring the sound as he so desires.

The doorbell rings again.

Rewan concedes to his fate and firmly closes the door to the writing room, walking across the apartment to answer the door.

Waiting on the porch outside is a very flushed and very sweaty literary agent laden down with bags. "Where the fuck have you been?!"

"Good afternoon, Hector."

Hector pushes past Rewan and strides into the main room, flinging his bags onto the dining room table.

"Yes, please, come in," Rewan says sarcastically, closing the door. "Make yourself at home."

"Don't be snarky with me Rew, it's my day off, I was shopping with Allison and the kid, who I only get to see every other weekend, let's remember, but no, even that's not sacred anymore, I had to –" Hector breaks off as he searches wildly around the main room. Rewan wonders if he is this dedicated to his other clients, or if he is the only one to be given this treatment. "Where the fuck is your fucking laptop?"

Hector is cursing even more than usual. It must be a bad day.

"Would you like a cup of tea?"

Hector pauses in his search to look at Rewan with disdain. "No, I don't want a cup of fucking tea. Gods, Rew, do you even know what's going on?"

"The Smitherson Prize…?"

Hector's glare becomes profoundly worse. "You ignorant –"

"Shall I put the kettle on?"

"Have you seriously not been online all afternoon?"

Rewan shakes his head and prepares for another admonishment but Hector sighs and runs a hand through his flat brown hair.

"Laptop, Rew. Now, please. Tablet. Anything with a goddamn internet connection."

Now Hector's ranting has died down, Rewan is beginning to think something might actually be wrong. He is quick to pull his computer tablet from the drawer in his living room table.

"What's going on?" Rewan asks as he turns on the device.

Hector groans as he sits down on the leather sofa beside Rewan. A sweaty handprint remains on the armrest.

"Don't know the full extent of it yet, but from the sounds of it, it's gonna be something that your agent ain't gonna be happy with."

"You are my agent."

"Aye," he says, wiping his forehead with a plaid shirtsleeve. "And don't I regret the day I made that decision."

Rewan knows he doesn't mean it. Or at least, he hopes he doesn't mean it, because Hector has been saying such things for years and they're still stuck with each other. He looks back down to the tablet and opens an internet browser. "What am I doing?"

"Video search for 'Elizabeth Brighton rant.'"

Rewan's fingers pause mid-typing. His stomach churns uncomfortably. "What?"

"Just do it."

Rewan does it. He finds the video instantly: **Smitherson Prize Rant**

"A rant?" Rewan asks Hector. "What does she have to be angry about? She won the damn thing."

Hector waves at him to be quiet.

There is a description underneath the video title from 'anon_student_14': *we heard Brighton went crazy this morning so we decided to secretly film our afternoon class...we were not disappointed...*

244

Rewan and Hector both hunch over the tablet as the video loads and then he watches with baited breath as it begins to play.

It's low quality, presumably taken on a phone, and the location is that of a fairly small and bland classroom. There are a couple of heads between the camera and the teacher and when a student turns marginally towards the camera, Rewan realises his mistake; they are too old for a classroom, these must be university students. But if this is a university then the fuzzy person standing at the front in a woollen dress and scarf must be the lecturer. "Is that Elizabeth Brighton?"

Hector waves at him to be quiet again.

Rewan acquiesces just as the audio clicks on.

Brighton speaks as she paces at the front of the class, "You need to remember that the Beat Generation were doing things that had not been done before. They were original for their time."

It sounds just like a normal lecture to Rewan. Her voice is more confident than Rewan imagined; Hector had gone to a reading of hers, incognito, and had painted a picture of someone quite socially awkward and scatty, but Brighton seems perfectly at ease in the classroom.

A voice in the video asks, "But what is originality?" The video pans to the back of a girl's head near the front of the room, a girl with red hair and glasses, presumably the speaker. The girl continues, "The Beats were all obsessed with Bonding, and, well… we're still doing that now, aren't we?"

There is a pause and the camera zooms to Brighton's face. She appears to be studying the girl, perhaps thinking about how to answer.

The red-haired girl continues, boldly and uninterrupted, "I'm sure we all read the controversy this morning about you and Rewan Pentaghast both writing about the same topic for the Smitherson Prize. You imply yourself in *StillBeat* that there is nothing new to say, don't you?"

Rewan holds his breath. It sounds like the class does too.

Complete silence. The camera is still focused on Brighton. Her blank face twitches into an expression and is gone again before Rewan can work out her emotions. He doesn't know how she is staying calm when his stomach is twisting with anxiety just watching.

Brighton licks her lips and then says perfectly flatly, "There are no new ideas in the world. Originality comes from how we choose to express them."

Rewan finds himself nodding along.

Another voice, female again, but closer to the camera, speaks, and the camera zooms out again to find a girl with pigtails. "Have you read Rewan Pentaghast then? I love the way he defamiliarised Bonding in *Eternity*."

The girl is obviously a fan. 'Defamiliarisation' is what you say to poets to flatter them.

It looks like Brighton has exactly the same reaction. Her nose crinkles in distaste. She collects herself and then replies, "Pentaghast is indeed a talented poet."

Rewan feels a small smile tug at his lips; the first since the news broke. Does he really have her respect? She has his, undoubtedly, despite *StillBeat*'s anti-Searching themes.

Brighton continues, "But I am going to have to disagree with you on his success at defamiliarisation."

The smile falls from his lips before it is even fully formed.

Brighton nods to herself before continuing. She knows exactly what she is doing. "My supervisor, Elijah, once said that it was a good poem if he was a different person when he'd finished reading it. But Pentaghast is not life-changing. He writes technically good poetry, but he is afraid to delve deeper. He claims his work is spiritual but does not address life as anything more than it first appears. Writers must first face themselves before they find truth, but he writes as if he is afraid of himself, or as if there is nothing there at all. It's possible that as a Searcher he doesn't believe he has a self until he has Bonded and for that, I pity him, but no amount of displaced romanticism is an excuse for lazy writing."

Rewan scowls at the video and the assertive woman strutting between desks as she gives her speech.

"It shows in his attempt at, what you called, defamiliarisation. Pentaghast uses in-depth descriptions of thought patterns during the moment of Recognition to great effect, but if you take, for example, the title sonnet of *Eternity*, line by line, there is nothing original about Pair Bonding there, only clichés in an appealing order. True defamiliarisation should enhance your perception of the familiar by showing it to you in a new way. The only *decent* method of defamiliarisation –"

Rewan cringes.

"– in Pentaghast's poetry collection comes in fact from his mother. It was folly for Pentaghast to attempt an original vision of the Bond without having Bonded himself; without any experience, and while afraid to truly examine himself, he only has clichés to draw from."

Brighton is leaning smugly against the desk by the time she has finished berating Rewan's work and the video clicks to a finish.

Rewan falls back against the sofa, processing. He has never felt so humiliated. How dare she assume anything about his life? He is not 'afraid of himself' whatever that means and, in any case, she can hardly speak, can she? Brighton is an academic poet, she hides behind literary figures and their language rather than finding her own, and surely that's equally as cowardly. He covers his face with his hands until he can only see an inch of the ceiling through a triangular gap in his fingers.

Hector exhales loudly and flops back against the sofa beside him. "Well, fuck."

Rewan nods and drops his hands. For once that curse word seems appropriate. "I need to…" he has no idea how to finish that sentence but he finds that he is standing up and walking towards the door.

"No!" Hector nearly trips as he rushes after Rewan towards the front door. He plasters himself in front of it like a Greek warrior shielding their beloved from the gods. "The press." He shakes his head. "You can't leave."

Rewan should be finding some irony in the fact that he has barricaded himself inside all day by choice but the moment he wants to leave, he is prevented from doing so.

Hector shakes his head again. "You can't leave, Rew. They'll be after you like a pack of wolves if you so much as step outside."

"Then could you please leave?" he asks Hector.

Hector looks taken aback. "Mate, you look wrecked. Are you sure?"

"Leave. Please." Rewan says. His voice is muted and scratchy but it still sounds far too loud in the apartment.

Brighton's words linger above the living area, poised, suspended in the stillness, but they shiver, vibrating with energy, as if they could start bouncing across the walls any moment. One word in particular towers above others: *Cliché*. The six letters grow behind his eyelids until they blind him. *Cliché*. Is there a worse criticism for a poet to hear?

Rewan hears the click of the door as Hector leaves; he doesn't know if he speaks, the only words he can comprehend are those hovering in the living room. They shudder violently. Pre-emptively. He has to leave this contaminated room.

He runs back into his writing room and closes the door behind him, protecting himself with these plain walls. He sits and lights a meditation candle, not looking away until the candle has burnt to its wick and a solution has presented itself.

There is a saying that to make right, you must first do right.

*

FROM: REWAN PENTAGHAST
SUBJECT: SMITHERSON

Dear Ms Brighton,

I apologise for using your personal email address but I thought that after today's debacle it was best for us to talk without our agents, your students, and the general populous interfering. I hope you agree.

I wanted to congratulate you on the Smitherson Prize. It was well deserved. I also wanted to take this opportunity to say that I agree with you – it was foolhardy of me to assume I could create originality without experience.

Forgive me for being so presumptuous but from your poetry you seem very sceptical of Bonding, which is natural considering your research area, but I am particularly curious as to your use of 'lonesome' in the title poem *StillBeat*. Is this a reference to Kerouac's *Lonesome Traveller*? Or did you wish to imply that it is the act of Searching that makes one 'lonesome'?

Your writing is your own of course and you owe me no explanation but your poem has been on my mind for days and I relish the opportunity to ask the creator. Forgive me if I have overstepped. I understand if you do not wish to discuss this matter, though I cannot promise that I won't pick your brains some more at the Smitherson Presentation on Saturday.

Lastly, let me reiterate that I take no offence from your spontaneous (and now widely spread) criticism of my work. I believe that is the nature of academia.

Yours sincerely,

Rewan Pentaghast.

FROM: ELIZABETH BRIGHTON
SUBJECT: RE: SMITHERSON

Dear Mr Pentaghast,

Thanks and all but I don't really discuss my work unless it's for academic reasons and particularly not through my private email address (I don't even know how you got hold of it). You can take any interpretation you like from *StillBeat* and I suggest that you read my paper on how Authorial Intent in the Technological Age is Destructive to the Progress of Modern Literary Theory: an analysis of how author response through social media is disempowering the reader.

Sorry about the video. Congrats. See you at the Presentation.

Elizabeth Brighton.

*

Lizzie regrets her reply to Rewan almost immediately. She plays around with the formatting of her thesis for an hour before deciding to call it a day and walk to her mother's house.

It's dusk by the time she knocks on the door. The little bungalow is still so familiar to her. Even when she had managed to scrape enough money together to rent a flat of her own she still visited her mother every other day. There used to be a house before this, she knows, but the only thing she remembers from their old house was the sight of a red bathroom and the memory of her mother hurrying her away from it, but Lizzie doesn't even know if that's real, or whether her mind has falsified a memory of the incident that forever changed them.

Her mum answers the door already dressed in her nightie. Lizzie is hardly surprised; since her mum stopped working, she tended to only get dressed for company, and that 'company' was usually only Ed when he managed to come home. He hasn't been home for three months now and it shows; her hair tangled and the weight of sleepless nights around her eyes. She always misses him more than she tells him she does. Lizzie wonders if he even realises the shell of the woman he leaves behind. She's got no one else. She doesn't even have any external support anymore, the counsellor and support group long gone, and she never did call the charities she was meant to. She's completely isolated when neither of them are home and Lizzie knows the guilt weighs heavily on the both of them. It's hard to encourage her mother to make friends though when she's afraid to even step outside the house.

Lizzie forces a smile that she hopes looks natural and lets her mum pull her into a hug. She's bustled through the door and then, before Lizzie knows it, she is rocking on the edge of the armchair, muffling her frustration into her hands.

"What was I thinking?"

"It's understandable," her mum says in an attempt to placate her. "You were upset, and you didn't know it would end up on the internet."

"No, but I should have done. Those damn kids and their phones. In any case, I shouldn't have ratted on Pentaghast so much, and I really shouldn't have sent such a prissy email."

"What email?" asks her mother and Lizzie forces herself to recount their exchange, growing hotter with humiliation as she does so. When she finishes she can't bear the look of disappointment in her mother's eyes and drops her face back into her hands.

"I was just so damn mad about that damn article – you know, the one that made it seem like I have some sort of *vendetta* against him – and then he had to be all *sincere* about it. The media were already pegging us as rivals and now... well, I suppose it's just a good story for them. But I swear, you say one bad word about Searchers and the press are on you like... like... oh, I'm too angry for this!"

"There, there. Drink your tea."

This time her platitudes include a pat on the back. It makes Lizzie realise how much her back aches from being hunched over. She sighs and sits straighter in the armchair, lowering her hands from the face that must look as red and blotchy as the patchwork blanket thrown over her. Her mum's obsession with knitting is unchanged from her childhood. There's a hand-knitted blanket over the back of the armchair, another over the sofa, doilies on the mantelpiece, a rug beneath the coffee table and a runner on top of it; gods forbid there is a single item in this living room not adorned with wool. Even the fishtank Ed got her has a blanket placed lovingly over the lid. Maybe her mum never leaves the house anymore because she physically can't climb over the amount of knitting that litters the place.

Lizzie numbly reaches for the cup of tea in front of her and takes a sip. The familiar clink of the floral china teacup against its saucer is even more comforting than the warm liquid that hits the back of her throat. How many times has she sat in this same chair drinking tea from the same cup? Countless.

Her mum is talking about plans for when Ed comes home when the exhaustion suddenly catches up with Lizzie. She wants to curl up in her mum's lap like she did as a child and fall asleep to the sound of game shows and the click of knitting needles. "Mum," she whines.

"Oh, Lizzie." Her thin lips tug downwards, and she wordlessly pushes a paper-dollied china plate towards her daughter adorned with chocolate digestives; the adult equivalent of a hug. "It'll be okay."

Lizzie accepts the comfort offered and obligingly picks up a biscuit, turning it in her palm until the chocolate topping begins to smear her fingertips.

Her mum is watching her with the same face of pity that she had upon opening her door twenty minutes ago. She turns away upon being caught, pretending that she was watching the television all along, but the television is on mute, and it's just adverts playing out. She used to make more of an effort when it came to hiding her worries.

Lizzie takes a small bite of the biscuit to appease her mum. "Thanks."

Her mum smiles broadly. "Least I can do, break out your favourite biscuits."

Chocolate digestives have not been Lizzie's favourite since she was thirteen and Ed introduced her to those posh squishy ones wrapped in foil, but she appreciates it nonetheless. "Thanks," she repeats. "Sorry I'm so…" she waves her arms around her in an attempt to explain her state of mind but it comes across as a chaotic flail, which is perhaps not so far from the truth.

"I'm just glad you came to see me." Her mum reaches across the armrest to pat Lizzie's knee. "Now you're so busy all the time, I hardly get to see you."

Lizzie nods, pretending that the words don't fill her with guilt.

She should make more time. She should have come here for the announcement on Monday. She just gets too wrapped up in her own mind sometimes that she can't carry her mother as well. *Like Ginsberg*, she notes with some irony. Her throat feels raw from ranting and her mouth is stuck together with biscuits but she drinks her tea until she can speak again. "By the way, I checked and they're streaming the Smitherson Presentation live online, so you and Ed can watch it together on Saturday if you want? Or, like, not *together* together, but at the same time."

Her mum shuffles uncomfortably on the sofa. "Oh I don't know about that Lizzie," she says stiffly. "He's very busy with the conference –"

"Not too busy for you," Lizzie interrupts. "And he already said it was fine so –"

"Lizzie!" she scolds.

"What? You want to see him, don't deny it. I know it's hard but I'm just worried you'll end up with a house full of Tolkien-named pets if I don't force you into socialising once in a blue moon. It's one evening, you don't even have to go out, you can watch the biggest achievement of my life, at home, with someone who means a lot to both of us, so unless you want to tell me what the problem is…?"

Her mum tugs at the frayed edges of the doily on the table for a minute, obviously disgruntled, but she doesn't actually come up with an excuse.

"Okay then," Lizzie says. "I'll set it up."

They didn't even have the conversation of whether she'd attend the actual Presentation, Lizzie realises. They both just knew she couldn't, at least, not without Ed by her side. It's become too difficult for her lately to be around people. A pity, as some new friends are probably exactly what her mother needs as Ed takes work placements further and further away.

They both resume drinking their tea and watch the silent TV for a while.

Then her mum spoils it with, "I hope you're taking a date at least."

Lizzie nearly chokes on her tea as she tries not to let it snort out of her nose. She subtly dabs at the couple of drops that stubbornly spewed over her chin with her pashmina.

"I don't want you to be there alone," she adds.

"Is this what we're doing now? Forcing each other into socialising?" Lizzie jokes.

Her mum taps the side of her cup while she waits for Lizzie to answer.

"What? I do date, you know!" Lizzie defends, trying not to think about just how long ago the last disastrous date was. A year ago? Two? The florist, wasn't it? Cute girl, but a little too obsessed with *Neighbours*. "It's just that I've decided to go alone to the Presentation," Lizzie says with more confidence than she feels.

"Decided, hmm?"

"Yes, *decided*," Lizzie insists. "And Carol will be there, annoying me enough, so there's hardly any need."

"Elijah would –"

"No."

"Someone else in the English department?"

"No."

"One of your students?"

"Mum!"

She laughs as Lizzie stares at her open-mouthed. It's good to hear her laughing though and Lizzie flops back in the armchair with an arm over her eyes so at least she doesn't have to physically see her mother laughing at her expense.

When her mum has recovered, she asks, "So what have you got to wear for it then? Has she chosen something fancy?"

It takes Lizzie a moment to realise the insinuation, "Wait, did you just *assume* that Carol's picking the outfit for me? I could find a dress myself, y'know."

This declaration only serves to provoke another round of laughter. Her mum raises a hand to wave at Lizzie's current outfit. "I love you, dear, but you are hardly the most fashion conscious –"

"Alright!" Lizzie shouts over her laughter. "Fine. You're right. Carol's in charge of the dress. It's blue or something."

"And I'm sure it will look lovely. I remember your first formal dress… you were so happy." A sad smile appears on her face and Lizzie knows she's thinking of Ed but between one blink and the next, the expression has disappeared. "I just hope the journalists aren't being too hard on you, I've read some articles –"

"Oh," Lizzie says. She was worried her mother might have seen some of the things they had been saying about their heritage.

"There's just so much pressure on you young ones in Mainstream," she tuts. "Sometimes I think the way Matthew was raised was kinder after all."

It takes Lizzie a moment to comprehend that her mum is actually talking about her father. They never talk about him. Lizzie shakes her head. "Don't say that, Mum."

But she is already gazing absently at the netting on the window. "He wouldn't even know what a poet was, I don't think," she muses. "I wonder if it would have been any better if we had stayed at the Outlie."

"I don't know," Lizzie says honestly. She can scarcely imagine living without the knowledge of Bonding. "I guess you can't hide from the world forever."

"Speaking of which," her mum says, jumping up from the sofa as if they hadn't just been discussing her innermost fears. "What are you going to do?"

Lizzie has to replay their conversation to work out what there was to speak of: *you can't hide from the world forever*, did she really say that? She watches her mum pour more tea before sitting down again.

"I suppose I should apologise to Pentaghast," Lizzie sighs.

"That seems sensible."

"I just don't know how to go about it."

"Why don't you ask Carol? She'll probably have some idea,

smart girl that she is."

If Lizzie didn't know any better, the way that her mum talks about her agent, she would swear that she wants her to Settle with Carol.

"She would just suggest something public. She doesn't know about the emails. Doesn't know how badly I screwed it up. Maybe I could just email him again?"

"What about in person?"

That startles a laugh out of Lizzie. "Sure, I'll just rock up to the Oracle's penthouse in a jumper my mum knitted and an apology pulled out my arse. Not bloody likely. There's probably some sort of protocol to follow... I dunno, I avoid the Elite like the plague. I've no idea how to actually socialise with those kinds of people. And he's the son of a Pair, at that, aren't they meant to 'glow with the blessing of the gods' or something?"

Her mum seems to find this hilarious, giggling away to herself.

"What?"

"You, my girl. Acting like it's all beneath you and then you come out with romantic gibberish like that. Ha! Like they actually glow."

Lizzie can feel her cheeks reddening. "Pairs always look bright on TV and stuff so maybe it becomes genetic or something, I don't know, I'm not a scientist."

Her mum slaps her leg in mirth.

"Oh, forget it."

"Darling, you're not entirely wrong," she says, wiping a tear from her eyes. "But you just made it sound like they walk around with their own generator or something. Besides, it's not genetic. Their children are just normal folk."

Lizzie huffs. *Normal.* She would like to see Rewan Pentaghast doing anything normal; she tries to imagine an animated version of his poised monochrome author photo folding laundry and fails.

"You know what I mean, dear," her mum says. "Nothing to be frightened of."

She doesn't need to say *unlike Bonded Pairs* but they both hear it anyway in the way her mum's voice has lost its levity. The sight killed Lizzie's father. They are both wary.

"Okay," Lizzie says with a deep breath, determined. "I can fix this."

*

"I just don't understand how you couldn't win," Rewan's father says. He puts down his coffee cup with enough force to make a harsh clink against the marble coaster. Rewan fights not to twitch at the sound.

His mother takes over the thought, "You're the Poet Oracle. I didn't think the Board *could* choose anyone but you. Another revered Temple writer perhaps, but an outsider like Brighton?"

Rewan flinches this time before he can stop himself. "Doesn't that strike you as a little unfair?"

His parents send a shared look of bafflement in Rewan's direction. They sit around the coffee table, sharing the sofa while he occupies the lonesome armchair opposite.

Rewan shakes his head to dismiss his straying thoughts and explains, "What's the point of a competition if others can't win?"

They blink in unison. "But you're Poet Oracle," they say.

"You're meant to win," his father adds.

Rewan groans and rubs his hands over his eyes. "That's not what I –"

"Poetry was a difficult career to pursue," his mother speaks softly. "It's very subjective. Are you sure you…?"

"Yes, I'm sure," Rewan says automatically. They've had this argument dozens of times before.

His father doesn't let it go this time though. "It's not too late to change your mind. Go into business. Join one of our papers perhaps, they could always use writers. More likely to meet your Pair too if you worked in the City –"

His mother hums in agreement. "Yes, all cooped up in here. You do still want to Search, don't you?"

Oh great, just what Rewan wanted this afternoon: ancient familial arguments, buy one, get one free. He drinks what remains of his cold coffee.

"You're ashamed of me," he wagers. His parents avoid his gaze and he knows he is correct. "You once spoke of the honour it brought to you, your son following the Arts, but I lose one competition and now you want me to change career? How would that look? Not honourable that's for sure. Cowardly," he spits out. He speaks with enough conviction that he even believes himself for a moment despite Brighton's cruel words from yesterday's video still dogging his thoughts.

His mother nods. His father licks his lips in thought. He can see a conversation happening behind their eyes, not with words, but a complex exchange of feelings, fleeting images, and rounded thoughts. Each senses what the other is thinking and they feel their way to a compromise before speaking. He cannot fathom how strong that level of understanding must be.

"The gods do not reward the idle," his father says. "You would do well not to presume so much of them."

His mother cants her head slightly in as much of a disagreement as Bonded Pairs can manage. He has never seen them fight – he knows such a thing is too painful for people that share emotions – but he has seen these little ticks from time to time that show a difference in thinking.

"Not that we're saying you're unmotivated, Rewan," his mother says. "But you can hardly expect the gods to send your soulmate to your door. You have a duty to Search – that's where your energies should lie, especially if things aren't working for you in other areas of your life."

"But –"

"And nothing can bring more honour to our family than a Bond. You know that," his father says coolly. Rewan holds his head in his hands, his shoulders buckling under the weight of their expectations. No wonder Arcadius told them all to sod off; he's very tempted to do the same.

"And your father is right," says his mother, oblivious. "You would thrive in business."

"Just promise us that you'll think about it, Rewan," his father says. "Losing a competition is one thing –"

"But losing to an outsider like *Brighton*?"

And the way her voice drips with disdain raises Rewan's hackles.

"Two days ago you didn't even know who Elizabeth Brighton was!" he exclaims. "Have you even read her poetry? This so-called unworthy work?" He doesn't wait for an answer because he knows it. "No! Of course you haven't. You're just belittling her based on prejudices that –"

"Enough!" his father shouts.

Silence falls over them, awkward and angry. After a minute, Rewan says, "So I take it you're too ashamed of me to attend the Presentation?"

"Of course not," his mother says briskly. "We have to attend."

His father nods in agreement. "The tabloids would have a field day if we didn't."

Rewan opens his mouth to say something, probably inflammatory and designed to provoke, when he is saved by the doorbell.

Elizabeth Brighton is standing on his doorstep, in the deserted hallway of the apartment complex, staring at the ground.

He startles at the sight and blinks a few times to make sure, but he's not imagining it, she's definitely standing in front of him.

"Hi, er, I'm Lizzie… Lizzie, er, Brighton."

"Rewan. And I know who you are." Rewan says and immediately cringes at how terse he sounds.

"Right. Your agent, Hector, told me where to find you…well, my agent did, but he told her and…" she trails off. "I'm here to apologise." At this she finally looks up, takes one quick glance at Rewan before fixing on some point over his shoulder. "I can get quite defensive."

"I can see that."

She blushes and shuffles on his doormat. "May I?" she asks.

"Sorry, I –" he says simultaneously.

She looks at him quizzically.

"My parents are here," he says by means of explanation. If he thought she was awkward before, it has nothing on the rigid posture that she suddenly adopts. She looks like she might bolt at any moment. He wishes he could join her.

"Right, sorry," she rambles. "I was gonna call ahead but I honestly didn't know if I was gonna make it up the stairs this time so…"

"I'm glad you made it, Ms Brighton," he says, although he isn't sure yet if he means it.

"Lizzie," she corrects. "Just Lizzie."

"Okay, Just Lizzie," he mocks gently and is happy to see that she smiles a little at his attempt at humour. "Why don't you come in?"

"Your pare– I mean, *Souls Pentaghast* are here. I…" she trails off again and picks at her woollen dress.

"I'll ask them to leave." He shrugs, trying not to look too pleased by the prospect.

She stares at him with shock. "No, I can –"

"Rewan!" calls a shrill voice from inside. "Are you going to let your friend stand outside in the hallway all day?"

Rewan cringes. At least Lizzie appears equally, if not more, uncomfortable than he is.

"Well, there's no escape now so…" Rewan jokes, holding the door open. Lizzie seems terrified. Perhaps she didn't understand the jest at his parents. "Please, come in."

Lizzie shuffles into the apartment and Rewan reaches around her to close the door. He has never seen someone so nervous. This is an entirely different creature to the one who lectured so vehemently or the one who sent that terse academic email. He can't quite wrap his head around it. He was ready to brush her off at the presentation, having made an attempt at reconciliation and been rejected. He had even fantasied about publicly humiliating her in a similar fashion but looking down at her hunched figure trembling in his foyer, he can't imagine any such cruelties now.

She blinks up at him and he realises he has been staring, and standing rather too close. They haven't shaken hands, in greeting or in Recognition, but now they are past the stage for such formalities.

"Rewan!" his father calls.

"Coming!" Rewan replies.

He walks the couple of paces from the doorway and into the open plan living area.

"Mother, Father, meet Elizabeth Brighton. Lizzie, meet Souls Thomas and Tara Pentaghast "

His parents noticeably school their faces into feigned politeness and then rise in tandem from the sofa to greet Lizzie, but she remains stock still behind Rewan even as they hold out their hands in greeting. Rewan gives them a curt shake of the head and they drop their hands obligingly.

Lizzie squeaks, "Hi," from somewhere over his shoulder. "I mean, hello, it's, um, an honour to make your acquaintance."

Rewan turns towards Lizzie just in time to see her make a half-aborted curtsey. He was wrong; this situation could get more awkward. Who curtsies to Souls anymore? Out of the corner of his eye, he sees matched surprise on his parents' faces, but he can't stop looking at Lizzie. Has she never met a Bonded Pair before? When she rises from the curtsey, her face is flushed and her eyes dart around the room.

It is then that Rewan remembers an article he read, one of those biographical columns hastily pasted together when the shortlist was announced a month or so ago. *Outlie*. Her family comes from an Outlie. This probably *is* her first time meeting a Pair.

Rewan cringes. Again.

"My mother and father were just leaving," Rewan says to Lizzie while attempting to have a silent conversation with his parents. "Right?" he prompts.

His parents thankfully seem to understand, or rather his mother does and touches his father, who raises his eyebrows moments later and nods his head. "Yes," he says, "We –"

"– have an –"

"– appointment."

Rewan closes his eyes in barely concealed embarrassment. His parents just shared speech in front of an Outlie descendant.

"Sorry!" they both say simultaneously.

This just keeps getting worse.

Rewan risks a glance at Lizzie. Her fists are clenched. She wobbles slightly on the spot. Her breathing is fast and erratic. She must be fighting every instinct just to stay in the room. He squashes the urge to reassure her; touch would only make it worse.

"Okay," Rewan says. "Well, it's been…" he can't bring himself to say anything positive to them and lets the sentence drop away. "I'll see you soon," he amends.

He practically pushes his parents out of the door.

When he returns to the living room, Lizzie is visibly shaking. He reaches out to her but something in her stance makes him instantly back off. He abandons the gesture and lets his hands fall limply to his sides. The only blessing is that Lizzie has probably missed this absurd show as her eyes are scrunched closed and taking deep breaths, like she's concentrating hard on her breathing.

"They're gone. I'm sorry. I forgot…" Rewan has apparently caught Lizzie's tendency to ramble. Her eyes open and now they're almost comically wide. He takes a step back. He tries to reassure himself that Outliers are usually only in danger after Witnessing a Bond; Lizzie's not a Lifetimer, only a descendent, and his parents have been Bonded for over thirty years. She must just be in shock.

"Why don't you sit down? I'll get you… do you want water? Or something stronger? Whatever you…"

"They really glow," Lizzie whispers.

"What?"

"Glow."

"Yes. Well, no, not literally, of course," Rewan sighs. "It's just all that god-given happiness rolling off them," he breaks off realising that that sounded bitter. "Just the way it looks. It's not important."

That gets Lizzie's attention. Her head snaps up.

"Was that really the first time you saw…?" he asks cautiously. "You study it. Teach it. Write it even. How have you never…?"

"No," she bites. "I write Searching. You write Bonding."

"Same thing."

"No, it's really bloody not."

Rewan steps back. Lizzie is seething. She must see something in his retreat because her defensiveness drops as quickly as it was raised.

"Sorry," she mumbles. "It's just…"

Rewan lets the pause carry until he is sure the sentence has been abandoned. "Sit down. I'll get you some water."

Lizzie seems relieved to have something to do. She goes to the armchair willingly.

When Rewan returns from the kitchen with a glass of water, Lizzie is perched on the edge of the chair, her knee bouncing relentlessly, her hands shaking and sweaty. He is thankful he only filled the glass halfway when it sloshes against the sides. She unsteadily brings it to her lips with both hands and takes a sip. He tears himself away from observing her like a doctor and makes himself sit on the sofa opposite, the coffee table firmly placed between them. She avoids his eyes, instead flickering over the apartment, lingering on the bookcases behind the piano. He finds himself eager to know what she thinks about his book collection but she says nothing. He wonders if she can make out her own poetry on the bookshelf. He honestly has no idea what to say to her.

"Okay?" he asks.

She nods, but still shakes.

For lack of anything else to do, Rewan also glances around the apartment as if he is also fascinated by the sight he sees every day. There is a stack of paper on the end table and with a sharp intake of breath he realises what it is. The essay that she had rather passively aggressively suggested he read in her email the other day. *Authorial Intent in the Technological Age is Destructive to the Progress of Modern Literary Theory.* He had actually read it, at first to see if there was anything he could argue against, and then when he had calmed down, purely out of interest. It must be new as it wasn't included in the work he first sought out when she had been nominated.

"I read your paper," he says, nodding to the stack.

She closes her eyes and exhales. "Shit, sorry."

"Don't apologise. It was interesting."

"I didn't mean to…" she rubs a hand through her tangled hair. "Honestly I was so horrible and angry on that video and then you sent that really nice email and I thought you were mocking me or something, I don't know, it just seemed impossible that anyone would be that nice after what I did, so I'm sorry I did that. The paper was just…"

"I know, but I enjoyed it anyway."

"You did?"

"Yes, definitely. A lot of the theory escaped me but I agree that social media is changing the way authors and readers relate to published works. I assume you wrote it in protest?"

Lizzie lets out a startled laugh. "How'd you figure that?"

"Hector says your agent is permanently attached to the internet. And in the paper you referenced your own experience of being cajoled into answering reader's questions about meaning. I put two and two together."

She smiles. "Yeah, Carol no longer insists on me having an internet presence. Readers –"

"Fans?"

"Yeah…" she scoffs, as if laughing at the idea of a fanbase. "Whatever. They expect instant gratification and by answering their questions about what I personally thought when I was writing something, critics take it to be the only possible interpretation of the poem. Once you've published something you should just… shut up."

"You should have finished your paper like that."

Lizzie looks bewildered at the fact that Rewan just made a joke. He chuckles at her expression and she laughs, probably more at him than the joke, but it's worth it to see her shaking for some other reason than shock.

"'Course I have no idea when to shut up," she mutters. "I really am sorry, Rewan. I shouldn't have run off on you like that."

"You were angry."

"I shouldn't have been. I just don't know how to handle this, you know? There's paparazzi outside my door and tabloids comparing our poetry and our personal lives like it's the same damn thing… but I shouldn't have taken it out on you." She looks across at him, in the eyes for the first time since she entered the apartment. "You should have won."

"Why? Because I'm the Oracle?" Rewan scoffs. "It doesn't mean it's the better work, and the judges knew that as well. You deserve it, Lizzie."

She blushes. Rewan can't recall ever meeting someone who gets flustered so easily. She opens her mouth to say something but remains silent and after a minute Rewan decides to pick up the slack.

"I'm sorry about my parents."

"It's okay," Lizzie says. "It was just unexpected."

"Just so you know, next time you meet a Bonded Pair, you don't have curtsey."

"Right. That was weird."

"A little bit," he teases.

She smiles. She seems calmer all round, which is a miracle considering her earlier shock. Perhaps she is not as sheltered as Rewan first assumed.

"You were right," Lizzie blurts.

"What? Sorry?"

"I meant... In your e-mail you asked why I chose the word 'lonesome' in *StillBeat* and it's not just because it's the name of Kerouac's book. It's because by Searching for your soulmate, especially in such a consuming manner, you are pushing others away because they can't measure up and so by its very nature it's an incredibly lonely thing to do if you never choose love. That's why in the last line..."

"It's a 'pitiful' sound," he recalls. "Because you pity them." *You pity me.*

"Not all Searchers," she corrects. "Not like my mother's companion and other Searchers who make connections. Just those that spend their lives 'howling never to be heard'. Those that don't bother making friends. Those that spend their whole life not living because they're fantasising about their soulmate like life is nothing without them."

Rewan wants to say something intelligent to rebuke her but finds that he is just watching her, hunched over in her seat and talking to the hands in her lap. "It must be lonely," she concludes.

It is. But she's wrong about why. "It's not only Searchers that are lonely," he says finally. "People can have all sorts of reasons for keeping their distance."

She looks across at him at last, curiously, as if she hadn't realised they were talking about anything more than the poem.

"Maybe some people reject love because the world rejects them," he says cautiously. "Maybe they try to make connections but they find it difficult, that there are boundaries in their way, expectations, or circumstance..." he trails off. He has unwittingly ended up talking about his own problems but he has a suspicion he might also be talking about hers.

She nods. "You're right. Of course, you're right. It's not just Searchers. I'm sorry."

He offers her a small smile, and he's surprised when she returns it, but even more surprised to find that he warms at the sight.

She leaves soon after, clumsy and flustered, and still at a distance. He pours away the rest of her water and puts the glass next to his parents' coffee cups in the dishwasher. He leans back against the kitchen counter and stares into the expanse of his living area; too large and too quiet.

*

Lizzie fidgets at the table. Carol has already slapped her hand away from playing with the wine glass and so Lizzie has resorted to fingering the woven edge of the tablecloth where the vulture-like eyes of her agent can't see.

Carol kidnapped Lizzie two hours before the Presentation; fussing over the cornflower blue dress that Lizzie could barely squeeze into and forcing a make-up artist upon her until she looked 'presentable'. Carol had grumbled her usual complaints about becoming Lizzie's personal assistant but even despite her worries they were still some of the first to arrive, and while Carol socialises, Lizzie makes use of the free bar. She now slouches in her designated chair, drinking and ignoring, counting down the minutes until the Presentation ends even though it's yet to begin.

The awards ceremony is taking place in a large function room of a rather swanky hotel. A jazz band is currently on stage, playing loud and pretentious covers of popular songs from about twenty years ago. It's the insufferable people that make it an Arts event though; the Elite, the upper classes, and the celebrities that are currently in favour, all of whom still look at Lizzie like dirt on their shoes.

So far tonight the only people Lizzie has spoken to are the staff members and the handful of people at her table who are representing her already. A few strangers ventured over to touch for Recognition, but most steer clear; not wanting to risk Bonding with someone like her.

Lizzie turns back to face her table. She watches, thoroughly entertained, as Carol's date – a blond-haired and well-toned man – attempts to make small talk with the publishers. He's clearly never picked up a book before in his life. Meanwhile, Carol is swanning between her contacts a couple of tables over, blissfully ignorant of the beautiful disaster that she's left behind. Lizzie is considering rescuing the poor man when the milling journalists suddenly seem to scamper towards the door.

Rewan Pentaghast has just walked in.

Lizzie checks the time; it's five minutes before the start of the presentation. Carol had Lizzie primed and ready, thirty minutes ago, and here Pentaghast goes, striding in confidently as if they wouldn't dare to start without him. He's the star attraction if the flock of fans and journalists around him are any indication. Lizzie grunts in annoyance before she can stop herself and is blinded by a flash moments afterwards. Of course there was a photographer waiting for her to pull a face. A youthful yet hard-worn woman appears from behind the camera and begins barraging Lizzie with questions in a shrill voice. It doesn't help that the journalist is only parroting back Lizzie's own thoughts.

Lizzie keeps her mouth shut. She knows that this is what the journalist wants. A tight-lipped photo looks like an angry photo which will fit their story perfectly. The press are meant to be on their best behaviour during the Presentation but perhaps they have a different understanding of that agreement.

Lizzie closes her eyes and tries to ignore the interrogation. Moments later she hears Carol swooping in, batting away the journalist with a couple of terse sentences.

"Thank you," Lizzie sighs gratefully.

Carol shrugs and smiles and then sits down next to her date, initiating a whispered conversation with him.

And then, Lizzie turns back to the empty chair beside her and, quite unbidden, sees Rewan Pentaghast lounging in it; his arm looped around the back of her shoulders, laughing, eyes bright, as his other hand plays distractedly with the place setting. She blinks away the image, embarrassed by her own daydreaming.

Finally, the tannoy cuts through the murmur, requesting the audience to take their seats.

The sea of press around Rewan clears to loiter at the back of the hall and Lizzie is granted her first full-length view of her competitor this evening; dark curls swept artfully back from his face and dressed in a fitted three-piece navy suit. Her breath hitches at the sight and she barely has time to admonish herself for the action before he catches her eye. A couple of tables stand between them but there is no questioning his eyeline, especially when his mouth quirks a little to one side in that self-assured way of his. He's looking straight at her.

Lizzie looks away, embarrassed, and down to her own clothes. The dress had looked fine on the hanger but on her body it seems to emphasise her every flaw; pale blue makes her skin look oddly pallid and the strapless shoulders only draw attention to her untoned arms, the shape too, does nothing to hide her belly, or anything in fact. She wraps her arms around herself self-consciously. She will never have the born confidence – quite literally – that her competitor has.

She keeps her eyes down as the speaker, dressed in ceremonial robes, reads the greeting and opening prayer. There is a quote about the gift of poetry and the Muses or something and then the speaker hands over to the Chair of the Board; a large, bald man who already appears to be sweating profusely under the bright lights.

Carol nudges her, and of course, it's her cue to go backstage. Lizzie tries to make herself as invisible as possible as she walks under the dimmed lighting past the tables of guests towards the curtain at the side of the stage. She hears the Chair begin to give his speech about the Board and the struggles they had this year in choosing a winner and for the first time during an award ceremony, Lizzie doesn't doubt it, but it all becomes a muffle as she slips behind the curtain.

It's dark backstage. So dark she can barely make out just how terrible she looks, which is probably a blessing in disguise. It's just a cordoned area of the hall, no more than scaffolding and thick blackout curtains. If she stretched out her arms, her fingertips would probably reach either side of the space.

In retrospect, she probably should have moved away from the entrance.

Instead, a prim and proper Rewan Pentaghast nearly falls over her as he enters the backstage area behind her. The movement in the curtain sheds momentarily light to the awkward encounter as they stumble around each other in the dark.

She turns towards him and sees his embarrassed smile. It's beautiful even in the darkness; enough to make her heart skip a little despite her determination not to like him. A man like him doesn't want to be *liked*; he wants to be Bonded. And she aches for him, because for the first time she wants someone to be granted their wish for completion. She doesn't want him to be alone. She doesn't want to see such a kind man broken like Kerouac; he doesn't deserve such a fate. If Rewan doesn't Bond, he will spend every day of his life trapped in that penthouse fortress and no one will ever see his smile. She decides in that split second that she's not going to let that happen. That maybe she can be his friend, just like Rebecca was to Ed.

As they right themselves, she feels his hand brush against her bare arm and then –

A sharp buzz erupts under her skin and blooms like spilt coffee. Warm. Marking. Light flares in front of her eyes, like stars, like galaxies. Everything is impossibly bright and vivid. There's the kind of silence that rings in your ears, like coming out of a loud concert into the still and expansive night. She feels like she's falling. A universe opening before her. She can barely see through the light but Rewan holds her steady; his hand now firmly grasping her forearm. There's a tangible static at the touch, an energy flowing between them, and it must be friction, she rationalises, because what else could it be?

Oh.

No, no, no.

Fear floods through her. But, no. No, they can't be. They've met before. They must have touched before.

It's impossible.

For an elongated moment, there only seems to be light and static and his skin on hers, time expanding with the universe, reaching in search of distant stars, for something indescribable... the white space filling... there is a pull, but it's too big, she feels sick with panic, she can't, *she can't...*

The universe disappears. He has let go.

Reality comes back in increments; the darkness falling back around them, his hand slipping slowly from her arm, the voice of the Chair steadily filtering back into her ears. Rewan is still looking at her with wide eyes. Her heart is beating so loudly she is afraid that he can hear it; that he may have felt its quick beat through her pulse. There is applause from outside that finally breaks the moment, and then a sliver of light that breaks their gaze. There is an assistant waving them through the gap in the curtain towards the stage. The Chair must have announced their names.

Lizzie shakes off the lingering intensity as Rewan casts his eyes downwards and walks past her to the stage. She's still feeling flustered when she steps out after him, moments later, to the sea of flashing lights below and the sun of spotlights above. Nothing like the light she saw in her mind; nothing quite as beautiful.

Rewan accepts his prize as gracefully as possible from the fumbling Chair and stands to the side. She tears her eyes away from him and focuses on crossing the stage, one foot after another, until she also receives her large award and prize money from the Chair. She feels dizzy and hot under the lighting but she smiles out at the cameras, imagining her mum and Ed beaming right back at her through the TV.

She is overwhelmed in every sense of the word. Her feelings are a jumbled mess and she both feels like laughing and crying. She looks across to Rewan as they receive applause and instead of feeling shaky as she had moments before, she feels almost doubly as strong and confident; brimming with energy.

I did it, she thinks, *I actually did it.*

She hurries off the stage afterwards, not sparing another glance at Rewan. This is silly. This is her day and she's spent the majority of the Presentation fantasising about her competitor. She slides back into her seat and finally places the heavy award on the table with a clunk. Whispered congratulations fly around the table – "that was magical" – and Carol turns to grin at her with a soft touch on her arm.

Lizzie shakes her head, downs her wine despite her continued nausea, and munches on the snacks as an excuse for not taking part in the conversation around her. She resents the pull, mere minutes later, that turns her head towards the table where Rewan sits. She resents even further her automatic reaction to what she sees; the uneasiness that trickles down her spine at the sight. Rewan's smile from before has drained from his face. She is too far away to know for certain but she has a feeling that he is being admonished for something. Perhaps she can tell from the slump of his shoulders or the matching scowls on Souls Pentaghast as they talk over him but something tells her that they are not pleased with him. A frown forms on her face before she can stop herself. She only realises she's been staring when Rewan looks up suddenly and catches her eye. It's impossible to know for sure over such a distance that he's looking at *her* but she feels that it's true nonetheless. Heat crawls up her spine.

This keeps happening, again and again, over mere minutes. Sometimes he is staring when she catches him, sometimes it is her, and then the heat burns too strong and she feels herself flushing. She actually fancies him, she realises abruptly. She finds herself looking at him again but this time it's him that's already staring. She can't stand this. There's still a couple of minutes before the speeches. Lizzie stands and runs to the ladies bathroom without looking back.

She splashes cold water on her face and then cringes when she remembers she's wearing make-up. Shit. She looks up into her tired reflection to see that the rest of her fares no better; her bun is practically redundant as hair falls out in every direction, the clasp of her dainty silver necklace has fallen to the front, and her strapless dress is dangerously close to slipping down to inappropriate levels, but... she can't help but look at her eyes. They look different. They seem brighter somehow. She felt fine earlier in the evening – nervous but in her own mind at least – now she feels dizzy and faint and sick all over, ever since that weird moment behind the curtain. But that happens sometimes after stressful periods, right? She hasn't been sleeping well. This is probably just the effect of being wound up too tight and let go too suddenly. Her mind runs through the metaphors, trying to recall some words to make sense of it, but nothing quite describes this strange anxiety that crawls underneath her skin, itching for something she can't define. The more she focuses on it, the sicker she feels. She needs to make her excuses and leave the Presentation but she still has her reading and speech to stumble through. She groans and only stops herself from banging her head against the cool mirror when a toilet door creaks open behind her. Right. She's in public. No freaking out in public. She's just going to have to grit her teeth, take advantage of the free bar, and somehow make it through the evening.

*

Rewan doesn't quite understand what happened backstage but he's thankful when he gets out from under the spotlight. Not quite so grateful, however, when he sits back next to his parents. They're scrutinising him worse than the journalists.

"What?"

"It's strange..." his father starts.

"...but you look..." his mother trails off.

They both tilt their head to the side like a demented pair of vultures.

"What?"

His mother looks out over the rest of the hall but Rewan keeps his father's gaze. His mother snaps out of their weird trance first and says to her Pair, "We were obviously mistaken, love. Maybe they've done something to the lights…"

His father hums in thought.

Rewan doesn't know what they're talking about. "Yeah, it's a weird evening," he says because it's the truth even though he doesn't know how it fits into their conspiring.

"You must be right," his father says to his Pair. "It would have happened at the house if she was his."

Rewan almost drops his red wine. "What? You thought I'd....? We'd...?" he splutters. Hope bubbles beneath the surface before his father's meaning sinks in. "But, of course, yes, we've met before. At my house. So it's impossible," he says, remembering the strange moment with Lizzie backstage, "Just an emotionally intense… evening." *Impossible*. The word that rang through his head as soon as the thought crossed his mind backstage. *Can't*. He knew even then that it couldn't have been a Bond. There's meant to be no doubts about it when you touch your soulmate for the first time; it's meant to be a certainty; impossible to deny. He reassures himself that they wouldn't be able to be apart right now if they'd Bonded; Separation Syndrome is renowned for its viciousness, even when the Bond is still new and forming. He looks towards Lizzie, where her agent, Carol Boots, is smiling at her and talking animatedly, reaching out to touch her arm. He narrows his eyes. "Impossible," he repeats to himself.

"Just as well," his father chuckles. "Imagine being stuck with a woman like that."

"What's that meant to mean?"

"She's hardly the most civilised woman in the room, Rewan," his mother says patronisingly just as Lizzie drops half a cheese cracker onto her dress. "Definitely not destined for the Elite," his mother is saying. "It looks like they scrounged up that dress from an M&S sale for godsake."

"There's no such thing as being 'destined' for this life. You either Bond or you don't. Class has nothing to do with it," he mutters, except that it *does*, because he knows that people like him are given more opportunity to Search than someone who has to work for a living, and that people like his parents are given more support from the Temples when they Bond. The gods may not care one whit about class and background when they merge Souls but the Elite *does* care. Greatly. "In any case, it's not like I can choose my Pair."

His mother clicks her tongue in admonishment. "Perhaps. But you *can* choose with whom to spend time."

Was that a dig at his association with Arcadius and Elena? Or another at Lizzie? Rewan opens his mouth to state that a true Searcher such as himself would welcome Recognition from a beggar on the street when his father changes the topic to one even less welcome, "And to think that she won. This'll be your last consolation prize, Rewan, and you know it."

Rewan sighs and settles in for a good long disparagement of his profession until, eventually, his parents run out of steam. His mother concludes with a brisk comment about "not being yourself this evening," and then they turn away to make small talk with others at the table.

Rewan looks out over the hall, unconsciously seeking out Lizzie. She is fiddling with the edge of the tablecloth that falls into her lap while the other occupants of her table are happily chatting away. A small smile comes unbidden to his lips as he watches. He should look away. He should really look away. But then, she's looking back at him.

He finds himself standing before he can stop himself. But whatever he had planned to say becomes irrelevant when Lizzie leaves her table without giving him a second glance. She stumbles out of the function room and out of sight.

"Rewan?" his parents ask in sync. His mother adds, "What are you doing?"

He has no idea. "Going to the Gents. Excuse me."

"But the speeches begin in a few moments –" his father says.

If they say anything further, Rewan doesn't hear it, already walking away from the table. Everything has been a blur since he left the stage and he still feels strange in a way that escapes description. He needs to clear his head.

The corridor is blissfully empty, only occupied with floral wallpaper and extravagant wall hangings. At one end is the reception hall, now cordoned off, but with a receptionist dozing behind the large oak desk, and at the other end of the corridor, past the bathrooms, there is a tall stone statue of Apollo.

Rewan goes to examine it. The god stands tall with a lyre in his hands and a bow and arrow at his feet, but his glazed eyes look straight ahead into Rewan's own.

Apollo is one of the most complex of the gods, with many qualities and connections, and although he is the god of light and should be treated as a good omen, he is also renowned for being unlucky in love. The gods do not have soulmates as they are whole in their own right but Apollo had dozens of consorts, both male and female, and never found happiness. It is rumoured that once Apollo begged his father, Zeus, to split him apart like a human so that he may find himself and become his own ideal lover. But Zeus refused. The gods don't want you to think that they are lonely; that they are, in any way, just as weak and malleable as humans.

He steps back just as the door from the Ladies swings open beside him. Rewan jumps in surprise and nearly loses his balance as he knocks into someone. Hands reach out to steady him and it's only when they have both righted themselves that he realises that he is standing inappropriately close to Elizabeth Brighton. Again.

He inhales sharply in surprise, not only at the sight of his company, but also at the unusual amount of touch between them.

Lizzie seemed reluctant to even share space earlier but now... he glances down to see their hands firmly grasping each other's forearms, just as he had done backstage, now perfectly mirrored, but their clumsiness has also resulted in them standing toe-to-toe with their knees brushing and their foreheads almost resting together. From this angle Rewan could find constellations in the freckles on her nose and give names to the individual pigments of her irises if he was afforded the luxury. They are so close that the warmth of her skin seems to thrum beneath his own. He looks down at her until she catches his gaze, shyly, and then she smiles. He should feel embarrassed, and he does a little, but his body seems instead to relax at her smile; tension draining from him so quickly that he feels lightheaded. It's her eyebrows drawing together that bring him back to focus and the fear of something being wrong that causes him to look away from her eyes. What he finds momentarily stuns him, because, quite unbeknownst to him, the pad of his thumb had begun rubbing circles on the inside of her arm; gentle, familiar, instinctive. He drops her arm, ceasing immediately and stepping back to a socially-acceptable distance.

"Sorry," Rewan says cautiously.

"It's okay," she whispers. He wouldn't be able to hear it over the clamour of the ceremony if he wasn't watching her mouth form the words.

He realises abruptly that although he has stepped away, he hasn't stopped *looking*. He is watching as her tongue darts out to wet her lips, and as her throat contracts with an audible swallow, and he understands for the first time the struggle with which Orpheus led Eurydice out of the underworld. Rewan would not make it as far as the gate he fears.

"The speeches are soon. We ought to –" Rewan starts. He hears the click of a camera and cringes. He rather hopes that the journalists only caught the tail end of this and not the entire awkward exchange.

"Yeah." She straightens up, seemingly thinking along the same lines. "We should go."

"Right," Rewan agrees. His body doesn't seem to be moving though. "Shall we?"

He doesn't know who is more shocked by the curved arm that he holds out to her. He really needs to reclaim control over his body – he is a Searcher and she a Settler, after all, so whatever spark lies between them ought to remain unlit. Still, she looks equally as surprised to find herself linking their arms together. They stare at each other, now caught in this arrangement under the watchful eyes of Apollo and half a dozen camera lenses. He walks towards the hall with her beside him and attempts to unravel what on earth he was thinking, and worse, what the journalists will think, and then, worst of all, what his parents will think. He considers letting go every second of the journey but he never does.

The din of conversation seems to drop a few notches as they re-enter the hall. He feels their eyes on him but instead of letting go, he holds on tighter. He leads Lizzie back to her table and doesn't miss the suspicious side-eye Carol Boots gives him. He turns back to Lizzie, rattling his brains for what a gentleman in his right mind would say at this point. He's got nothing. It takes all his concentration to step away.

"I'll see you on stage in a minute then," Lizzie says.

"Right, yes," Rewan mumbles. "See you then."

Rewan walks back to his table, attempting to shake off the strangeness that seems to have taken over his higher brain functions this evening. His parents look suitably disappointed in him when he sits back down.

"What was all that about?" his father asks.

"You shouldn't encourage her like that," his mother chides. "You'll give her the wrong idea."

Rewan suppresses the urge to snap at his parents. He takes a large swig of wine and watches Lizzie fidget at her table, her fingers curling the hair that has fallen from her bun.

Finally, Rewan says firmly, "I was just being a gentleman."

His parents look at him suspiciously and open their mouths but thankfully the tannoy cuts through the hall, calling Rewan, Lizzie and the three others from the shortlist to the stage.

It's a gift from the gods that everyone by this late stage of the evening is too merry to listen attentively to the speeches. Soon it's only him and Lizzie on stage. They still have to get through a reading, a speech, and then the dreaded Q&A when even more press will be let through the door. The only solace is that however unwilling he is, Lizzie is probably equally as unenthusiastic.

He reads out his poem and it falls from his lips without thinking; it's the title poem and always the one requested. He performs and receives applause and then returns to his seat on stage to watch Lizzie.

He can see her legs shake when she stands to do the reading and he wishes there was some way he could calm her. This time it's his turn to fidget anxiously, as if taking her nerves upon himself as she cannot presently do so. She clears her throat and as soon as she begins reciting *StillBeat*, Rewan finds himself mouthing along. By the time Lizzie is reciting the concluding couplet, Rewan has a smile on his face.

The hall explodes into applause, and rightly so. This is the recognition that she deserves; the Elite and their traditions be damned. It is only then that Rewan realises that it hadn't just been him enthralled; the whole hall had been silent during the reading. He wonders if she's finally broken through to them; if she's somehow convinced them of the worthiness of her poetry that he's seen all along; if they've finally realised how much bigger their world could be if only they let it. And all because of her.

Lizzie shakily steps back around the table on stage and walks into Rewan's open arms. He must have given a standing ovation and now he is hugging his competitor, on stage, in front of a hundred guests and a dozen photographers and a live TV camera, as if it is the most natural thing in the world. He can feel his heart beating impossibly fast and knows that this time his crush may not be so easily abated.

Just let me get through this evening, he begs the gods, *then I will never have to see her again.* He ignores the pang of pain at that thought and then continues to ignore it all night as he does his best to avoid her.

*

Lizzie wakes the morning after the Presentation with a pounding head, a foul taste in her mouth, and a twisting anxiety in her gut. She aches all over and every bone feels exhausted and weak, like the start of the flu.

She groans and curls further into the warm duvet. This has got to be the worst hangover of all time. Then she thinks back to the Presentation; the sweaty shaking of her hands, the knee-rattling reading, the cringeworthy Q&A... and of course, Rewan Bloody Pentaghast with his perfect bloody hair and life and... Fine. She drank a lot. But it seemed like a sensible thing to do at the time.

She needs tea and painkillers. She doesn't want food yet but decides that bacon definitely needs to be consumed before too long. The digital numbers that blink at her from the microwave inform her that it's only just past ten o'clock. She checks her phone to see a couple of missed calls from both her mother and Ed but she can't bring herself to call back just yet. Instead, she pads around the kitchen in her flannel pyjamas, thankful at least that she had the mindfulness to change clothes last night, and fixes herself some tea.

She ambles back to bed shortly afterwards as the caffeine did not have the desired effect. She still feels *heavy*, for lack of a better word, as if something is pressing on her from all sides. As if she's forgotten something; missing something; needing something... It makes no sense but the weight sits on her shoulders and the anxiety stirs in her stomach. She leans back against the headboard and closes her eyes in an attempt to abate the nausea, the second cup of tea steaming between her fingers, and this time the words that nudge at her from her subconscious aren't poetry at all, but prayer: *Almighty Zeus – fair ruler and father of all, hear my prayer…*

Lizzie shakes her head to dispel the words, but it only makes her nausea worse. She is surprised that she still knows the words as she has not heard the customary prayer since secondary school festivals. It must have been spoken last night at some point when Lizzie wasn't paying attention and weaved its way into her subconscious.

When Rewan wakes in a puddle of his own drool it's not his most promising start to the day. He groans and pushes himself away from his pillow only to find himself toppling onto the hardwood floor instead. He lands with a loud thud.

He groans louder and lets his head fall into his hands until the room stops spinning. He has never felt so rotten in his life. He doesn't tend to get hangovers as he always makes sure to moderate his alcohol intake and then drink water before bed but he doesn't know what else this could be. He feels weak all over. An incoming sickness, perhaps.

He hauls himself up from the floor, thankful at least that he missed the coffee table during his fall and wipes the drool from the leather sofa with the sleeve of his rumpled shirt. It's late morning already; too late for his routine morning worship, but he doesn't feel overly guilty for missing it, only guilty for wondering why.

He checks his messages and is surprised to see his name added to a group chat – a quick scroll through the messages confirms that it's Elena, Archie, and the rest of their 'disgraced' party that he has so casually been invited to join. Attached is a snapshot of a tabloid with an article entitled **'Oracle Fallen from Grace?'** and he notes with numb detachment that it is from a paper owned by his own parents. The article is smattered with various compromising pictures of him and Lizzie from last night. Beneath the link is Elena's witty comment, welcoming him into their group: *fraternising with an Outlie girl? congrats, nerd. even Archie hasn't managed that one.*

It seems that one night consorting with Elizabeth Brighton was enough to evict him from the Elite and fall into the lap of the disgraced.

He doesn't know how he feels about this development; the opportunity for friends over a career. Rewan deigns not to think about it until he has ingested some caffeine. He shuffles over to the kitchen and makes a cup of tea. He usually drinks black coffee but this morning he has tea. He even adds milk. His whole morning routine feels off-kilter.

Bacon. Bacon will fix it, as it always does.

Rewan listens to the radio as he cooks, hoping that the music will ease the twist in his stomach or the pounding in his head or the strange sense of *not right* that has been dogging him, but instead it only serves as a distraction. So much so, that he doesn't notice when the pan begins to spit hot oil.

He swears in surprise when a splattering of it lands on the back of his right hand. He instinctively pulls back, dropping the spatula in the pan of sizzling bacon. He turns off the hob and runs his hand under cold water but there is already a scattering of red blotches standing stark against his pale skin.

"Shit," he whispers. And a second later, wonders when he began to swear so much.

Lizzie is browsing the internet back in bed when her right hand suddenly flares with heat.

"Shit," she whispers, cradling her hand to her chest.

She looks down at her laptop for a sign of what could have caused it but unless the image of Rewan Pentaghast taking up her screen is literally scorching hot, there is nothing to blame. It must have been static or something. The pain is gone as soon as it comes but her hand remains warm like a reminder.

Despite Rewan's earlier enthusiasm for bacon, he still only eats half his sandwich. He feels too nauseous to stomach the rest but leaves the other half on the kitchen counter just in case. He sits on a stool at his kitchen island and scrolls through this new group chat, willing himself to make the connection. He considers Lizzie's implication that he should make friends but it's harder than he thought even though the opportunity is now presented to him. For a moment his thumb hovers over Lizzie's name; at the contact she put in his phone before they parted last night. What would her reaction be if he called her? He shouldn't talk to her, he knows, his crush is already dangerously distracting, but he wants to, and she was the one that suggested that he try to make connections.

The phone vibrates in his hand and he almost drops it in shock. A message from Lizzie is displayed on the screen.

Sometimes I think scientists are lying about deep-sea fish. How can this be natural?

Attached is a low-quality picture of a terrifying and disproportionate eel creature with the title *saccopharyngiformes*. Rewan re-reads the message and the image for a good three minutes, wondering how he's meant to respond to that. Finally, he decides:

Poseidon was drunk.

He stares at the screen, nervously waiting for a response.

LOL

That's it. One goddamn acronym. Is she actually laughing? Or is it a quick way to end the conversation? He is dreadful at this.

He groans and drops his head onto his arms that are crossed on the table. His hands come up to run his fingers through his tangled hair. He needs a shower. He needs to stop thinking about Elizabeth Brighton.

Lizzie feels more embarrassed than she thought possible after sending that spontaneous message to Rewan. It's the type of friendly nonsense that she usually sends to Ed or her mum. Also, she's not going to overanalyse her giddy reaction when he messaged her back. It's like she's fourteen again and talking to her first crush at that house party in Brixton. His joke is kind of funny though, even if she is too humiliated to continue the conversation.

She drags herself out of bed shortly after that and into the shower to try and wash away the embarrassment.

By early afternoon, Rewan feels no better. His stomach is still twisted into knots and his head is pounding as if raging a war with itself. At least he now looks outwardly presentable, if nothing else; dressed in a suit and tie, and his stubble trimmed to its usual length. His reflection in the mirror is awfully gaunt and his eyes are strangely wide and hollow; as if he is withering away. After the festival, he will take himself to the doctors, but Apollonia is one of his favourite events of the year and not even his mysterious illness will prevent him from attending.

Apollonia is the Hellenic Spring Festival where offerings are given to the gods to petition for a pleasant summer; it's a celebration of the good weather to come. Athena Temple will host live music, poetry, dancing, and fine art from late afternoon until midnight, but pigs will also be given as offerings; the organs sacrificed to Apollo, and the flesh roasted and eaten by the worshippers. Lizzie would probably call it a glorified hog roast and she wouldn't be wrong.

Rewan tells himself he'll be fine once he's there. It helps that his parents will not be present this year as they've spontaneously decided to visit the family estate in the Lake District (thus avoiding the spotlight on Rewan's recent fall from grace). There will still be a fair number of Elite present, which will no doubt keep their distance, but there will be more worshippers and artists than bureaucrats and entrepreneurs for which he's grateful. He may finally be able to talk to Archie without looking over his shoulder for cameras. He may even have the opportunity to make new friends. He turns away from the mirror and smiles in anticipation; Apollonia really is his favourite time of year and he is determined to enjoy it.

Lizzie can't stand it anymore. There is a constant thrumming beneath her skin, a strange energy, and it's completely illogical but she needs to get *out*. She hopes that fresh air will ease her nausea, but it shouldn't be enough to justify leaving the house when a pack of journalists are probably outside waiting to pounce. She could leave through the underground car park without too much trouble but then her options are limited. She needs to go somewhere where she won't be bothered. Somewhere big like a park or quiet like a Temple. She doesn't know but she has to get *out*.

Athena Temple is a good fifteen minute walk away and so Rewan finds his music player and turns it on to keep his thoughts calm during the journey. He would normally take a taxi, even for the short distance, but today for some reason, he relishes the idea of a walk. He also realises that the headphones have the advantage of dissuading the reporters outside the apartment complex from excess interaction. The numbers of journalists have dwindled since the Presentation but there is still an optimistic handful whose voices he can hear over his music, asking after Lizzie, asking if they secretly Bonded. He's tempted to snap at them with a brisk Lizzie-esque explanation that if he had Bonded, he would be too weak from Separation right now to function, but then he recalls how deathly pale he looked in the mirror and realises it would rather undermine his point.

Lizzie grabs her music player and leaves the flat. She runs past Cat Lady, nearly tripping over the tortoise cat, Frodo, as she goes. There are five flights of stairs down to the carpark. She can hear her footsteps echo, the clunk of trainers against concrete, audible above the quiet stirrings of music in her ears.

She emerges onto the street but the fresh air isn't helping as much as she'd hoped. She lets her feet guide her through the suburbs of the city. It's easier than usual to avoid people; most don't even reach out to touch her as if they can sense her bleak mood. Her stomach rumbles and she realises that she didn't manage to eat much today, only half a sandwich. It's tempting to duck into one of the takeaways but her feet seem to have other plans, taking her further and further away from the area she knows.

The Temple is a hive of activity and Rewan feels better with every minute he spends surrounded by art in the cella. The chatter echoes across the tall stone chamber and he feels at home upon seeing a child's painting hanging next to the Art Oracle's; there is no hierarchy here, only offerings of love, none more worthy than any other. There is excitement in the air; he can feel it buzzing under his skin, dancing across the stone slabs, and curling up the marble columns to envelop the arches of the cella.

Lizzie is calmer after walking for so long. She doesn't know this area of London well but the clean streets and Georgian buildings with brass door knockers and potted roses signal that the Elite might consider this home. In fact, Rewan's penthouse must be somewhere in this district; she recognises the postcodes on the street signs. She turns and walks down a road where the houses appear to get smaller. Dusk is approaching and she hears the distant sounds of a party.

As enjoyable as the festival is, Rewan finds himself craving fresh air within the hour and excuses himself from an engaging conversation with Archie to walk through the open Temple doors. He stands at the top of the stone steps and sighs; both in contentment and in melancholy.

The sun is setting, just beginning to disappear behind the tall pine trees that envelop Rewan's favourite shrine in the Temple Gardens. From the top of the stone steps he can watch the worshippers in the bandstand set up their instruments, a couple of teenagers climbing trees to hang the last of the fairy lights over the square, and a chef as he prepares the feast at the edge of the large marquee. The evening part of the festival will begin soon, with dancing into the night. He remembers last year, when he played the piano for the dozens of couples dancing under the fairy lights, and praying to the gods that next year – this year – he would have his

Pair in his arms as well.

Rewan aches so suddenly it feels like a wrench in his gut. He needs her here. He *needs* her.

The album finishes playing. Lizzie stops walking. A colossal Temple towers over her, its pillars casting shadows over the street. The streetlights are beginning to come on, painting everything pink, and she hears the whisper of the last track in her mind. She knows this Temple, she realises; it's Athena Temple. These are the gardens that she visited with her mum after her father's death; her one clear memory of that time. Ed and Mum still come back here every Solstice. She looks up over the gardens to the stone steps of the Temple and sees none other than her so-called rival, Rewan Pentaghast, standing before her.

Rewan opens his eyes, and unbelievably, Lizzie is before him; like he wished her into existence. She's standing in the street in jeans and a jumper, her hair tied back and her face clean of make-up. She's the most beautiful thing he's ever seen. He grins, giddy at the sight of her, and runs down the steps towards her.

Lizzie is too shocked to move. Of all the places she could have gone, she ended up finding Rewan. She puts away the silent music player and the full sound of the festivities roar across the street towards her. Rewan is smiling like a madman and she feels a smile of her own responding in kind. For the first time all day, her nausea abates and she can breathe in the clean spring air. She crosses the street to meet him halfway.

Rewan envelopes her in a hug like it's the most natural thing in the world. He breathes her in and feels her relax against him. "Hi," he whispers against her ear, and his stomach flutters with something other than sickness when she returns the phrase, so close he can feel her warm breath on his skin.

"Missed you," she whispers. Her head has stopped aching and is instead fluttering like her stomach; she didn't know that was even possible. It's only when he sighs contentedly that she realises with horror what she just said. She cringes and tries to pull away but he only holds her tighter. It's stupid. It's mad. She can't have fallen for him so quickly. She turns her head in the embrace, her cheek brushing against his stubble, until they are so close that she can see the pigments in his irises. They look like autumn leaves. He smiles down at her softly, his eyes flickering from her eyes to her lips. She can't deny his unspoken request. Her heart beats loudly as she closes her eyes and tilts her head just slightly until her lips brush against his.

She kisses him and a spark flares and ignites every part of his body. Electric in the same way it was yesterday when he held her backstage. Suddenly connected like a plug in a socket. But more than that; it's the feeling of vastness and yet isolation, as if the universe exists only for them. It's his first kiss, and it's perfect. He tugs her closer, kisses her deeper, and he feels overwhelmed with feeling, with uncontainable completeness, just as he felt yesterday when she fell into his arms...

They don't know who realises first. They break the kiss and stare at each other in shock.

"Yesterday was the first time we touched," Lizzie gasps. "At yours, I didn't..." she trails off, her eyes darting back and forth and her breaths getting lost in her growing panic.

He follows her in hastily trying to remember their actions at his house. He was afraid to touch her, he realises, so although they had met before yesterday, they hadn't actually touched, which means that the intense moment they had backstage yesterday was actually… actually...

"Shit," they both swear simultaneously.

Their shared speech only seems to scare Lizzie further. It takes Rewan a minute to realise that it's not his panic he's feeling but hers. Bonds are like a constant feedback loop, he remembers his parents saying, so he needs to calm down. She backs away from him, pale and shaking, just as she had done at his house. He forces himself to tamp down his trepidation. If they are Bonded then nothing can happen; they'll be fine, no matter what.

"No," Lizzie says. "No, I can't." It's too big, too scary, and she realises that this is exactly what she thought at the Presentation. She's so terrified of being Bonded that she must have denied it to the extent that Rewan didn't accept it out of some stupid protective instinct. "No." It can't have happened. She shakes her head, trying to shake herself out of it, trying to shake him out too if he's in there. "Take it back."

Rewan feels her panic attack like it's his own. He has no idea how to fix it. He's never had one before. They're just standing opposite each other, freaking each other out. It has to stop. One of them has to break the loop. He could kiss her again –

She steps back, away from him, out towards the street again. She can't do this. She can't leave her mum alone. She can't be with a man she hardly knows for the rest of her life with no way out. She can't. And she won't accept it because there's no evidence they actually Bonded, dammit. That weird moment backstage was just because she was excited, and she felt sick today because she picked up a cold or something, and that only felt like the best kiss of her life because it's been a while, but that doesn't mean anything. She can walk away now and forget about him. She backs away but her eyes remain locked on his, they seem to get duller with every step she takes and her heart aches at the sight but *she can't –*

He knows he has to let her go but now he's acknowledged the Bond, he can feel it like an elastic band direct to their hearts being stretched apart. The pull of the universe. They had been fighting the effects of Separation Syndrome all day and not realised it. How is that even possible? He can feel the sickness already building with every step away she takes. The Bond must be stronger now than it had been. He doesn't drop her gaze even as she backs out of the gate and onto the street.

Lizzie looks at Rewan, dwarfed by the stone Temple behind him and he seems so small, so lost, she can almost hear him beg for her to stay. She nearly gives in to his plea. She hears nothing but the howling void between them, still the only two in the universe, but the universe is expanding quickly and it's deafening.

A sharp sound breaks through the void. A screech of tyres. Screaming. Then, an almighty pain sends Rewan to his knees.

*

Rewan gasps. Noise. Pain. *Silence.* The pain in his leg subsides to throbbing and his mind feels a vortex where there had been an expanding universe. He's not the one hurt, he realises. He jumps back to his feet, vision swimming, and sight returning to see a car swerving out of sight.

Lizzie is thrown against the far side of the pavement; sprawled awkwardly, leg crooked and bleeding through her jeans, her head cracked on the curb, and the music player fallen out of her pocket and smashed to the ground. It was her pain he felt, and her silence he hears now. With an anguished scream he runs past the gate and falls to his knees at her side. His hands hover over her prone body, needing to touch but scared of hurting her further.

Another hand is on her wrist. Rewan blinks and looks around him frantically to see through blurry vision that a bystander is next to him; taking her pulse, talking to him, "I'm calling an ambulance, Soul, don't panic."

Rewan can't bring himself to speak a single word to thank him even as the bystander tells him not to move the body and makes the call.

"No," he whispers. "No, no," but he means: *no, you can't die; no, don't leave me.* They're meant to be dancing, and laughing, and...

Desperately, he opens his mind to the vortex – the place in his mind that he now realises Lizzie has made hers – and he searches through the darkness until he finds what he didn't know he was looking for: a little thread of light, pulsing weakly in the depths. "No," he orders it. It vibrates under his command and he attempts to pull the light towards him. He has no idea if this is the right thing to do. This is how Bonded Pairs always die – from Soul Break – one follows the other into the darkness until they both fade. But he has to trust his instincts and his instincts say that the thread tastes, smells, feels, like Lizzie and if it means she's alive, he will cling to it indefinitely. "No," he orders again, and this time the light seems a little brighter.

He finally lets go, exhausted, when the doctors take her into surgery.

"When she's out you can see her," a gruff ginger-bearded nurse called Nate explains as he steers him towards the waiting room. "Emergency Certificates grant you the same rights as married folk but it's too risky to have new Pairs in the operating theatre; you gotta have your Soulmate Certificate for that."

Rewan grunts. He understands but he's not happy about it. "Will she be okay?"

He makes a derisive noise. "What did the paramedics tell you?"

"I don't know. I wasn't listening. I was in her head, sort of, holding on to her spirit, or soul, or something… it's hard to explain."

Nate harrumphs. "You were being an idiot. Alrighty then." Nate practically pushes him onto a red plastic chair. "Cliff notes version: her broken leg should straighten out, her cuts and bruises will heal, but… there could be spinal damage 'cos of the way she fell and it's a head injury so brain damage is a possibility. The doctors should be able to say more after they've finished patching her up in surgery and taken her for a scan, okay Romeo?"

Rewan swallows his nerves and nods. He has to stay calm. He has to ignore the vortex in his mind and the weight pinning him down and the panic simmering under his skin and *stay calm*. "How, er, how long?"

Nate shrugs. "Probably a couple of hours. Take a nap if you can and we'll wake you when she gets out. You need to rest after focusing on the Bond like that."

Rewan shakes his head. "No, I need to get her mother." Does he? He doesn't know where that thought came from but he feels its importance nonetheless. "I'll rest when I get back. But Lizzie will need her here. Will you call me if anything changes?"

Nate furrows his eyebrows. "You are a funny one, aren't you?" It's not a question. "I dunno a single Soul that would leave right now. You sure you're Bonded, mate?"

Rewan doesn't know how to respond to that. There's still a sliver of doubt in his mind but with everything that has happened in the last twenty-four hours and now his delve into her mind, he's fairly certain that it's true. He always thought the mental connection between Souls would be more than that tiny thread of light but he doesn't know what else it could possibly have been. Maybe it will build when they are permitted more than a minute to nurture it.

Nate pushes him into the Gents to get 'cleaned up' before he lets Rewan leave and once Rewan sees his reflection he understands why. He looks half-dead from exhaustion and his eyes are empty but there's also blood everywhere: on his face from where their foreheads rested, on his hands from where he touched her, and then smeared everywhere since. His trousers are damp to the touch from kneeling on the road in her blood. *Her blood.* He heaves over the sink but his body has nothing to throw up. The fear and panic start to encroach but he pushes them away. He has to stay calm for Lizzie. If his mind is calm then hers will be, he has to believe that. He begins to clean with shaking hands and by the time the sink is empty of blood he has regained a little of his composure.

When Rewan emerges, he finds Nate again and the nurse agrees to keep him informed if anything changes. Rewan gives one last look at the closed surgery doors before running out of the hospital.

Lizzie's ancient mobile phone at least has the capability to store addresses so he uses the map on his smartphone to locate her mother's house. He doesn't question why he has to visit her in person; he has faith that there is a reason behind his hunch, or else he would still be at the hospital with Lizzie.

His head begins to spin as he sets off and he can feel the Bond even in its weak state making him uncomfortable at the separation. It is always pulling him towards her. Now he understands the constant sickness as Separation Syndrome, it's even harder to ignore.

He calls Carol to tell her about the accident as soon as he gets into the taxi because the Bond says that's the right thing to do. There is immediate chatter and movement to be heard on the other side of the phone. She says she'll be there in ten minutes. Rewan breathes a sigh of relief; he needs someone to be there with Lizzie in the hospital as he doesn't know how long Ms Brighton will take.

"Why was Lizzie even at the Temple?" Carol asks.

"I don't... I don't know." Rewan says. He has a feeling that the Bond led her to him but he doesn't want to tell anyone about the Bond just yet, not until Lizzie is okay. She'll want to be there and see their faces, and she will, when she wakes up, he reassures himself.

"Okay, well, I'm on my way to the hospital," she says. "Once I'm there I'll call Ed if Rebecca doesn't beat me to it."

"Call Hec as well, will you? He'll want to know where I am."

There is a brief silence on the other end and then, "Actually, er, Hec is here," her voice has gone rather squeaky. "We had a, um, thing. A Post-Presentation agent meeting thing."

"A meeting?" Rewan asks sceptically. "On Apollonia Sunday evening?"

Rewan can hear Hector laughing in the background as Carol squeaks out an affirmative.

If this was any other time, he would have something to say about their agents' love lives but right now there are bigger things happening. "Okay, whatever, I'll meet you two at the hospital. Thanks Carol."

The taxi lets him out at a row of terraced bungalows at the edge of a small derelict park. He fully realises for the first time how different their paths have been and how hard Lizzie must have worked to have the career that she does. Not just battling the Elite who have denied her recognition for so long but her path to university could not have been easy either when she lacks the funds that he takes for granted. His path in comparison has been easy and expected; already laid out before him, ready to take, but she must have battled for every step.

He runs down the houses until he comes across number 9. He stops outside and checks the address stored in Lizzie's phone again. It's the right one. He takes a deep breath, wipes the sweat from his brow, and attempts to fix his tie before he realises that his trousers are still stained with blood and all attempts to look presentable are ultimately futile. He swallows his discomfort and knocks on the door.

The door opens on the latch and Rewan is afforded an inch-width view of a woman in a nightie and curlers.

"Hello Ms Brighton –"

She seems to cower as soon as he speaks. He was born and raised in the Elite, he realises, and he must also sound like it. He winces. He remembers vividly how anxious Lizzie was meeting him for the first time and he knows that her mother is likely to be even more wary of Bonded Pairs and their kind.

He tries to tone down his accent as he continues, "I'm Rewan Pentaghast, I'm afraid something's happened to –"

The door shuts and then opens fully before he can finish his sentence. The woman behind the door has paled at least three shades and stares into the distance like she's scared of looking straight ahead. "She Witnessed?"

Her voice is so quiet that Rewan thinks he must have misheard before his mind catches up to exactly who is talking to. Her husband died from Witnessing. Of course her worst fear is that it would happen to her daughter as well. "No! Not at all, Ms Brighton. She Bonded."

Rewan clamps his mouth shut. He hadn't meant to say that; he'd been in such a hurry to reassure her that the words had slipped out unintentionally. He holds his breath in anticipation for Ms Brighton's reaction.

"Oh," she says simply, her face crumpling in despair. "I suppose she's yours now, isn't she?" She sounds wrecked, like her heart is breaking. "Is this what you're here for? To take her things? Where is she?" she asks, harsh and untrusting, scrutinising the space around him like she'll appear out of thin air. "Where's my daughter?"

Rewan tries to speak but words fail him. The woman in front of him is utterly distraught.

"She, uh, she's not here," he manages to say. He sees Lizzie's mother begin to panic; he recognises the signs now having seen them so often on Lizzie. He swallows and tries to speak again, though his voice comes out deep and scratched, "She's at the hospital. She was with me and there was a car accident and now… Will you come?"

"You left her there?!" Ms Brighton exclaims. "She's alone?!"

Rewan opens his mouth but no words come out.

Ms Brighton looks away. "I can't leave, I can't –"

Rewan has heard those words far too often recently and this is one too many. He snaps, "Yes, you bloody well can."

She visibly recoils.

He really is doing a terrible job. She hates his kind already and with every word he speaks is making it worse but he *needs* her; he needs her because Lizzie needs her. He pinches the bridge of his nose with his fingers trying to tamper down the anger born of fear. "I'm sorry," he says, and doesn't care how panicked his voice is as he pleads with her. "Truly I am. But I left her to come and get you because she's scared and she wants you there and please will you just come with me and see your daughter because the only thing I *can't* do right now is explain to her when she wakes up why her mother isn't there beside her. Please."

Ms Brighton's face falls, her body language no longer defensive. "It's true isn't it? You two really did Bond," she says in quiet awe as she studies him. Absently, he wonders what evidence she sees; if he glows like Souls are meant to or if the Separation or Lizzie's unconsciousness is preventing the natural flow of the Bond.

Rewan can't speak anymore, too fraught from containing his panicked emotions but he nods sadly at her because he knows they didn't want this and he didn't want to cause Lizzie pain but he seems to have done that anyway. He wishes he could go back in time to the Presentation and listen to his instincts and take Lizzie somewhere quiet where she can scream and kick about being Bonded but would be *safe* and he could hold her until she accepted their fate. He never wanted to be here, barely able to stand with the fear of losing her, on her mother's doorstep.

"Oh, you poor Soul," Ms Brighton says, and then surprises both of them by stepping outside her door and wrapping her arms around him.

"I can't believe you left her," she says, but this time it's not in anger, but in compassion, "that can't have been easy." She soothes him with a hand on his back as he hunches over and cries into her shoulder. He feels instantly comforted by the gesture and he doesn't know if it stems from Lizzie's own familiarity of her mother's touch or his own desperate desire for a loving parent. "We'll go back and see her, okay dear? We can do that. We can go to Lizzie."

Rewan nods and leans against the doorframe in utter exhaustion, his eyes closed, the fight gone out of him now he has what he needs. When he next opens his eyes Ms Brighton is standing outside her bungalow with him, fully dressed, with an oversized handbag in her arms. He blinks, and vaguely remembers her running around the house muttering to herself, "Oh, what if Lizzie needs...? I should probably take... and just in case..."

"Right," she says as she nods to herself. Then, "You won't let anyone touch me will you? I haven't been outside without Ed in so long..."

Her sudden trust in him warms his heart. "I won't let anyone come near you, Ms Brighton, I promise."

"Rebecca," she amends. "Just Rebecca."

"Okay, Just Rebecca."

*

Lizzie wakes to bright lights dancing before her eyes and swirling in her head.

She feels sleepy and surreal; as if she is still dreaming. She doesn't remember being anywhere so white and so full. She closes her eyes against the brightness. Her hand reaches out in reassurance but it's not until her fingers scrape across a mop of soft curly hair and she senses, more than feels, the body beneath it relax, that she realises exactly why. Rewan must be beside her.

She tears her eyes open and blinks against the blinding light until she can see his head pillowed against her legs on the bed. Or rather, one leg, as her other is suspended above her in a cast. The accident. She remembers now – she panicked, she stepped backwards, into the road... yes, she must have been in an accident and Rewan... she remembers his presence in her mind. It's too much to think about and the painkillers are making it difficult to think at all but she lets her fingers curl in his hair and feel the softness between her fingertips and feels grounded. He looks beautiful when he's sleeping, even hunched over at this angle, but she's beginning to think that she will always find him beautiful whatever the occasion. He is exhausted, she can feel it.

A soft cough startles her from focusing on him and Lizzie turns with some difficulty (her neck is apparently very stiff from the fall) to see her mum in the other chair. Lizzie's smile is in danger of breaking her already damaged face at the sheer joy of seeing her here. "Mum!"

Her mum looks sheepish. "Hello dear, how are you feeling?"

"Mum, what are you doing here? How did you...? Why?"

"Your gentleman came to get me." Rebecca smiles. "He was quite adamant."

It takes Lizzie a moment to understand and when she does, she looks down to where her hand is still instinctively stroking Rewan's hair, calming him. He did that for her?

"Did he tell you?" she whispers. She's talking to her mother but she's finding it hard to look away from Rewan.

"Yes," her mum says.

Lizzie closes her eyes and turns towards her, bracing for the worse. "You're not mad?"

A number of emotions seem to pass over her mum's face before they settle into a small smile. "No. It was quite a shock but there's nothing to be done, and, in any case, you liked him before the Bond, didn't you?"

Lizzie thinks back to his timid politeness, his bad attempts at jokes, and how good he looked in that tailored suit... "Yeah," she acknowledges with a smile. "I liked him."

"Then it's okay." Her mum smiles back. "Souls have overcome worse. Besides, you may be battered and bruised, sweetheart, but you're glowing like one of your father's angels and it's hard to begrudge you that."

Lizzie didn't realise how anxious she was about her mother's reaction until relief floods through her at this demonstration of her unwavering support. "You'll be able to stand being around us, right? I don't want to never see you again –"

"Lizzie," she says, placing her hand over her daughter's, "Of course I will see you again, as often as I can. You are my daughter and I love you far too much to let you go. They say that the Bond adapts to those it binds, adjusting to your fears and your desires. I trust that you are stubborn enough to sway it."

Lizzie supposes that's true. If she can motivate her Pair to find her mum while unconscious, she can probably negotiate with Rewan even better while awake. She *would* find a way to traverse these two worlds. She'd find a way. "Good. What about Ed?"

She laughs, and it's such a bizarre reaction that Lizzie sits up straighter, immediately worried.

"What?" she pushes.

"His plane landed an hour ago," her mum says.

"I don't...?" Lizzie tries to make sense of it through her drug-addled brain but it doesn't make sense. Ed's not meant to be back for another month. "What?" she asks again.

"We were watching the Presentation yesterday and he said..." she trails off, shaking her head with another laugh, "He didn't say it in so many words – probably knew I wouldn't believe a word of it – but Lizzie... he *knew*. I don't know how. I think he tried to call you to find out for certain but when you didn't answer he got on a plane. He just called to say he's in a cab, right now, coming to see you both."

Lizzie huffs a breathless laugh, overjoyed with the familial support she can't believe she doubted, and pulls her mum towards her into a hug. The movement wakes Rewan and she turns in time to see him stretch and rub his eyes like a sleepy child. It's strange, but she can feel his waking consciousness in her mind, like it flickers to life a little further with every second.

"Hey, sleepyhead," she says.

Rewan's eyes open suddenly and the light flares in her mind. "Lizzie!" he says and nearly falls over his own two feet from trying to stand up too quickly. Her mum sneaks out of her arms and out of the door mumbling something about finding a doctor. Lizzie fights the urge to laugh at Rewan's clumsy display only because she can feel Rewan's confusion and panic and relief and knows he still needs comforting.

"Lizzie! Are you okay? I'm sorry about the Bond, I know it's not what you want, but I… Are you still upset? I can sort of feel that you're not angry right now but maybe you're just tired and you'll shout at me later and that's okay too. I just… I planned this whole speech out, I did, and now I'm messing it up, but basically –"

She kisses him before he can finish. He startles for a minute and then his fingers ever so gently come to cradle her bandaged forehead.

Lizzie pulls back to grin at him. He stays close, nuzzling into her hair. She can feel his worry like it's her own. She whispers into his ear, "I'm here. It's okay. I'm sorry. I'm never going to leave you. We'll be okay." The words terrify her at the same time as they comfort her. It feels all too fast and yet all too right. She feels the warm buzz of Rewan's love through the Bond.

"I love you," he whispers against her ear. "Never going to leave you. I'm sorry you were scared. I'm sorry you were hurt."

The words are just as terrifying but she feels the truth in them. He has seen her very soul, all of it, and knows that he loves every part.

He pulls away suddenly and presents her with a plastic cup of water. Lizzie searches the Bond trying to work out why, only to find that she's thirsty and he realised before she did. There are some perks to this shared mind and soul thing it seems. She drinks it. But then she looks up into Rewan's hopeful smile and it all comes crashing down on her. She's going to ruin that. Already his forehead is wrinkling with worry. This is how it's going to be from now on: shared *everything*. She gets to have him, and that's wonderful, but he gets *her*, and that's not a good deal. What happens when her thoughts aren't pure and academic? When they're rude, or inappropriate, or daft? He'll realise how deranged she is; what he has tied himself to for eternity.

"Stop it," Rewan begs. "Whatever you're thinking about. Please. Don't think of yourself like that." He takes both of her hands in his and runs a thumb over the bandaged palm. "It'll take a while for us to get used to this, I know, but right now, I'm just happy you're you."

"Well, of course I'm me! Who else would I be?"

He is laughing now and pressing his lips to her forehead. She stubbornly ignores the flutter her heart makes at the gesture.

"Don't ever change," he whispers, and that's just obtuse, because Lizzie knows what Bonded Pairs do. She knows that they will merge until the only disagreements they can have are those silent headshakes that Rewan's parents exchange. She hopes not. She hopes they will stay like this forever.

His hand leaves to trace the outline of the bandage on her head, and she realises, rather belatedly, why Rewan had been so anxious. She could have had brain damage. She can taste his relief through the Bond. He continues, "I am grateful for every ridiculous thought you have, even if it's about deep-sea fish, or a scathing review of my work, or –" he breaks off.

He doesn't need to continue because she can feel the shape of his thoughts in her own mind. Their Bond is growing stronger with every passing moment, like their minds and souls are testing the strength of the threads between them and fusing them together. She's not as scared of it as she thought she would be. She thought having someone else Bonded to her would be like an intrusion but instead it's like he's filled a part of her she didn't realise was empty.

He smiles, because he knows, of course he does. Now, there will always be someone who understands her.

*

They don't actually have the discussion of where to live, at least not

301

out loud. Rewan's apartment is bigger and a good halfway point between Lizzie's university and Rebecca's house. Lizzie is still on crutches when she moves in, and once again, logic tells her it's too soon but the Bond won't have it any other way. It feels right putting her books – her Ginsberg – beside Rewan's on the shelf. The wooden angel from her father becomes the sole ornament in the writing room. The Soulmate Certificate, signed by Ed himself, is hung above the mantelpiece, amidst framed photos of their friends and family; a purposeful reminder that they can, and will, co-exist. Her mum was right it seems; the Bond *does* adapt, and much faster than the attitudes around them.

On their first evening in their new home, Lizzie sits on the piano stall – tinkering, but mostly just resting her broken leg – as Rewan cooks dinner. She still marvels that they can spend time apart like this, unlike all the Souls in Rewan's mind, but it suits them – it stops her from feeling overwhelmed and stops Rewan from feeling trapped – and it reassures them to know that the Bond really has adapted to their needs. It lets them love how they need to; not how they are meant to. There's a thought there... one that is building into something, one that she wants to chase.

For now, she sits by the piano and pushes down a key, intrigued by a related idea. "I wish I could play," she says, letting the unvoiced question skitter across their Bond.

Rewan looks over at her, equally as curious by her silent question, and comes to join her on the bench; his side pressing against hers as if it's the most natural thing in the world. He pushes down two other keys, making a chord.

"You want to know if..." Rewan murmurs and Lizzie hums her agreement. She closes her eyes and focuses on the Bond. There is an orange rhythmic pulsing that is unusually strong and she knows it's the right one to follow. It's easy then to give in to the instinct that tells her what movements and sounds are needed. *Moonlight Sonata* begins to play. When she opens her eyes, his right hand is dancing towards hers, playing the bass notes, while hers play further up the keyboard. She gasps at the sight. She didn't realise they could do this, that they could be synced enough in their minds to be this proficient, to produce something so wonderful.

They pause in their playing to look at one another and they can feel the Bond quake in anticipation. They smile shyly, and without looking away, close the piano lid. They have much more to share together, for the rest of their lives.

Forever. The word is so strong that it has a taste in their minds, but it's more than that, it's almost as if they can see it, hear it... *Forever.*

"Affecting Change"

a comment on what the Outsider Award means for the future of the Arts

Elena Morenzo

Souls Rewan and Elizabeth Penton, the first joint Poet Oracles of Great Britain, rocked the Arts world this week by announcing a new poetry award specifically targeting those normally overlooked by the Elite. The annual prize of £20,000 will be open to any published collection of poetry which addresses "any aspect of the human experience" and will be judged, not by a chosen panel, but by the public themselves.

"The attitude we have towards the Arts is outdated and in dire need of revision," Souls Penton said in a joint statement, "The Temples have historically had a huge cultural influence on society, and that's not to be forgotten or in any way discounted, but we must also recognise that poetry can exist outside of these confines and is equally deserving of recognition."

This is a struggle that Soul Elizabeth Penton knows all too well given that she was once the most infamous outsider poet in the UK. Some critics even argue that it was the Bond, not the work, that finally bought her begrudging acceptance into the Arts world. It is unsurprising then, to see their ambivalence towards the Elite – the historic Arts Institution of Great Britain.

"Too long have the Elite overlooked exceptional work just because it didn't fit within their parameters," Souls Penton continued, "We cannot, as two people, rewrite the rules, but we can, as two people in a privileged position, start to affect change."

The implication being of course that the Outsider Award is only the beginning of what I'm sure will be a very interesting term as

Poet Oracles. Perhaps given Soul Elizabeth Penton's Outlie and Non-Trad upbringing, and Souls Penton's reportedly cavalier attitude toward their Bond, it is almost tempting to believe they are speaking of something grander than poetry in this statement – that perhaps they intend to "affect change" on a much wider scale – but only time will tell.

For now, perhaps Souls Penton have demonstrated their courage simply by daring to step outside the status quo. It would have been easy for them to be enchanted by the advertised glitz and glamour of the Elite, to fall into the narrative they were expected to take, but instead they looked beyond the world they knew and started to write their own narrative. The future they have affected is not one to fear, but one to embrace, and one which sets a brave precedent for us all to strive after.

Acknowledgements

This book would not have been possible without the instrumental advice, input, and support of Maggie Gee at Bath Spa University and Nelle Andrew at Peters, Fraser & Dunlop.

The author would also like to thank Rewan Tremethick and Nicki Foley for their advice, and her parents & friends for their invaluable support over the years, especially Lindsay Schiro and Sophie Meyer.

With thanks to Brown Bear Art for the cover image.

About The Author

caseybourne.co.uk

Casey Bourne achieved a Distinction in Creative Writing (MA) from Bath Spa University in 2014. She was soon picked up by a literary agency and her debut novel *Pair Bonding* was optioned by a major TV company.

Casey has spent the majority of her life working retail by day and writing by night. She's a nerd who loves science fiction, music, and strategy board games.

She lives with her partner and their gremlins in Cornwall, UK.

Printed in Great Britain
by Amazon